"Come, creature—take my fear. Take it all. I have no use for it. The sea is yours, and the land is mine. Let us share them. Do you not see? You yearn for my land, but you cannot walk. I yearn for your sea, but I cannot swim. So here—take it. Take it all."

- The Unsettled Sea, by Myra Okombuur

M.R. ISAIA

Tales of EVIIRI

Reclamation

Lyrnathor

White Isls

Kordas Desert

Dron Mountains

Bay of Zenithal

Zenithal

Latijh

Feniq Belt

Besti'Qa

Bryll

Ton-Basin

Weaver

THE WORLD OF EVIIRI

Eviiri, meaning *turquoise* in the ancient tongue, is a world shaped by its boundless oceans—turquoise seas that stretch endlessly, their vastness dotted with five great continents. These lands, as if sculpted by the gods themselves, are a blend of towering mountains and unfathomable valleys, forests and rolling grasslands that stretch as far as the eye can see, contrasted sharply by uncrossable deserts and windswept plains. Rich in nutrients and mineral deposits, Eviiri is a world of beauty and boundless possibility, a cradle for life that has flourished for millennia.

The Faith, which spans the breadth of Eviiri, devotes itself to the five primordial Gods. Those within the Faith believe the Gods are responsible for the creation of the heavens, the seas, the earth, and all life within it. At the head of this religious order are the five High Priests, known as The Ancients, who are believed to have inhabited Eviiri since the moment their god, Qyma the Creator, first bestowed life upon the world. To the people, The Ancients are seen as the very embodiment of the gods they serve, their wisdom and long lives regarded with reverence. Some sceptics say they are mere mortals, their longevity attributed to the consumption of the rare and mysterious Fire Orchid essence—a substance derived from a sacred flower that The Ancients have kept closely guarded for millennia.

At the helm of Eviiri stands the Imperium, a vast empire ruled by five monarchs, each governing a continent of their own. At the heart of the Imperium is House Aprya, whose rulers have held dominion over all for two centuries. From their seat in the towering Citadel of Zenithal, Emperor Jannon Aprya III has maintained a fragile peace—one that has endured only through careful balance and diplomacy. Yet this peace, so long upheld, has begun to show signs of fracture, as whispers of unrest ripple throughout Eviiri.

The Architects, a prestigious guild of scientists, mathematicians, engineers, and artists, are tasked with overseeing the advancements that benefit the Imperium's growth. They are the creators of Eviiri's wonders—machinery, infrastructure, and technology that elevate the lives of its people. But even their creations are not without their own shadow, for the betterments they forge may be used as tools of war.

* * *

And so, the balance of power is delicately poised, threatened not only by those who would seek to usurp the throne, but by darker forces that may arise from within the very institutions that once safeguarded the realm.

CHAPTER 1

The people of Zenithal gathered along the Path of Peace, a five-kilometre-long stone boulevard connecting the Citadel to the Sanctuary of Qyma. The milky-white marble thoroughfare was lit only by honey-coloured trail-lights that lined the entirety of the avenue. Flanking the Path were two rows of enormous date palms, planted two hundred years ago to proclaim the newly established peace between the Faith and the Imperium. Each palm rose proud and towered high. Their fronds stretched out over the crowds that had begun to fill the impressive spectator stands.

It was a balmy night. The cloudless sky offered limpid views of the stars. The two moons of Eviiri sat bashfully crescent on the horizon to the northeast. A quietness blanketed the city.

Along the Path, the sweet aroma of orchid incense permeated the air as the Faith Partisans strode down the expansive road holding golden rods topped with ornate bowls. Smoke flowed out of small openings in the sides, undisturbed by the calm of their surroundings. The two hundred hooded figures were dressed in the familiar garb worn by members of the Faith, pure ebony gowns, long and flowing, beaded with onyx gems and laced with gold stitching. A single strip of blood-orange silk trailed from opulent headdresses atop their hoods. Their gait, as if nonexistent, made them appear to be gliding over the marble street as they moved towards the towering Citadel.

Princess Alysse Aprya could only see tiny shadows moving over the trail-lights on the avenue, some 600 metres below, as she stood on her balcony. The rest of the sombre expanse was gifted little light by the stars. The last of the city lights dimmed one after another until the entire capital vanished under the blanket of night. Her chamber's broad balcony looked north over the city and towards the distant Drom mountains.

Growing up, she spent considerable time here studying the intricacies of the streets and the allure of the buildings lining them. However, tonight the city did not offer her the warm comfort it so often did.

She closed her eyes and searched her memories for a moment when she felt her city's warmth. At the forefront of those memories was her father, Emperor Jannon Aprya III. She recalled a moment, only a few weeks earlier, where she and her father admired their lively city together from this very spot.

'You danced well tonight, Little Wren,' he said, a wide smile curling his thick moustache.

'I fumbled the steps, Pa,' she laughed. 'I'm certain the entire city saw. What are they to think of me?'

'Nonsense, you did great,' he assured, playfully nudging her off balance. 'May I suggest one less cup of wine next year?'

Alysse regained her footing, giggling as the sweet summer wine toyed with her senses. She wrapped her arms around her father and squeezed him.

'Another wonderful Summer Festival, Pa. This was the best one yet. You have the people's gratitude and admiration, along with mine.' She paused, her tone turning sombre. 'I only hope that I am one day viewed with the same regard.'

Jannon lowered his head to meet her eyes.

'The people adore you, Little Wren,' he said sincerely. 'You will make a fine Empress. I am so proud of the woman you have become, as I know your mother would have been too.'

Alysse gave a faint smile as a well of emotion formed in her eyes.

'I miss her,' she whispered.

'Me too.'

'Someone once told me that time would ease my sorrow, but ten years on, I know that was just a story to comfort a frightened child. A lie.'

'Well then, tell me who this storyteller is and I will have them flogged down the Path,' Jannon said, puffing his chest.

'It was you, Pa,' she chuckled. 'Good luck ordering the people to flog their Emperor. You've never so much as received a foul look from them. They call you *Jannon the Peacekeeper*.'

'I merely adhere to foundations our ancestors implemented, and kept peace with the Faith,' he said. 'The Thousand Year War was devastating to both sides, a fact upon which all can agree. Only a madman would want to see Eviiri plunge back into darkness.'

'What if I cannot hold the peace?' She asked, a deepening doubt forming in her mind.

'My girl, do not allow fear to guide you. The paths we take to avoid our fears often lead us directly to them,' he said, shifting the curl of hair that hung in front of his daughter's face.

He hugged her.

She pressed her head against his chest and listened to his heartbeat in the silence. It was calm, steady, pure. In the centre of his chest, beneath his muted green suit, she felt a solid lump. She pulled back and eyed the area. The pressure of her cheek had outlined the circular object.

Jannon followed her gaze to the object, then reached for the gold chain around his neck and slipped it over his head. At the end of the chain was a dulled golden pendant, no larger in diameter than a walnut. On its flat face was the sigil of House Aprya surrounded by intertwining vines and odd geometry.

'This pendant has been passed down through every generation of our House. It has been worn by every Emperor before me, all the way back to Jannon the First who had it made for his son. You see, I inherited it *after* my father's death, so he never got a chance to see me wear it. I wish not to make the same mistake. Here.' He placed the chain over Alysse's head and adjusted the intricate pendant. 'It suits you.'

Alysse felt its full weight. Though it was solid gold, that was not what weighed on her. The thought of her father's title and responsibilities inevitably passing to her was frightening.

'Whenever you feel doubt,' Jannon continued, 'this pendant will be a reminder of those who came before. They will be with you, to guide you on your path.'

Alysse looked down at the pendant, gripped it in her hand, then closed her eyes.

'Alysse?'

The soft voice from behind startled her, snapping her mind back into the present. She opened her eyes. The vision of her father was gone and the darkness of the city had returned. She quickly wiped the single tear rolling down her cheek and took a long breath.

'They're waiting,' the voice said.

Alysse turned to see her brother standing in the doorway.

Jaxon Aprya was of generous stature. Despite being two years younger than Alysse, he stood half a head taller than her. His silhouette was unmistakable. The soft curls of his dark, jaw-length hair and his slender figure framed his perfect posture amidst the glow of the night lights. She could barely make out the muted green of his suit, the signature colour of House Aprya.

'I'm ready,' she said faintly as she smoothed over her exquisite ceremonial gown, lowered her black veil, and adjusted the gold pendant around her neck.

Jaxon extended his hand to her, and she took it.

The dim lights of the hall softened his sharp features. She looked into his deep hazel eyes and saw the pain he so selflessly masked behind a gentle smile.

Alysse cherished her brother's comforting presence. After their mother's passing almost ten years ago, the two had formed an inseparable bond. Children of the imperial family were not often granted opportunities to consort with people outside the walls of the Citadel grounds. As children, they had spent what little leisure time they had playing in the gardens south of the towering bastion they called home. The rest of their time had been spent with their father, Emperor Jannon III, who had taught them the great histories of Eviiri and the ways of rule. He had often read them tales of the Thousand-Year War that ended the holy reign, the ceaseless downpours of the Middle Ages that submerged mountains under seas, and the romantic lore of the five primordial Gods.

As he led Alysse through the Citadel's hallways, Jaxon couldn't help but reflect on their father's achievements. He was a valiant ruler who carried on the peace held by his father and his father before him. Beloved by the people, he would often tour the great schools of Zenithal and sit with the children as they learned. He visited the ill in the infirmaries to offer prayer and comfort. His generosity was well known throughout Eviiri.

'How are you?' Jaxon asked, breaking the silence as the soundless elevator descended the tower.

Alysse's words escaped her. She said nothing, dropping her head and taking a series of deep breaths.

Jaxon did not ask again. Instead, he gently squeezed her hand as the elevator reached its intended floor.

Beyond the doors of the elevator was the grandiose Entrance Hall, a single room of formidable size. Twenty-metre-high ceilings and warm stone walls harmonised with fluid and geometric carvings, the architectural style adorning most buildings in the capital. On the walls hung banners of House Aprya. The sigil, a sharp-lined diamond flame comprised of four quadrilateral portions atop a segmented base, sat boldly towards the bottom of the colossal, muted green drapes.

Descending the main staircase, Alysse and Jaxon looked around at the mass of people gathered in the hall. Familiar faces of council members, noble families, military generals, and the High Priests all turned their gazes to the pair as silence gripped the space. The clack of their every step echoed in the hall.

In the centre of the room was a transitory altar, a single block of commonplace marble, unadorned. The crowd had gathered around it. Upon the arrival of the Prince and Princess, they parted. It was then that Alysse focused her gaze on the altar. For there, atop the heavy stone, lay the body of their father, Emperor

Jannon Aprya III.

As Alysse and Jaxon stepped onto the lower landing, they were greeted by solemn bows. Still holding her hand, Jaxon ushered Alysse down the remaining steps and towards the altar.

In front of the altar stood the head of the High Priests, Reverend Kalax. Young to the eye, Kalax appeared no older than Alysse herself. He possessed an androgynous face with pale ivory skin, flawless, yet seemingly void of the life that animates the living. His eyes were as black as a moonless night. His fixed stare on the princess unsettled her, as it did any who returned his gaze. His obsidian robe dripped with opulence, coloured only by its gold detailing and the vibrant orange sigil of The Ancients, a single Fire Orchid flower.

'Alefre'a,' Kalax said as he lowered his head, the other four High Priests echoing the gesture.

Alysse had grown to disfavour The Ancients' address. *Alefre'a*, meaning *royal child* in the ancient tongue, was not used by the common folk, nor by any within the Imperial ranks, only by the Faith. It felt foreign to her, and carried with it a whiff of condescension.

She remained silent as she moved past the High

Priests and approached her father's still body. She stared down at his face. He had very few aging lines, despite his years and the stresses of his position. Through his thick moustache, his once bright smile drooped in sorrow, his deep hazel eyes shielded behind closed lids, never to open again. She paused for a moment before lifting her veil. Laying a gentle hand on his jet-black hair, she leaned down and kissed his forehead. A single tear rolled off her cheek and landed perfectly next to his left eye, making it appear that he too was mourning their sudden disconnect. She straightened and lowered her veil. Turning back to the High Priest, she gave a nod to proceed.

A moment later, the four great horns of the Citadel sounded outside. The deep, harmonic rumble saturated the hall as the massive golden-arched doors cracked open.

Alysse, now back by Jaxon's side, stared out through the doorway. The night appeared endless. Only the warm trail-lights illuminated the Path before them.

Reverend Kalax headed the procession as it filed out into the night. Directly behind him was the Emperor's body upon the now levitating marble altar. Alysse and Jaxon followed first and the rest came after them. Two young boys at either side of the drifting altar began to belt ethereal chants that echoed in the silence.

Along the Path of Peace, the people kneeled as the cortege passed, like a shockwave in slow motion. Acknowledging his father's loyal crowd, Jaxon could see the glint of tears on their faces as he fought back his own. He eyed each of the two hundred hooded Faith Partisans stationed at each of the two hundred palms, their heads lowered, their onyx gems shimmering in the dim light, incense flowing from their golden sceptres. He turned his gaze to Alysse, but hers never left her father.

Be strong, he thought, fighting his sorrow. *For her.*

The walk to the Sanctuary felt never-ending for Alysse. The colossal temple in the approaching distance was almost invisible in the darkness. She lifted her gaze towards it. The Sanctuary of Qyma was one of the most opulent structures in the city. Its pentagonal edifice, capped by a copper dome with an expansive oculus, was guarded by the five personifications of the Gods at each corner of the complex. Copper doors that matched the vaulting dome were already open as the procession approached the entrance.

Passing into the towering void of the Sanctuary, the trail-lights of the Path of Peace faded behind them. Alysse felt the air grow cold as the doors closed, shutting out the faint cries of her father's mourners outside.

The altar drifted to a stop in the centre of the Sanctuary as the entourage accompanying the body filled the galleries. Turning his attention to the altar, Reverend Kalax spoke aloud in the ancient tongue.

'Your life in this world has ended. Your journey to the next shall now begin.'

Alysse reflected on the ancient tradition. The Faith taught that, upon death, the soul departs the body and journeys to Tharpys—the heavens. Plunging the city into darkness ensured the soul could make its voyage unencumbered. This tradition was greatly respected by those within and outside of the Faith.

'Go now, Jannon Aprya. The Five await your return,' Kalax said, raising his hands towards the heavens.

As the final glow of the internal lights diminished, sinking the hall into darkness, the two chanters wailed the Soul's Hymn, an ancient song said to release the soul from its worldly vessel and begin its transcendence.

Blackness surrounded everyone. Alysse looked up at the stars through the sizeable opening in the dome's apex, directly skyward of the body, and muttered her prayer.

Jaxon felt his sister's grip tighten around his hand as she laid her head on his shoulder and wept. Now free to mourn in the darkness, he released his sadness. The echoing hymn drew his mind back to their mother's final journey. As a boy of ten, his then fragile emotions had consumed him. Despite the devastation he had felt for the loss of his mother, he couldn't help but recall the fear that had sat alongside it. The fear had not come from death or from loss, but from the colossal statue of the patron deity, Qyma the Creator, that towered over all within the Sanctuary. Standing before it now, he dared not meet her gaze. Instead, he kept his eyes shut and focused on the echoing tones of the hymn resonating throughout the expanse.

The howling hymn, however, was not all he could hear. He turned his head slightly to place the sounds, first left, then right, but the sounds were not coming from within the sanctuary. He turned his head back towards the closed doors as he heard them grow louder.

Screams.

His eyes shot open to no avail. Knowing where he stood in the sanctuary, he turned sharply in the darkness and ran towards the entrance. He felt Alysse stumble as his shoulder slipped out from under her. Fumbling for the doors, he found them and pushed. Light poured into the sanctuary as the screams intensified. Dismay gripped him as he bore witness to the unthinkable scene. Staring down the Path of Peace, he watched in horror as each of the two-hundred palms erupted into flames, one by one.

CHAPTER 2

A thunderous crack woke Thio. The night's storm had made it difficult for him to sleep. He imagined he would have grown accustomed to it by now. It had been three months since he arrived in this curious burg. He rolled to face the narrow window that sat just above his bed and stared out into the night. Craning his neck, he saw the two slivers of moonlight atop the horizon, offering little to no light to the city below.

Nestled within a sloped valley, wedged between two great mountain ranges, the small city of Ton-Basin spent most of its days and nights battered by downpours and storms. With a population close to ten thousand, Ton-Basin was cherished for its rare mineral deposits and mountain salts.

Thio rolled over again and stared into the darkness of his seemingly unfamiliar room. He slowly gathered his bearings as his weariness began to fade, spotting a faint glow of light creeping under his door from the hallway. Unable to settle his mind, he lugged himself out of bed and slipped on his night robe. A silvery flash of lightning briefly illuminated the cramped space he had been occupying of late.

He dragged his weary body towards the small nook in the east corner. With a wave of his hand, a soft glow filled the tight area. The light, he noticed, was significantly dimmer than usual. He tried again, but the lamp grew no brighter. Confused, he turned on the water from a tiny basin and splashed a handful of it over his face. He looked up at his reflection in the slender mirror on the wall. It revealed the shadowy rings under his vivid blue eyes. His strong, youthful features looked worn and dull in the dingy light. His fresh buzzcut did well to soften his sandy-coloured hair. He retrieved his worn spectacles from a small ledge and put them on.

Stepping out of the nook, he walked a few paces to the door and opened it. The hallway's dimmed lights struggled to illuminate the barren sleeping quarters. He stepped out and closed the door behind him, making his way down the narrow corridor toward the main library.

It was a short walk. Ton-Basin's Athenaeum was not of notable size. It housed in the vicinity of one hundred students, and a possible twenty Architects. Of all the guild's Athenaeums Thio had visited, however, this one was his favourite—not for its aesthetic or the books in its library, but for its location. His latest research had led him to this town and to the possibilities buried within the mountains.

He turned the final corner and arrived at the modest expanse. The walls of the library were stacked with countless books and scrolls. The shelves surrounded an assortment of oak desks in the middle of the room, one of which was lit by a delicate table lamp. It was the desk Thio had been working at only hours ago. He noted that the lamp was, like those in the halls, dulled. A figure sat at the table. It was the unmistakable, round frame of Dalos Okombuur, his mentor.

Dalos was a jovial older man, plump and light-hearted, renowned for his witty quips. His intellect was often misjudged due to his round face and soft eyes, yet his mind was sharp and brilliant.

Adjusting his spectacles, Thio noticed another figure standing next to Dalos, hooded and whispering in his ear. He did not recognise the person at first. As he drew closer, he could just make out the soft lines of her face. *Deni.*

Deni was the Athenaeum's caretaker. She was uncommonly short for a middle-aged woman, standing no higher than an average child. Her stout figure paired well with her pudgy face. She was stern and a woman of few words. She would often ignore the greetings of others as they passed her in the halls.

The interaction struck Thio as odd for this time of night. He watched as Dalos gave her a small nod to which she responded with a pat on the shoulder, then turned away from the table and headed towards the hallway. Spotting Thio approaching in the darkness, Deni gave him a fleeting glance before disappearing into the shadows.

Thio moved closer to the table, his bare feet making no noise on the frigid marble floors. The desk was covered in loose papers.

'Can't sleep either?' Thio asked, breaking the silence.

He waited a moment for the cheerful greeting he regularly received from Dalos. Instead, a sombre voice spoke.

'Sit, Thio.'

Confused, Thio rounded the table, pulled out the chair opposite Dalos, and sat.

'Sir? Is everything okay? What did Deni want at this hour? And what's with the lights?' Thio took another look around at his gloomy surroundings.

'Tell me,' Dalos said as he passed a single sheet to Thio, 'what is wrong with this?'

'Sir?' Thio countered as he took the page, noticing it was one of his own research theories.

'This new energy source, what is wrong with it?'

Thio was puzzled by the question. *Is this a test? Have I made a mistake?* Without further question, he lowered his head and reviewed the page.

'Ah, the um, the…' Thio's forehead scrunched and his eyes narrowed as he surveyed the equations.

Dalos leaned back in his chair, studying the young man. The boy's broad shoulders and athletic build contrasted sharply with most members of the academic guild. Despite the young man's hard exterior, Dalos could see Thio's timidness. Having taken him on as his apprentice a year and a half ago, the two had travelled from city to city, studying each of the land's unique forms and resources. They had discussed Thio's new theory at length, but had not yet landed on a practical means of testing it. Dalos saw its potential, even through the young man's own doubts. He knew the most rigid blockade to its success was Thio himself.

It had become apparent to Dalos that Thio thrived in solitude, away from the watchful eyes of his teachers and mentors alike. In the relatively short time they had spent together, Thio did more observing than he did applying his crafts. Despite Dalos' efforts to encourage action, the boy spent most of his time scribing in his notebook. On rare occasions, Dalos would observe Thio testing his theories in private, unaware of his keen observer. That was when he produced his best work.

Minutes passed as Thio mumbled the equations to himself.

'Give up?' Dalos asked, knowing full well that the boy would not surrender until he was sure of the answer.

'There... there doesn't appear to be anything wrong with it, sir,' Thio said as he continued to scrutinise his work.

A grin broke the placid staleness of his mentor's face.

'Exactly!' he said proudly with boisterous energy. 'This is exceptional work, m'boy. Destabilising simple mountain salt into an exoergic state—astounding!'

'Thank you, sir,' Thio said bashfully.

A wild flash lit up the darkness as another whip of lightning clapped over the leaded glass ceiling. Raindrops began to dance upon the lofty domed roof.

'It seems the Gods would agree!' Dalos chuckled.

Thio rolled his eyes. He found it strange that a man who had dedicated his entire life to researching the very fabric of the known world had such a strong belief in the Faith. Despite the countless books Dalos had written himself, he always carried two others around with him. One was a children's storybook, written by his late wife. The other was the book of the Faith, the Ancient's Codex. Thio struggled to see how the conflicting foundations of both the Faith and the sciences could reside peacefully within one's mind. Nonetheless, he respected his mentor's beliefs.

'How 'bout you ask the Gods to turn this theory into practice,' Thio joked.

Dalos closed his eyes and outstretched his arms. 'Oh wise and omnipotent Qyma, I ask you to grace my young apprentice with a hefty pair of balls and allow him to step back from his notebook and actually *try* to make his work… work.'

'Very funny,' Thio said, playfully tossing the loose page across the table.

Dalos had all but forgotten about the news he had just been told as the two discussed the details of Thio's work. In a moment of silence, he heard the patter of rain and a rumble of thunder. His smile faded. Morbid imagery sprang to the forefront of his mind. He pressed himself back in his chair and let slip a sigh.

'Sir, what's wrong?' Thio inquired, noticing the sudden shift in his mentor's demeanour.

'Thio,' Dalos said before taking a long pause, 'the

Emperor is dead.'

Thio struggled to grip the words. A whirlwind of queries flooded his mind.

'The Emperor? What? When?!' he asked.

'Tonight. Not a few hours ago. Deni just delivered the news.' Dalos instinctively shuffled the papers in front of him in an attempt to distract his thoughts.

'But we saw him here only a week ago. He seemed in perfect health. How…' Thio halted his barrage of questions when he saw the sadness swelling in his mentor's eyes.

The Emperor often travelled around the lands of Qymathor to visit the noble Houses that governed parts of the land. He had come to Ton-Basin with a small entourage the previous week after word of a terrible accident in one of the ore mines. Nine people had lost their lives in the collapse. He had visited the families of the perished and held counsel with Dalos and the city's governor. Thio was not privy to such meetings; however, he had been introduced to the Emperor as Dalos' principal apprentice in a brief audience with the travelling company.

'That is all the information I have,' Dalos replied. 'I'd say the funeral will be taking place right about now. Hence the lights.'

Thio eyed the darkened library and recalled the old tradition. *The soul's final journey.* He was not much of a follower of the Faith anymore. He felt his time and talents were better spent researching the technologies and natural processes of Eviiri. His true inspiration came from The Architects, a guild made up of bold men and women possessing intellectual mastery.

They were responsible for how the Eviirian harnessed the strengths of this world. At the head of the guild were three Chief Architects, one of whom currently sat opposite him.

Thio stood up and moved around the table, placing a consoling hand on Dalos' shoulder.

'Sir, I'm… I'm sorry.'

'Thank you, m'boy,' Dalos said as he shifted in his chair, 'though it is not me you should feel sorry for. I have lost a dear friend, yes, but my heart weeps for his now parentless children.'

Princess Alysse and Prince Jaxon, Thio recalled. Prince Jaxon had accompanied the Emperor on his recent expedition to Ton-Basin. During their brief meeting, Thio had caught himself staring at the handsome prince for most of their encounter, oblivious to the conversations happening around him. It was only when the Prince had returned his gaze that Thio lowered his stare in a panic.

Dalos cleared the lump in his throat, jolting Thio's mind back into the library.

'Dawn is still an hour from breaking,' he said. 'You should try to get some rest. We shall begin exploring your new theory come daylight.'

Thio, still with unanswered questions, gave a soft nod of agreement. He offered his mentor a few gentle pats on the shoulder, then retired to his dorm.

Dalos sat still for a moment, reflecting on the sudden loss of his long-time friend. Moving his hand across the table lamp, it dimmed into obscurity. Silence paired the darkness as the rain ceased. He looked up through the glass ceiling as the clouds beyond parted briefly. The distant twinkle of starlight stared back at him.

'Safe travels, old friend.'

CHAPTER 3

The screams of the city folk echoed along the Path of Peace as Jaxon leapt down from the sanctuary's entrance. Chaos was abundant. People clambered over the tiered stone spectator stands, desperate to evade the scorching licks of the burning trees.

Without hesitating, Jaxon raced towards the flames. The crackling fronds spat embers over the marble pathway as the fires roared. He scouted the area for any sign of the cause, shifting his attention from one flaming palm to another as they continued to erupt down the Path towards the Citadel. He ran towards the fleeing crowd and clutched the nearest person.

'What happened?! What did you see?!' he pressed.

The woman's face, drenched in fear, turned paler still at the sudden appearance of the Imperial Prince. She struggled for words but managed a few.

'I don't know, Your Grace. Only darkness… then

flame. Forgive me, I must find my son,' she pleaded before twisting out of his grasp and fleeing into the darkness of the city.

Jaxon stood in place as the people evacuated the area. He continued to assess the situation unfolding around him. He watched as the masses dispersed into the darkness. He stood alone amongst the flames, shielding his eyes from their fiery radiance. It was then that his gaze fell upon an object at the base of the nearest palm—a lump of black cloth. Fearing it was a casualty of the flames, he crouched as low as he could and scampered towards the heap.

The heat intensified as he neared the obsidian pile. Shielding his face, he drew closer. Suddenly, he recognised it as an ebony gown, one he had seen during the precession covering the Faith Partisans. The cascade of onyx gems echoed the ravishing flames just metres above him. The fine gold stitching began to singe. The blood-orange silk streamer curled and warped, contorting like tortured skin as the heat gnawed at its threads.

Wasting no time, Jaxon leapt forward, clutched the garment, and heaved it backwards. Expecting the full weight of a body, he exerted his full force. To his surprise, the cloth moved freely, his own momentum throwing him backwards. There was no weight to it. There was no body.

Jaxon stumbled back from the immense heat with the robe still grasped in his hand. He inspected it, puzzled. There was no sign of blood or flesh, or any evidence of a victim at all, only twisted cloth and jewels. Peering down the boulevard, he saw another pile of black cloth, then another, then another. At the base of each palm, clumps of black silk squirmed in agony beneath the flames.

—

Alysse saw only a glimpse of the flames before the doors were heaved closed again, the image of Jaxon's silhouette framed by the inferno burnt deep in her sight. As the Sanctuary returned to darkness, she encouraged her eyes to adjust. The sound of panicked nobles scurrying about the echoing rotunda drowned out the screams from outside. She fumbled in the dark. Her hands probed the empty space around her, searching for anyone or anything nearby. Suddenly, she felt a hand grab hers and her body was pulled sideways.

'Your Grace, I have you. Hurry, this way.'

The voice was deep and aged, yet she recognised it instantly. It belonged to her uncle, Cyrus Thenta. He sheltered her as they hurried in an unknown direction. Disoriented by the turmoil, she struggled to make sense of the events unfolding around her.

'This way, Princess!' she heard in the darkness as she felt another arm wrap itself around her back. This time, a woman's voice—her Aunt Fayh.

Ahead, a door opened. The light behind it reoriented Alysse. She now knew where she was and where she was headed. It was the hidden door that led to the array of tunnels below the city, a vast network of travel ways connecting major landmarks, and offering safe transit for those privileged enough to have access.

Stepping out of the darkness and into the narrow corridor, she turned to each of her escorts. Her uncle was a stout man. His silver hair matched his thick silver moustache, which cascaded down to his well-groomed silver beard. He had a naturally stern expression and prominent wrinkles about his eyes. The gold embroidery adorning his deep purple suit sparkled as he passed each wall lamp.

Cyrus Thenta was the Commander of the Imperial Forces and had commenced his position shortly preceding Emperor Jannon's coronation. Brother to Empress Palymma, Alysse and Jaxon's mother, Cyrus had long upheld the security of the capital and nation cities throughout Qymathor.

Her aunt, Fayh, was a genteel woman in her late sixties. Despite her witch-like face, she exuded an air of grace and intelligence. Her frosted updo fought to hold intact as she rushed Alysse towards the approaching stairwell, then began their descent.

The stairs were broad and spiralled downwards into a seemingly bottomless pit. Behind Alysse, she heard the crowd of unnerved nobles clambering their way to safety. The voice of Reverend Kalax did its best to calm the swarm.

Finally reaching the bottom landing, Cyrus steered Alysse to one of the six tunnel entrances. The sizeable circular shaft stretched far beyond the field of sight. It was lined with two strips of trail-lights that appeared to converge in the distance. Just past the opening was a carrier—a roofless vehicle, fitted with no more than a dozen seats, which rose a few centimetres from the pale stone floor as they approached. Cyrus lent a steady hand to Alysse as she stepped onto the driverless platform. Fayh followed, then himself.

'Go now. The rest will follow behind.' A senior general spoke above the gathering crowd.

Without command, the carrier began to accelerate down the endless cavern.

Alysse, now allowing herself a moment to catch her breath, sat in the warm embrace of her aunt. The gathered nobles at the tunnel's entrance fell away as the carrier picked up speed. Scanning their faces in the light, she realised one was absent.

'Jaxon?!' she exclaimed as panic set in. She recalled him standing in front of the flames, but knew not whether he had returned inside the Sanctuary.

'Stay calm, Your Grace. Jaxon is a smart boy. He will be fine.' Cyrus said softly, taking her hand.

The words did nothing to ease her fear. She stared wide-eyed at the vanishing entrance as the tunnel winds caressed her veil.

He will be fine, she tried to reassure herself.

'Are you hurt, Princess?' Fayh asked.

Alysse attempted to sense her own body through the numbness her panic had caused. She felt no pain —nothing of her physical form—and shook her head.

'Uncle, what happened?' she asked, prying herself from her aunt's grip and turning to Cyrus.

'It is impossible to say at this moment, Your Grace,' he said. 'We have men on the Path. I will gather their accounts as soon as you are safe within the Citadel.'

'The Path is not my prime concern,' she said, temper rising in her voice. 'What happened to my father?

His health was sound.'

Cyrus took a deep breath. 'I only had a brief moment to confer with the examiner. He concluded there were no marks of treachery, Your Grace, if that is the true nature of your question. A chambermaid found him in the hall outside his quarters. There were no signs of struggle, nor blood. It appears his heart simply failed him.'

Alysse found the account difficult to believe. She and her father had enjoyed their evening meal together only hours before his body was found.

'I cannot settle on these facts,' she said, staring ahead at the empty void, the pendant around her neck caged in her grasp.

'Your Grace,' Fayh spoke, placing a gentle hand on Alysse's arm, 'this wound is fresh, for all of us. But now is not the time to let your mind sew wild threads. Perhaps the dawn will shed light on the matter. Until then, it is best to keep your sight level.'

Alysse felt comfort in her aunt's words, as she always had. From a young age, Alysse would often seek out Fayh for a woman's point of view. Following the death of her mother, she felt the Citadel had become overcrowded with men. She had great respect for her aunt, for Fayh had never tried to step into a motherly role. Instead, she spoke to Alysse as an adviser, propagating her years of wisdom to the young princess.

'You're right,' Alysse said, hesitating a moment. 'But are we sure the examiner had enough time to perform a thorough investigation? My father's body will be sealed within his altar before daybreak. Perhaps we can…'

'Alysse, knowing the cause will not bring him back,' Cyrus stated. 'His soul is with the Gods now. It is best to lay his body to rest too.'

'Can we be sure his soul made its journey?' Alysse rebutted, 'You saw what is happening up there. What if the flames have obscured his path? What if…'

'Hush, my girl, hush,' Fayh whispered as she pulled Alysse back into her embrace.

Cyrus saw the turmoil in his niece's eyes. He pursued a remedy but arrived at none. He did not possess the same craft of comfort as his wife did, instead, opting for a logical solution.

'I will reconfer with the examiner come daybreak. Perhaps tests can be performed with the body absent. Rest assured, Your Grace, I will initiate a full investigation.'

'Thank you, Uncle.'

'Cyrus,' Fayh turned, speaking directly to her husband, 'I think it also wise to increase security for Alysse and Jaxon. Until we understand these matters wholly, we cannot risk their safety.'

Cyrus gave her a fleeting sneer, as if offended by the obvious measures suggested by his wife. He moved quickly to uncurl his lip.

'Agreed,' he said, straightening his posture. 'I will see to it.'

'Jaxon,' Alysse muttered, her mind now focused on her brother. 'Please find Jaxon. He is alone up there.'

Fayh pulled away from the shivering Princess and stared into her hazel eyes, cocking her head to one side.

'Alysse, do you recall your excursion to Penyth with your father?' she asked. 'You were just a child.'

The question struck Alysse as odd. 'I do. He brought me with him to settle the riots over the destruction of their farming lands.'

Fayh nodded. 'The farmers were outraged that your father had permitted the Architects to lay a new rail line directly through their crops. It halted all production in Besti-Qa for a month.'

'I recall... but I do not see its importance,' Alysse responded.

'Your brother begged your father to accompany you. He insisted that you needed protection in the event the farmers turned their rage towards you.' Fayh scanned her memory. 'He said they may order their cattle to trample you, if I'm not mistaken.'

The recount of Jaxon's fantastical childhood dramatics made Alysse let slip a brief laugh.

'After your father's final refusal of his request,' Fayh continued, 'Jaxon scurried off in a huff down into these tunnels. Your father ordered the entire Citadel to search for him whilst he was away. We spent days scouring each and every corridor. But Jaxon had left the tunnels just as fast as he had entered them. Unbeknown to us, he had crossed the city, stolen a fisherman's boat, and sailed it across the bay to the foothills of the Drom Mountains. From there, with nothing but the clothes on his back, he trekked blindly through the Western Passage, a perilous feat not even the bravest would attempt, let alone a boy of eight. Yet, by the Gods' will, he made it through. All he had left to do was to cross the Besti-

Qa Plains. Of course, by this time, you and your father had settled the quarrel and had begun your return journey.'

'We spotted him trailing the tracks a short distance from Penyth,' Alysse remembered.

'His shoes had all but worn through,' Fayh chuckled. 'He would have continued barefoot had the train not stopped for him.'

'Father was both furious and impressed.'

Fayh leant in close. 'Jaxon's dedication to your safety has always stood above all other traits. He is resourceful—perhaps foolish at times—but wise in his motivations. The Gods favour him. He will be fine.'

Alysse knew her aunt was right. Jaxon had always had a propensity to escape death. Nevertheless, she still worried for him.

What took an hour to walk, the return journey to the Citadel was completed in minutes. The speeding carrier delicately slowed as it approached the opposite end of the tunnel. Standing by the exit, two imperial guards waited in their deep purple suits. Their heads cocked as deep rumbles from the Path above permeated the solid ground looming above them. The rumbles caused everyone to turn their attention skyward.

As the carrier came to a stop, Cyrus stepped off first, again offering a hand to his niece. The moment her feet touched solid ground, Alysse took flight, clutching her hefty gown and barging past the guards there to receive her. Cyrus and Fayh had little time to call out to her before she disappeared up the staircase.

Bursting through a concealed door attached to the entrance hall, Alysse ran for the private elevator. She stepped into the confined space, and the doors closed behind her. Her breath was rapid as the noiseless cubicle ascended the tower.

Within seconds, the elevator doors opened to a large foyer directly adjacent to her chambers. She headed straight into her room and slammed the door behind her. The delicate sheers partially covering her expansive window mindlessly danced in the warm breeze. Cutting through them, she exited onto the balcony where she had stood earlier in the night.

The scene below drew all the breath from her lungs. The city was alive with chaos. Two hundred blazing torches lit the entire boulevard and the areas surrounding it. She could hear the faint screams of the people still scattering below. The fiery aisle stretched out before her, converging at the foot of the Sanctuary. She could only think of her father's body lying within, in darkness, in solitude. She forced the images out of mind and searched the Path for any sign of Jaxon. Though, from this height, it was near impossible to distinguish one person from another.

Amidst the throngs of panicked city folk, Alysse spotted a single figure sprinting down the centre of the street towards the Citadel. The familiar muted green suit illuminated as it passed each fiery palm. It was him. A tidal wave of relief hit her with tremendous force. She barely noticed the warm hues of the approaching daylight to the east as she dropped to her knees and pulled off her veiled headdress.

* * *

—

It felt like an eternity before Jaxon swung open the bedroom door. Without pause, Alysse jumped to her feet and ploughed into his arms. He held her tight as she wailed uncontrollably.

'I'm here, Alysse. Shh. Everything will be okay.' Jaxon whispered, striving to console her.

'His soul is lost, Jax. I know it,' she spluttered through her cries.

'Shh, he is with the Gods now,' Jaxon reassured, uncertain of his own statement. His eyes focused on the brightening sky framed by the tall windows, comprehending what he had just witnessed.

'Are you okay?' he asked Alysse as her breath began to slow.

'I'm okay, but Jax, what is happening? Our father was here, alive just hours ago. And now this? I can't make sense of it.'

'Me neither. On the Path, the...' He swallowed his words in an attempt to avoid any additional unrest on his already unrested sister. 'I should speak with Uncle Cyrus. And you should get some rest. Once all of this has settled, we will visit father at the shrine.'

Jaxon released his grip on her.

Alysse nodded, wiping her face with her draped sleeve. She closed her eyes and felt a kiss on her forehead. Listening to Jaxon leave the room, she gathered her thoughts. Taking a few deep breaths in the silence, she felt the growing warmth of morning around her. The sun had ushered away the darkness and begun filling her room with light.

36

CHAPTER 4

The vibrant colours of dusk decorated the city below as Jaxon pressed his head against the towering glass window. His gaze was fixed on the Path of Peace. The entire avenue seemed deserted but for a few caretakers who had begun to scrub the ashes from the marble thoroughfare. His fixation on the meticulous process had allowed the day to slip by. He had been pacing this expansive room since midday, reflecting on the morning's chaos. It was clear that the two-hundred charred columns of withered palms pointed to something more sinister than a mere act of vandalism. His eagerness to investigate their destruction had all but overshadowed the funeral itself.

He stood in the Session Hall. It occupied an entire floor positioned halfway up the Citadel. It served as the primary council chamber where most of the realm's governing matters were discussed. Walled by glass, it offered expansive views of the vista beyond.

The sprawling city below, the distant Drom Mountains to the north, and the boundless ocean to the south were all in clear view. In the centre of the room was the council table. The robust circular stone mass tapered towards the base and was encircled by fourteen slender matching chairs gently suspended off the floor.

Jaxon studied the city for a moment more. The Citadel, rising from the southernmost tip of the north island, overlooked all. The entirety of Zenithal sat on six artificial islands forming the shape of The Ancients' sigil, a fire orchid. Channels of turquoise waterways divided the six districts as broad, concentric bridges connected them. Each island represented one of the five primordial Gods, respectively. In the centre of each rose the Sanctuaries of Qyma, Kapry, Shaavy, Doma, and Aanka with their brilliant domed roofs of varying hues. The sixth was reserved for the Architects and their Grand Athenaeum.

The silence of the hall was broken by the cracking of the doors as Cyrus Thenta stepped through, clad in his familiar deep purple suit. The noise jolted Jaxon's awareness.

'Uncle! Thank the Gods,' he sighed with relief. 'I called for you hours ago. Are you hurt?'

Cyrus shook his head as he approached his nephew. 'My presence was needed elsewhere. I'm sure you understand.'

'And Aunt Fayh, is she…'

'She's fine.' Cyrus interrupted in pursuit of more pressing concerns. 'Have you spoken to Alysse?'

'Briefly, this morning. She was addled, but intact.'

'Good.' Cyrus replied, striding over to the council table and standing behind the northernmost chair. He drew a long breath then turned his head towards the young prince.

'Her safety is paramount, now more than ever. When my duties demand my attention elsewhere, I need you to be vigilant in my stead. No more daring acts, do you hear? It was foolish of you to rush danger like that. You cannot be so reckless.'

'Yes, uncle, but…'

'No buts, Jaxon!' Cyrus barked, thrusting his face mere inches from his nephew's. 'I have a sworn duty to uphold. How do you expect me to shield you from the scorch when you throw yourself so heedlessly into the fire?!'

Jaxon held firm, restraining his response. His uncle had always been his idol, his mentor, especially in his father's absence, as Emperor Jannon dedicated most of his time to teaching Alysse the ways of rule. Jaxon respected Cyrus greatly, often shadowing his every move to learn the duties of an Imperial Commander.

'I'm sorry, uncle,' he said, acknowledging his faults.

Cyrus eased backwards and placed a hand atop Jaxon's shoulder.

'You are in line to inherit my post as Imperial Commander,' he said gently, 'but a man in such a position cannot act on impulse, despite the chaos before him. When danger declares itself, you must not only see what is within your view, but also anticipate what lies beyond your sight. The moment you narrow your focus on a single threat, another charges from behind.'

The words weighed heavily on the young Prince. He felt defeated, as if he had learnt nothing from his years of training.

'Yes, Uncle,' he sighed.

Cyrus echoed his nephew's sigh.

'I understand,' he said. 'She is your sister. You would cross the Kordas Desert on foot if it meant keeping her safe, as I would have for my sister. I would have waged war to protect your mother. I would have given my own life to the Gods in place of hers. But a decade ago, when the Dusk fell and Kapry came for her, my focus was elsewhere, and she was taken from me.'

Jaxon fought back his emotion. No loss ever compared to the loss he felt for his mother.

'You and your sister are all that remains of her now,' Cyrus continued. 'I see her eyes every time I look into Alysse's, as if she is standing before me once again. Alas, she is not. That is why I will do all in my power to ensure her memory lives on.'

He took a few short steps and peered down at the wake of destruction that scarred the city below.

'Anyway,' he straightened, 'enough on that matter. What is it you called me for?'

Jaxon cleared his throat and refocused on the issues at hand, striding to his uncle's side.

'Uncle, I have spent the day contemplating what happened down there. I fear what it may mean for the Imperium.'

'How so?' Cyrus questioned.

'When I stepped out onto the Path,' Jaxon began, 'I

saw panic—panic in the city folk, panic in the guildsmen. The only faction I did not see panic in was the
Faith. I did not see the Faith at all. They were absent
entirely, all two hundred of them. Only their robes
remained.'

'The Faith? The Ancient's Partisans, you mean?'
Cyrus corrected. 'We are of the Faith. The people are
of the Faith. The guildsmen, for the most part, are of
the Faith.'

'You know what I mean, Uncle. Yes, we all carry
the Faith, but we serve the Gods, not The Ancients.
The Partisans, however, cast aside all else to serve
The Ancients directly.'

'Yes, yes. State your point,' Cyrus snapped, his
patience waning.

'Those palms were planted as a proclamation of
peace between The Ancients and the inaugural Emperor. We all know this. Precisely two hundred of
them,' Jaxon stated as he began pacing the area.
'Now, correct me if I'm wrong, but does this year not
mark the two hundredth anniversary of the war's
end? The Summer Festival was dedicated to com-
memorating this significant milestone.'

'That is correct,' Cyrus said, his face utterly void of
enthusiasm as he began piecing together the prince's
theory.

'Strange, no?' Jaxon said with passion. 'Do you
think it possible that this was some form of message
from The Ancients, an announcement of their desire
to cast aside peace and regain power over Eviiri? I
simply cannot see how this is mere coincidence. An
act of this scale is not contrived in a single night. It

would take a great deal of planning. All involved must be united in the cause. Cohesiveness, loyalty, devotion, all things The Ancients demand of their followers.'

Cyrus grabbed Jaxon's arm and pulled him in close.

'These are bold accusations, Jaxon,' he said, his voice projecting louder than before. 'Do not speak of them lightly.'

To the surprise of both men, a soft voice called out from across the hall.

'What accusations?'

'Your Grace!' Cyrus gasped as he bowed sharply at the sudden appearance of Alysse. 'Your brother and I were just debriefing.'

Alysse plodded closer to the pair, her restless eyes straining in the dwindling sunlight. She reached the council table and settled her weight against the back of a chair.

'You look exhausted,' Jaxon stated. 'Did you sleep?'

'For an hour, maybe two, it's hard to say,' she said, massaging her forehead. 'My mind, it's… I feel I am beginning to distrust my own thoughts. Each time I close my eyes, I see the flames, and in them, I see him there, standing lost under a starless sky.'

Cyrus stepped lively to her side.

'A telling product of your grief, Your Grace,' he said, offering her a comforting hand. 'It is common to experience these inner visions in such somber times.'

'They do not feel like inner visions, Uncle. More like apparitions. I have also seen him with my waking eyes. He appears as real in my sight as you do here and now.'

'Perhaps the herbalist can brew you a tea to settle your mind?' Jaxon suggested.

'I don't need settling.' Alysse bit back, her weariness shifting her mood. 'I need to understand what happened to him. Uncle, did you meet with the examiner again?'

'I did, Your Grace. He is presently on his way to the Sanctuary to extract a vial of blood. I have instructed Reverend Kalax to delay the sealing of the body.' Cyrus paused. 'The request was met with reluctance, but he eventually acceded to it.'

Alysse looked up in confusion.

'Why would he be reluctant?' she quizzed.

'The Faith, as you know, abide unwaveringly by their traditions. They believe that if a body is left unconcealed for too long, the soul may yearn to return to it, re-enter it, and be confined for eternity.'

Jaxon snickered and muttered under his breath. 'Or perhaps *they* have something to conceal.'

'What makes you say that?' Alysse asked.

Cyrus stepped in front of the disgruntled young prince, blocking his next words.

'Your brother is weary, Your Grace, his words are best left unconsidered,' he encouraged.

Alysse shifted her head sideways, catching a glimpse of Jaxon. She identified the intensity in his eyes.

'Thank you, Uncle,' she said, motioning him to step aside, 'but I wish to hear what he has to say.'

Cyrus dared not disobey her request. He turned to

Jaxon as he stepped back and expressed a stern glare of disapproval.

Jaxon caught the glare. Although loyal to his uncle, his sister took precedence. He stepped forward and spoke.

'The Faith Partisans were absent during the chaos. They had stripped themselves of their robes and vanished into the night. There was no trace of them after that.'

'How could two hundred Partisans vanish?' Alysse asked, struggling to grasp the notion.

'Perhaps you didn't see the thousands of mourners in the stands,' Jaxon explained. 'They could have easily slipped into the crowd and spread throughout the city during the panic. We only recognise the Partisans by the robes they wear and the services they perform. Have you ever truly looked upon their faces? They are perpetually veiled and hooded. Remove those veils and they would appear as common as everyone else.'

Alysse agreed with her brother. The Faith Partisans were themselves a mystery, sworn only to obey The Ancients and carry out their duties in service of the Gods.

'Surely someone in the crowd saw something?' she queried.

'You would think so,' Jaxon answered. 'I asked whomever I could, but the people were in darkness. The ceremony shed all light from the city. It was the perfect disguise.'

He stepped closer to his sister.

'Alysse, I cannot see any perpetrators other than

The Ancients. I believe they ordered the torching of the palms. If this is true, then perhaps they also played a hand in our father's death.'

'This is absurd! Hold your tongue, boy.' Cyrus scolded, shoving the young man aside. 'Your Grace, do not allow him to conjure such suspicions. The Ancients have…'

Alysse could hear her uncle's voice but could not process any of his words. Confusion began to overwhelm her. Her thoughts blocked out all audible inputs as her mind raced, leaving only her vision sharp. Within that vision, she caught movement beyond her uncle's shoulder. It was not Jaxon—he stood to her right. It was not the sheers; there were none in this room. Alysse tilted her head, peering behind her uncle as he continued speaking to her.

The figure standing against the setting sun stepped into view. The sunlight outlined a muted green suit. Bushy curls of a familiar moustache lifted as a bright smile caught the contrasting light. It was her father.

She sought to beckon her brother's attention, but felt herself rooted in place.

Her gaze remained fixed on her father, unsure whether her eyes were deceiving her. She knew he was gone—she saw his body. Yet despite all of that, she cared not. He was here, right now, in this moment. He was with her.

A comforting air blew over her. She opened her mouth to speak, but no words came out. Instead, it was her eyes that conveyed the words she wanted to say, and he saw them.

'You're confused, Little Wren,' he said. 'Don't be.'

He lifted his hand to his chest and lightly clasped the dulled gold pendant around his neck.

'Remember your lessons. Remember the histories.'

Still confused, she searched her memory for meaning. Her eyes pressed her father for answers. His response was three words.

'The Lost Prince.'

Alysse looked down at the same pendant that now hung around her neck, her father's words repeating in her mind. She lifted her gaze to ask for clarity, but he was gone.

'Your Grace? Your Grace?' The persistent voice grew louder. 'Are you listening?'

Alysse followed the voice, her eyes landing on her uncle's puzzled face as he stood directly in front of her.

'What?' she said, scanning the room for her father, the pendant still in her grasp.

'The Ancients have forever been loyal to your House,' Cyrus repeated.

'Not forever,' Alysse said in a moment of clarity, her memory landing on a page from her history books.

'What do you mean?' Jaxon queried.

'The rise of the Imperial rule toppled the religious reign,' she began, 'a reign headed by the High Priests themselves. Emperor Jannon the First was met with heavy resistance upon his ascendancy. I read that he requested an audience with the High Priests for months in an attempt to broker any form of peace.'

She sighed and looked down at her pendant. 'It wasn't until the Emperor's first-born son, Jarrys, was murdered at their behest that the resistance ceased.'

'The Lost Prince?' Jaxon probed. 'You believe the High Priests killed him?'

'The prince was murdered by religious fanatics, Your Grace,' Cyrus interjected. 'The Ancients had no part in it.'

'The prince was murdered in the Sanctuary of Qyma by the Faith Partisans,' Alysse asserted. 'They are the High Priests' army in all but name. When has history ever recorded the Partisans carrying out the will of anyone other than the High Priests?'

'I fail to see the logic,' Jaxon said. 'Why would the High Priests murder the prince only to concede to peace immediately after?'

'The memoirs of Jannon the First state that his request for an audience was finally granted just prior to the death of the prince. A truce was brokered between himself and Kalax,' Alysse stated. 'None of the accounts speak of it in any detail. Only the two of them knew its terms.'

'*Know*,' Jaxon corrected. 'Kalax is still living.' He stepped forward towards Alysse. 'Grant me an audience with him and I will ask of these terms.'

Cyrus scoffed. 'The Ancients do not answer to the whims of a curious prince, nor to those of an emperor for that matter. Your father attempted the same without result. They answer only to the Gods, except during a...' He paused short.

'During a what?' Alysse probed.

Cyrus sighed at his own overstatement. 'The only juncture they can be brought to question is a Qyx-Iriyan.'

'A Qyx-Iriyan?' Jaxon queried.

'A Meeting of the Heads.' Alysse said as she began to pace the room. 'The leaders of all three factions convene in this very room. I believe Empress Xenna was the last to call one after the King of Kaprythor went rogue and sent his armies to destroy all major ports around the world. That was a century ago.'

'There has been no cause for such a gathering since then, Your Grace,' Cyrus stated, 'nor do I believe there is cause for one now.'

'Whether you believe it or not, The Ancients must be questioned, Alysse,' Jaxon asserted. 'If they…'

Alysse raised her hand to silence her brother, still pacing the room. She had reached the south-facing windows and looked out to the vast southern sea.

'Uncle,' she said, 'I take it you have informed the Great Houses of their emperor's death?'

'I have, Your Grace,' Cyrus confirmed. 'Houses Iibryn and Tennyr are expected to arrive in the Capital within the week to pay their respects. There has been no word yet from House Frailyn or House Peryx.'

Alysse pondered her next move carefully.

'Good,' she began. 'Send word again to House Frailyn and House Peryx. Inform them that their presence is required in the Capital come the week's end. And notify the Chief Architects. Mia and Gorryn are here in the Capital. Dalos is still lodging in Ton-Basin, if I'm not mistaken. Be sure he receives the summons.'

Jaxon's eyes lit up in excitement. 'Are you really doing it? Are you calling a Qyx-Iriyan?'

'With respect, Your Grace, I must caution you against this.' Cyrus pleaded, striding over to the princess. 'These meetings should not be called on impulse. The Great Houses, The Architects, The Ancients, they will all see this as weakness on your part. A Qyx-Iriyan is reserved only for affairs of great significance.'

Alysse turned sharply towards her uncle. 'Do you not find my father's untimely death, and the burning of our city *affairs of great significance?*'

'Of course I do, Your Grace,' Cyrus cowered, 'I simply mean...'

'Send word, Uncle,' Alysse said calmly.

'Yes, Your Grace.'

Cyrus bowed and began heading for the exit. Arriving at the golden doors, he halted.

'One more thing, Your Grace,' he said, 'and I mean not to overstep, but what if the Great Houses or any other faction choose not to recognise your authority to call this gathering? You are to become Empress, yes, but you are not Empress yet, not until your coronation.'

Alysse smiled and dropped her head. 'You're right, Uncle, that is why the summons will be signed by you. By law, you hold the realm until I am coronated. They may choose not to comply with my orders, but they must comply with yours.'

Cyrus took a deep breath.

Alysse lifted her head and locked eyes with her uncle. 'Ensure everyone arrives on time.'

CHAPTER 5

The last glimmer of dusk crawled in through the oculus atop the Sanctuary of Qyma, gifting faint light to the cavernous hall. Orchid incense ebbed and flowed within the space, pouring out of the mouths of the five colossal statues of the Gods. The greatest statue was that of Qyma the Creator. Standing 25 metres tall, it towered over the other four Gods. The feminine figure wore a flowing gown and an elaborate woven gold headdress that sat atop her hairless head. Her hands nestled a teal-coloured orb against her cheek, her eyes fixed on the delicate warm stone inlay of The Ancients' sigil in the centre of the room. In the centre of the sigil was the pale off-white altar Jannon Aprya still laid upon, cloaked in an ebony shroud, one arm bare and exposed to the dwindling light.

'One more vial should suffice,' the examiner said as he secured a glass vial to the opaque line of tubing that pierced the Emperor's skin. 'Then I will be out of your hair.'

Reverend Kalax gave an unimpressed smirk at the examiner's attempted joke. Having removed his headdress, his hairless scalp was clearly visible to the man. He watched the examiner inspect the grand Sanctuary, his eyes perusing its fineries. The Emperor's dark, oxygen-deprived blood snaked through the tube, appearing black in the dim lighting.

'You are an Architect, no?' Kalax asked, taking slow, methodical steps towards the altar.

'I am a member of the guild, yes.'

'Tell me, do you remain in reach of the Gods, child?'

'Child?' The examiner laughed. 'I am approaching my 84th year of life. I could be no farther from a child.'

'We are all children in the Gods' eyes,' Kalax said, showcasing the mammoth statues surrounding them, 'but I did not ask your age. I asked about the Gods. Do you still pray to them?'

'I've spoken the words from time to time, but to what end?' the examiner stated. 'In all my years, I've yet to hear them speak back.'

'Perhaps you have not been listening. Perhaps you have silenced them in your mind. They may be speaking to you now. If you listen, you will hear.'

The examiner chuckled, his voice reverberating off the solid stone interior of the Sanctuary. 'I hear nothing but my own echo.'

Kalax grinned. 'And you choose to ignore these echoes? That is unwise, child. Whose voice is loudest in one's mind than his own?'

The examiner spent a moment decrypting the High Priest's words.

'Hah,' he scoffed, 'what are you saying, that my own voice is the voice of the Gods? Could I simply speak a thing and it will be? Spare me. If that were true, I'd be Emperor.'

'So that is your desire? To be Emperor?' Kalax asked, taking another slow step towards the man.

'No... I... I simply meant that with such power, one could control the world.' The examiner stammered, feeling the looming presence of Reverend Kalax.

'Then power is the ultimate goal?' Kalax probed.

'I didn't say that.'

'Oh, but you did, child.' Kalax knelt down beside the old man and commanded his attention. 'You spoke not of healing the sick or feeding the hungry, but of the unspoken lust for control—the very desire so many strive to bury.'

The examiner stared into the abyss of the High Priest's onyx eyes, his words consumed by their void. He felt powerless to escape their hold. His hands began to tremble. It was the growing sensation of wetness crawling across his skin that jolted his focus. Looking down, he saw the dormant emperor's blood spilling from the thin opaque tube, drenching his aged hands.

'Ah, shit!' the examiner shrieked. He pinched the tube sharply, creating a tight kink that halted the flow. Reaching into his carryall, he produced a wide roll of cloth and began cleaning his blood-stained hands.

Kalax stood, amused by the frantic flurries of the old man as he attempted to wipe his mishap from the polished, sandy-stone floor.

'I have allowed you enough time to perform your duty, child, now allow us to perform ours.'

Kalax guided the rattled man towards the massive copper doors with a slow outstretching of his arm. The examiner said nothing more as he collected his equipment and hurried out of the Sanctuary.

Kalax turned to the body and approached it. He drew the black shroud over the Emperor's exposed arm. As he brushed over the cold skin, he collected a small droplet of blood on the tip of his finger. Examining it, he first took a whiff of the crimson dollop, then stretched out his tongue and smeared it across his taste buds. His eyes quivered as a metallic twang filled his mouth. He explored the evolving flavours, noting several oddities amongst the natural taste. Turning his gaze to the door, he wondered what, if anything, the examiner would discover within the blood. Having lived for thousands of years, Kalax had encountered a vast array of poisons, all of which he was able to endure. Returning his attention back to the body, he called out for the other High Priests to join him.

—

After completing the body's concealment within

the altar, Kalax motioned to Reverend Thyta, who approached with silent poise. She was the smallest of the High Priests. Her cascading auburn hair framed her youthful face. To an outsider, Thyta might appear as a child no older than thirteen, yet she possessed a mind that had lived through millennia.

'We are done here,' Kalax said.

With a soft bow, Thyta ushered in ten Faith Partisans that had been stationed within the Sanctuary's extremities. The collection of veiled servants converged on the altar, silently awaiting further command.

'You will escort the altar to the Shrine,' Thyta said in a delicate, yet well-annunciated voice. 'It is not wise to use the Path. Travel via the tunnels instead. When you arrive at the pier, a vessel will carry you the rest of the way.'

The ten Partisans bowed in unison, each taking their place around the altar as it gently began to levitate off the stone floor.

'Be prompt,' Kalax added. 'Make sure the altar is secured in its place.'

Once again, the circle of Partisans bowed, then moved off. With every step they took towards the tunnel entrance, the altar drifted silently at their centre, its weightless motion a stark contrast to the finality of its destination.

A deep groan caught Kalax's attention, prompting him to turn towards its origin. There, his gaze settled upon the apathetic face of Reverend Dakaar, whose square jaw tightened as he ground his pristine teeth.

'Why do we toil in vain for them?' he snickered.

'This city was ours long before these usurpers arrived and built their tower. If they wish to honour their dead, let them do so themselves.'

'You know why, brother,' Kalax said calmly as he approached the broad-shouldered priest. 'If we refuse to play our part in this world, then all we have built will wither.'

'And all they have built will crumble.' Dakaar returned. 'Their tower is fracturing. It is only a matter of time before it falls, then we reclaim Eviiri once again.'

Kalax rushed towards his counterpart, stopping a nose-length short of his face.

'Silence!' he hissed. 'Know your place, brother. Speak not on this matter.'

Dakaar's mouth stretched into a wide grin as the stale breath of Kalax wafted over his dark skin.

'You are ashamed, *brother*,' he teased. 'You have always been ashamed. Two hundred years have done little to hide that. You gave it away, all of it, the day you bowed to that man and called him Emperor. And now a path to our old world has been laid and you ponder?'

'Enough.' Thyta pleaded, staring up at her squabbling peers. 'Your minds are out of sorts. Hithema, the essence?'

Reverend Hithema turned at the call of her name, her sleek, jet-black ponytail whipping across her narrow shoulder.

'The extraction is almost complete,' she said confidently.

'Very good,' Thyta commended. 'Brothers, it is

time.'

Kalax delivered one last scowl towards Dakaar before retreating from the immense gallery, the remaining High Priests following close behind.

At the north end of the sanctuary, hidden behind the towering statue of Qyma, lay a spacious vestry. This opulent chamber was adorned with intricate carvings depicting the tales of the Gods, all encircling a pentagonal table at its centre. Windowless, the room was illuminated solely by the warm glow of lamps affixed to the sparse marble columns. Secluded from the view of the main chancel, this vestry served as the private meeting chamber of the High Priests.

Hithema continued onward to a locked den as the others took their seats around the table in the vestry. Within the den, a single shaft of light pierced the darkness, illuminating a circular pedestal beneath it. Atop the pedestal rested a delicate and shallow urn, cradling a cluster of five long-stemmed orchids. Each bloom spanned twice the width of a human hand, their fiery orange hues radiating brilliance. These were Fire Orchids—rare treasures thought lost to time. Amongst all living beings, only the five High Priests had laid eyes upon them. To the rest of the world, they were little more than myth.

At the heart of each Fire Orchid sat a cluster of translucent, bulbous sacs, like teardrops of molten amber. These delicate pouches glistened with a luminous liquid, as if they held the very essence of sunlight within. Fine veiny lines of tubing pierced each sac, extracting the nectar into five opaque vials. Once the last drops had fallen, Hithema collected the vials and returned to the vestry.

She handed each High Priest their own vial before taking her own and joining them at the table. Raising the glowing orange liquid, she spoke in the ancient tongue.

'A gift from The Five. May it light our way.'

In unison, the High Priests repeated the chant.

'May it light our way.'

Together, they brought the vials to their lips and consumed the glowing essence. A rich, sweet aroma filled their nostrils as the fluid emptied from their containers.

Stillness consumed the room as they sat motionless, eyes closed in reverent silence. Moments passed before Kalax opened his. In place of his hollow onyx irises, a crystalline fire-orange glow emitted from his eyes as his skin breathed life again.

CHAPTER 6

The rains had subsided that morning as Dalos and Thio strolled the gardens of the Ton-Basin Athenaeum. The grounds were moderately sized. Lush, manicured foliage lined its snaking paths. The entire area sat high up in the western elevation of the city. No other building sat higher than the Athenaeum. Cascading down from the peaks of the Ton Ranges were channels of spirited rapids, all converging into a single river that cut through the centre of the town. The churning river rumbled amidst the lively city activity.

Thio took leisurely steps to allow his heavy mentor a chance to keep pace. Dalos' dark wooden cane methodically clicked on the stone pavers as he hobbled alongside his apprentice. His other hand held an elegant parasol, shielding the man's receding white hair from the sporadic droplets of rain.

'Sir, with your permission, I would like to visit the

salt mines to obtain a sample. I was thinking I could begin testing…'

'What?!' Dalos exclaimed, turning to a nearby fruit tree and leaning in close to it. 'Did you hear that? Thio wants to begin testing! Oh, Qyma the magnanimous, thank you. Thank you!'

Thio dropped his hip and cocked his head, watching as Dalos began playfully dancing in jest. Despite being the butt of his joke, he couldn't help but smile, relieved to see his mentor's vibrancy return.

'Okay, okay. Settle down, sir. I would hate for you to slip.'

'Quit calling me sir!' Dalos joked. 'I'm not that old. Even if I did slip, I would hop right back up.'

'Or bounce.'

Dalos halted in place and slowly turned to Thio. The two exchanged challenging looks for a moment before bursting into laughter.

'Cheeky shit,' Dalos chuckled as they continued their stroll. 'So tell me, how do you propose to test your theory?'

'Well, that's what I was hoping to confer with you about,' Thio responded. 'In order to destabilise the minerals, I would need an apparatus that can produce very precise frequencies across multiple wavelengths.'

'Hmm,' Dalos pondered, 'a pulse resonator should do the trick. They are extremely complex and a pain to tune.'

'Is there one here?'

'I'm afraid not, m'boy. At least not one suitable for your needs. The Grand Athenaeum in Zenithal has the largest in the country. Perhaps you can pray to the Gods for a pair of wings to match your new pair of balls.'

Thio ignored the joke, his mind donning a heavy cloak of discouragement which began to smother his previous excitement. Self-doubt crept in, growing ever stronger. Before either of them could say another word, a hooded figure rounded the corner and strode briskly towards them.

At first, Thio thought it was a child—perhaps one of the students seeking Dalos' aid. It was only when the figure drew closer that he realised it was Deni, the caretaker, her stumpy legs struggling to keep pace with her hurried momentum.

'Dalos!' she called out, her breathlessness clear in her broken voice. 'There has been word from the Capital, sir.'

'Don't call him sir,' Thio yelled, offering a cheeky grin to his mentor.

Dalos returned the grin, but his expression quickly shifted when he caught the disturbance in Deni's eyes. His face straightened as he lowered his head to meet her gaze.

'What is it?'

'During the funeral, sir… there was… an incident,' she panted, struggling to speak as she fought to catch her breath.

'What kind of incident?' Dalos questioned.

'The Path of Peace was set alight. All two-hundred palms are ash.'

Both Thio and Dalos stood motionless, gripped by the unsettling news.

'Alysse and Jaxon, are they safe?' Dalos pressed, panic rife in his voice.

'They are safe.'

'Who would do this?' Thio asked.

'That remains uncertain,' Deni said. 'The letter was sparse on detail.'

Dalos took a few steps away from his apprentice and the caretaker. He pressed himself against the balustrade of the viewing platform that overlooked the entirety of Ton-Basin. His mind churned. He felt helpless in that moment. Taking a few deep breaths, he calmed himself and returned to the pair of worried companions.

'It will all be fine. Alysse and Jaxon have their uncle to protect them. Good luck getting past Cyrus the Serious,' he joked, attempting to lighten the mood.

Thio rarely saw Dalos in a state of worry, but on those rare occasions, he observed how swiftly Dalos would shift the atmosphere to prevent his concerns from spreading to others. It was admirable, yet Thio couldn't help but worry about the emotional burdens Dalos silently carried.

'There's more,' Deni said, reaching into her fleece overcoat and producing a small black scroll.

'What is this?' Dalos probed. 'A new lunch menu, I hope! I'm growing rather tired of the river trout. People say Ton-Basin is a terrible place to live on account of the weather, but no—it's the damn river trout.'

Deni remained silent, a staunch look on her face. She turned the scroll to reveal the golden wax seal, its surface bearing a flawless imprint of the Imperial sigil.

Dalos looked down at the scroll and took it from Deni. He carefully pried open the parchment and began reading the gold text. His face relayed no emotion to his curious onlookers. Calmly, he turned to Thio and smiled.

'Well, m'boy, it seems the Gods have granted you your wings,' he said. 'We're going to the Capital.'

—

The rainless morning was short-lived as a moderate drizzle began to fall upon the city. Thio shouldered two hefty rucksacks and carried them effortlessly through the main doors of the Athenaeum.

'Oi! Over here!' Dalos yelled over the increasing downpour, already sitting in the carrier to the right of the steps.

'Yeah, yeah, I'm coming. No need to yell,' Thio replied.

'I wasn't sure if you saw me.'

'You're hard to miss,' Thio quipped, hauling his bags into a recess at the back of the carrier. He stepped up onto the small vehicle and took a seat opposite Dalos. Once secured, the carrier lifted off the ground with a deep hum and began drifting down the winding street.

'My finest work,' Dalos chuffed as he patted the side rail of the cart.

'Acoustic levitation. Very impressive,' Thio complimented.

'The earlier prototypes were louder than the four horns of the Citadel. I almost gave up,' Dalos said.

'Well, thank the Gods you didn't. I don't think you would have made the walk.'

Dalos waved a dismissive hand to Thio as the carrier powered towards its destination.

The streets of Ton-Basin meandered down the valley. Factories, shops, and homes lined the narrow roads. City workers pulled wagons of ore and minerals from the towering mountains flanking the busy town. Children played in large puddles, occasionally splashing unsuspecting passersby. Thio and Dalos chuckled as they witnessed the children drench an elderly man enjoying his lunch.

'No, not the river trout!' Dalos said sarcastically. 'Ah, I almost forgot. Here.'

Dalos produced a small leather pouch from his pocket and lobbed it towards Thio. The boy clutched it midair, almost dropping it from the carrier. Thio loosened the drawstrings of the petite sack and opened it. Inside was a palm-sized chunk of unrefined mountain salt.

He smiled. 'Thank you, sir,' he said, tightly gripping the rock.

'Don't go using it all at once. It's not like there are mountains of the stuff,' Dalos said, jokingly pointing at the entrance to the salt mines halfway up the southern mountains.

The journey to the city station took less than half an hour. It was positioned at the base of the city. Two rail tracks stretched out from either end, fading into the distance of the vast land. The two men disembarked the carrier. As they did, they were greeted by a thin middle-aged man in formal attire who collected Dalos' bags and ushered the men to the opulent carriage stationed at the platform. The train was short. No longer than five or so carriers, with sleek lines and tinted aqua glass, embellished with gold trim.

'Where's our driver?' Dalos pressed the station steward. 'You don't expect me to do it, do you? I designed the bloody thing!'

Nervousness struck the steward as he fumbled for a response.

'Leave the poor man alone,' Thio said. 'You also designed the navigation system. No driver needed.'

Dalos laughed, patting the steward roughly on his back.

The two men stepped into the empty carriage. Plush carpets lined the floor. The furniture resembled that of a royal chamber, simple yet refined. Rain pattered on the arched roof, constructed entirely out of glass, offering unobstructed views of their surroundings.

The doors closed as Thio stowed the bags towards the rear of the cabin. He studied the interior. It was nothing like the common trains he and Dalos had used to traverse the country. He watched as Dalos plonked himself on an oversized couch, resting his cane beside him.

'It's a day's journey to the Capital. Get comfortable.' Dalos said, pointing at the opposite couch.

Thio sat as the train departed the station heading east. The rain dancing on the roof was all he could hear. No engine sounds. No wheel friction on the track. Just faint raindrops.

'Sir, the letter from the capital,' Thio said, 'what did it say?'

'It was a summons, m'boy. There is to be a Qyx-Iriyan.'

'A what?' Thio said, trying to repeat the foreign words.

'In the ancient tongue, it means *Meeting of the Heads*,' Dalos said, staring out at the broad vista now whirling past them. 'The Iriyana are a council of the fourteen members of the world's highest-ranking factions.'

'And you are one of these… Iriyana?' Thio asked.

'Of course! I am a Chief Architect,' Dalos replied, adjusting his coat and puffing his chest.

'Who else attends?'

'Well, the three Chief Architects,' Dalos began, 'the five High Priests, the Emperor, of course, the Imperial Commander, and the four monarchs of the other continents. It's quite a grand affair, y'know.'

'Strange, I've not heard of one before,' Thio said.

'And nor should you again. An Emperor gathers the Iriyana only when a matter poses a severe threat to the realm. These meetings are highly secret—few know of their existence. I couldn't tell you when the last one was held. During Empress Xenia's reign?'

'Do you think the realm is in danger?' Thio questioned.

'Hard to say, m'boy. With Jannon gone, the Imperium now passes to Princess Alysse. It would be a heavy burden at such a young age. Perhaps she is only seeking counsel.'

'So the Princess summoned you?'

'In fact, no,' Dalos replied. 'The Princess is only that—a princess. She does not have the authority to call a Qyx-Iriyan until she is crowned. This summons was from the Imperial Commander, Cyrus Thenta. He is in charge in the interim.'

'I see. And what about the flames? It was clearly an attempt to sabotage the ancient tradition,' Thio said.

'It would appear so,' Dalos said. 'Those palms also represented peace in the Capital. Whoever set them alight is trying to send a message—one I can only imagine comes with ill will.'

'The Imperium is safe though, right?' Thio asked.

'Cyrus heads the Imperial Forces,' Dalos said. 'He is the greatest commander Qymathor has seen. His connection to the Princess gives him more cause than any to keep her safe. Her brother too.'

Jaxon. Thio's mind wandered as he recalled briefly meeting the handsome young man in his muted green suit, his smile pinning soft dimples in his cheeks. He recalled the way the wind had swept across his soft curls. And his eyes, his piercing hazel eyes. Lost in thought, Thio barely heard Dalos' voice.

'Am I speaking to myself?' Dalos shouted, his question snapping Thio's mind back into the carriage.

'Sorry, you were saying?'

'You will be staying with us at the Grand Athenaeum,' Dalos continued. 'The dorms there will feel like the Citadel itself compared to the sparrow nests you're used to.'

'Thank you, sir,' Thio said, his eyes lighting up in excitement at the thought of seeing the grand structure.

'Now, be a good lad and fetch me some lunch. Just through that door.' Dalos requested as he pulled out a small book from his carry bag and flicked to his marked chapter.

'Yes, sir. One plate of river trout, coming right up.'

CHAPTER 7

The two imperial guards escorting Alysse and Jaxon through the gardens south of the Citadel's base were dressed in deep purple uniforms intertwined with muted green panels. Gold-plated armour pieces covered vital areas and gleamed in the sunlight. Their thick black boots hammered on the pavement with each step. Alysse felt a sense of security as she eyed their mid-length swords that hung sheathed on wide utility belts. She brushed her hand over the thick, lively foliage of the garden path as they headed for the southernmost tip of the island. Wearing a light, flowing beige suit, she strode in silence alongside her brother, the green of his jacket now vibrant in the sunlight.

Ahead of them were two more guards waiting by the pier. Just below the stone ledge was a small open-top boat. Cream-coloured with gold trim, the vessel sat delicately on the crystal-clear turquoise water of the Bay of Prosperity. The perfectly circular lagoon lay at the centre of the city's six main islands.

Arriving at the pier, Jaxon offered his hand to Alysse as she stepped onto the watercraft. The vehicle's stabilisers planted it in place, making it feel like she was stepping onto solid ground. The two guards accompanying them embarked behind.

Sitting on the front seats, Alysse looked out ahead. Far in the distance was a small island in the centre of the bay. *The Shrine of Old.* She had visited it many times with her father to pay respect to the past Emperors and Empress whose marble coffins lay at rest there.

As soon as the two guards took up their posts at the rear of the vehicle, it slipped away from the pier and began the crossing to the shrine. The winds were gentle. The salty smell of the water stirred in Alysse's nostrils as she drew a long breath.

'The city feels quiet,' she spoke.

'The people are uneasy,' Jaxon said. 'Perhaps they fear a rebellion of sorts. They look to you now for leadership.'

Alysse's gaze stayed fixed on the distant island.

'I'm not ready, Jax,' she said, a slight tremble in her voice.

'Is anyone ever ready?' Jaxon replied.

'I thought I had more time. Father's death has come without warning. The cause is still unknown.'

'The examiner has tested the blood and found nothing,' Jaxon stated. 'Perhaps it is true that his heart just… stopped.'

A tear fell from Alysse's face as she fidgeted with

the pendant around her neck.

'I need him. I don't know how to rule, Jax,' she said, feeling the weight of the world pressing down upon her.

'You have Uncle Cyrus for guidance. And me,' Jaxon said, placing a hand on her shoulder. 'The position is not served alone.'

His words brought her little comfort.

'I have received word that Dalos is nearing the Capital,' Jaxon continued, pep in his voice. 'His wisdom helped father countless times.'

Alysse cracked a faint smile as she reminisced. She and Jaxon were very fond of the rotund man and his lively persona. Dalos was always a welcome sight in their often sombre imperial lives.

'Have I made the right choice in calling a Qyx-Iriyan?' Alysse asked. 'The Great Houses may view it as weakness.'

'The Great Houses will rally behind you to weed out this threat, if it is indeed a threat,' Jaxon said. 'This is your chance to show them you are the strong leader father believed you to be. The Imperium will continue to hold strong, I know it.'

'If The Ancients are indeed behind this, it will split the world in two,' Alysse said. 'The Faith has a devout following. Many will flock to their cause out of fear of the Gods' wrath.'

'The Gods do not intervene, Alysse,' Jaxon said.

'The Great Flood would disagree,' she rebutted.

'The Architects say the flood was an inevitable natural phenomenon,' Jaxon stated, 'and is sure to one day happen again.'

'And The Ancients once ruled this world. Are we sure that isn't going to happen again?' Alysse asked.

Jaxon contemplated the thought as they continued their transit.

The island ahead grew larger as the raft neared. A towering stack of eight marble altars stood proudly in the centre, their father's now resting atop.

Both Alysse and Jaxon stared ahead at the shrine in silence as the boat approached the pier. Alysse, familiar with the shrine, noticed something odd in the distance—something out of place. Squinting in the sunlight, she leaned forward in an attempt at a clearer view. Towards the highest altar, she spotted a pale stain on its northern face—an object of sorts. *A shroud perhaps, left by one of the Faith Partisans who ushered the altar to the island,* she thought. She focused in on the drooping form. A pit formed in her stomach. Before the vessel could come to a stop, she leapt up and onto the pier.

'Alysse!?' Jaxon called out, instinctively trailing her.

The Princess was now running at full sprint towards the monument. Getting closer, her fears were confirmed. The object was not a shroud, but a body, naked and upside down. Jet-black hair hung from his head.

She screamed as her father's face came into view. Jannon Aprya swung twelve metres off the ground from a rope tied to his feet; his arms pinned out wide, the sigil of House Aprya painted in blood on the altar behind the body.

Jaxon caught up to Alysse, grabbed her, and spun her away from the horrific scene. He held her firm as she wailed and attempted to break free.

'Pa!' she screamed.

Standing directly before the shrine, Jaxon looked up at his father's mutilated body. In the middle of his chest was a blistering branded icon. The symbol formed an elongated "X," split by a vertical spine and a sharp horizontal crossbar.

Jaxon used all his might to heave his sister away from the shrine and back towards the pier.

'Guards! Help me with her!' he yelled over her screams.

One of the guards, still on the boat, attempted to step off before he was suddenly halted, the other behind him grappling his collar. Jaxon looked over in confusion. In one swift motion, the rear guard unsheathed his sword and drew it across the neck of his unsuspecting comrade. Blood poured from the hairline slit as the body dropped to the floor.

Jaxon stopped in shock. Alysse, now bearing witness to the murder, also halted in fear.

'Jax!' she managed to shriek.

'It's okay, I'm here. I'll distract him. Once you have a clear path, get to the boat and go back to the Citadel,' Jaxon whispered as he slowly moved Alysse towards the island's western edge.

The guard's stare was fixed on the two. He leaped off the boat and ran towards them.

'Go, now!' Jaxon yelled as he shoved her backwards. Alysse found her footing. There was no clear path to the pier. Scanning for a solution, she ran towards the water and dove in.

Within seconds, the guard was swinging his blade at Jaxon. The Prince darted around the stone courtyard, avoiding every attempt made by the traitor. Weaponless, Jaxon swung an empty fist at the man, making contact before dodging another attack.

The two fought viciously as Alysse swam for the boat. Arriving at the pier, she hauled herself up. Leaping onto the boat, she looked down at the pool of blood at her feet, then to the lifeless body from whence it came, then to the sheathed blade on the guard's belt.

Jaxon landed another blow to the guard's torso. The man grunted in pain as he thrust his sword forward. His blade slipped across Jaxon's face, opening a small cut on his cheek. Jaxon stumbled backwards as the man prepared another attack, rage rife in his eyes. Right before the guard could advance, Jaxon spotted a glint of metal pass alongside the man's neck. In an instant, the guard's eyes widened. A moment later, his head toppled off his shoulders, hitting the pavement with a bone-cracking thud.

Alysse stood behind the collapsed body, the sword in her hand dripping with blood. The two exchanged tremulous looks as each fought to catch their breath.

'We must get back to the Citadel, now!' Jaxon panted, motioning to the boat.

'No!' Alysse said. 'Our Imperial Guard has been compromised. Whoever is behind this does not want us alive.'

'We must inform Uncle Cyrus!' Jaxon exclaimed.

Alysse paced the area. She looked over at her father's body, numbed by the image. Beyond the towering shrine, past the bay, was Zenithal's southern island. That was when the idea struck her.

'We will go to the Grand Athenaeum,' she said.

'The Athenaeum?' Jaxon questioned.

'The Architects do not involve themselves with politics, they have no desire for power, therefore they pose no threat,' Alysse stated. 'Plus, you said Dalos is almost here.'

Jaxon watched as Alysse turned and made for the boat. He leant down and unhooked the belt from the headless corpse, then persisted towards the pier.

Alysse leapt onto the raft and approached the dead guard. She crouched over him and mumbled a prayer as she softly closed his vacant eyes, then cleaned her blade on his purple jacket.

'Help me with him,' she said as Jaxon stepped onto the boat.

The two scooped up the limp body and lugged it over the side rail. The body plunged into the water, floating for a moment before sinking. Rich crimson blood permeated the turquoise water as the body disappeared into the depths.

Jaxon moved over to the control module and activated the manual override. He pulled at the control wheel, and the vehicle began to ease away from the pier. Turning the vessel southwards, he levered the throttle to full speed.

CHAPTER 8

The train snaked widely through the sprawling Besti-Qa farming plains. Bountiful crops and grazing fields covered the lands to the west of the Drom Mountain range. These lands produced the main supply of food throughout Qymathor. Small homes and processing plants dotted the region.

Dalos sat quietly, his favourite book capturing his thoughts.

'What are you reading?' Thio asked.

'The Unsettled Sea, by Myra Okombuur—my wife,' Dalos replied, his eyes staying fixed on the pages.

Thio found it odd that Dalos rarely spoke of his late wife. All he knew was that she had died nearly three years ago, but he did not know how, nor did he dare ask.

'What's it about?' he probed carefully.

Dalos huffed, then folded the top corner of the

page he had just read and closed the book, shifting his attention to his prying apprentice.

'It's about overcoming one's fears,' he began, 'and recognising that our desires are not always to our benefit, despite how much we desire them. When I'm done with it, you should give it a read.'

Thio accepted the offer with a nod and said no more about it. He looked out over the plains at the towering slopes ahead of them. The Drom Mountains were the largest in Qymathor, visible from hundreds of kilometres away. Thick flora covered most of the foothills. Remnants of the winter's snow channeled down from the peaks, carving through the pale rock of the near-vertical alps.

'A little bigger than the Ton Ranges, wouldn't you say?' Dalos said, observing the young man's wander-lust stare.

'My mother read me tales of these mountains, created during the Great Battle of the Gods,' Thio said, his eyes not parting from the scenery. 'They say Kapry threw Qyma down from Tharpys, the heavens themselves. The impact was so formidable it shifted the lands into the sky, creating these forms.'

'Curious. Do you take these tales as fact?' Dalos asked.

Thio turned to the old man with an incredulous look.

'The people of the Capital call them the Soaring Shield,' Dalos stated. 'They protect the city from the abrasive northern winds. They also form an impene-trable arc around the Bay of Zenithal. Only three tunnels bore through them. The East Passage, which leads to the White Isles and the eastern seaboard. The North Passage, which heads towards the Kordas Desert and beyond. And the West Passage. We will be traversing it soon. You should be able to see it.'

Thio's eyes traced the line of tracks ahead to a circular stone opening in the approaching distance. The elaborate tunnel entrance was carved into the slopes of the mountain. It appeared as a speck against the sheer size of the alpine giants. He spotted The Ancients' sigil cresting the finely polished stone portal.

'To protect the city from any who would wish harm against its people,' Dalos said, noticing Thio's inquisitive stare. 'Although, it wasn't The Ancients that built these tunnels, it was The Architects. An incomprehensible achievement—sturdy and true, not even the Gods could buckle them.'

The cabin lights woke as the train approached the circular entrance. Thio could now clearly see the intricacies of the sigil carved atop the entrance—a leap above the simplified icon used in most textbooks these days. He peered down the pitch-black void ahead. Within seconds, the view outside the glass ceiling turned black, plunging the cabin into darkness.

'No lights?' Thio asked.

'They keep the tunnels unilluminated to ward off unwelcome travellers,' Dalos stated. 'A handheld lamp would diminish long before it reached the other side.'

'The world has been at peace for 200 years. Surely some light could be granted?' Thio said.

'Peace is a naked flame on a windy night. It must be shielded, or darkness will take its place,' Dalos said.

Thio sat in silence, reflecting on his mentor's words. The recent events in the Capital had all but left his thoughts since departing Ton-Basin.

The darkness of the tunnel endured for several minutes. Spotting a faint light ahead, Thio stood and moved towards the nose of the train. He held his face close to the glass. The light expanded rapidly as they sped towards the exit.

Thio stood motionless, squinting at the ever-brightening wall of light. The train suddenly became consumed by daylight as it burst out into the expanse of the bay. His eyes widened in awe as they adjusted. The city of Zenithal was illuminated in the midday sun. The gleaming white marble of the buildings glistened above the spirited turquoise waters. At the centre of the city, he saw the Citadel soaring gallantly above all.

'Welcome to Zenithal, m'boy,' Dalos said, now standing behind Thio.

The train shot over the short foothills of the mountain before continuing over the water. The thin rail track stood on stone pillars that led the train towards the city. Thio did not move from his position, absorbing the views as the city approached.

The train slowed to a low cruising speed as it turned towards the waterway between the two western islands, lowering closer to the water's surface. The channel spanned 100 metres with pale-white stone quay walls lining each side. Solid arched bridges crossed overhead, boasting ornate carvings of the histories of Eviiri.

A smile was fixed on Thio's face, like a child receiving a new toy. Well-dressed city folk strolled the paths on either side. He caught some staring at the opulent carriage as it passed by. Elegant buildings with gilded trimmings rose multiple stories from the tidy streets. Everything felt new to him. The Capital was unlike any city or town Thio had visited. It was refined, polished, yet portrayed no sense of arrogance or condescension.

A few short minutes passed as the train continued through the city, still levitating over the water. Ahead, at the end of the channel, lay the Bay of Prosperity, the central fulcrum of the city. The waters here were much shallower than those encircling the exterior. The purity of the white sandy sea floor amplified the vivid turquoise hues of the bay. It was a beauty unrivalled.

Thio turned his attention north to the towering Citadel—a tall, slender monolithic icon, dwarfed only by the distant Drom mountains. Its polished white exterior reflected sunlight across the city. Colossal green banners adorned its base, the sigil of House Aprya clearly visible even from this distance. Beyond the Citadel, faint smoke still rose from the Path of Peace.

The train turned southeast as Thio moved his gaze to the centre of the bay. There he noticed a small island in the middle.

'The Shrine of Old,' Dalos spoke. 'Every Emperor and Empress since the birth of the Imperium lies there. Seven marble altars stacked one atop the other.'

Realising he had not accounted for his dear friend's recent addition to the monument, Dalos sighed and corrected himself. 'Eight.'

'The city is shaped as a Fire Orchid? Was it built by the Faith?' Thio asked.

'It was. This city was established just prior to the Thousand-Year War at the centre of the world. It stood to symbolise the Faith's presence and to reflect the religious significance of this sacred site. Colossal sanctuaries to each God were constructed on each of the five main islands. The Citadel was erected following the fall of the religious reign and the rise of the Imperium. The Architects later claimed the sixth, the southernmost island, detached from the rest as an assurance that their work could continue without the interference of either faction.'

Thio turned to the southern island. It was greener than the others. Tall oak trees spread across the district, shielding many of the buildings.

'Look, there,' Dalos said, pointing towards the island's centre.

Rising above the foliage was an immense structure. A brilliant blue dome reflected sunlight in every direction. Great sandstone pillars encircled the building.

'The Grand Athenaeum,' Dalos said, placing a hand on Thio's shoulder.

Thio stared in silence, the excitement in his eyes clearly visible. He had dreamed of studying in the great library ever since he was old enough to hold a book.

The train caressed the outer edge of the bay as it approached its destination. A solid gateway in the periphery of the south island's quay wall opened to receive them, the familiar crest of The Architects guarding overhead. The passageway beyond was lit with warm-coloured trail-lights. In the distance, the underground station became visible.

Standing on the platform was a naturally curvy young woman in her thirties. Her kind, youthful face brimmed with joy as the train approached. The soft curls of her honey-brown hair flowed loosely as the tunnel draft swept through. Spotting the two men at the head of the carriage, she waved in excitement.

The train came to a stop at the platform, and the cabin doors opened. Dalos stepped out first and was greeted by a tackling hug that almost knocked him over.

'Dalos, you old fool, welcome home!' the young woman exclaimed.

Thio trailed out of the carriage, chuckling to himself at the overpowering gesture of affection forced upon his mentor.

'M'girl!' Dalos said, finding his balance and embracing her. 'It's good to be home. Ah, allow me to introduce Thio. Thio, this is Mia, Chief Architect and my lovely daughter.'

'Chief?… Daughter? It… It is an honour, ma'am.' Thio said bashfully.

'Ma'am? Careful who you're talking to, boy,' Mia said as she playfully greeted him with a tight squeeze. Thio instantly felt comfort in her embrace. *His daughter indeed.*

'I see you share your father's distaste for formality,' he said.

'Indeed! I share a lot of my father's traits,' she said.

Thio looked over at Dalos then back at Mia. 'I'm guessing you share your beauty with your mother then.'

Mia burst into laughter.

'Cheeky shit,' Dalos mumbled. 'Go fetch the bags.'

CHAPTER 9

Jaxon pulled the boat up alongside one of the piers of
the south island after navigating the generously sized
port. Having manoeuvred around a collection of
small exploration vessels docked alongside the
throngs of jetties, he brought the boat to a stop and
helped Alysse disembark. Before disembarking himself, he reengaged the autopilot and set the controls
to return the boat to the Citadel. Once on the pier, he
and Alysse were surprisingly greeted by the pier
master, Koris.

'Princess!?' he said, bowing his head. 'I don't believe we were expecting you. You're drenched. Is
everything okay?'

'Apologies for the unscheduled visit, sir. We're here
to see Dalos at the Grand Athenaeum,' she said calmly, deliberately avoiding the pier master's enquiry.

'I'm afraid Dalos is not here. He has not been in the
Capital for some time now,' the man said timidly.

'We have word he will be arriving today,' Jaxon said with a forced smile. 'We are happy to wait for him inside the Athenaeum. Please arrange a carrier for the Princess.'

'At once, Your Grace,' Koris said with a sceptic eye, spotting the unusual blade at Jaxon's side.

Koris stepped aside as Alysse and Jaxon headed towards the administration building at a brisk pace. He stood in place a moment, staring at his unexpected visitors, trying to piece together a reason for their unannounced arrival. He looked back at the boat that had begun pulling away from the pier until something caught his eye. Through the side rails, he spotted the pool of blood on the deck. Alarm set in as he turned and hurried to catch up to the two who were already entering the port building.

Trailing them, Koris motioned to an officer. He approached and whispered in his ear. The officer nodded and hurried off down the east corridor.

'Princess,' the pier master called out.

Alysse and Jaxon froze in place as the man caught up to them.

'Princess, might I suggest we take the tunnels instead?' he said, his hand directing them to the corridor.

Alysse turned to Jaxon. The two contemplated the suggestion for a moment, assessing any possible risks. Placing a reassuring hand on his sword, Jaxon gave her a soft nod.

'Thank you, sir. Perhaps that is best. Which way?' Alysse said, feigning a smile.

'Follow me,' Koris said, turning to the east

corridor.

He approached a solid stone door where the officer from moments ago stood guard. He methodically poked various points on the carved inlay. Low hums sounded with every press until a high-pitched chime rang softly. A brass handle appeared from a cavity in the door. He grabbed it and heaved. The door swung open to reveal a narrow passageway, void of natural light. He ushered Alysse and Jaxon through, the officer following behind.

The walk to the hidden stairwell was brief. Koris led them down the spiral shaft at a moderate pace. The air grew thick as they descended. The distinct smell of rust became apparent. Alysse could sense that these tunnels were seldom used.

Nearing the stairwell's terminus, Koris paused briefly and turned to his companions.

'One moment, please,' he said with a smile, then continued further down the landing.

The two watched as he approached another officer posted at the base of the stairwell and exchanged a few short words with him. He dismissed the man with a nod then motioned for Alysse and Jaxon to advance.

'How much further, sir?' Jaxon called out, his scepticism ever-growing.

Alysse, too, felt uneasy, sensing the presence of another officer behind her.

'Just down this passage. There is a carrier there,' Koris said.

Alysse clutched Jaxon's arm as they continued to follow the old man.

'Jax, I don't like this. What if it's a trap?' she whispered.

'I won't let anything happen to you. I swear it,' he said, firmly gripping the short sword on his belt.

Koris turned a corner towards the end of the passage.

'Here we are,' he said, activating the tunnel's traillights with a wave of his hand.

To the relief of Alysse and Jaxon, in front of them sat a four-person carrier. The petite cart hummed as it lifted off the ground.

'Allow me, Princess,' he said, offering his hand to Alysse.

Alysse stepped up; Jaxon behind her. Still cautious, he scanned the carrier for anything out of the norm. Nothing.

'I will take them from here, Jonna. You're dismissed,' Koris said to the officer.

Koris hopped up and took the leading seat, then pulled at the control wheel. The vehicle shifted to the right, then eased into motion down the dimly lit tunnel.

'Princess,' Koris said, 'now that we're alone, we can speak freely. I have my officer sending word to the Athenaeum as we speak. If indeed Dalos has arrived in the capital, I've requested that he meet you down below.' He paused for a moment. 'I am not sure what is happening, Princess, but you are safe here. I can promise you that. Your father was a good friend of mine. He would often stop in on his way to the Athenaeum for a tea. My deepest condolences for your loss, both of you.'

A comforting tide of relief washed over Alysse.

'Thank you, sir,' she said. 'I must emphasise the need for discretion. Our business with Dalos is strictly our own.'

'Of course, Princess,' Koris acknowledged as the carrier sped through the underground network towards the Grand Athenaeum.

—

Dalos navigated the tunnels as fast as he could, the hurried rhythm of his cane echoing throughout the narrow corridors.

'Slow down, Pa,' Mia exclaimed, pacing beside the hobbling man.

'Something's wrong. I feel it. Alysse and Jaxon would not arrive unannounced otherwise,' Dalos said with a heavy breath. 'Thio, stay close.'

The three continued down the corridor towards the main thoroughfare of the subterranean maze. Rusty staleness filled the air. Ahead, Thio spotted movement in the dim lighting.

'Sir, there,' he said, pointing at the approaching vehicle.

The group arrived in the main tunnel as the carrier came to a stop. Alysse and Jaxon stepped off with haste.

'Alysse,' Dalos said as he embraced her. 'M'girl,

you're soaked? What happened?'

Alysse remained silent, relieved by the heavy man's presence.

Mia approached Jaxon and offered a comforting hug. 'Jaxon, are you okay?'

'Mia, it's good to see you,' Jaxon said, exchanging a faint smile then turning to Dalos. 'Sir, perhaps we should speak in your quarters.'

'Of course, m'boy. This way,' Dalos said, pointing down a side corridor before turning to the hovering carrier. 'Thank you, Koris. No one is to know they are here.'

Koris nodded then rounded the carrier back towards the port.

In the flurry, Alysse and Jaxon had not yet noticed the young man accompanying Dalos until they began their ascension into the Athenaeum.

'Dalos?' Alysse said cautiously, motioning with her eyes to the unfamiliar companion.

'Forgive me, this is Thio, my apprentice,' Dalos said.

Both Alysse and Jaxon turned their attention to the young man.

'Your Grace. My Prince.' Thio said coyly.

'I know you. We met in Ton-Basin,' Jaxon recalled as the lights of the tunnel caught Thio's strong features.

'We did, My Prince,' Thio said, a soft smile tugging at one corner of his mouth, surprised by the Prince's recollection.

'Dalos speaks very highly of him. A future Chief Architect, I think he said,' Mia added.

Thio sheepishly adjusted his spectacles as they continued their way through the hidden passages within the Grand Athenaeum.

Reaching the top of the slender stairwell, Dalos unlocked the hefty door. It opened into a modest reading room. Sunlight poured in through two ceiling-high windows, casting warmth across a lavishly embroidered rug. Cluttered bookcases lined the walls. With a determined effort, Thio contained his excitement as he beheld the extravagant study.

'Through here,' Mia said, guiding the party down a short hallway and into Dalos' chambers.

The room was a spacious octagon. The walls alternated between sandstone and glass. The wide-open picture of the city beyond was tinted by the faint sapphire hues of the window panes. Each piece of furniture sat with purpose and sophistication. An octagonal oak table stood sturdy in the north-west corner.

'Please, sit. It seems we have much to discuss,' Dalos said, guiding one of the floating chairs out for Alysse.

Mia offered Alysse a towel to dry herself as the four sat. Thio remained standing by the door, afraid that his presence was not appreciated by the Princess.

Dalos noticed Alysse's uneasy stare at his young apprentice. 'Fear not, Princess. I trust Thio with my life,' he said. 'You are safe to speak freely.'

Alysse hesitated a moment, then spoke.

'I fear we are facing a great threat. A threat to the peace of this country and to our House.'

She paused, her words caught in her throat.

'The Shrine…' she continued, taking a deep breath. 'The Shrine of Old has been desecrated. My father's body hangs mutilated from his altar with a strange sigil branded into his chest.'

Dalos and Mia sat silent in disbelief.

'One of the Imperial Guards escorting us to the Shrine murdered his comrade, then attempted to take our lives,' Jaxon added.

'By all the Gods!' Dalos exclaimed as he battled with the scenario in his mind. His thoughts conjured images of his dear friend, and the horrific scene his two children had just borne witness to. He rose from his chair and moved towards the window overlooking the bay. The Shrine of Old appeared peaceful in the distance.

'I will send guild members immediately to retrieve your father,' Dalos said.

'No,' Alysse replied. 'The fewer people that know about this, the better.'

Mia reached over and rested her hand atop Alysse's.

'My girl, I am so sorry,' she said as a tear rolled down her cheek.

Alysse fought back her own grief as she reciprocated the touch.

'Your uncle…' Dalos began.

'He is unaware,' Jaxon interjected. 'We came straight here. I prompted our boat to return to the Citadel at low speed. It should arrive shortly. I can only assume there will be panic when it does. He needs to know we're safe before then. Can we send word from here?'

Dalos quickly turned to Thio.

'M'boy, over there,' he said, pointing across the room.

Thio hurried in the direction of Dalos' gesture. Inside a small cavity in one of the walls was a weighty black box. He picked it up with ease and brought it to the table.

'Here, give it to me,' Mia said pressingly.

Thio peered over as Mia lifted the lid to reveal an intricate cube. He looked down curiously at the peculiar object. He had never seen anything of the sort. It was a mixture of wood and brass surrounded by a set of coin-sized marble buttons. With a system of rhythmic presses, Mia entered the message. Smooth harmonic tones whispered out from the device.

Thio continued to look on, puzzled.

Finishing the encrypted message, Mia pressed another button on the front face of the object. A soft glow from an indicator light began to pulse.

She gave Jaxon a reassuring nod.

'What is it?' Thio blurted, enthralled by the strange apparatus.

'It's one of mine,' Mia said proudly. 'A sonic transmitter. I discovered how to cast frequencies over great distances when I was fourteen. The discovery was profound and is kept heavily guarded. They are only used in times of urgency or distress.'

'The message is translated into tones,' Dalos added, 'like the melody of a song. Only a select few are taught how to interpret them. A secret language of sorts.'

Paying no attention to the conversation, Alysse

stood from her chair and walked over to the window. She could see the minute outline of the shrine in the middle of the bay. A wave of despair flooded over her as she dropped her head and closed her eyes.

'Little Wren?' a voice spoke.

Alysse kept her eyes shut. She knew it was her father's voice, yet dared not look at him in fear of seeing his branded skin.

'Do not fear,' the voice continued.

'What is happening, Pa? Why is this happening?' she whispered, a tear rolling down her cheek.

'Our paths are fraught with obstacles, many of which we cannot avoid,' he said. 'But does that mean we stop moving forward? Or does it grant us the chance to forge new paths, ones that wind towards horizons unseen? Each obstacle we encounter prepares us for the next. Knowledge is your true power, Little Wren. What would an empress be without the knowledge of her empire? In time, the way will become clear.'

Alysse felt a hand on her shoulder. The touch startled her as she opened her eyes to see Dalos and Mia at her side. The voice of her father faded in her mind. She fell into their arms and wept.

Jaxon remained at the table, curiously watching Thio study the transmitter.

'So you're his apprentice,' Jaxon said. 'We had doubts he would ever take one on.'

Thio lifted his gaze from the box and met Jaxon's stare. The luminance of the Prince's hazel eyes glimmered now in the daylight. He suddenly felt weak and lost for words.

'Um… yes… It came as quite a shock to everyone in Latyth as well,' he managed to say. His hands smoothing over his creased, off-white linen tunic.

'So you are from Latyth?' Jaxon asked.

'No, My Prince. I was born in Syka, a small village just south of the port city.'

'Then how did you come to study in Latyth?'

'My mother. She wrote to the Athenaeum when I was twelve, begging for one of the mentors to admit me into the guild.'

Jaxon observed a sudden sadness in Thio's eyes, even through the young man's worn spectacles.

'She had fallen very ill, you see. Growing up, we had very little. My father died right before my younger sister was born. I guess my mother was trying to find a home for us before… the inevitable,' Thio said, adjusting his posture, fearful he was rambling to an uninterested audience.

'And the guild accepted you, just like that?' Jaxon asked.

'Not at first.' Thio replied. 'For months she wrote to them as her sickness grew, pleading more and more. The sickness then took hold of my sister, Y'mara. I was lucky to avoid it. I spent most days gathering herbs for them to ease their pain. I tried everything I could.'

Jaxon's attention was fixed as the young man spoke. He hadn't noticed that Alysse, now calmed, was listening in on the conversation from across the room.

'Then, a week before my thirteenth birthday, my mother…'

Thio's words were cut short as the transmitter on the table sounded, commanding the room's attention. A mixture of frequencies pulsed from the wooden gadget. Mia ran to the box and placed her ear close to it. Her face scrunched as she focused on translating the emanating tones.

'What does he say?' Dalos asked, pressing Mia to translate faster.

She struggled to decode a handful of the words, allowing the message to repeat a few times.

From across the room, Alysse spoke. 'He is coming alone via the tunnels. *Tell no one of our presence here,*' she said, still staring out the window. The room fell into silence as the tones ceased.

Jaxon and Dalos looked at her stunned.

'You understand this language?' Jaxon asked.

'Father taught me,' Alysse replied. '*What would an empress be without the knowledge of her empire?* So I learned. I absorbed every bit of knowledge I could, but now, it seems not enough.'

Dalos moved towards her. 'My dear Alysse. Your father believed in you. We believe in you. This world will flourish with you leading its people. You are not alone.'

Alysse said nothing.

'We are here for you,' Mia said.

'Always,' Jaxon added.

CHAPTER 10

The sunset gilded the interior of the Session Hall, bathing it in a warm glow. The boundless Southern Sea shimmered as it slowly faded into the cool hues of the approaching night. Alysse, now back within the comforting walls of the Citadel, peered down at the Shrine of Old.

'Your Grace,' Cyrus spoke, entering the room, 'your father has been re-entombed within his altar. I have stationed my most trusted men on the island to safeguard it until we are sure such acts of profanation will not happen again.'

'How did this happen at all?' Jaxon asked in frustration as he sat at the robust council table. 'It was my understanding that once the altar is sealed, it's sealed. Unless, of course, it wasn't.'

Cyrus huffed as his patience with the young Prince waned.

'Speculation invites more harm than resolution,

Jaxon,' Cyrus barked. 'I can only relay the reports I have gathered thus far.'

'Let us not forget, uncle, that one of *our* men tried to kill us!' Jaxon growled. 'What report can you offer on that matter?'

'The Imperial Guard has never before been breached,' Cyrus asserted, his tone edged with pride. 'This was no man of ours. I have ordered a thorough investigation to uncover the identity of this insurgent and the forces that drove his intent.'

'What of the brand on his chest?' Alysse spoke softly, almost inaudible to the squabbling men. She had not moved from her vantage point since arriving in the Session Hall.

'Your Grace?' Cyrus probed, confused by her question.

Saying nothing, Alysse expelled a lungful of warm breath across the cooling glass, fogging a small area. With a delicate finger, she traced the scorched sigil that had burned itself into her mind, just as it had been seared into her father's flesh. She willed herself to unbind it from the memory of his ruined form.

Cyrus watched on with intrigue as Alysse composed the sharp-lined icon. Completing the final downward stroke of its piercing spine, she stepped back from the glass. Now, clear of view, Cyrus viewed it in its full form as his eyes widened.

'It can't be,' he whispered.

'You've seen this before?' Jaxon asked, quizzically staring at his bewildered uncle.

'Not entirely, but those lines are unequivocal,' he said.

'Tell me more, Uncle,' Alysse urged.

'A decade ago,' he began, 'not a few weeks before your mother's passing, your father came to me with a letter. He said he had received it anonymously. There was no name signed to it, nor any clear sigil. The only markings were the flanking lines that encased its words.' He paused. 'The author of the letter called it *The Reclamation*.'

'I don't understand. What did the letter say?' Alysse probed.

'It was rather cryptic, Your Grace,' Cyrus admitted. 'I pondered its meaning for weeks yet failed to decipher it. It alluded to past decisions made by your father and the potential repercussions they might yet bring. I'm afraid its true meaning eluded me.'

'So an old enemy has waited ten years to enact their… what… grievances?' Jaxon questioned.

Cyrus ignored the Prince's words, instead honing his attention on Alysse.

'Your Grace,' he said timidly as he approached her, 'I have been awaiting an opportune moment to share something with you. In light of what has happened today, I see no better time.'

'What is it, Uncle?' Alysse asked, a pit forming in her stomach.

'Your father received another letter, only a few days ago.'

Alysse felt the blood retreat from her face, leaving only a hollow chill. She watched as Cyrus reached into his coat pocket and produced a tightly rolled scroll. Dread coiled around her limbs, keeping her rooted where she stood. Even as he extended it toward her, her senses refused to acknowledge the offering.

Jaxon strode in and took the scroll, carefully unravelling it. Then, he read it aloud.

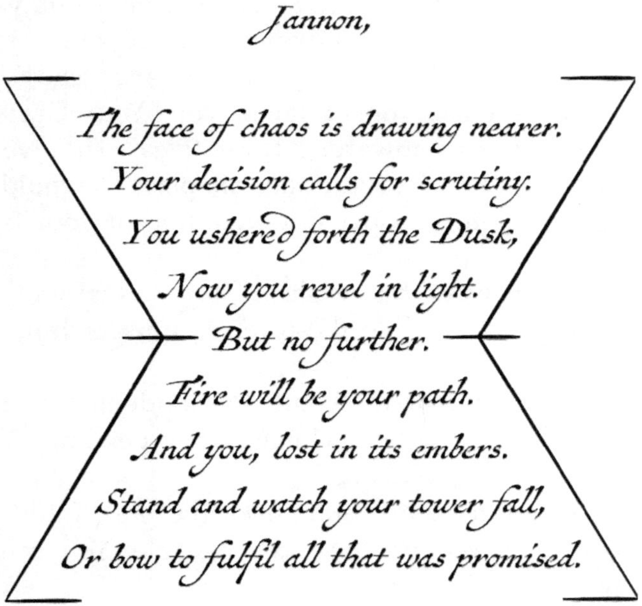

'So it *was* murder.' Alysse's voice cracked.

In an instant surge of rage, Jaxon rushed his uncle, clutching his collar and driving him backwards into the thick glass window.

'And where were you, Uncle? His sworn commander and his brother by law!' Jaxon erupted, fury spilling from his clenched jaw. 'Only yesterday you told me to pay mind to all beyond my sight, yet you failed to see what was right in front of you?'

'You're right!' Cyrus yelled as Jaxon shoved him aside. 'I failed him. I failed you, Your Grace.' He moved swiftly towards Alysse. 'Please, forgive me if you can. I had precautions in place. I would have spoken of this sooner if it were not for your father's wishes.'

'What were his wishes?' Jaxon snarled. 'Stand blindly aside while these rebels murder him in the night?!'

Alysse fought to silence the loudening feud. She closed her eyes and clutched her pendant. That is when she heard his voice.

'Take only the lessons from the past, Little Wren. Do not dwell on the unchangeable. You can only write what has not yet been written.'

'It doesn't matter now!' she yelled over the two men.

Jaxon halted. 'What do you mean it doesn't matter?'

'Father is gone, Jax,' she said, turning to her enraged brother, 'there is nothing we can do about that now. But this does not mean the threat has passed. Judging by this letter, its author intends to bring an end to our House—to the Imperial rule itself.'

Braving her fears, Alysse took the scroll from Jaxon and reread it.

'*The Reclamation is upon you,*' she read, pondering its words. 'To reclaim, one must first have been deprived. But who among us has suffered such a loss that vengeance became the only means of solace?'

'The Ancients were divested of their reign,' Jaxon answered. 'But why seek to reclaim it now, two hundred years on?'

'That is for us to determine.' Alysse replied, turning to her uncle. 'Any word on the Iriyana?'

'Yes, Your Grace,' Cyrus informed. 'Queen Marcia Iibryn arrived this afternoon. Her accommodations on the guest levels have been arranged. Houses Tennyr, Frailyn, and Peryx are set to arrive by morning. The Chief Architects await your call.'

'What word from The Ancients?' she asked.

'Anticipating their response is like waiting for a statue to blink, Your Grace,' Cyrus remarked. 'That said, I do not doubt their attendance—the very laws of this world demand it.'

'Very well.' Alysse said. 'I will hold onto this. Let no word of this letter, nor any of the recent events, be spoken of until I permit it.'

'A wise choice, Your Grace,' Cyrus agreed.

'What now?' Jaxon asked.

'The Qyx-Iriyan is in two days. Uncle Cyrus will continue his investigations. Jaxon, I want you to take command of the Citadel's security. Begin by shutting the gates.'

CHAPTER 11

Thio meandered around his new quarters, his internalised excitement now freely spilling out of a wide, uncontainable smile. The room was as Dalos had promised. It had ample space with a seating area, study table, and broad feathered bed. Three narrow windows offered views of the manicured gardens below, gently kissed by the last light of the day.

He moved to his rucksack and began unpacking what little he possessed. He pulled off his tunic and slipped down his trousers. A muted thud sounded as his pants hit the floor. He bent down and pulled out the leather sack from a pocket. *The mountain salt.* He smiled in appreciation at the simple gift from his mentor.

After donning a night robe that he found in one of the drawers, he pulled out his notebook and sat at the study desk near the windows. The warm table lamp woke with a wave of his hand. He held the small chunk of grey rock under the lamp and watched it shimmer in the light. Opening his notebook, he flicked through the pages, each filled with equations and drawings, until he landed on his latest work. He read over the pages for a few minutes before a knock at the door startled him.

'Come in,' he called out.

The door opened. Mia stood in the dim hallway holding a tray of food, her tender smile lighting up her face.

'How are you settling in?' she asked, entering the room. Thio immediately stood from his chair.

'I've never slept in a room this grand. It's going to take some getting used to,' he said, eying the lavish space.

Mia smiled, 'We're thrilled to have you here, Thio. Dalos has not stopped talking about you all afternoon. Chief Gorryn must have sore ears. Apparently, you're working on something quite profound,' she said, giving him a playful nudge as she set the tray before him.

The two sat.

'It's just a theory. I doubt it'll even work,' he said. 'I had hoped to begin testing it in Ton-Basin, then Dalos received his summons, and, well, here we are.'

'You will have plenty of opportunity for that now,' Mia said, picking up the small rock and turning it in the light. 'He has instructed the guild to grant you full access to all necessary resources. Not even Chief Gorryn's apprentice has received such endowments.'

'He is more than generous,' Thio said, shifting in his seat. 'Although, I'm still not entirely sure what I have done to warrant such kindness. I mean not to sound ungrateful, not in the slightest, but many students in Latyth showed far greater promise than me. Yet I was chosen, and have received everything I could possibly ask for. I don't know why.'

'He never told you, did he? Amazing.'

Thio looked quizzically at the gentle-featured woman. 'Tell me what?' he asked.

'Why he selected *you* as his apprentice.' She smiled and leaned closer to the table. 'Earlier, you spoke to Prince Jaxon of your mother and sister falling ill. The Dusk, they called it. It was wildly contagious and incurable.'

The Dusk. Thio had heard its name only a few times before. The word sparked visions of his dying mother and sister. He fought to rid his mind of the imagery.

'Our guild spent countless years researching it to no avail,' Mia continued. 'Even the highest-ranked herbalists and physicians could not find its weakness. Then one day, word began to spread of a possible cure—a cure from a small village in the north. And within that village in the north, a boy, no older than twelve, who had produced a very special tonic for his ailing mother and sister.'

'I...' Thio stuttered.

'The boy had spent mere weeks combining herbal compounds into a tonic. The techniques he had used were far beyond anything the practical minds of The Architect could come up with.'

Thio tried to speak but words did not form.

'You gave that tonic to your sister, Y'mara, and she got better, didn't she?'

'No… I mean, well, yes, but… how do you know all this?' Thio asked, confusion fogging his mind.

Mia placed her hand on his. 'Your mother's last letter to the Athenaeum spoke of a medicine. It was almost disregarded at first. To think a child of twelve may have discovered a cure was unfathomable. But as you know, our guild demands that any new findings be investigated. So a guildsman was sent to study your sister and this *cure*.'

'Forgive me, but it was no cure,' Thio said with conviction. 'I gave it to my mother, also. It made no difference. I lost all hope in my ability to help them, so for the first time, I prayed. But it was too late for my mother, so I asked the Gods to allow my sister to live, and they answered.'

His eyes swelled with emotion.

'My sweet boy,' Mia said, placing her hand atop his as it began to tremble, 'your mother never recovered because she did not drink the tonic. Knowing there was very little, she gave her portions to Y'mara.'

Thio felt the hairs on his arms stand on edge.

'Thio, it worked. It was your discovery alone that saved your sister's life. If the Gods shared any part in it, it was delivering you and your brilliant mind.'

'No… I don't believe it.'

'Believe it. Not long after your discovery, the Dusk found its way to the capital, into the Citadel itself. Fortunately, Emperor Jannon had taken Alysse to the White Isles a few days prior. His wife, however, was not so fortunate. The sickness took hold of Lady Palymma, along with the person she held closest, young Prince Jaxon. The two fell ill swiftly. Emperor Jannon demanded the High Priests call upon the Gods for aid. Their prayers, of course, went unanswered. The Imperium began preparing for their deaths. The Emperor was distraught beyond measure. He then turned to his closest friend for aid. So Dalos sent word to every Athenaeum across Eviiri, hoping for some sort of miracle.' Mia offered a sincere smile. 'Only Latyth replied. A few days later, a small vial arrived at the Citadel. Sadly, it was too late for the Empress. The Dusk took her during the night. Prince Jaxon was on the brink of death until....'

'Impossible.' Thio managed to say.

'You saved his life, Thio, as well as the countless others who faced the same fate. The Emperor vowed to reward the person that discovered the cure. Dalos ensured that you and your sister were well cared for at the Athenaeum in Latyth until the time was right.'

'I don't understand. Why was I never told this?' he asked.

'Dalos believes that early awareness of one's achievements can hinder progress. He warns that excessive pride may blind individuals to their untapped potential. Thus, he sought to ensure your training was complete before allowing you to fully embrace your talents under his guidance.'

'Does the Prince know?' Thio questioned.

'No. Only a few within the guild. And the late Emperor, of course.'

Thio sat in silence. The room around him disappeared as his mind churned through the information he had just received. He barely noticed Mia slide the tray of food closer to him.

'Eat up, then get some rest. Tomorrow you'll have the freedom to explore the city,' she said, trying to calm his mind. 'Us Chief Architects have the Qyx-Iriyan to attend. The Great Houses will arrive tomorrow so Princess Alysse has brought the gathering forward. Gods only know how long we'll be up there. I've heard some have lasted days!'

Thio barely heard her as she stood and made for the door. The hallway lights filled the dim room as she opened it, bringing Thio's mind back into the space.

'Thank you, Mia, for everything,' he said. A tear rolled down his cheek and into his gentle smile.

Mia smiled back at him, 'Goodnight, Thio.'

CHAPTER 12

The main library's lifter hummed as it elevated Deni and a stack of tomes up the face of the ceiling-high bookcase. The small platform navigated the plethora of shelves while the short-statured caretaker slipped books back into their respective sections. Students packed the desks in the centre of the room. The majority were young adults, aged from mid-teens to early twenties. They discussed that morning's lessons, debating and chuckling amongst themselves.

To say Deni loathed the ruckus was an understatement. She would often wait until late hours of the night to sort through the shambles left by the students, opting to care for the gardens instead. However, the day's downpour in Ton-Basin extinguished any opportunity to escape the noisy halls.

'Deni! Deni!' A young girl called out from below. 'Deni!'

Deni peered over the side of the lifter at the persistent teen some four metres down, saying nothing, the look of disdain clear on her face.

'Seafloor Geology: Q'Tenka Trench! It's not in its section,' the young girl shouted over the bustle of the library.

Deni turned to the stack of aged books on the lifter. She scanned the spines for *Seafloor Geology: Q'Tenka Trench* and found it, third from the bottom. *Great,* she thought. One by one, she shifted each book into new piles. Finally reaching the thick collection of pages, she heaved it up onto the side rail. Peering over the ledge again at the young girl, she gestured subtly to it.

'Here. Move,' she said sharply before sliding the tome over the edge.

The young girl below leaped out of the way of the plummeting slab of paper before it slammed onto the stone floor. The thud echoed across the room, startling most of the noisy crowd. Everyone turned in unison, curious as to what just happened.

'Thanks!' the young student shouted, giggling as she collected the tome off the floor.

The room joined her in laughter before continuing their boisterous chatter, many gathering around the young girl, hoping to prove their arguments correct with the Seafloor Geology textbook.

Deni huffed as she knelt, glancing at the disorganised pile of books next to her, her meticulously crafted cataloguing system now in disarray. As she began rearranging them into her preferred order, another deafening thud blasted across the room.

'Hey! What's the deal, Deni?' One student yelled.

'Careful with those!' shouted another.

Deni pulled herself up and looked over the railing for the fallen tome, yet saw nothing but empty floor. Another loud thud sounded. She scanned the room, searching for its source. *Perhaps they are detonating crumblers up in the mines,* she thought.

A young boy sitting alone stood from his desk with an inquisitive stare. He motioned to the nearby window bay and stepped up into it. The city beyond was misted by rain. He peered left then right, his face pressed up against the glass.

The library quaked as a deep rumble resonated through the walls. A few students let out shrieks as a thunderous clap blew through the air, louder than the previous. Deni reached for the lifter's control unit and navigated it to the ground. Before it reached the polished stone, she leapt off and darted for the window. The uncharacteristic nimbleness of the middle-aged caretaker stunned the surrounding students.

She stepped up onto the window bay and shoved the young boy aside, then stared into the heart of the city. She gasped as an abrupt plume of blue flame and debris surged violently from the town centre—another from the station at the city's base. The delayed shockwaves rattled the thick glass.

'Students!' she belted. 'Get to your dorms! Bar the doors and windows!'

Panic set in as the crowd scurried to the nearest hallways. A collection of consecutive blasts shook the ground, accompanied by screams from the young students.

Deni ushered the young boy off the window bay

and towards the east wing. Spotting a tall, burly pupil, she called out.

'You, go to the main entrance. Seal the door.'

The young man nodded, fear rife in his eyes. He sprinted down the main hall towards the hefty, sapphire-stained doors. Beyond was a clear view of the chaos unfolding in this ever-peaceful town. He grasped the large door handles and slung them shut. Unlatching the barricades, he slid one into position, then the other. The sound of the other student's screams dissipated as they scattered from the main library. He leaned forward to inspect the bars, ensuring they were secure.

The doors suddenly ruptured inwards. Hefty chunks of wood and copper wrapped in blue flame belted the young man, slamming him against the solid sandstone walls.

Deni sheltered her face as rubble blew through the main hall and into the library. Dazed by the pressure wave, she clambered to her feet and took flight for the west wing. Her stumpy legs struggled to keep up with her panic-driven injection of adrenaline.

Navigating the halls, she reached the administrative quarters. She approached an ornate wooden closet and flung the doors open. Inside sat a small wooden cube with brass wires and marble buttons. She frantically pressed combinations into the cube as it emitted harmonic tones.

Hurry, hurry! she pressed herself. A nearby explosion shook the room, jostling the sonic transmitter precariously on its shelf. Dust and stone trickled from the ceiling as slender veins of fracture webbed across its surface.

With the last few melodic inputs, Deni struck the large marble stud on the front-facing side of the cube. The small indicator light flashed to life. Stepping back from the closet, she took a deep breath. She closed her eyes and quietly chanted a prayer, her words barely audible.

Within a heartbeat, her world shattered into blue flame and rubble.

CHAPTER 13

'The botany wing is down there to the right, fluid dynamics to the left,' Dalos stated, guiding Thio through the labyrinth of corridors within the Grand Athenaeum, his cane clicking on the pristine marble floors. 'Our agricultural sector is further down that hallway. The mineral and geo-purification facilities are opposite. That's where you should take your little mountain rock. Be sure to speak to Britt, she knows those machines better than anyone.'

Thio barely heard Dalos speaking, his eyes surveying every inch of the advanced complex. Through one door he saw a team of engineers testing the hydro efficiency of a new water blade prototype—through another, walls lined with complex equations. In this moment, heaven seemed second best. He was in his element.

'Got all that?' Dalos asked.

'Huh?' Thio responded, only hearing the old man

after the buzz of drilling in an adjacent room ceased.

Dalos shook his head and chuckled, then pointed the way to his chambers.

After a brief walk, the two arrived back in Dalos' reading room.

'Feel free to read anything from here. These books aren't in the main library,' Dalos said, showcasing the vast array of his private collection. 'Ah, this one, my favourite.' He pulled a thick tome from the bookcase and handed it to Thio.

'*Utilising Resonance,*' Thio read aloud. '*By Dalos Okombuur, 3013.* Very funny.'

Dalos chuckled. 'From crumblers to carriers! What? Not on your *wavelength?*'

Thio palmed his face in embarrassment. 'Shouldn't you be heading off?'

Dalos laughed, 'Yes, yes. Just as soon as Mia…'

'As soon as Mia what?' the jovial voice blurted as she rounded the corner. 'Good day, Thio,' she said, greeting him with a tight hug. 'Oh, what's this? *Utilising Resonance.* That's sure to shake things up!'

Thio stiffly turned to Dalos who stood silent, clearly unimpressed by his daughter's attempted pun.

'Shall we?' he said, attempting to skip over the awkwardness, motioning to the door.

'Now, Thio, my boy,' Mia said, 'if there's anything you need, you just go right ahead and help yourself. If anyone gives you grief, tell them Chief Architect Mia Okombuur will have them expelled from the guild.'

'Thanks,' Thio said, offering a quaint smile.

'Who knows how long this gathering will last.

While you wait, make yourself at home. Perhaps explore the city. Go see Koris at the port; he will arrange transport across the bay,' Dalos said, patting Thio roughly on the shoulder.

'But most of all, be safe,' Mia added. 'The events of the past few days have left me feeling quite uneasy. Zenithal is a secure city, for the most part, but still be on guard. Just in case.'

Dalos nodded in agreement as he hobbled over to the hidden door and unlocked it. Mia stepped through into the dim passage, Dalos following behind.

'Bye for now, m'boy,' he said, closing the door.

Thio stood for a moment looking around at the luxurious room. Besides the countless books, small prototypes of Dalos' inventions dotted the shelves. They appeared to be a collection of his finest works—trophies of the brilliant man's achievements. Towards the south wall, he spotted more obscure objects, one of which he immediately recognised. It was a small wooden cube with brass wires and marble buttons. *A sonic transmitter*, he thought to himself, still amazed by its simplistic form, yet complex function. *These must be all of Mia's works.*

He walked up to the apparatus and curiously poked one of its small marble buttons. A low, steady tone emanated. He pressed another. This time, a medium-pitched tone sounded. He pressed the two together, and a soothing harmony of the two tones caressed the air.

He pondered how words could be derived from such simple tones. There were no visible markings on the buttons to indicate any form of alphabet, nor were there enough buttons to accommodate every letter. He also found it curious that a device such as this was only used in times of urgency and its language kept so heavily guarded.

Walking over to the sizeable reading desk, Thio sat, placing Dalos' *Utilising Resonance* book in front of him. He flicked through the pages. Intricate drawings of odd devices filled each leaf, some he recognised, but most of them were strange and foreign.

He stopped on a familiar object, *a crumbler*. Dalos had shown off his powerful little contraption in Ton-Basin when they had toured the mines. The device was set against mine walls. Once remotely activated, it would pulse a variety of frequencies until one matched that of the cavernous rock. Once the device found the correct frequency, it rumbled to life, crumbling the surrounding rock into rubble.

Thio continued through the pages, again spotting a familiar object—a carrier.

From crumblers to carriers, he recited in his head, laughing to himself.

He began reading the thick paragraphs accompanying the imagery, curious as to how Dalos had been able to control the volume of such vibrations without compromising their strength. Engrossed in the literature, he barely heard the sounds emitting from the adjacent room.

A few minutes went by before the tones became apparent to him. He peered around the room, carefully honing in on the curious melody. Standing from the desk, he quietly walked over to the entrance of

Dalos' chambers and pressed his ear to the locked door.

Frantic harmonic tones danced around within the room. He instantly recognised the noise as that of the sonic transmitter. *They're only used in times of urgency or distress.* He ran for a nearby sheet of paper and a coal pen. Returning to the door, he closed his eyes and focused on the message. Not knowing how to translate it, he scored the harmonics on the page. High, mid, and low dashes combined with their symphonic counterparts began filling the page.

The message was short. Thio quickly realised it was playing on a loop—the song now imprinted in his mind.

I have to tell Dalos, he thought, inferring the importance of the message. He ran to the hidden door and pushed it to no avail. *Fuck.* Knowing his sloppy notes could prove difficult to transcribe, he dashed over to the transmitter prototype, clutched it, and sprinted out of the room into the nearby corridor.

Racing through the lengthy passageways of the Grand Athenaeum, Thio reached the central atrium. The splendid hall was alive with activity. Architects and students moved leisurely across the geometrically intricate inlaid floor, the dazzling sapphire glass roof painting colour across the space.

Turning for the main entrance, he bolted through the crowd, knocking over a handful of passersby.

'Sorry!' he yelled as he continued his sprint.

'Thio!' A deep, booming voice echoed through the hall.

Thio immediately halted.

'What in the Gods' name are you doing?'

Thio turned to see Gorryn Venidor, the third Chief Architect. The forty-four-year-old man stood some six and a half feet tall, towering over his entourage of colleagues. His broad shoulders were accented by his sharp, tailored navy suit, decorated with gold brooches and twisted cord.

'Chief Gorryn, I'm… my apologies. I'm on my way to the port. I must speak with Dalos at once,' Thio said through his heavy breath.

'He would have reached the Citadel by now. What is so urgent it requires your blatant disregard for your fellow comrades?' Gorryn said, his tone harsh.

Thio surveyed the atrium. A small crowd of students were helping a young girl to her feet, her face wincing in pain, pages scattered around her. Others shot him indignant stares for his obtrusive act.

'I…'

'Come with me,' Gorryn commanded before turning to his entourage. 'Have those results sent to my chambers, and commence work on the nano-fuser. I expect to begin testing in a month.'

The group nodded and dispersed.

Gorryn strode past Thio, his impressive gait moving his imposing form swiftly across the atrium. Thio followed behind, mouthing another apology to the stricken girl collecting her papers.

The two exited through the colossal main doors of the Grand Athenaeum. The high noon sun warmed the light sandstone pavement as they approached a carrier.

'Get in,' Gorryn demanded.

Thio submissively stepped up onto the humming carrier. The gargantuan man followed behind, sitting opposite as the vehicle shifted into motion.

'So you're a thief too?' Gorryn said, eying the transmitter clutched at Thio's side. 'Where did you get that?'

'No, sir. It's the prototype from Dalos' reading room. I...'

'So you wish to discuss sonic transmitters with Dalos?' Gorryn pressed.

'No, I...'

'Or do you need to talk about your little rock?' he mocked.

'SIR!' Thio shot out, his patience snapping.

Gorryn, taken aback by the young man's sudden outburst, stared speechless.

'A message came through to Dalos' transmitter. I believe it may be of importance,' Thio blurted.

Confusion then concern struck the Chief Architect. 'What message?'

'I don't know the language, but I managed to score the tones,' Thio said, producing the crumpled page from his pocket and handing it to Gorryn. The man snatched the paper and examined the scatter of dashed lines.

'This makes no sense to me,' Gorryn stated.

'That's why I brought this.' Thio lifted the small wooden cube. 'I don't know how to transcribe words, but the melody is certain in my mind. If you will allow me a few moments, I can try to reproduce the message.'

Gorryn stared quizzically at the young man as he

began systematically pressing the marble buttons, eyes closed, one ear turned to focus on the soft tones.

'What are you…'

Thio dismissed the question with a raise of his hand.

The carrier continued down the main boulevard of the guild's island for a few minutes as Thio honed in on the operation of the transmitter.

'Ok,' he said, opening his eyes. 'I think I'm ready, please listen carefully.'

Thio began massaging the small box. A flow of frequencies filled the open-aired carrier—an exact replica of the message he heard emitting from Dalos' chambers.

'Astounding,' the Chief Architect muttered, 'how did you…'

'Please, sir, the message,' Thio pressed the seemingly distracted man.

Gorryn leaned in and focused on the tones. First, a look of confusion, then shock. He turned a slow gaze up to Thio, his skin stripped of colour.

'What does it say?' Thio asked.

'Are you certain this is what you heard?' Gorryn queried.

Thio gave a confident nod.

'Here, hand that to me,' Gorryn said, motioning for the transmitter. 'Return to the Athenaeum. Tell no one of this. I will confer with Dalos.'

The carrier came to a stop in the middle of the busy thoroughfare. Thio gave an obedient nod and disembarked the platform.

'Good work, Thio,' Gorryn said, reciprocating the

nod as the carrier quickly hummed into motion again.

Thio stood a moment in the foreign surroundings. The streets were teeming with life. A warm breeze moved around him. Ahead, the carrier continued north towards the port. Beyond, the Citadel rose proud. He traced the simple lines of the tower up to banded sections of turquoise glass, pondering as to what the Qyx-Iriyan had planned for its attending council.

CHAPTER 14

The city below gleamed under the midday sun, its colourful activity muted by the thick turquoise glass surrounding the Session Hall. Alysse stared out at the world she was soon to govern and the millions of lives that looked back at her for leadership. She felt as if the weight of the Drom Mountains were pressing down upon her, expelling the very breath from her lungs. She squeezed her pendant and closed her eyes.

'Pa, be by my side. I need you today,' she whispered.

The silence of the hall fractured as the doors cracked open. Jaxon stepped into the room, his military suit perfectly framing his slender form.

'The hall is secure. We will proceed at your behest,' he said.

'Thank you, Jax,' she said, her hands trembling.

Jaxon stepped closer to his sister and held her hands tightly.

'I've seen you command the attention of the entire city.' He began to comfort her. 'Trust in that confidence now and it will see you prevail.'

Alysse dropped her head. 'The people of this city never questioned my place. But these are rulers, High Priests, and scholars of great renown—they will demand more from me.'

'Once you bring the High Priests to heel, the others will support you,' Jaxon assured. 'Their involvement is undoubtable.'

'It is clear Uncle Cyrus has his doubts. He has countered every one of your contentions.'

'Uncle Cyrus barely listens when I speak,' Jaxon sighed, 'but when you speak, his attention is absolute.'

Alysse took a deep breath as she smoothed her formal gown. Yards of muted-green fabric draped delicately over her slender body. Broad beige panels encased her bust. Gold details lined each seam. She adjusted the ornate diadem resting on her head. Strings of rare stones and metals hung softly over her up-swept hair.

'Best we begin,' she said. 'Call them in.'

Jaxon nodded and headed for the foyer adjacent to the Session Hall.

First into the room was Cyrus Thenta, dressed in his deep purple military suit. As he approached, his gaze lingered on the Princess, captivated by her elegant beauty. The likeness to his late sister was striking, and for a fleeting moment, he felt as though he were looking upon her once more.

'Your Grace,' he said, bowing in her presence before standing by her side.

Within the foyer, the elevator doors opened. Through them, Jaxon was greeted by the comforting sight of Dalos and Mia.

'All good, m'boy?' Dalos asked jovially, offering a heavy-handed pat on Jaxon's shoulder.

'Pay close mind to her,' he said in low volume. 'She's struggling to hide her nerves. Your presence alone should be enough to comfort her, but if it does not, back her every word.'

Mia gave a small, affirming nod, as did Dalos.

Jaxon peered behind the pair, noticing the absence of the third Chief Architect.

'Chief Gorryn?' he asked.

'Perhaps he's having trouble finding the place,' Dalos joked.

'Let's hope he arrives soon,' Jaxon said, turning to face the hall. 'Alysse is eager to begin and will proceed without him, if need be. Come, follow me.'

Jaxon stepped forward into the hall, straightened his posture, and announced the attendees.

'Your Grace, the Chief Architects.'

Dalos and Mia stepped forth, arm in arm. Upon seeing the Princess in her formal gown, Mia playfully mouthed the word 'wow' before offering a respectful bow.

'Your Grace,' she said.

'M'girl.' Dalos followed.

Mia nudged her elbow into his side, drawing a brief grunt from the round man.

'Shit, sorry,' he blurted, 'Your Grace.'

Alysse couldn't help but chuckle at the duo's easy

camaraderie. Even amid the troubles surrounding them, they always found space for levity. She composed herself before inquiring about the absence of the third Chief.

'Where is Chief Gorryn?'

'Not far behind, I'm sure,' Dalos said. 'We all know how enthralled he gets in his work.'

Alysse nodded, then motioned for them to find their place within the hall.

'Queen Marcia Iibryn of Aankathor,' Jaxon announced.

Through the doors strode a delicate woman, robed in a peach gown. She was short, in her fifties, with long silver hair cascading down to her lower back.

'Princess,' she said with a gentle smile, 'what a vision you are—an exact semblance of your mother, Gods nurture her soul. May I offer my most sincere condolences. Your father was truly an impressive man.'

'Thank you, Your Grace,' Alysse returned, 'for your kind words and for travelling so far on such short notice. It has been too long since our last meeting.'

'How long has it been?' Marcia pondered. 'Five years? Ten? I don't recall.'

'I believe it was my mother's funeral,' Alysse stated.

'Tharpys,' Marcia scoffed, 'I'm beginning to wonder if the Gods take pleasure in casting the shadow of death over all our meetings.'

'Well, let us work together to cast light on those shadows,' Alysse offered with a smile.

Marcia reciprocated the smile and continued past

the Princess.

'King Lyro Tennyr of Shaavythor,' Jaxon announced.

A middle-aged man in a black suit stepped in, the deep yellow koi sigil of House Tennyr stitched proudly across his chest.

'Your Grace,' he said, bowing. 'Shaavythor grieves your father's passing.'

'Thank you, King Lyro. I trust the good people of Shaavythor will regain their spirits before long.'

Jaxon watched as Lyro Tennyr moved deeper into the hall before announcing the next monarch.

'King Lex Frailyn of Kaprythor.'

Alysse observed a staunch figure stride into the hall, his ivory suit accented with soft blue details. She immediately noted the hardness in his face. Without a word, he offered a half-hearted nod before moving immediately past her. The gesture made Alysse shift uneasily, sensing his disdain.

Jaxon moved quickly to usher in the last of the four monarchs. He turned to the young king, who seemed preoccupied, awkwardly murmuring a practiced script to himself.

'King Benin Peryx of Domathor,' he announced, startling the king.

To Alysse's surprise, a young man of thirteen appeared through the doorway. His soft rosy face made him appear even younger than his years. Standing half a head shorter than the princess, he took her hand and bowed.

'Princess,' he began in a rehearsed tone, 'your beauty shines so brightly it has crossed the Q'Tenka

Sea and captured my gaze. I may still be a boy, but my heart longs as fiercely as any man's. I humbly ask that you consider uniting our Houses, so that together, we may share our love with the generations to come.'

The earnest attempt at courtship brought a wide grin to Alysse's face.

'You flatter me, Your Grace,' she said, 'allow me some time to consider your proposal.'

'Certainly, Princess,' he said as his face lit up. 'Might I also suggest a tour of Domathor? Its beauty pales only in comparison to your own.'

Before Alysse could politely decline his suggestion, a gentle voice called out from across the hall.

'King Benin,' said Marcia Iibryn, 'the Princess has heard your requests and will announce her decisions in due time. Until then, please allow her to continue greeting her honoured guests.'

The young king bowed sharply before striding toward the gathered crowd, his newly appointed title as King of Domathor evident in his self-appointed pride.

Minutes elapsed without any sign of the High Priests. With each passing moment, Alysse's uneasiness deepened. Jaxon, who had been waiting by the elevator, strode into the hall and approached his sister.

'This is an undeniable mark of their betrayal, Alysse,' he stated. 'Should they refuse to attend, we will have no choice but to arrest them and force...'

Within that breath, a chime echoed through the foyer. Without hesitating, Jaxon hastened back to his post. As the solid doors of the vertical carrier slid open, the sweet aroma of incense immediately filled the air. Stepping out of the spacious cabin were the five ethereal High Priests, their obsidian robes dripping in onyx pearls. Each had donned elaborate headdresses that framed their youthful faces. As they neared, Jaxon caught sight of their eyes, shimmering with an eerie orange glow.

'Alefre'am,' Reverend Kalax spoke, curtsying to the perturbed young Prince.

Jaxon restrained himself from speaking out of turn. Instead, he spun to face the hall's entrance and spoke his announcement.

'Your Grace, The Ancients.'

The pentad of pearl-plated priests entered the hall. Curious stares met them from most of the room's occupants, none more inquisitive than Alysse's.

'Alefre'a,' Kalax said with a half-grin. The other priests simply bowed, then continued towards the robust council table.

Alysse motioned to Jaxon. She watched as he heaved the doors shut, sealing the room off from the outside. Turning to Cyrus, she gave a nod to proceed.

The council of Iriyana stood behind each of the suspended chairs encircling the marble table. The five High Priests occupied the southwest quadrant with Dalos and Mia to their left. Opposite stood the leaders of the Great Houses. Alysse proceeded to her northernmost position, the backdrop of the distant Drom Mountains framing her while Cyrus Thenta took his position to her left.

'Please, sit,' she said, outstretching her arms.

The group of nobles sat, their chairs gently guiding them closer to the table. As custom, each produced a palm-sized orb from their garments and placed it in a spoon-sized divot on the stone table, signifying their participation and authenticity in such gatherings. Each orb was crafted of local ores or gems from their respected lands.

'Thank you, Iriyana, for joining me here,' Alysse began. 'I know the travel can be quite demanding; however, your presence and counsel do not go unappreciated. I trust your stay in the capital is comfortable. Should you desire anything, please...'

'Enough with the formalities, girl,' Lex Frailyn shot out. 'Let your uncle speak. We are here at his request, not yours.'

Cyrus stood to address the agitated king.

'In my capacity as regent, I hereby relinquish my position as head of this council and grant Princess Alysse full authority to preside.'

'I knew it the moment I received that black scroll,' Lex Frailyn scoffed. 'This is her calling. The little girl couldn't endure a single tribulation before succumbing to panic.'

'You will hold your tongue until called upon!' Dalos ruptured in anger with a venomous tone uncharacteristic of the jolly man. 'You are addressing the Empress. You will respect her as such.'

'Crown Princess, you mean?' the deep voice of Reverend Dakaar corrected. 'Her coronation has not yet taken place.'

'Nor should it,' Lex challenged. 'The Prince should inherit the heirship.'

'Alysse is the firstborn child. She is next in line by law,' Mia stated. 'Gender plays no role in these matters. Besides, she will not be the first empress to ascend the Imperial throne.'

'That is true, Lady Architect,' Lex mocked. 'It is also true that Empress Xenna was the last ruler in a century to call a Qyx-Iriyan. Can you not see the correlation? Women are not fit to rule. They are timid and cower at the first sign of disorder.'

'Shall I relinquish my crown too, Lex?' Marcia Iibryn suggested, the sharpness of her words cutting through his argument.

'Aankathor is but a tiny fragment of the realm,' he rebutted. 'My concerns lie with the governance of the entire world. If they wish not to budge, then perhaps it is time House Aprya relinquished their rule entirely.'

'You insolent snake!' Dalos said enraged. Mia clutched at her father's arm as he shot up from his chair.

Control of the gathering began to slip from Alysse's grasp as emotions flared and voices clashed across the room.

'Enough!' she exclaimed. The room fell silent. 'You were not called here to question my father's succession. Nor were you called here to insult my House.' She turned her gaze towards Lex Frailyn. 'May I remind you, Your Grace, that House Aprya and House Frailyn have stood as allies since the birth of the Imperium *and* before. For centuries, our House and lands have supported the good people of Kaprythor. I implore you do nothing to falter that.'

Mia turned a short smile at the Princess's command of the room.

'We cannot afford division at such a crucial hour,' Alysse continued. 'It has become clear that the Imperium is facing a threat that we have not seen in two hundred years.'

Quizzical glances darted across the hall, exchanged in silent inquiry as the tension thickened, each pair of eyes seeking understanding amidst the rising discord.

'Princess,' Lyro Tennyr began to speak, 'what threat do you speak of? The palms? A disgraceful act, yes, but not one to indicate any credible insurgency.'

Alysse took a short breath. 'You may be right, King Lyro. However, the murder of the Emperor, his desecration, and the attempt on his heirs—all in the name of reclamation—tell of a much larger plan.'

Shock gripped many of the nobles.

'Gods...' Lyro uttered as murmurs spread across the room.

Alysse fixed her gaze across the table, where Reverend Kalax sat in unbroken silence, his expression unreadable.

'The Gods indeed,' she spoke. 'The true purpose of this gathering is to call the High Priests into question.'

As if controlled by one mind, the crowd of nobles all turned their gaze in unison to the silent mystics. They watched as Kalax leaned back in his chair, his expression as indifferent as a child unwilling to heed a scolding.

'Speak your questions, Alefre'a,' he drawled.

'Reverend Kalax, correct me if I'm mistaken,' she began, 'but was it not your Faith Partisans who stood beneath the palms? Was it not they who laid my father's altar to rest upon the Shrine of Old? It was your dominion over Eviiri that was stripped from you, and now you seek to reclaim it.'

'It was,' Kalax replied plainly.

'I'm sorry,' Cyrus spoke, 'to which question is that your answer?'

'It was our Partisans who stood beneath the palms. It was they who escorted the altar to the shrine. And yes, it was our dominion that was stripped from us.'

'So you declare your treason?' Cyrus pressed.

'I am merely conveying the truth as I know it, child.'

The condescending address ignited a simmering rage within Cyrus. He held onto his words out of respect for the Princess.

'These are serious indictments, Reverend,' Lyro explained. 'How can you sit there so calmly and confess?'

'Confess?' Kalax said, tilting his head and leaning forward. 'I have done no such thing, child. If you wish for me to confess, then hear this. Our two-hundred Partisans beneath the palms have not been seen since. The ten that escorted the altar through the tunnels have not been seen since.' He turned his attention to Alysse. 'Forgive me if I speak out of turn, Alefre'a, but by my count, our losses far outweigh yours.'

'For all we know, you silenced them once they had served your purpose,' Alysse surmised.

'You are quick to assign blame, Alefre'a,' Reverend Dakaar declared, 'yet you withhold a key detail in your report. Why don't you tell the Iriyana of the failed assassin cloaked in purple?'

Cyrus shot a look of bewilderment at the request. He shifted in his seat, ready to speak before Alysse placed a soft hand on his arm.

'You're right, Reverend. The man who attacked Jaxon and I was disguised as a member of our Imperial Guard, that much is known,' Alysse stated, audible gasps sprouting around the table. 'I do find it curious though, Reverend Dakaar, how you acquired this information. As far as I am aware, The Ancients were not privy to this detail.'

Dakaar leaned over the table. 'The Gods see all, Alefre'a,' he replied, the hint of a grin lifting the corner of his mouth.

'Cyrus, how could this happen?' Lyro Tennyr asked. 'The Imperial Guard is meant to be impenetrable.'

'Just prior to this gathering,' Cyrus spoke, 'I was informed of the assailant's identity. An officer turned rogue, it seems.'

Alysse turned to her uncle, her surprise evident at this unexpected revelation.

'He was part of a unit sent abroad on assignment not three months ago,' Cyrus continued. 'Belief is that he may have been compromised there. The accompanying officers are being held for questioning.'

'Abroad?' Lyro enquired. 'Where exactly?'

'It is mere speculation at this time. I do not wish to make hasty assumptions.'

'Where, uncle?' Alysse pressed.

Cyrus took a deep breath then answered. 'The East Garrison in Kaprythor.'

All eyes turned to Lex Frailyn.

'Kaprythor?!' exclaimed the young Benin Peryx. 'That is your domain, King Lex. Do you share involvement? What say you?'

Lex Frailyn looked void of concern. 'There is nothing to say, Young King. This is a spurious claim. Not a whisper is uttered in my country without my knowledge of it. The Princess can point her finger elsewhere.'

'You are under no accusation, Your Grace,' Alysse assured. 'Our investigations have only just begun.'

'And yet, we are so quickly condemned,' Kalax opposed. 'Shall we take blame for the Emperor's death? Your father was not the first to meet the Gods before his time. Your great-grandfather, Emperor Alyx Aprya, was taken by Kapry at the age of thirty-nine.'

'Yet, I do not recall Prince Brenn rushing to call a Qyx-Iriyan, crying murder,' Lex Frailyn added.

'Princess,' Marcia Iibryn spoke, 'you say your father was murdered? What evidence do you have to support such a claim? Last report made no mention of malfeasance.'

Saying nothing, Alysse inserted her hand into a concealed pocket in her gown and retrieved the small scroll she had acquired from her uncle. She reached past Cyrus and handed it to the concerned woman.

Marcia Iibryn skimmed over the words and muttered them under her breath. A few lines were audible to the group. 'Fire will be your path. And you, lost in its embers… The Reclamation is upon you.' She lifted her head, searching for clarity in her mind, then passing it along to King Lyro who read it to himself.

'This is clearly a threat,' he announced. 'But who…'

A clatter at the door stole the room's attention. Alysse looked over as the clicking and sliding of metal continued. Once they ceased, the doors swung open.

'Your Grace!' The deep voice of Gorryn Venidor called out between his panting breaths.

'Chief Gorryn?' Alysse said, standing. 'Where have you been? What's wrong?'

'Forgive me, Your Grace. Qymathor is under attack.'

'Impossible!' Cyrus exclaimed as Gorryn hurried over to the council table.

'I wish that were true, Commander, but a distress call was received from Ton-Basin,' he managed, approaching his fellow Chief Architects. 'Dalos, your apprentice intercepted the message.'

'Thio?' Dalos quizzed. 'But how?'

'He memorised the transmission and recreated it on an old prototype. The message itself is unknown to him, but I heard it clearly.'

'What did it say?' Alysse asked, dread consuming her.

Gorryn dropped his head, the message clawing at his mind. 'Ton-Basin burns. The Blue Flame.'

A pit of fear settled deep within Dalos. 'Deni…' he whispered.

'The Blue Flame? I don't understand,' asked the curious young King Benin.

'The Blue Flame was a weapon,' the childlike voice of Reverend Thyta answered, 'a fire forged by The Architects during the war, made to consume field, flesh, and stone alike. Even in sleep, I cannot escape the horrors it unleashed on our people.'

'Such weapons were forbidden after the war's end,' Lyro interjected. 'The schematics were destroyed.'

Alysse turned to her dear friend. 'Dalos, is this true?'

'Indeed,' he assured, 'they were destroyed. Not even the highest ranks of our guild possess the knowledge of their craft. The technology was lost to time.'

Without pause, Alysse motioned to Cyrus. 'Uncle, send scouts to Ton-Basin to assess this claim. In the meantime, make safe the Capital and dispatch units to all surrounding cities. I want the Passages shut and all transport throughout Qymathor halted.'

'At once, Your Grace,' Cyrus confirmed as he stood and rushed out of the hall.

Lyro Tennyr shook his head, contemplating the emerging events. 'If all of this proves true, then Qymathor is no longer safe. Remaining here is not wise. I beg pardon, Your Grace, but I feel it best we return home. This matter is not ours to resolve.'

'Not yours to resolve?' Mia rebutted. 'These rebels murdered your Emperor! What makes you think that Shaavythor, or any other country, is safe if Qymathor falls? It matters not who sits atop the mountain.

Should its base crumble, all will fall.'

The room erupted in argument.

'Iriyana!' Alysse called out. 'Should this message hold true, I ask that you uphold your vows. Stand with Qymathor. Stand with me. Chief Mia is right, if the foundations of the Imperium collapse, Eviiri will fall back into chaos.'

The gathered monarchs lingered in thought, the weight of her words settling upon them as they grasped the gravity of the situation. Marcia Iibryn spoke first.

'The Aankathorian forces are yours, Your Grace.'

'Domathor stands with you, Princess.' Benin Peryx followed.

'You have our support,' added Lyro Tennyr.

Alysse looked to Lex Frailyn, who sat silent. 'And House Frailyn? Can we count on Kaprythor for aid if called upon?'

King Frailyn pondered for a moment, fondling the light blue topaz orb he had placed on the table earlier. Closing his palm around it, he looked around the grand hall, then to Alysse.

'For two centuries, we have lived in the shadow of this erroneous tower. Despite the malice that takes aim, I cannot risk the lives of my people. I will not bring peril to my country. At the Coalition of Crowns, our forebears elected your House to govern...' he pocketed the orb, 'so govern.'

'This is treason! You invoke war,' Benin protested.

'You coward,' Dalos remarked.

'Iriyana,' Alysse said, holding her hand up to silence the room, 'King Frailyn has made his decision clear. I will not press the matter further.'

Holding formality, she bowed at the stern King. 'I wish you safe travels home, Your Grace.'

Lex Frailyn scanned the crowd, noting a few ominous stares aimed back at him. He pressed himself up from his chair and moved towards the door, silently.

'You let him leave without consequence?' Lyro questioned. 'Kaprythor holds the world's largest infantry.'

'Then let us pray we won't need it,' Alysse responded. 'As for the rest of you, the hospitality of the Capital is yours for as long as it pleases. If you wish to return home, you are free to do so. I ask that you consider my coronation. By tradition, the monarchs are required to attend to affirm the ascendancy. You will be notified of its commencement. Again, I thank you all for coming.'

She outstretched her arm towards the door, eager to rid the room of them. The council stood as one, bowing to formally conclude the proceedings.

Once the room had emptied, Jaxon entered, approaching his sister gradually, acknowledging the turbulence in her eyes. 'How did it go? Did The Ancients answer for their crimes?'

'Nothing went as planned.' Alysse sighed. 'Kalax danced around every enquiry. I am now more uncertain of which direction to look. The Ancients, the Great Houses, The Architects…'

'The Architects?' he questioned.

'That apprentice intercepted a message from Ton-Basin. It claims an attack on the city. It spoke of a forbidden weapon once crafted by The Architects.'

'What?!' Jaxon exclaimed.

'Uncle Cyrus is investigating.' Alysse sat down, her legs weakened by the day's efforts.

'What can I do?' Jaxon asked.

She pondered a moment, her mind drawing an image of the young apprentice. 'I wish to speak to Thio. Will you call for him?'

'At once.'

CHAPTER 15

Gorryn Venidor stood silent in the gardens south of the Citadel as he reflected on the troubling news he had just delivered to the Iriyana. The mid-afternoon sun bounced warmth off the vibrant waters of the Bay of Prosperity. Each shimmer mimicked whips of blue flame, conjuring imagery of the perils in Ton-Basin.

'Chief?'

The soft voice of Mia Okombuur brought his mind back to the bay.

'Mia,' he said, noticing the two figures approaching, slowed by the hobbling gait of Dalos' aging body.

'Are you well, my friend?' Dalos asked.

'That apprentice of yours,' Gorryn said in awe, 'I underestimated him. I recall hearing on the wind that your choice was widely contested.'

'It's a good thing I pay no mind to the wind,' Dalos

returned with a wink.

'Thio is a very special boy,' Mia added. 'He has a brilliant mind.'

'For him to deduce the workings of your transmitter in a matter of minutes, and produce the message he heard only a few times is impressive,' Gorryn said with conviction.

'Thio does things his way,' Dalos stated. 'He may not fit the mould of our teachings, but he produces outstanding work nonetheless.'

Mia nodded in agreement, referencing the cure in her mind. 'Indeed he does.'

'He is an asset, especially in these uncertain times.' Dalos added. 'We must all work together now, for the Princess.'

Gorryn shifted uneasily at Dalos' comment, unsure whether to address the concerns that had begun to plague his mind. He pondered a moment then spoke.

'Dalos, I trust you will pardon my frankness. The guild has always aided the Imperium in bettering our world. Yet we were sworn to take no sides in its politics, only to provide what is best for the people.' He took a deep breath. 'I fear your affections for the late Emperor and his children may be compromising your objectives.'

'I have not forgotten our purpose, Gorryn,' Dalos said firmly, 'but Alysse and Jaxon are akin to family. Jannon entrusted me to keep them safe should anything happen to...'

He paused as a lump of emotion caught his words. Mia placed a comforting hand on her father's back.

'We are still capable of continuing our work while

minding the wellbeing of the Crown Princess and her brother,' Mia stated. 'These matters may yet affect us all, Chief Gorryn. It is only by the consensus of the Faith, the Imperium, and our guild that we are able to continue our work freely. If this threat proves to be of significance, we may come to know that freedom no more.'

Dalos cleared his throat and straightened his posture.

'Our work will continue as normal,' he said. 'Zenithal will stand strong as it has for two hundred years. This is all merely a small obstacle in our path.'

Gorryn gave a hesitant nod of acceptance as he turned his eyes south towards the brilliant blue dome standing proud in the distance.

'Very well. We should get back to the Athenaeum,' he said, motioning for the docks at the island's point.

'You go ahead,' Dalos encouraged, 'Mia and I have some small business to attend to.'

Gorryn delivered a faint smile then proceeded to the same watercraft he had arrived on.

Dalos and Mia stood a moment as they watched their colleague board the vessel and set off for the guild's island. Mia turned her head towards her father and noticed beads of sweat accumulating on his forehead.

'Pa?' she said out of concern.

'This is bad, m'girl. Poor Deni. If what she said is true, then most of Ton-Basin will be rubble by now. Her life, along with countless others, will be no more.'

Mia closed her eyes and dropped her head in

mourning. A thousand thoughts danced within her mind.

'Who do you think is behind this attack? The Ancients?' she asked.

'The Faith never waged war with such weapons,' Dalos replied. 'Yes, The Architects crafted the Blue Flame, but it was gifted to the Great Houses of the time. Its use, however, was not at all what the guild intended.'

'Surely the Great Houses wouldn't risk open war to take hold of the Imperial seat?' she responded.

'There have always been subsurface tensions between the Great Houses,' Dalos stated. 'House Frailyn is one to note. After the war, Lien Frailyn stood confident to sit at the head of the Imperium. Kaprythor's forces far outnumbered those of the other countries and played a pivotal role in the success of the campaign. Yet, when put to a vote, House Aprya was elected to hold the realm. Ever since that day, House Aprya has been met with resistance from House Frailyn, made clear today by Lex Frailyn's foul, treasonous remarks.' His last few words were delivered with a sharp bite.

Mia played with the idea, sorting through reasons for the possible revolt. The two made their way to the docks and boarded another golden vessel suspended atop the lucid water. The craft, unmanned, sat two and was reserved for the Emperor and his wife to visit the Shrine of Old. When they had taken their seats, the craft buzzed and hummed, then began to move over the undulating water.

'Now that Alysse sits her father's throne,' Mia

began to speak aloud, 'House Frailyn seizes the opportunity to claim what they feel was taken from them?'

'Perhaps. It seems the only plausible theory,' Dalos expressed.

'And Alysse today…'

'She handled herself perfectly. Her father would be proud.'

Mia agreed with her father's statement, smiling with her own pride in the young Princess's strong presence at the council.

'She is very much like him,' she added. 'It seems his lessons were not wasted on her.'

'I agree, although I do not envy her. Nor any of the Imperial children, past, present, or future. Their lives are so carefully planned from the outset,' Dalos said, eying the marble shrine in the approaching distance. 'When I was a young boy, Jannon and I would only have brief moments to play amongst the gardens, or scurry around the Citadel before his father whipped him away to learn the ways of his future kingdom. Being an only child, I was the closest thing Jannon had to a brother. I was his window into a normal life, free of expectation. I'd often bring him gifts from the Athenaeum, you know. New prototypes.'

'Father!' Mia exclaimed playfully. 'You shared confidential research with someone outside the guild?'

Dalos chuckled. 'He was to be Emperor anyway, might as well give him a head start.'

'You're lucky you were never caught,' Mia warned.

'Hah, I was a lot more agile back then. Good luck

trying to catch me. Plus I was Chief Hyllan's apprentice, nobody would dare question such a prestigious pupil,' Dalos said proudly.

Mia shot her father a condescending eye.

'Now, now, Pa. You were his second choice, remember?'

Dalos sighed. 'Must you remind me of your mother's genius?'

'Well, she was smarter than you. It's just a shame she chose a different path.'

Dalos drew a long breath. The smell of salty sea water triggered memories of his late wife, her beauty radiating in his mind's eye.

'A marine explorer cannot hold the title of Chief Architect,' he muttered. 'It is far too dangerous, all those months out at sea. What a waste. Everyone tried to reason with her.'

Mia placed her hand on his. 'Yet *you* managed to ground her, wed her, and have me. Was it truly a waste?'

Dalos stared at his daughter with a full heart and soft smile, the resemblance to her mother written clearly in her features.

'Only the Gods know how much I miss her,' he said, watery-eyed.

'Me too, Pa.'

The watercraft adjusted its thrusters to position itself alongside the dock of the small island, then shut off. Mia aided her father from his seat and up onto the stone landing. He offered her his arm as they walked the path towards the stack of marble altars. The freshly manicured gardens breathed sweet floral scents into the air.

Mia approached a large planter lining the pathway and plucked two white orchids. She held them under her nose to enjoy the peaceful aroma they emitted.

Dalos' gaze stayed fixed on the shrine ahead. His eyes followed the sharp lines of the simple marble blocks skyward. Grief set in when he noticed the remnants of bloodstains on their faces.

Arriving at the monument, Mia leant down and placed one of the white orchids at its base, bowing respectfully to the past rulers.

'Oh Jannon, old boy,' Dalos said as he placed a flat hand on the shrine.

'I'll give you a moment,' Mia said.

Dalos nodded in appreciation.

Mia turned east and made her way to the graves of the Imperial consorts. Their shrines, although well kept, were no spectacle. Simple marble headstones with gold plaques dotted the area. Singling out the furthest stone block, she approached it and read the words engraved on the plaque.

Lady Palymma Aprya, the Gentle.
Honoured Empress, wife, sister, and mother.

She knelt in front of it, brushing off dried salty deposits left by the sea air. Smiling, she placed the other white orchid atop the stone.

'My Lady. You would be so proud of your children. Your boy is doing a gallant job,' she spoke aloud. 'He has grown into a remarkable young man. He has your brother's sternness, yet your gentle heart, and handsome, like his father. He will make a fine Imperial Commander one day. No harm will ever come to Alysse while Jaxon is there to protect her.'

A tear rolled down her cheek as she reminisced about the unbreakable bond between this mother and son.

Dalos approached from behind and bowed in the Empress' presence. Mia stood and wrapped her arms around her father.

'Come, m'girl,' Dalos said as he comforted her. 'There is something I wish to tell you.'

CHAPTER 16

The gold plaque beside the open set of double doors read *Geology: Mineral Research*. Thio peered into the vast room before stepping inside. Towering machines glowed and hummed. The smell of rock and soil was carried amongst the steady flow of air within the space. Cabinets brimming with varying mineral forms lined the outer walls. The entire ceiling was illuminated with a bright white light.

There were ten or so researchers scattered around the room, each heavily invested in their work. Towards the centre was a small group hovering around a desk. Standing at the head of the desk was a young woman, tall and blonde.

'Ah, you must be Thio!' she shouted excitedly across the room, noticing the shy man entering. 'Dalos has spoken a great deal about you.'

She pranced over to him, her golden ponytail swinging joyfully with every step.

'I'm Britt, Britt Pensyr. Head of Geology and apprentice to Chief Gorryn Venidor,' she announced, shaking his hand. Her dazzling blue eyes and wide smile lit up her face. Thio noticed the gold and royal-blue brooch pinned to her beige coat, the Architect's sigil crested at its centre.

She is no mere student, he thought.

'It's a pleasure to meet you,' he said, matching her energy.

'Welcome to the Capital. First time?'

'It is. A tad grander than imagined, and I'm yet to explore beyond the Athenaeum,' he replied.

'Straight to work, hey? I was the same when I arrived. My sole focus was beginning my research here in this facility. The Athenaeum in Beq'a wasn't as well stocked.'

'Beq'a?' Thio questioned.

'All the way across the Q'Tenka Sea, in Domathor. Quaint little town, but no Zenithal.' She laughed. 'Well, I guess you're eager to get started. Let me show you around, then you're free to begin.'

Britt led Thio around the room, explaining the functions of each apparatus. Crushers, incinerators, sieves, resonators. Each filled Thio with wonder as his mind churned at the possibilities.

Circling back to the entrance, Britt placed her hand on Thio's shoulder.

'And that's the mineral research sector. I'll leave you to it. If you need anything, I'm right here.' She winked, drawing her hand down his arm.

Thio returned a soft smile, sensing the flirtation in her gesture as Britt danced off back to her colleagues.

He spotted an empty desk in the back corner. Feeling more comfortable sitting alone, he pursued the vacant spot.

He emptied out his satchel onto the broad desk. A notepad, a few loose pages, and a brown leather pouch sprawled across the table. He sat and reviewed his notes for a moment. Running over his equations, he eyed the pulse resonator across from him. Retrieving the chunk of mountain salt from the pouch, he headed towards the machine.

The collection of twisted copper tubes and a symphony of wires stretched high towards the ceiling. Nearing its centre, in a broad niche, was a solid iron disc, round and thick.

Thio approached the array of tools in a nearby cabinet and plucked one off its hook. He chiseled off a tiny fragment of salt from his clump and placed it on the testing pad, precisely nudging it into the centre. Moving to the controls unit, he studied the dials for a moment, then fine-tuned them and switched on the instrument. A mechanical whir sounded as a thin probe lowered onto the fragment. Making contact with the raw mineral, the machine buzzed to life.

Low vibrations permeated the ground at his feet. The frequency slowly increased into a high-pitched thrum. Thio leaned in to get a closer look. Suddenly, the tiny piece of salt evaporated with a solid pop. A plume of thick black soot expanded out from the pad where the piece once sat. Thio bore the brunt of the debris, coughing violently as acrid fumes filled his lungs.

'Make sure to close the guard screen next time!'

Britt yelled out from across the room, laughing alongside her colleagues.

Thio felt stupid, removing his blackened spectacles and wiping the lenses clean. His face was covered in black dust—a surprising amount from such a small sample.

The frequency was off, he thought to himself. He reached for the palm-sized rock and chiseled off another sliver. Marking the results in his notepad, he retuned the dials, then started the machine again, this time sliding the guard screen down.

The vibrations felt more stable this time—the pitch more acute. He peered closer as the prong drew near to the specimen.

In an instant, a brilliant flash of light illuminated the already well-lit lab, temporarily blinding him.

'Woah! What in Korpys was that?' Britt called out again, heading over to the station.

Thio's vision slowly returned. In front of him was no longer a small piece of mountain salt, instead, a melted divot in the solid iron testing pad. The tempered metal prong was dripping into beads of molten iron, glowing red-hot.

'Fascinating!' Britt exclaimed, leaning over Thio's shoulder.

'I'm so sorry,' Thio said nervously, scoping the damage he had just inflicted on the apparatus.

'Don't worry, it's easily replaceable,' she reassured. 'So what are you testing anyway?'

'The excitation of crystalline structures,' Thio clarified. 'Certain minerals possess lattice bonds that store immense potential energy. By applying the right resonance frequency, we can trigger a controlled phase shift, releasing vast amounts of energy. If we can contain and channel that energy, entire cities could be powered with only a fraction of the resources.'

'Wow,' Britt gawked, picking up Thio's notebook and examining the pages. 'I'm impressed. This could have endless potential.'

'I doubt it,' Thio sighed. 'The process is too unstable. If done incorrectly, it could potentially cause a catastrophic discharge.'

'I see.' Britt pondered.

Thio began cleaning up his blunder before a voice called out from across the room.

'Thio? Is there a Thio here?' the voice shouted.

Thio and Britt turned in unison to see a young student standing in the doorway, scanning the room.

'Here.' Thio said, raising his hand.

The young girl spotted him and walked over. 'You've been requested to return to your quarters. Someone is here for you.'

'Who?' he asked.

The girl shrugged.

'Probably Dalos. They must be back,' Thio surmised.

The young girl said no more, then walked off.

Thio turned back to the mess in front of him and groaned.

'You go. I'll clean up,' Britt offered.

'Thank you. I shouldn't be long,' Thio said, dusting himself off as best he could, then heading toward the exit.

* * *

Thio rounded the corner of the dorm's corridors, nearing his room. Reaching the door, he turned the unlocked handle and pushed it open.

'Thanks for the warning. That machine has covered me in shit!' he blurted, expecting Dalos to explode into laughter.

But instead of his heavy mentor, Jaxon Aprya stood in his room.

'My Prince!' Thio exclaimed in shock. 'I thought you were Dalos. Please forgive me.' He bowed sharply, embarrassed by his crude remark.

Jaxon looked down at his flat, trim stomach and patted it. 'An easy mistake,' he said jokingly.

Thio simpered. 'What can I do for you, My Prince?'

'The Princess has requested a meeting. I am here to escort you to the Citadel,' he said.

Thio grew nervous at the thought of a private meeting with Princess Alysse.

'Certainly, My Prince. At once,' he said, straightening up his tunic and adjusting his spectacles.

'Perhaps you should wash that *shit* off first,' Jaxon suggested playfully, pointing at the young man's face.

Thio wiped at his forehead, producing a smear of black soot across his hand.

'Fuck… I mean! Please spare me a moment.'

Jaxon chuckled softly. He felt a sudden calm around this boy, but wasn't sure why. The pressing matters facing the Capital seemed to slip away momentarily.

Thio fumbled to the washroom in the corner of his

quarters and half-closed the privacy screen in his rush. He pulled off his blackened tunic and dropped his trousers.

Jaxon heard water begin to stream from the stall. Meandering around Thio's generous quarters, he shot a quick glance at the half-opened screen. Beyond, through a mirror, was the reflection of the young apprentice. Ripples of sun-bronzed muscle shimmered as water trickled down his back. Jaxon caught himself staring for a moment before quickly moving to distract his thoughts.

'How are you finding the Capital?' he called out.

'A truly astounding domain, My Prince!' Thio yelled over the running water, his vocabulary now formalised after his earlier blunders. He finished scrubbing his body and shut off the water. Towelling himself dry, he realised he had forgotten to grab his fresh garments out by his dresser. He thought of ways to sneak around the wandering Prince but could not risk insulting him should he be seen. He had no choice but to ask.

'Um… My Prince…' he said, nervous to ask the simple request.

Before he could continue, Jaxon reached his arm around the privacy screen, a fresh tunic and a pair of trousers in his hand.

Thio smiled in private at the gesture. 'Thank you, My Prince.'

'We shouldn't keep my sister waiting,' Jaxon pressed.

—

Jaxon led Thio through the underground tunnels beneath the Architect's island. The smell of rust was rich in the air.

'My Prince,' Thio said, breaking the silence, 'the Qyx-Iriyan?'

'Suspended for now. More pressing matters have come to light,' Jaxon replied.

'Does it have anything to do with the message I intercepted?' Thio asked.

'Those are matters reserved for the highest ranks. Concern yourself not with them,' Jaxon said politely.

'Of course. Forgive me, My Prince.'

Thio punished himself for asking such an intrusive question.

The two young men coursed through the labyrinth of passageways before reaching the main tunnel. The small carrier at its entrance sat idle as Jaxon ushered Thio aboard.

Lifting off the ground, the vehicle shifted into motion. The tunnel's trail-lights woke to reveal the lengthy voyage ahead. Nothing but the hum of the carrier could be heard.

Jaxon looked over at Thio, who was nervously fidgeting with a loose cord hanging from his tunic.

'Our conversation the other day, you were speaking of how you came to be Dalos' apprentice,' he said, shifting Thio's attention. 'Would you mind continuing that story?'

'Of course, My Prince,' Thio said, calming his

hands.

'Jaxon. Call me Jaxon.'

'Of course… Jaxon.' The name caught in his throat. He cleared it and continued. 'After my mother's death, my sister and I were taken to Latyth and boarded at the Athenaeum. The Architects seemed very interested in my sister. They performed a number of physical exams on her. I, on the other hand, was tested mentally. Trial after trial, assessing my knowledge, creativity, thought processes. It was fairly overwhelming. Quite frankly, it left me little time to mourn my mother.'

Jaxon felt Thio's pain. His own imperial duties had prevented him from adequately dealing with the passing of his own mother, Lady Palymma, and now, his father.

'A few weeks later,' Thio continued, 'I was accepted as a student of the Athenaeum. I was no better than any other student, in fact, quite the opposite. The Architects paid me no mind. I was merely a slow pupil falling behind. My sister was placed in the infirmary where she learnt to care for the sick. She's still there to this day, having managed to work her way up into the top ranks of senior physicians—the youngest Latyth has ever seen.'

'It appears your family is blessed with intelligence.' Jaxon inserted. 'That is quite a powerful tool. Please, go on.'

Thio acknowledged the compliment with a soft smile, then continued. 'For eight years I studied there, learning the ways of the Architects. Then one day, in mid-winter, all the students were brought into the main hall to welcome Chief Architect Dalos Okombuur, the great man we had heard stories about. Rumours spread throughout the students that he was on the search for an apprentice. To see the man in the flesh was one thing. To consider the possibility of him selecting one of us was something else entirely. But I knew it would never be me. He spoke to the cohort for what seemed like hours. I don't think I've ever laughed so hard.'

Jaxon chuckled at the thought of Dalos' jokes.

'Once the lecture was over,' Thio went on, 'I was called to meet him personally. As you can imagine, it came as quite a shock to me and the cohort. We spoke briefly. He made it feel as if he had known me for years. Before I knew it, I was gathering what little I had and saying goodbye to my sister. I must have been the most unpopular person in the Athenaeum that day. The other students, some my closest friends, made no effort to conceal their disapproval of Dalos' choice.'

'Did you not question him as to why he picked you?' Jaxon asked, curious himself.

'Of course I did,' Thio stated, 'many times. His response was always the same. *There is greatness in you, m'boy,*' he said, perfectly mimicking the old man's tone.

'Interesting,' Jaxon said softly, his mind searching for a reason.

The carrier approached the end of the tunnel, slowing steadily before coming to a halt. The two disembarked and turned for the west corridor.

'My Prince... I'm sorry... Jaxon.' Thio corrected

himself. 'I'm not sure if I am the right person to tell you this, but I have since been told…'

'Jaxon!' A loud voice echoed through the caverns.

The prince turned in the direction of the voice. 'Uncle?'

Cyrus Thenta strode towards them at speed with two guards trailing him.

'What in Korpys are you doing?! You are not to leave the Citadel without my knowledge, do you hear?' he asserted as he approached the prince.

Jaxon stiffened in defence as his uncle drew closer.

'I was sent at Alysse's request,' he said sharply.

'It is not safe for…' Cyrus paused as he noticed Thio standing a few paces behind. 'What business does she have with the apprentice?'

'I'm afraid you will have to ask her yourself, Uncle,' Jaxon said with a condescending inflection.

Cyrus studied Thio, unimpressed by his casual appearance. 'Very well. He will need to be screened before entering the Citadel.'

'I can assure you he bears no arms,' Jaxon stated, momentarily picturing the young man in the mirror.

Frustration grew in Cyrus' tone. 'He is to be questioned.'

'And he will be,' Jaxon shot back, 'by Alysse. Now, if you please, Uncle, step aside.'

For a brief moment, they stood locked in each other's gaze. Thio remained frozen as the tension gripped the space around him.

With a huff, Cyrus conceded, then stormed off through the dimly lit corridor.

Jaxon's frustration slipped from his clenched

mouth in a single word. 'Cunt.' He took a deep breath, then turned to Thio. 'Please, this way.'

Thio dared not comment, opting to follow in silence instead.

'Apologies,' Jaxon said after calming himself. 'I don't know why he holds such disdain for me. He often forgets that I am to one day take his place as Imperial Commander, yet he still treats me as a child and undermines my ability to protect myself and my sister.'

'I'm sure he is only concerned for your safety,' Thio suggested.

'Ever since my mother's death, he has grown cold towards me.' Jaxon's tone shifted to sorrow. 'He lost a sister that day, I understand. Yet I feel he places blame on me. I was a child, stricken by the Dusk. What could I have done?'

Thio searched for words of comfort but found none.

Jaxon straightened his posture and lifted his chin, then continued to lead Thio through the tunnels towards the Citadel entrance.

CHAPTER 17

Alysse stood at the edge of the Skyhold—the open-air terrace crowning the pinnacle of the Citadel. Nothing but the towering spires flanking its eastern and western borders rose higher. Perched 800 metres above the city, Alysse felt the air's purity—untouched, as if no breath before hers had ever drawn it in.

She fondled the scroll in her hands before looking down and reading the words once again.

Your decision calls for scrutiny.

She searched her mind for a meaning that made sense of the words. She had always known her father to rule with fairness and integrity, his judgement revered by monarchs and common folk alike. *What decision could have led to such malcontent?* she thought. Staring out towards the Sanctuary of Qyma, she explored various reasons why the Faith would challenge his rule—what grievances they might hold, what ambition his death might serve.

The whirring of the Skyhold's elevator to her left shifted her focus. She pocketed the scroll and smoothed over her fine silk blazer.

The doors hissed, then slid open. Inside stood Jaxon and, a step behind, Thio.

The young apprentice stood in awe of the towering terrace. A ring of potted lemon trees encircled the courtyard. At its centre was a large iron basin—an unlit fire beacon that spanned metres across the patterned stone landing.

'Your Grace. Thio, the apprentice,' Jaxon announced, stepping out into the open air.

Thio followed closely, mindful not to let the grandeur and sheer scale of the Skyhold divert his attention.

'Your Grace,' he said eloquently as he bowed with rehearsed form.

'Thio, thank you for meeting with me,' Alysse said with a soft, welcoming tone to her voice. 'I recognise that the conditions of our first meeting were far from ideal.'

'It is a relief to see Her Grace and the Prince safe,' he responded, his eyes fighting his curiosity to admire the view beyond the precipice.

Noticing his failing attempts at self-control, Alysse directed Thio towards the southern perimeter.

'Go ahead,' she said.

Thio approached the balustrade slowly, an unfamiliar pit forming in his stomach as his legs began to tremble. Jaxon looked on in amusement—first-timers often found such heights utterly unnerving.

Looking out over the Bay of Prosperity, Thio let slip an audible gasp at the scale and beauty of the world below. He spotted the Shrine of Old, the glowing sapphire dome of the Grand Athenaeum, and the sheer expanse of the Southern Sea. He studied the intricacies of the city blocks, meticulously planned from their inception.

'I could get lost up here,' he spoke aloud.

'As I have many times,' Alysse responded playfully. 'You never quite get used to it.'

She allowed Thio a moment longer to admire the scenery before speaking again.

'I hear you possess quite a curious mind, Thio, may I explore it for a moment?'

'Of course, Your Grace,' Thio replied, anticipating a question perhaps intended to provide strategy.

'Say you were to build a structure that can withstand time itself,' Alysse began. 'It has to be defiant, proud, but most of all, strong. How would you go about its design?'

Thio stepped back from the balustrade, confused by the question.

'Your Grace?' he queried. 'Forgive me, perhaps that question is better asked of the builders.'

Alysse smiled softly. 'I speak only theoretically.'

Thio pondered the question again, looking out over the city at the structures that lined its streets. Cubes, domes, spires, arches—nearly every shape imaginable. He pictured the slender tower he currently stood atop. His mind wandered back to his days studying in Latyth—equations, complex mathematics, formulas. He continued to scan the city, looking south, then west, then east, then south again. *Ah, of course, it's simple,* he thought.

'Well,' he began, 'if strength is paramount... a trigon. Three equal sides. The strongest shape there is. Any force weighed upon it is evenly distributed between all three sides.'

Alysse smiled at his answer. 'Now, say one side were to be compromised, what would happen to the structure?'

'It would severely weaken its integrity, even to the point of collapse,' Thio responded swiftly.

'Precisely.' Alysse approached the young apprentice. 'Thio, the foundations of our working world are held together by the triadic nature of the Great Factions—The Ancients, The Architects, and the Great Houses. The people look to all three for guidance, prosperity, and peace.'

Now standing beside him, Alysse looked out at her city. 'It seems cracks have formed of late. It is my duty to see that they do not fracture.'

Thio felt the weight of her words as he reflected on them.

'How may I aid, Your Grace?' he asked, sensing the Crown Princess was arriving at her point.

Alysse peered across the bay towards the Grand Athenaeum, its sapphire dome prominent amongst the green foliage dressing the flat island.

'Dalos,' she began. 'It is clear that time has not treated him well. His health is fast declining. But it is not this that I fear. His loyalty to my family is well known, and that puts him in danger.'

She turned to the young man with a direct stare, her rich hazel eyes glazed with emotion.

'I simply ask that you protect him from harm should he face it,' she requested. 'Can I count on you, Thio?'

Thio gave the request little thought before responding.

'He has given me everything. It is my honour to serve him and House Aprya. You have my word.'

'*Your* honour?' Alysse said, producing a smile. 'No, Thio, the honour is ours. I have come to learn that a great debt is owed to you, one I fear we cannot repay.'

Jaxon stared quizzically at his sister. 'A great debt?'

'Dalos told me why he chose you—a poor boy from a town few have even heard of,' Alysse said. 'A tragedy once befell my family, and an unknown saviour prevented my brother's death. My father swore to find the one responsible and reward them.'

Thio attempted to communicate his reluctance for Alysse to disclose this information through his gaze. 'Your Grace, I...'

Before he could say more, Alysse flung her arms around him in embrace.

'Thank you, Thio,' she said, tenderly.

Jaxon, confused, looked on as his sister held the young man.

'I'm sensing a key detail is eluding me,' he said.

Alysse released her hold and turned to her brother.

'If it were not for Thio, you would not be with us today,' she said.

'What are you saying?' Jaxon asked.

'It was he who cured the Dusk,' she said. 'He denied the Gods your life, as if a God himself.'

The revelation struck Jaxon with force, rendering him speechless.

'Please, Your Grace, I seek no praise,' Thio said quietly in an attempt to avert attention. 'I have already been given opportunity well above my worth.'

'You shall have every opportunity you desire. House Aprya will see to it,' Alysse said.

Jaxon could only stare at his unveiled saviour, newfound emotions surging within him—gratitude, admiration, but also something else—something he had not felt for anyone before. He readied himself to say something—anything—but was suddenly halted by the hiss of the elevator doors.

'Your Grace!' Cyrus Thenta called out, urgently striding towards them.

'Your Grace, a few of our scouts have returned report,' he said.

'Speak them.'

Cyrus caught sight of Thio and hesitated.

'Perhaps in private, Your Grace,' he suggested.

'Speak them, Uncle,' Alysse repeated, this time accompanied by a reassuring nod.

Cyrus sensed a trusting tone in her voice. He took a breath, then spoke.

'The message spoke the truth. Ton-Basin is lost—blue flame still burns. The few survivors have sought refuge in the foothills.'

Thio listened on in disbelief. *The message.* Images of Ton-Basin's quaint beauty shattered in his thoughts. The peaceful place he had called home for the past few months was no longer.

'And the rebels?' Alysse pressed.

'A station just outside the city was attacked earlier this morning. Reports suggest they are heading north. We have sent precautions to Bryll, the West Wall, and Latyth.'

Fear instantly gripped Thio. *Y'mara is in Latyth*, he thought as his sister's face sprung to mind.

'Your Grace,' Cyrus continued, 'if the port city falls, trade between the countries will cease.'

'We have large forces in Latyth, do we not?' Jaxon asked. 'Surely enough to defend the city.'

'The fort has been inadequately manned of late. The majority of the troops were sent to Aankathor to settle the mining feud. I will order men from…'

'How long before they reach Latyth?' Thio interrupted.

'Our military movements are not of your concern,' Cyrus responded with arrogance.

'Not the troops, the rebels!' Thio shouted.

'How dare you raise your voice to me,' Cyrus challenged, advancing on the boy with rage in his eyes.

Before Cyrus could advance further, Jaxon instinctively stepped between them, halting his uncle with a steely glare.

'Answer the question, Uncle,' he said.

'We don't know how they are travelling around. If by foot, a month. By rail, less than a few days. Three at most.'

Thio pushed past the Prince and his uncle and hasted for the elevator.

'Where are you going?' Alysse called out, halting

Thio in place.

'I am going to get my sister,' he said with clenched teeth.

'We have suspended all civilian transport throughout Qymathor. The Passages are shut. No one passes in or out of the Capital. Our troops will deal with the rebels. You will remain here,' Alysse said firmly.

'Forgive me, Your Grace, but I am not asking for permission,' Thio tried to say politely, suppressing his growing rage. 'Y'mara is the only blood I have left in this world. Hold me prisoner, if you can, but I *will* protect my family.'

'Your Empress has spoken,' Cyrus interjected. 'It is far too dangerous. Plus your skills may be needed here.'

'Skills?! I have no skills!' Thio exploded in anger. 'I am only here because I happened upon some cure for a disease I knew nothing about. I am not special. I am no God. I am alone, as is my sister. I will scale the fucking Drom Mountains to get to her if I must!'

Enraged, he ploughed his fist into the elevator door. The combination of flesh on steel and cracking bone resonated through the open air.

Alysse and Jaxon stood in shock at the timid boy's sudden outburst as Cyrus placed a readying hand on his short sword.

Thio clutched his throbbing fist, closed his eyes, and took a series of deep breaths. Once calm, he spoke.

'Your Grace, I am going to Latyth, one way or another. If you wish to repay your debt, allow me access through the North Passage. I will ask nothing more of you.'

Alysse sensed his fear and took a moment to think.

'I will allow it,' she said. 'But it is too dangerous to go alone. Uncle, prepare an escort.'

'I will take him,' Jaxon said softly.

'What?' Alysse questioned, unsure if she had heard correctly.

'I will take him,' Jaxon repeated louder.

'Out of the question!' Cyrus responded immediately.

'It is a day's travel by rail,' Jaxon argued. 'We can reach the city and return before the rebels step foot in Latyth. Thio can retrieve his sister, and I can speak to Commander Rodyn at the fort.'

'Jaxon, I…' Alysse found herself lost for words; the thought of her brother not by her side was inconceivable.

'Alysse, I am alive because of Thio,' he whispered to his sister. 'It is the least I can do for him. You and I both know the importance of protecting family. Besides, if I can secure an accord with the forces in Latyth, it may prove to Uncle Cyrus that I am deserving of his position.'

'I need you here, Jax,' she pleaded.

'Uncle Cyrus is here to protect you. So are Dalos and Mia. We will return before you know it.'

'My Prince,' Thio interjected, 'I cannot ask this of you. Your place is here.'

Jaxon stepped closer. 'You are not asking. It is my duty to protect the people of this country. I know these lands better than most. Plus, I am proficient in combat, should it come to that. It would be my father's wish to see you well protected.'

A tear formed in the corner of Thio's eye.

'Ok.' Alysse conceded. 'You will travel after dark. No one can know that you have left the Capital. You will retrieve Y'mara and return immediately.'

'Princess, I must insist you reconsider,' Cyrus said with concern. 'Your brother's safety is tantamount to yours.'

Alysse took a deep breath and motioned her uncle to approach.

'Make the arrangements,' she said. 'Tell the station stewards that the last train leaving this evening holds valuable supplies. It is not to be halted before its destination. Open the North Passage only once the train has departed, and close it immediately after it has exited the mountain.'

'Yes, Your Grace,' Cyrus said with hesitation, opening the elevator doors and beginning his descent of the tower.

'Thank you, Your Grace,' Thio said softly.

Jaxon gave Alysse a nod of appreciation and a reassuring smile. He turned to Thio.

'Gather what you need from the Athenaeum. We will meet in the tunnels below the Citadel at dusk. Do you remember the way?'

'My Prince, I…'

'Do you remember the way?' Jaxon repeated.

'I do.'

'At dusk,' the Prince reiterated.

'At dusk,' Thio echoed.

CHAPTER 18

Dalos sat in his armchair by the window in his reading room, his favourite book in hand: *The Unsettled Sea by Myra Okombuur*. Throughout her early explorations, Dalos' wife would imagine tales of fantastical sea creatures and heroic voyages into the forbidden oceans. Her creativity was unmatched, and her books were exceedingly popular amongst children and adults alike. He could nearly recite this book word for word, yet never lost the joy of reading it from beginning to end.

He picked up his cup from the ornate side table and brought it to his lips. The sweet aroma of the tea seduced his senses as he took a sip. Its warmth consumed him. It was his most cherished luxury, imported from Aankathor, where it was solely grown on the slopes of the Perdys Valley.

'Knock, knock.' A cheerful voice broke the peace.

Dalos looked over at the door to see Britt Pensyr

peering into the room, a bright smile lighting up her youthful face.

'Britt, m'girl,' Dalos greeted her cheerfully, 'come in.' He placed his cup back on the side table and closed his book.

The spritely young woman entered the room, curiously scanning the elaborate shelves of the opulent space.

'What can I do for you?' Dalos asked, drawing her attention back to him.

'I met your apprentice this morning, sir. He's a handsome fellow,' she said with a playful wink. 'He performed an experiment with one of the pulse resonators. I have never seen anything like it.'

'Ah yes, he's been working on this for some time now. What were his findings?'

'Pure energy. I'm talking about blinding light and ferocious heat. All from a mere speck of mineral. The most perplexing oddity, though, was that the flare was completely silent. It suggests that the resonation was able to isolate the kinetic energy of the blast into only radiant and thermal energy. Dalos, this could be a huge breakthrough.'

Dalos grinned proudly.

'I've since tried to recreate the anomaly to no avail,' Britt continued. 'I looked over his notes but couldn't make sense of them. I would have gathered insight from him if you had not called for him, but...'

'Called for him?' Dalos interrupted.

'It wasn't you? Someone was awaiting him in his chambers. We all assumed it was you.'

A moment of fear set in as Dalos stood from his

armchair. He lifted his left wrist and pressed a small disc on the leather band wrapped around it before hobbling to the door. Britt stood in place, confused at the Chief's sudden panic.

By the time Dalos reached the other side of the room, Mia had appeared in the doorway.

'Pa? What's wrong?' she asked with trepidation.

Britt looked on as Dalos whispered in his daughter's ear. Without a word, Mia gave a sharp nod and hurried off down the hallway.

Dalos stood a moment, his breath rapid and deep. He grabbed the door frame to steady himself. Concerned, Britt collected his teacup and brought it over to him.

'Here, sir. Drink,' she said, handing it to him as beads of sweat rolled down his forehead.

Dalos took the cup and consumed what was left of the honey-coloured liquid.

'Sir, I think you should sit,' she said, assisting the large man back to his armchair.

'Thank you, m'girl. It's nothing. Now, what were you saying?'

'It's not important,' she replied. 'Perhaps you should rest. I can come back later.'

'No, no, please continue,' he insisted, patting his forehead with a pocket cloth.

Britt hesitated a moment before speaking. 'Sir, news has reached the Athenaeum of the attack in Ton-Basin. Word of a rebellion is spreading throughout the guild. I was thinking...' She paused. 'This discovery of Thio's, besides its clear potential as a new energy source, could be harnessed as a countermeasure should the city be attacked.'

'We do not make weapons, Britt,' Dalos said firmly.

'I understand that, sir, but an advantage such as this could secure our…'

'We do not make weapons!' Dalos repeated, exerting more energy than he had intended.

He felt his chest tighten as his heart pounded.

Britt conceded. 'Yes, sir. My apologies. I will leave you be. Thank you for your time,' she said as she feigned a smile and made for the door.

Dalos watched the young blonde stride across the room. Heart still pounding, his vision began to shift, seeing multiple images of the girl's figure before she exited. He fought to focus on a single point. A daze fell swiftly upon him. He reached for the pot on the side table and poured another shot of tea, spilling most of it in his attempt. Gulping down what little was in the cup, he heaved himself up from the chair and staggered to his quarters.

The room swayed around him as his gaze latched onto the portrait of his late wife, Myra, hanging solemnly on the eastern wall. With unsteady steps, he tottered toward it, his already burdened frame growing heavier as his legs fought against collapse.

Lunging at the painting, he grabbed the frame and pulled. The solid piece of wall on which it hung shifted and swung open. Behind it, within a deep recess, sat a large iron box, decorated with intricate metalwork and etchings. Dalos traced his fingers around the ornaments, pushing some and pulling others as he worked his way around the box. As he pressed the final pieces in the combination, the box's front cracked open with a hiss.

In his failing vision, he saw a stack of journals and two glowing orange vials inside. Without hesitation, he clutched at one of the vials, but in doing so knocked the other. It rolled out of the iron box and fell to the ground, shattering on impact. Taking no heed, he opened the successfully retrieved vial and consumed the sweet liquid.

Disoriented, Dalos stumbled backwards, his legs finally buckling. It felt like an eternity before his body hit the marble floor. Then darkness.

The old Architect lay motionless on the floor of his chamber, his mind drifting from reality. In the black of his vision, small orange flashes burst in his mind's eye. He felt warmth in his veins as the Fire Orchid essence he had just consumed began coursing through them.

With a sudden gasp, his eyes snapped open. Where once dull brown had resided, a luminous orange now blazed, rekindling the life that had almost abandoned him.

CHAPTER 19

Thio peered through the narrow window in his quarters. The warm sun began to kiss the western ridge of the Drom Mountain range as it lowered in the sky. *I have an hour at most,* he thought.

He crammed a fresh tunic into his rucksack, paying no mind to its neatness. The pain pulsing from his clearly broken hand made him wince. Coupled with the shame of his outburst before the Crown Princess, Thio hesitated at the prospect of journeying alongside Jaxon. *What must he have thought?*

Scanning the room, he noticed his leather satchel neatly atop his study table. Someone had returned it from the geology wing earlier that morning. Before he could reach for the bag, a knock sounded at the door.

He made his way across the room, unlatched the door, and swung it open. Before him stood Mia, panic in her eyes.

'Oh Thio!' she exclaimed as she wrapped her arms around him. 'You had us worried sick. Where have you been?'

'I… I was called to the Citadel. Princess Alysse…'

'Do excuse me, your business is your own. We just —anyway, thank the Gods you're alright,' she said, loosening her grip on the young man. She let out a sigh of relief. Calmed, she looked down at his swollen hand.

'What have you done? Here, let me wrap it for you.'

She entered the room and fetched a medic kit from a small cabinet near the door. Retrieving a roll of linen, she began tending to his injury. The constriction of the cloth had an instant effect on his pain.

'There we are,' she said, securing the tail end of the wrap with a thin metal clip. Looking up at him, she noticed the rucksack atop his bed.

'You're going somewhere?' she asked, concern returning to her voice.

'Mia,' Thio said, drawing a long breath, 'I'm leaving for Latyth tonight.'

'Latyth?'

'I need to get my sister out of there before…'

'The rebels.' Mia spoke with dawning awareness. 'But transport has been suspended. How will you get there?'

'Princess Alysse has granted me passage.'

'Are you travelling alone?' she asked with concern.

Thio hesitated, recalling Alysse's insistence that no one know the Prince was leaving the Capital.

'Yes,' he said, uncomfortable with the lie.

'Oh, my boy. Is there anything we can do to aid you?' she offered wholeheartedly.

'I need access to the tunnels. I know they are off-limits, but I…'

'The door in Dalos' reading room is unlocked. Be sure to close it behind you.' Mia wrapped her arms around him once again. 'Please be safe.'

Thio returned her embrace with warmth, as if it were their last. He swiftly pushed the unsettling thought from his mind.

'Oh, will you let Dalos know? I'm a little pressed for time,' he asked.

'Of course. In fact, you may see him. He was in his reading room last I saw, but he never stays still for too long,' Mia replied with a smile. 'See you soon, my boy. And be safe.' She patted his shoulder then proceeded down the hallway.

Thio walked back into the centre of his room, listing the necessary items in his mind. He approached his satchel and opened it. Inside were his familiar items. His notebook, a scribe, and the small leather pouch. As he began to close the bag, he noticed something extra. A note.

Retrieving it, he opened it and began reading the words.

Handsome Thio,
I was extremely impressed by your work this morning.
I would love to speak to you in private about it.
I hope you don't mind, but I've kept a small chunk of your sample.
I promise I will replace it.

I look forward to our next meeting.
Yours, Britt.

'She's confident, I'll give her that,' Thio said aloud, noting the flirtatious undertones. He reached into the bag and pulled out the leather pouch. It felt significantly lighter in his hand.

He untied the string and poured the piece of mountain salt onto his palm.

'A small chunk?' he exclaimed to himself as he inspected the remaining quarter of the mineral. Unimpressed by Britt's self-helping, he repacked what was left of his mentor's gift and slid it into his pocket for safekeeping. He moved to the dresser against the north wall and picked up a silver locket. It was slender—about a finger's width, with a rose etched on its face. Opening it, he looked at the two drawings inside. One, his mother, fair-faced, picking flowers in the garden outside their modest cottage. The other, his sister, young and jovial, laughing as she often did. He closed the locket and slipped the chain over his head, tucking it into his tunic. Putting on his spectacles, he stared at himself in the mirror. *Ok, I'm ready,* he thought confidently as he shouldered his rucksack and tightened the straps.

Winding his way through the corridors, Thio reflected on the mission ahead of him and the thought of seeing his sister again. During their time in Latyth after their mother's death, Y'mara would often check in to make sure he was eating adequately, as he often forgot about his meals while he worked on his ideas. They would spend countless hours at night discussing their learnings and reminiscing about their hometown. As children, the two would often trek through the lush forests to the Syka Falls, a natural beauty known only by the native folk of the town. Its picturesque waterfalls cascaded into a deep basin of crystal-clear water where the children would come to swim during the summer months.

Thio couldn't help but smile as he pictured his sister's face. All thought of the looming rebellion vanished from his mind.

Arriving at Dalos' reading room, Thio noticed the door slightly ajar. He gave a polite knock as he pushed it open. The room was empty. He made for the hidden door. As he passed Dalos' reading chair, he noticed a puddle of tea on the side table. *Clumsy shit*, he chuckled to himself as he pushed against the section of wall. It cracked open. A waft of rust-scented air brushed over him as he peered down the lightless staircase, then entered.

Arriving at the main tunnel, Thio spotted the carrier. He hesitantly stepped onto it and studied the control unit. The array of buttons and knobs intimidated him. Trying his luck, he pressed the uppermost button. The carrier began to vibrate as it hummed to life, lifting gently off the ground. He pressed another which produced a small control wheel that emerged from an opening in the unit.

'That's a good start,' he commended himself.

He grabbed the control wheel and gently eased it forward. With a faint buzz, the vehicle crept into motion. The tunnel's trail-lights illuminated the path before him. Pressing harder, the carrier accelerated, faster and faster. Thio felt an exhilarating rush as the still air now whirled around him.

The tunnel stretched endlessly before him. Thio closed his eyes for a fleeting moment, savouring the rush of wind against his skin. In that brief reprieve, his mind felt weightless, unburdened. A few moments passed before he opened them. In the nearing distance was a black object—the end of the tunnel.

Instinctively, he pulled back on the control wheel to no avail. The carrier did not slow. He tried again. Nothing. Panicked, he slammed his hand on the uppermost button. The carrier suddenly dropped to the ground, skidding along the smooth marble thoroughfare. Ahead, a stone wall drew closer. The sound of metal and stone grinding together echoed loudly down the tunnel behind him. Smoke and dust billowed around the vehicle. He braced himself for impact. Arriving mere centimetres from the facade, the carrier came to a complete stop.

Thio stared ahead at the wall in front of him, his skin pale, beads of sweat forming on his brow. Eager to disembark, he reached for his rucksack, only to find it missing from its hold. His hands swept through the dust in vain, searching blindly. He scanned the surrounding darkness, but it yielded nothing.

'Lost something?' A voice startled him.

Thio turned to his left to see a silhouette emerge from the shadows, his rucksack in hand.

'My prince! I'm sorry... the carrier...' Thio fumbled.

'I care not about the carrier. Are *you* okay?' Jaxon

asked as he stepped into the light.

In place of his formal green suit were common garbs. Loose trousers were paired with a beige woven tunic topped with a hood that masked his soft curls. Thio found himself lost for words as he looked the handsome man over.

'I'm… I'm fine, My Prince,' he managed.

'Jaxon,' the Prince playfully insisted.

Thio bashfully dropped his head as he adjusted his spectacles and stepped off the grounded vehicle. Jaxon handed him his rucksack and brushed off the dust that had settled on Thio's shoulder.

'Are you ready?' he asked.

Thio nodded.

Jaxon led the apprentice through a series of corridors beneath the Citadel before arriving at another large tunnel to the north. The sight of another carrier suspended off the ground made Thio shudder.

'You drive,' he joked.

Jaxon laughed as he slipped off his own rucksack and flung it onto the platform. Within moments, the two were hurling down the passage at speed.

Reaching the terminus at the opposite end of the tunnel, Jaxon eased the carrier to a gentle halt.

'See, that's how it's done,' he said with a wink.

Thio rolled his eyes and grinned as they disembarked.

Passing through a few more corridors and ascending a staircase, the two men surfaced into a small yet opulent room. At the back of the room were a cluster of statues depicting the Gods. In the centre stood Qyma, arms outstretched, a turquoise orb in one hand and a freshly cut orchid in the other. Beside the feminine figure was Kapry, hunched, turned away from his mother and reaching for the blue orb. Figures representing Shaavy and Doma wept at the feet of the two rivalling deities. Last was Aanka, a child, eyes closed with both hands on her heart. Thio concluded that this was a shrine. Dalos had once mentioned that these ancient sanctums dotted the Capital.

Thio followed Jaxon toward the door leading out onto the street. As they stepped outside, he took in his unfamiliar surroundings, his gaze settling on the distant silhouette of the Citadel to the south.

The city lay in an eerie quietness, a silence that, oddly, reassured Jaxon. Moving swiftly, they made their way toward the station a few blocks ahead. Jaxon kept his head low, avoiding the eyes of passing city folk.

The station came into view, its scarlet dome aglow from the building's night lights. The grand doors stood firmly shut, a lone sign affixed at their centre.

Suspended operations.
No entry.

'Follow me. Hurry,' Jaxon said as he diverted left down a small alley, out of sight of any onlookers. The external walls of the station rose some five metres from the street and extended all the way to the island's northern tip and slightly beyond.

Reaching the water's edge, Jaxon removed his rucksack and rifled through it, producing a coil of rope. On one end was a self-releasing grappling hook. His eyes traced the crown of the wall as the light began to fade, landing on a perfect anchor point. Unraveling the rope, he began swinging the hook. After a few rotations, he flung it towards the top of the marble wall. With perfect accuracy, the hook hit its mark and burst open, gripping the stone with its slender iron fingers. Jaxon gave a few reassuring tugs, then looked to Thio.

'I'll go first. Do as I do.'

Thio stepped back as Jaxon tightly gripped the rope. With a few swift strides, he launched himself over the water. The rope tensed, bearing his weight as he swung in a fluid arc around the jutting section of the wall—then vanished from view.

Thio, impressed, waited for a sign that the Prince had landed safely. Moments later, the rope swung back around the wall. He caught it, secured his ruck-sack, and adjusted his spectacles. Mimicking Jaxon's movements, he sprinted toward the water's edge and leaped. The rope tensed, yanking against his injured hand. Pain flared, and his fingers instinctively re-leased their grip. Panic surged as he clamped down with his other hand, narrowly avoiding a plunge into the bay. The sudden shift in momentum sent him into an uncontrolled spin, twisting wildly in the air.

Rounding the edifice, Thio spotted Jaxon waiting on the platform. Calculating his trajectory, he re-leased his grip on the rope. He tumbled onto the platform, his rucksack breaking his fall, the small leather pouch flinging out of his pocket and landing at Jaxon's feet.

'Are you okay?' Jaxon asked.

Thio nodded in embarrassment.

'Here,' the Prince said as he picked up the small pouch and extended a hand to help Thio to his feet. He collected the end of the rope and performed a series of short tugs, unlatching the grappling mechanism from the wall. He wound the rope and stuffed it back in his rucksack as Thio dusted himself off, once again ashamed by his clumsiness.

Before them stretched a network of rails. Four massive rail carriages, each spanning 50 metres, sat idle in the empty station. Only one glowed with the faint illumination of interior lights.

'There,' Thio pointed towards the glowing carriage.

The two men scanned the area for any sign of movement. Nothing. Crouching, they navigated over the rail lines to the train. Reaching under the doors, Jaxon activated the manual opening latch and the doors whispered open. Interlocking his fingers, he offered Thio a boost up onto the carriage. Once up, Thio extended his hand to Jaxon. Gripping tightly, he heaved the young Prince up.

'Now what?' Thio asked.

Jaxon peered across the station at the large clock suspended from the apex of the dome.

'Three, two, one.'

With exact precision, the doors to the carriage shut. A warm tone rang out across the station as the train shifted into motion.

'These civilian trains don't travel as fast as our private ones, so settle in,' Jaxon said. 'We should reach the Kordas Desert by morning. From there we'll pass through it, and continue north to Latyth. Let's eat, then get some rest.'

Thio agreed, watching the sprawling lights of the city recede behind them through the train's glass ceiling.

CHAPTER 20

Britt Pensyr sat in her spacious chambers. The small wooden box before her chimed, the message within its harmonious tones immediately clear to her trained ear.

'Is it done?' the message translated.

'I poisoned his tea. He should be with the Gods now,' she replied, inputting her response into the sonic transmitter.

'And his apprentice?'

'A work in progress. He is a clever boy but has no sense of awareness to him. Once I understand his work, he shouldn't be hard to silence.'

'Good. Continue with the others. I want them dead sooner than planned.'

'Yes, my liege.'

Britt switched off the sonic transmitter and stowed it back in the hidden slot beneath her bed, then moved into her washroom. In front of the mirror, she brushed her buttery blonde hair and tied it up into a ponytail. Within her side cabinet, she released a false backing panel and located a small hidden box. The box contained a small glass jar filled with a mirky balm and a smaller vial of pale blue liquid.

She applied a generous amount of the balm to her lips and rolled them for an even coverage. After pocketing the vial, she unbuttoned her blouse half-way and adjusted her well-formed breasts. She couldn't help but produce a malicious grin. *Perfect.*

The walk to Chief Gorryn Venidor's chamber was short. Britt noticed a handful of male students gawking at her beauty. She awarded them a seductive wave as she passed. Arriving at her mentor's door, she smoothed over her blouse and gave her breasts one last adjustment, then knocked.

'Come in,' said the deep voice from within the room.

Britt opened the door. Gorryn looked up to see the sultry figure perfectly framed in the doorway.

'Britt! Um… what can I do for you?' he managed through his sudden arousal.

'Good evening, sir,' she said brightly as she entered the room. 'I just wanted to know if you had made any headway on Thio's notes?'

Gorryn took a second to refocus on the work in front of him.

'I must admit, they are extremely complex. These frequencies are so precise, it would be near impossible to replicate consistently.'

Britt walked around the desk and leaned in over her mentor's shoulder, her bust level with his eye line.

'Not impossible,' she said with sweetness in her tone. 'I saw him execute it this morning.'

Gorryn quivered at the young woman's alluring perfume. He cleared his throat.

'Well, I've managed to rewrite the formula into a somewhat comprehensive model. I may have to run it by Dalos first, but I'm fairly confident this will work.'

'I can run it past him myself if you like, first thing in the morning,' she said as she slowly drew the page from his hands and placed it back on the table. Gorryn looked up at the seductive beauty leaning over him. Britt placed a soft hand on his shoulder.

'Thank you for doing that for me,' she said, stroking his arm. 'Now, allow me to return the favour.'

With a forceful push, she spun the huge man around on his chair. Before Gorryn knew what was happening, the young woman was straddling him.

'Britt, this is highly inappropriate,' he stated, fighting every primal urge.

'I know,' she whispered in his ear as she licked his lobe slowly.

The sensation resonated through his body. He felt the swelling of his manhood press against her as she continued to tease his neck. Against his better judgement, Gorryn conceded to her seduction and stood, carrying the slender woman with him. Her legs wrapped around his waist as he rubbed his hand up her back.

The two locked lips in a fit of passion. Blindly,

Gorryn slid his hand across the table to clear it. Stacks of pages sprawled across the floor as he laid her down on her back. Britt stared at him with lust-filled eyes, sliding up her skirt. The Chief aggressively tore at his belt to remove it, then slid down his trousers. He pulled at her hips to draw her closer to the edge of the table, then eased himself inside her. Britt moaned in pleasure as she felt his pulse grow deep within her.

'I want you to fuck me like I'm the last girl you will ever have,' she encouraged as his pace quickened and his ferocity grew.

Their indulgence went on for a few minutes, each groan and grunt louder than the last. Britt watched as her towering companion began to sweat, beads dripping on her exposed breasts.

Gorryn felt his heart racing. Little did he know that the poison had already begun to take effect. His vision started to blur. Entranced by the pleasure, he took little notice.

'I'm ready for you, sir,' she invited.

Her words were enough to propel him to climax. With a few last thrusts, he emptied inside her. The euphoric moment encapsulated his mind and body as the poison coursed through his veins. He swayed, losing strength, until he finally collapsed on top of her. His weight expelled the air from her lungs as he became limp.

Britt reached for the small pocket in her skirt and produced the vial of light blue liquid, uncorked it, and consumed the antidote. Using her victim's shirt, she wiped off the remaining balm from her lips. With all her strength, she heaved his hulking body off her. It dropped to the ground with a solid thud.

Taking her time to redress, she looked down at her motionless mentor and grinned. She knelt down next to him and stared directly into his lifeless eyes.

'Such a shame,' she whispered as she brushed over his hair. 'Let us hope your seed takes. The world could use another mind like yours.'

With that, she caressed his face, shutting his eyes. She fixed his clothing and placed his hand over his chest. Looking around next to him, she spotted the formula he had rewritten. She picked it up and tucked it between her breasts, stood, and made for the hallway.

'Good night, sir,' she said as she shut the door and locked it.

CHAPTER 21

An abrupt jolt threw Jaxon awake, and he sat up, sweat covering his body. The train's cooling system struggled to counter the penetrating desert heat. Bringing himself to focus, he surveyed the dim, empty carriage. A faint orange hue permeated from the glass ceiling. Beyond, he saw nothing, struggling to discern what time it was.

Dazed, he looked over to where Thio had settled himself in for the night, but saw only empty sheets. He scanned the carriage once more. Panicked, he called out.

'Thio?'

The train shifted violently again.

'Thio?!'

Jaxon stood. He began making his way up the carriage, quickening his pace as another silent blow rocked the train. Before he reached the end, the partition between the carriages opened. There stood Thio, a pot of tea in one hand and two cups in the other.

'Thank the Gods. What's going on?' Jaxon asked.

'Sandstorm,' Thio replied, fatigue in his voice. 'It's worsened in the past hour.'

'How long have you been up?'

'Since daybreak, I think. I can't tell.' Thio looked up at the opaque hues beyond the glass ceiling, catching his balance as the floor shifted beneath them. The plumes of sand thrown up by the storm obstructed all view of their surroundings. He motioned to the table centring the carriage and placed the pot and cups atop it.

'These storms are common here,' Jaxon stated. 'The northern winds stir up the desert. If it weren't for the Drom Mountains, Zenithal would be under a blanket of sand.'

'The Soaring Shield,' Thio recalled, pouring a cup for the Prince.

The two sat in silence for a time as they enjoyed the sweet tea, both peering out for any break in the storm.

'Once we reach Latyth,' Jaxon said, turning to his travel companion, 'what is your plan?'

'The infirmary,' Thio said instantly. 'Y'mara will be there. It isn't far from the station. I can get there and back within an hour. Perhaps you should wait on the train.'

Jaxon could still sense the fear in Thio's tone. A fear he knew well.

'I understand your haste, Thio, but I too have business in Latyth. As future Imperial Commander, I must speak with the commanding officer at the barracks.'

Thio had all but forgotten that the imposing threat stretched far beyond his own need to protect his family.

'My uncle says their troops will be arriving back from Aankathor within the day,' Jaxon continued. 'I need to make sure they are well prepared for an attack.'

'The barracks are across the port,' Thio said, recalling the city's layout. 'You'd be exposing yourself. Latyth doesn't have hidden tunnels.'

Jaxon cracked a smile. 'I'm glad they have remained hidden, even from the smartest of folk.'

Thio's eyes widened. 'Latyth *does* have tunnels?'

'Long before Zenithal was established, the port city was this nation's capital. Its first king built tunnels without the people's knowledge. These were different times, however. After their construction, the king ordered the builders be killed, ensuring no one outside the royal family knew of their existence.'

'Was that really necessary?' Thio asked, taken aback by the story.

'The world before the Imperium did not hold to the same accord as we do today,' Jaxon stated as he took another sip of his tea. 'Houses fought Houses for lands and resources. Poverty befell most of the world. That was when The Ancients rallied the people to uprise against their oppressors in the name of the Gods. And uprise they did. Once The Ancients took control of Eviiri, they implemented their holy laws. All progress and development ceased for decades, until a secret consortium of esteemed minds was formed.'

'You're talking about The Architects?'

Jaxon nodded. 'Five of the chief members established themselves amongst each nation and worked with the noble Houses to overturn the religious reign. Of course, a war ensued.'

'The Thousand-Year War,' Thio said, piecing together the history.

'A misleading title,' Jaxon inserted. 'The war did not span a thousand years. Plainly, it was the war that ended the thousand years of unrest. When it was over, the people rejoiced. As a reward for this conquest, the five leaders of The Architects were appointed monarchal seats at the head of each nation. They met at what is now called the Coalition of Crowns to elect a ruling House to oversee all others. Thus the Imperium was born and initiated the rise of Houses Frailyn, Tennyr, Peryx, Iibryn, and…'

'Aprya,' Thio said in revelation. 'You're saying that your ancestor was one of the first Chief Architects?'

'Jannon Aprya the First, the inaugural Emperor of the Imperium and former Chief Architect. With the four newly appointed kings under his guidance, each could govern with fairness and humility, encouraging progression and propelling Eviiri into the paradise it is today.'

Thio stared at Jaxon in awe. A thousand thoughts flooded his mind. History had never been a primary focus of his. Instead, he dreamed of the future and the advanced technologies he envisioned for the people. His recent work with the mountain salt fuelled his drive to create—to tap into the vault of ideas that furnished his every thought.

'How's your hand?' Jaxon asked.

Thio looked down at his bandage. 'I'll live,' he said with a playful grin.

Jaxon smiled back.

'Your bandage is coming loose,' he said, reaching for Thio's hand. 'Allow me.'

Thio extended his hand to the Prince, a timid hesitation slowing its movement. He stared into his hazel eyes as Jaxon began to unravel the loose linen. Despite the Prince's sharp features, his touch was soft.

'I wouldn't have suspected a member of the guild to possess such a temper,' Jaxon teased, a smirk tugging at his lips.

'Believe me, I am as shocked as you are,' Thio replied, his tone light. 'It's not in my nature to react that way.'

'You're worried about your sister,' Jaxon stated. 'It was an understandable response.'

'Still, it was no way to act in front of the royal heirs.'

Jaxon chuckled softly.

'Do you think that being of royal descent makes us immune to emotion?' he asked, raising an eyebrow.

'Of course not…'

'We are all human, Thio,' Jaxon said, his smile wide. 'This world has a strange way of evoking feelings within each and every one of us, without exception. Sometimes the feeling is anger, sometimes pain.' Jaxon playfully squeezed Thio's hand, making him wince slightly. 'Other times, it is joy and happiness, sorrow and woe—even love has a way of catching us off guard.'

Thio's gaze dropped from the Prince to the carpet at his feet, his toes seemingly dancing within his shoes. He let his mind wander for a moment as Jaxon completed the swaddling of his swollen hand.

The conversation had left both men oblivious to the violent shakes of the train as it hurled through the desert storm. It was the sudden flicker of the cabin lights that drew their attentions to it.

With another powerful jolt, the cabin lights blinked once more—then again, and again. With one final flash, they shut off completely. The carriage suddenly dropped, slamming onto the rail tracks with a thunderous bang. The sound of steel on steel screeched through the air as the vehicle shook violently. The rapid deceleration knocked both Thio and Jaxon from their seats, the pot of tea crashing to the floor.

After metres of violent rumbling, the carriage came to a complete stop. Silence prevailed. Only the muted whooshes of the raging storm could be heard through the thick glass. Thio rushed over to aid Jaxon.

'The storm must have jammed the train's power output,' Jaxon said, getting to his feet.

'No, these trains don't generate power onboard,' Thio corrected. 'It's supplied through the tracks. The fault would lie in the track's generators.'

'So the storm has knocked them out?'

'Unlikely. The generators are at the stations. Unless the storm has spread further than the desert, I can't see how it would affect them.' Thio walked over to a large map of Qymathor that hung near the partitions. 'Considering our speed, I estimate we are somewhere

here. That would mean the nearest station is…'

'Fenniq,' Jaxon inserted. 'That may still be a hundred kilometres away.'

Thio paced the carriage, fearing this delay may cost his sister's life. He motioned to the door and searched for its release latch.

'You can't go out there, not in these winds. You'll be cut to shreds,' Jaxon asserted.

'Fuck!' Thio yelled as he pounded his broken hand into the glass door. The pain momentarily crippled him, forcing him to drop to his knees. Jaxon approached him in an attempt to offer comfort.

'It will be okay. We will wait out the storm. They're fierce but short-lived.'

Thio detested the notion but conceded, knowing there was nothing he could do while the savage winds roared outside. They would have to wait.

CHAPTER 22

Alysse had always relished the morning breeze in the gardens below the Citadel. The smell of the fresh sea air that struggled to ascend the height of her chambers was abundant down here. A symphony of golden-crowned wrens adorned the grassy terrace, each note of their cheery songs sung in flight.

Little of the city could be seen from here. At most, the architecture that lined the quay walls of the surrounding islands. To the south, she could trace the circular Bay of Prosperity, with the Shrine of Old at its centre. Beyond was the sapphire dome of the Grand Athenaeum, rising above the dense forestry of The Architect's isle.

Drawing her gaze back to the gardens, she felt herself relax. This space allowed her respite from the sometimes suffocating nature of the city. The Drom Mountains, encasing most of the Bay of Zenithal, also served to remind Alysse of her place at the centre of her people.

Sitting on a stone bench at the garden's centre, she allowed herself a moment of peace as she closed her eyes. The placid rustling of the lemon trees and the songs of the wrens pacified her angst. Emperor Jannon had often found his daughter here, drawn by her need for a brief escape from the relentless demands of her lessons. She imagined her father sitting beside her as she longed for his counsel and reassurance.

'How are you, Little Wren?' she heard him say.

'I'm failing, Pa,' she whispered.

'How so?'

'It seems I have sown discord amongst the monarchs,' she signed, 'the very people I am supposed to keep united. I have placed blame on those that may be blameless. I have allowed an entire city to be destroyed. The people will hate me. Perhaps Lex Frailyn is right. Perhaps I am not fit to rule.'

'Being Emperor does not mean you rule the world,' he said. 'Each nation governs itself. Our role is not to dictate, but to oversee—to ensure they do not stray from the greater good.'

'But how can I oversee that which I am blind to?'

'Do the wrens see every branch in the garden before they take flight?' he asked, tilting his head toward the birds flitting about the trees. 'They listen, they watch, they feel the shifting wind beneath their wings. They know where to land before they even set out. A ruler must do the same. You may not see all, Alysse, but if you listen well and trust in the signs around you, you will always know where to guide your people.'

Alysse opened her eyes, watching the delicate birds weave through the gardens, each moving with purpose and grace—never colliding, never in conflict. She allowed her mind to settle and her ears to open, savouring the wren's melodies. From some distance behind her, she tuned into an approaching rhythm. *Footsteps.* Remaining calm, she turned her head slightly. Through her peripheral vision, she caught sight of a figure approaching—an indistinct blur at first, until the peach-draped silhouette of Queen Marcia Iibryn emerged, her leisurely stride producing soft clicks against the stone path.

'Queen Marcia,' Alysse said, standing to greet her guest, 'I assumed you had returned home with the others.'

Marcia Iibryn met Alysse with a sweet hug and a soft kiss upon her cheek.

'Your coronation is a scant few days ahead,' Marcia said. 'I see no point in making the journey home only to return once I arrive.'

Alysse felt comfort in the tender woman's embrace.

'That is kind of you,' she said with a smile. 'You may be one of the few who wish to see the ceremony proceed.'

Marcia sensed the defeat in the young Princess's voice.

'Oh, sweet girl, do not let those men dull your spirit,' she said, motioning to the bench and taking a seat.

Alysse sat beside her.

'They undermine my rule,' she voiced. 'Lex Frailyn would have never challenged my father the way he did me.'

'Lex is a miserable old man,' Marcia chuckled. 'His ego is fuelled by his army, but commanding vast lands and legions does not make him a great man. He lacks compassion. His bold statements rest on the hope that his claim prevails should your House fail.'

'What do you mean?' Alysse asked.

'It was declared during the Coalition of Crowns that should House Aprya fail to meet their duties, the throne would pass to House Frailyn,' Marcia explained. 'But do not pay heed to such hopes, they are reserved only for fools.'

'Even if he were content with my House remaining in power, he made it clear that he favours my brother. You heard him.'

Marcia took Alysse's hand in hers.

'You sit on the highest seat, my dear, and proud men do not like to look up. I know full well the difficulties of being a ruling woman,' she stated. 'They call us soft, weak, lacking in drive.'

'I am trying to avoid war,' Alysse said sternly. 'They can call that what they want.'

'Oh my dear, the kings would have waged war long ago if it weren't for the sensible hearts of their queen consorts. It is the women that possess the compassion. To men, it is all a game. They puff their chests and splay their feathers like peacocks vying for notice,' Marcia said, miming the motions with theatrical flair, 'all to prove who has the biggest cock.'

Alysse couldn't help but laugh at the queen's statement.

'Trust me, my dear,' Marcia said, lowering her

voice, 'none of them measure up.'

The two giggled at the remark. Marcia Iibryn had long been known for her persuasive nature—wielding both intelligence and an effortless charm that swayed those around her into submission. Among the other monarchs, she was respected not only for her sharp mind but for her unyielding and unapologetic approach.

The thought of the kings squabbling over matters of government brought Alysse's mind back to her father.

'My father was never driven by power or pride,' she said, solemnly. 'His intentions were always for the good of the people.'

'Your father was indeed an outlier. He faced many challenges, yet always held true to his values,' Marcia said in agreement.

'You knew him well, how would he have dealt with this?' Alysse asked.

'Diplomatically,' Marcia answered, simply.

'An idyllic prospect,' Alysse chuckled, 'but how does one engage in diplomacy with a faceless adversary?'

'Faceless?' Marcia leaned in, peering into the young Princess's eyes, her voice now drawing serious undertones. 'Think, my dear. Who stands to gain from the fall of your House?'

The sudden question took Alysse aback. She sifted her mind for answers but found only one.

'House Frailyn,' she said.

'If House Frailyn should attack the Capital, who will aid in its defence?' Marcia pressed.

'I trust the other Great Houses will answer the call,' Alysse responded confidently.

'And what happened the last time the Great Houses fought one another?'

Alysse could sense Queen Iibryn was guiding her to something she was missing. She recalled her knowledge of the history books, searching for the answer until it dawned on her.

'The Faith rose to power,' she said. The revelation caused her eyes to widen as she turned to the Shrine of Old.

'Divert, divide, ascend,' Marcia said firmly, leaning back from the Princess. 'They have done it before, and if you cannot secure the realm, what stops them from doing it again? I think you already know your next move.'

'Kalax,' Alysse spoke in a fierce whisper, her eyes fixed on the topmost marble altar where her father's body lay at rest.

'Your adversary watches history repeat from the murk. Expose them now before…'

'Your Grace!' A voice in the distance called out.

Alysse whipped her head around to see Cyrus Thenta rapidly approaching them.

'Uncle, what is it?' she pressed, sensing his urgency. Her mind instantly flew to Jaxon, anticipating a negative turn in his current undertaking.

'Your Grace,' Cyrus repeated, heavy of breath as he arrived before her. 'It's Chief Gorryn.'

The absence of her brother's name came as a relief.

'What of him?' she said, concern still her prime emotion.

'His apprentice found him in his chambers this morning,' Cyrus announced. 'It appears his heart failed him during the night.'

Alysse felt her own heart race in response to this news. She struggled to believe this was a simple act of nature. Like her father's death, the news seemed unnatural. Unsure of her next move, she turned to Marcia Iibryn, who had reached for her hand.

'What does this mean?' Alysse asked.

The bold woman, emotionless, stared up at the unnerved Princess and repeated three words.

'Divert, divide, ascend.'

Faster than Marcia or Cyrus could say another word, Alysse bolted for the tower. She snaked her way through the gardens, sweeping past the Citadel guards posted evenly along the paths. Entering through the private lobby, she navigated the large hall to the elevators in the western wing. Performing a specific set of motions on the control unit, she activated the silent capsule. Stepping inside, it began to propel the young Princess skyward at a speed only used in urgent times. The ascension brought Alysse to her knees as she battled the forces dragging down on her body.

In seconds, the elevator came to a stop in the foyer beside her quarters. She leapt out and sprinted through her chamber doors. On the western wall of the room were a series of shelves. Reaching a particular shelf, she retrieved the bespoke sonic transmitter Mia had gifted her the previous year. Atop the delicately decorated device was a golden disk with an engraved image of two golden-crowned wrens, the birds favoured by Alysse and Mia alike.

Bringing it to the large marble table in her room, she placed it down and activated its power. With slow but precise rhythmic presses, Alysse entered her message.

The Athenaeum is not safe. Make for the Citadel now. Tell no one.

Confident in her inputs, she hit the transmission button. The indicator light confirmed its workings with a series of rapid blinks. Taking a moment to catch her breath, she looked over at the two portraits that hung beside her bed. The delicate paintings of her mother, Palymma, and father, Jannon, watched over her as she navigated her new role at the head of the Imperium. Fighting back tears, she continued to process the day's events. The words of Marcia Iibryn looped in her mind.

Divert, she thought, recalling the distraction caused by recent events—flashes of the flames scorching the Path of Peace during her father's funeral—his body strung from his altar as an assassin moved to strike. And now, the death of a Chief Architect.

Divide: Discord between the Great Houses. Distant attacks to draw forces away from the Capital. Her brother absent from her side.

And ascend.

Alysse slowly stepped towards her balcony. The warm air permeated through the thin drapes as she parted them. Stepping out, she looked down over the balustrade. Her eyes traced the grandeur of the Path of Peace stretching out from the base of the tower. City folk went about their day, ignorant of the impending danger the city faced. At the opposing end of the thoroughfare, the Sanctuary of Qyma glistened in the sunlight. Rage built within Alysse as she glared towards the resplendent structure.

'I will draw you from your murk, Kalax. And I will do it… diplomatically,' she snarled.

CHAPTER 23

Thio sat hunched on the carpeted floor of the train, his head rested in his hands. The sweltering heat within the cabin had risen to an unbearable temperature. Time seemed to slip away as his mind wandered far from the desert. His palms were slippery with sweat and his body felt heavy. Lurching forward, his head slipped from his hold, jolting the apprentice back into a disoriented awareness.

His eyes stung as pure sunlight bore through the glass ceiling. The entire cabin was luminous. Outside, a blinding white veil shrouded the scenery as his eyes adjusted to the light. He stood, weak. Out of one side of the carriage he saw a vastness of desert, endless to the eye. Out of the other, a wall of sand piled against the train.

Water was his sole focus now. He stumbled to the galley, took a cup and filled it to the brim. He devoured it in seconds. The scorching water burnt with every gulp, providing little relief. He forced down another cup, then another. Once more he filled the cup and exited the galley. On the floor beside the central table lay Jaxon. His near-naked body coated in perspiration.

Thio approached. Despite his disorientation, he couldn't help but note the young Prince's toned physique. He was built like a fighter, nimble yet solid. Each muscle, perfectly sculpted, glistened in the sunlight. He knelt down and gave the Prince a soft nudge.

'Jaxon.'

The young man shifted slowly, groaning as his stiff body ached. He could barely open his eyes as light saturated his view. Dazed, he looked up at the figure lurking over him. The silhouette of Thio's buzz cut and rims of his spectacles planted Jaxon's mind back within the train.

'Here, drink some water,' Thio offered.

Jaxon sat up and accepted the cup. He took a generous sip and winced.

'It's too hot,' he recoiled.

'I know, but you must drink.'

Jaxon forced the rest of the water down then surveyed the change in their surroundings.

'What time is it?' he asked, still battling the harsh light.

'Midday,' Thio concluded. 'The storm has well and truly passed.'

Thio helped Jaxon to his feet. With his vision now clear, Jaxon too noted the wall of sand on one side of the train. Thio had already moved to the doors on the opposite side, cluelessly searching for the emergency latch.

'Allow me,' Jaxon said as he redressed, then moved to assist Thio. Shifting a panel near the door's base, he pulled at a concealed lever. A strong hiss blew puffs of fine sand into the cabin from the seals as the doors parted. Through them, a wave of heat struck the two men.

Both stepped out onto the blistering sand to examine their surroundings. The air outside was harsh on their lungs, stinging with every breath. Thio scanned the horizon. A seemingly endless mirage stretched out to the distance. Beyond, the hint of green mountain ranges.

'The Fenniq Belt,' Jaxon surmised. 'It stretches the entirety of the desert's western edge. It is difficult terrain to navigate, so the tracks were built through the desert.'

He turned back to the train, puzzled. 'I can't see the tracks anywhere. Did we derail?'

'I doubt it,' Thio said. 'They will be buried under the sand.' He dropped to his knees next to the carriage and began to dig. The heat of the sand on his broken hand made him grimace. Jaxon knelt down beside him to assist. Shifting a sizeable amount of sand, the two revealed a section of track.

'How does the train navigate safely over this much sand?' Jaxon questioned.

'They are equipped with clearers, front and back,' Thio explained. 'They emit fluctuating air waves to blast any debris from the tracks.'

Jaxon looked out at the expanse of torrid desert.

'What are we going to do? We won't survive this heat much longer.'

Thio had already begun to pace the length of the train, occasionally crouching down to inspect the underside of each carriage.

'See anything?' Jaxon called out, his head throbbing from his dehydration.

Thio didn't answer, instead focusing solely on a solution. 'Surely the… if I can…' he mumbled.

'If you can, what?' Jaxon shot out impatiently, the heat toying with his mood.

'We need to uncouple these carriages. I can strip this one for parts,' Thio called out confidently. 'I need a knife. Do you still have that rope?'

Jaxon pulled himself back into the train and opened his rucksack. He retrieved the rope and un-strapped the short sword he had concealed inside a hidden sleeve. Exiting the carriage, he trudged back to Thio and handed him the requested items.

'Here.'

Thio unsheathed the sword and looped the end of the rope over it. With a swift draw of the blade, he severed the grappling hook from its end. Jaxon surged forward to stop the act but was too late.

'Trust me,' Thio said, noting the Prince's panic.

Inspecting the fastened catch, he jammed the thin apparatus between the two coupling hooks holding the carriages together. Nudging it into a precise position, he hit the release mechanism. The grappling hook burst open. A boisterous clang pinged off the train's joiners as the two plates separated.

'Perfect,' Thio revelled.

Jaxon, although impressed, looked down at the disfigured hook in displeasure. 'Now what?'

'The clearer,' Thio answered. 'They run off a battery and are set to shut off once the train comes to a stop. I'll remove the one from the rear carriage. If I can manipulate the frequencies, it may be able to generate enough energy to power the front carriage.'

'A clearer could power a whole carriage?' Jaxon asked, puzzled.

'Not the clearer,' Thio said, reaching into his pocket, 'this.'

He pulled out the small leather pouch containing the mountain salt.

'I'm confused,' Jaxon stated.

Thio smiled confidently as he moved to the rearward carriage. Inspecting the rear panel, he beckoned Jaxon over.

'Help me with this.'

The two men grabbed each side of the curved sheet of metal. With a nod from Thio, they yanked backwards. The panel dislodged with a pop. Behind the covering was an array of instruments and wires. Thio probed at the parts, some he recognised, others he did not. Spotting what he sought, he reached in through the tangle of steel and dismantled the securing bracket of a moderately sized copper box.

'Hold this,' he said, carefully removing it from its place and passing it to Jaxon. 'Be careful, the ionic liquid inside is extremely toxic.'

Jaxon hesitated before gently grasping the container.

'What is it?' he asked.

'The battery,' Thio said as he continued to extract components.

Unlatching the final piece, he cautiously removed a weighty chunk of the apparatus. The item was composed of a small control unit, from which sprouted a thin metal needle. Pressed against the needle was a broad but thin membrane spanning just shy of a metre.

'This is it,' he said excitedly. 'See that needle? It resonates against this membrane which diffuses the vibrations evenly across an area. It's generally dialled in quite low but with a few tweaks, I can alter the frequency to destabilise the salt compounds. Then...' He noticed himself rambling and stopped.

'Onwards?' Jaxon asked, attempting to conclude the impromptu engineering lesson.

'Onwards,' Thio confirmed with a smile.

The two carried the necessary parts back to the front carriage. Thio, entering first, reached down and took the battery pack from Jaxon, then offered a hand to pull him up.

Once back inside the train, Thio began stomping his foot along the carpeted floor, shifting gradually from side to side. As he neared the nose of the carriage, one final stomp yielded a distinct thunk— deeper and more resonant than the rest. He crouched, scanning for a seam in the carpet. Finding it, he pried at the joint until the edge lifted. With a forceful pull, he tore back the strip of carpet, revealing an access panel beneath.

Jaxon looked on, intrigued by the workings of this young apprentice's mind. He watched as Thio peeled open the panel. Beyond was a multitude of gears, wires, and motors, all filling the void beneath the cabin. After a few moments of inspecting, Thio began wiring the clearer to the main drive motor. Fashioning a clasp at the base of the needle, he removed the remaining chunk of mountain salt from its pouch. Placing it precisely at the needle's tip, he meticulously scrutinised his contraption, checking that every wire was tight, every dial calibrated, and every part secure. Confident, he turned to Jaxon.

'Have you done this before?' Jaxon asked.

'Not quite,' Thio answered. 'I got close but... I suggest you stand back. You might also want to close your eyes.'

Concerned, Jaxon took a few steps backwards. Thio placed his hand on the clearer's power switch, took a deep breath, then closed his eyes. *Click.*

A piercing ring emanated from the clearer. Both Thio and Jaxon winced in discomfort. The frequency bounced around the carriage then began to alter its pitch, lower and lower until the sound was bearable. Thio opened his eyes to see the pebble of salt glowing red-hot. In that same instant, it ignited with a noiseless flash of immense light.

Jaxon, blinded by the flash, felt a sudden shudder at his feet. As his vision returned to him, he noticed the carriage lights flicker. A moment later, a chilled breeze from the cabin's cooling system swept over him.

Thio stood and raised his face to the vents, relishing in the chilled air. The wall of sand that covered the right side of the train began cascading down the glass as the carriage reverberated into life once again. Then, movement.

Thio pressed himself up against the front window. Below, the train's leading clearer activated and sand splayed away from the tracks before them. The train crept forward on the exposed tracks, gaining speed metre by metre.

Elated, Jaxon grabbed Thio.

'You did it!' he exclaimed, wrapping his arms around the surprised apprentice. Thio gleefully embraced the hug, relieved at his own success. Jaxon held him tight for a moment, then slowly released his hold, caressing Thio's arm. The two stood face to face for what seemed an eternity. A silent lust built within Thio as he stared into the Prince's hazel eyes. Jaxon, feeling a swell of desire, eyed his saviour's tempting lips and inched forward. In a moment of panic, Thio turned away from his Prince.

'I best keep an eye on this,' he said nervously, 'just in case.'

'Sure,' Jaxon said, hastily avoiding the reveal of his embarrassment. 'I'll grab us some water.'

Thio watched Jaxon walk off to the galley. *Fuck,* he thought, regretting his recoil as the train powered on at full speed through the desert.

CHAPTER 24

The past hour had felt like many as Alysse paced her room, the sonic transmitter sitting dormant on the stone table. Fear grew within her at the thought of Dalos and Mia encountering the same fate as that of Gorryn Venidor. A warm breeze played at the flowing green gown that she had donned moments ago. Her dark hair hung loosely with slicked-back sides, held in place with a thin rope of jewels crowning her head.

In the silence, she heard approaching footsteps. *Only one of them,* she determined, expecting to hear two sets. Fear roiled in her stomach as the hurried steps reached her chambers. The door swung open to reveal Mia. Both elation and alarm set in.

'Oh, my girl,' Mia said as she moved to embrace Alysse. 'We came as quickly as we could.'

We?

Alysse looked past Mia to the foyer adjacent to her room. Gliding silently across the marble floor was a suspender chair. Atop the chair sat Dalos, a thin bandage around his head and shaded spectacles masking his eyes. Relief washed over Alysse.

'Thank the Gods,' she breathed. 'Dalos, what happened?'

'Ah, don't worry yourself,' he said jovially. 'I had a simple fall. I'm old and clumsy.'

'I found him in his quarters struggling to get off the floor. He told me he slipped on some *spilt tea*,' Mia said, raising an eyebrow, clearly suspicious of her father's explanation. Dalos waved a dismissive hand as the two refocused on the Princess.

'About Chief Gorryn, what do you know?' Alysse asked.

'The examiner concluded no foul play,' Mia stated. 'It just doesn't make sense. Gorryn has always been in good health.'

The account raised suspicion in Alysse's mind as she recalled similar reports after her father's examination.

'I believe that which killed Chief Gorryn may have also killed my father,' she surmised.

'A logical suspicion,' Dalos acknowledged. 'There have been known poisons that leave no vestige, but they are old and long forgotten.'

'The Ancients are responsible, I know it,' Alysse asserted.

'I must say I concur, Princess,' Mia said. 'The coincidental nature of the recent happenings all seem to indicate their involvement. But why? And why now?'

'Perhaps to reclaim their power,' Alysse replied. 'Perhaps the truce they struck with Jannon the First has run its course. Whatever it was that settled the war may have died alongside my father. And with that, The Ancients are free to oppose the Imperium.'

Dalos sat silent, pondering the thought as Mia moved towards the broad balcony. Alysse took a deep breath.

'That is why I intend to storm the Sanctuary,' she declared, 'and see that each of them is brought to inquiry—this time, before the public eye. No more private talks.'

Mia and Dalos exchanged unsettled looks.

'M'girl, are you sure that is wise?' Dalos asked out of concern. 'If you are wrong and the people side with the Faith, you will lose their adoration.'

Alysse shook her head and closed her eyes.

'I have to try,' she said. 'I am running short of alternatives. I *must* quell this insurrection immediately. Not for me, nor for my House, but for the people, as my father would have.'

'A very noble thought, Princess,' Mia said, placing a tender hand on Alysse's arm.

'Indeed.' Dalos agreed. 'How can we help?'

Alysse moved to the suspender chair and crouched beside the feeble-bodied man.

'Stay with me,' she pleaded. 'I have amassed my most trusted guards. We will take the Path to the Sanctuary. No tunnels. The people need to see that I am willing to risk my safety for them.'

'And Jaxon? Perhaps it's best he too accompanies us,' Mia suggested.

'Jaxon is engaged in other matters,' Alysse said, regretting her decision to let him leave the Capital.

'Of course. We will be with you,' Mia offered with a smile as she stood beside her father, 'now and always.'

Standing atop the main staircase that descended into the entrance hall, Alysse, Mia, and Dalos looked down at the near-empty space. The colossal draped banners hung gallantly beside the towering doors, the House Aprya sigil impeccably stitched at their base. Alysse had not stood in this room since the night of her father's funeral. Stillness enveloped the air.

In place of the noble crowd, twenty imperial guards stood in perfect unison, flanking the pathway to the exit. Each wore the signature purple of the Imperial Army, intertwined with House Aprya's muted green. Their polished armour plates reflected pale gold light around the hall. Each wore a sharp helm that sported a lengthy purple-dyed horsehair plume, and all carried a sheathed short sword.

The trio above made their way down the stairs. Dalos' suspender chair effortlessly hovered over the steps as they reached the landing. Alysse and Mia strode arm in arm past each pair of guards.

'Alysse?' A voice echoed across the hall.

'Uncle?' Alysse said, recognising the voice of Cyrus Thenta. She turned to see him descending the staircase behind them.

'What are you doing?' he asked, concerned.

'My duty,' Alysse said confidently. 'The Ancients must be held accountable.'

'The Ancients? But...' Cyrus held his opinion. 'Allow me to escort you,' he insisted.

'There is no need, Uncle,' Alysse politely declined. 'They will never harm me before the eyes of the people. I need your focus on the attacks outside the city.'

Cyrus eyed the two Chief Architects and the surrounding guards. 'Yes, Your Grace.'

Alysse gave him a soft smile of appreciation, noting the fatigue in his eyes. Turning to a guard posted by the door, she gave an affirming nod. A moment later, the four horns of the Citadel rumbled, signifying a royal procession. A deep crack emanated from the doors as they peeled open, flooding the hall with sunlight.

Alysse stared ahead as they exited into the warm summer air. Nearby city folk began to gather along the Path of Peace, curious at the unannounced sounding of the Citadel horns. Shouts of admiration rang from the skirts of the Path.

'Princess!'

'Empress!'

'Your Grace!'

Alysse smiled at the adoring people as the small procession continued their way towards the Sanctuary. Children waved and ran alongside the entourage, catching glances of the Princess' beauty and poise. Alysse felt the warmth of her people, a unity and spirit unbroken by the looming threat.

The city's caretakers dotted the Path, attending to the charred palms, a somber reminder of the sudden loss of the world's leader. Alysse studied each as she passed, recalling the inferno she had briefly seen through the Sanctuary doors that night. Halfway down the Path, she spotted new fronds emerging from the scorched tip, a sign of resilience and new growth amidst chaos.

Reaching the steps of the Sanctuary, Alysse turned to see the large crowd that had amassed since departing the Citadel. A thousand or more spectators stood curious to learn of the events unfolding. Making her way up the steps, she stopped at their apex and turned again to her people. Smiles and waves rippled across the crowd as she acknowledged their loyalty. Raising a soft hand, she silenced the congregation.

'People of Zenithal, I speak to you now with truth in my heart,' she began. 'Our beloved world faces war—a war we have not seen in two hundred years. Your Emperor's passing has presented an opportunity for those who oppose us to attack the very peace we all hold dear.'

Worried whispers spread throughout the masses.

'But I wish no fear upon you,' she continued. 'House Aprya will continue to provide, protect, and nurture our ever-growing world. Believe in me, as you did my father, and Zenithal will hold strong.'

Applause erupted from the crowd as many bowed in support of their Princess. The gesture overwhelmed Alysse. Mia wiped the trickle of tears from her face as she grasped at her father's hand. Dalos sat proud, acknowledging the growth he had seen within the Princess.

Two members of the Imperial Guard approached the doors of the Sanctuary and heaved them open. Once the crowd had settled, Alysse spoke again.

'I am here today to deliver justice to those who

have wronged my House, our city, and Eviiri. I invite you all into the Sanctuary to witness the deceit unfurl,' she said.

The gathered people of Zenithal exchanged inquisitive stares as the Princess and her company made for the entrance.

Within the monumental void of the Sanctuary, the five High Priests encircled the central altar. Kalax, at the end of the marble block, stood with his back facing the entrance. The other High Priests turned in unison to inspect the disruption of their prayers.

'What is going on? Why is she here?' Hithema queried in the ancient tongue.

Kalax remained motionless as a sea of city folk flooded the circular pews of the sanctum.

'What is the meaning of this?' Siiva hissed, the censer clutched in her hand billowing orchid incense.

'Explain yourself,' Dakaar barked.

'Silence,' Alysse shouted as she moved towards the altar, her guards holding tight rank around her.

The demand angered Dakaar. 'You dare command us in our holy house!' he rebuked.

Kalax raised a pacifying hand to his fellow priests, then turned to meet his approaching guests. His gaze met Alysse's. She saw the hint of fire-orange burning within them. His eyes scanned the faces of those around her before landing on Dalos. The stare made the round man shift in his suspender chair.

'I expected you sooner, Alefre'a,' Kalax said calmly.

The statement surprised Alysse. *He expected my inquiry?*

'Your conspiracy is clear, Reverend,' she announced.

'And what is it you think I have conspired?' he responded passively.

'Do not play the fool with me,' she said with sharpness in her tone. The throngs of spectators sat silently observing the exchange.

'Then speak your accusations, Alefre'a, before the people and the Gods.'

Alysse felt confident in her objective and of the support of Mia and Dalos.

'You murdered the Emperor,' she accused. 'You destroyed Ton-Basin, killing thousands of innocents. You have plotted to overthrow my reign and claim rule for your own.'

The crowd of onlookers murmured amongst themselves at the revelation of her indictment. Dakaar shifted into motion towards Alysse.

'An accusation such as this requires proof, Alefre'a,' he sneered, 'yet you stand here with only allegations.'

Alysse directed her gaze at the riled priest. 'Archaic poisons,' she referenced, 'and weapons seen by none alive today but the five of you. My allegations, despite the absence of proof, hold merit.'

'Just because one has seen a thing, does not mean that one possesses it,' he rebutted.

'It seems you also see things beyond your sight, Reverend Dakaar,' Alysse said in reference to the priest's knowledge of the assassination attempt on her and her brother.

Dakaar snickered, 'We speak a thing to the Gods, and the Gods speak a thing back.'

The response angered Alysse. 'Did the Gods speak instruction to kill an innocent child?' she bit.

'Of what child do you speak?' the soft voice of Hithema questioned.

'You know of whom I speak,' Alysse scorned. 'Emperor Jannon the First's son, two hundred years ago in this very Sanctuary!'

Dalos studied the group of ancient beings through his shaded spectacles for any telling signs of admission.

'The Ancients have never taken a life, Alefre'a,' Siiva inserted. 'It is not our place. Only the Gods can decide when a soul is ready for liberation.'

'Whether the life is taken by your hand or by your order, the blood still stains,' Alysse said.

Growing impatient, Kalax turned his back on the Princess and muttered in the ancient tongue. 'Foolish child. You know not of what you speak.'

As soon as the words had left his mouth, Alysse responded with precise vocabulary. 'The only fools are those who challenge the Imperium!'

The High Priests reeled in shock at the Princess' knowledge of their ancient language.

'She speaks our tongue?' Thyta gawked.

'Impossible,' Hithema concurred.

Kalax stopped in his tracks, then turned back to Alysse, slowly approaching her. The surrounding guards shifted into defence of the Princess. She raised a hand to dismiss the action, allowing the androgynous man to draw near.

'You continue to surprise us, Alefre'a,' Kalax said with an admiring smile.

'And yet you continue to mock me,' she replied. 'What threatens you, Reverend? My seat? My House? That I am a woman, perhaps?'

Kalax let out an audible laugh. 'Our creator is a woman,' he said, turning and pointing up at the enormous statue of Qyma that towered over the sanctum.

'Then what?' Alysse pressed.

Kalax stepped away from the Princess and towards the centre of the room, peering out to the assembly of city folk.

'I trust you are familiar with the tale of our creator,' he said, commanding the room's attention. Alysse stood in place, allowing the priest a chance to speak.

'In the boundless expanse, a solitary glimmer of light fractured the eternal void,' Kalax began. 'From which, our beloved Qyma arose in corporeal form. By her first breath, she birthed two stars. Their splendour evoked joy in her heart. She tended to them as a mother would her children. Yet after some time, the stars repelled one another as they sought freedom in the emptiness.'

Kalax paced the sanctum, becoming more animated as his story went on.

'Fearing solitude,' he continued, 'Qyma plucked a strand of hair from her head and tethered the two stars. But the stars resisted, tugging and heaving until the strand fractured, its shards circling the blazing orbs. Qyma wept, and in doing so, shrouded the shards in tears. For eons she searched for her children. When finally she came upon them, she saw life had flourished on the soaked fragments of her hair. Elated by her progeny, she drew another breath and two more stars were brought into existence. Eager to create more beauty, she plucked another strand from her head and sowed discord amongst her new children. As intended, the struggle tore apart the strand and tears of glee covered the shards. On and on she bore stars ceaselessly until the void was stripped of darkness. Space dissolved, and chaos ensued. Qyma began to suffocate amid her creations. In desperation, she wailed. From her scream, Kapry was born. Fearing his mother's demise, he began to devour the stars, one by one, until few remained. The desolation incited Kapry's thirst for destruction. Horrified at his consumption, Qyma restrained him. But his hunger was too great. They clashed for an eternity as Qyma bore stars and Kapry consumed them.'

'Enough!' Alysse exploded as her patience wore thin. 'I did not come to listen to tales. I have come to uphold peace.'

'Can you not see, Alefre'a?' Kalax questioned as he approached her once again. 'Like our creator, you fear solitude. You endeavour to hold together things that cannot maintain relation forever. There cannot exist balance without opposition.'

'My father and those before him created a just and prosperous world free of opposition.'

'Yet you suffocate in your pursuit of peace,' he said. 'The thread has fractured. Now you bear witness to the destruction of your screams.'

'Kalax!' Dalos exclaimed. 'End this now.'

The High Priest turned a slow gaze to the immobile Chief.

'I have no means to end this, old friend,' he said with condescension. 'Only the Gods can rule over all.'

'So you deny any part in this?' Alysse asked sternly.

'Unequivocally,' Kalax answered.

'Do you swear it before the Gods, knowing their wrath should you speak falsehood?'

Kalax leaned in close to the hostile Princess.

'I swear it.'

CHAPTER 25

The Fenniq Belt spanned most of the central corridor of the continent. The lush mountain range began to the northwest of the Besti-Qa Plains and trailed up to the city of Latyth's southern border. The thick forests that lined the foothills clawed their way up the rocky shoulders of the alps, blanketing the dark-stone giants.

The shroud of green surrounding the train was a comforting sight for Jaxon as the harshness of the desert faded from his mind. It had been a few hours since the train had crossed out of the parched lands, advancing ever closer to their destination.

'We're close,' Jaxon said in the calmness, his attention fixed on the gorge walls whipping by the glass enclosure.

The train snaked through the tight valley. The towering ranges flanking the passage eclipsed all view beyond. The tracks appeared only a hundred metres or so ahead before becoming obscured by the next winding bend.

Jaxon peered down at the torrent of water that kept pace with the speeding train. The turbulent river that carved its way through the valley offered the only pathway through these impassable monuments. Erected precariously some ten metres above the raging current, this stretch of track was the Prince's favourite. As a child, he had imagined himself as a bird, gliding freely at speed through the twisted valley.

He had almost forgotten that Thio sat at the table beside him. The silent apprentice had buried himself in his notebook since they parted from the desert. The sporadic scratches of his coal pen were faintly audible with every stroke.

'What are you working on?' Jaxon pried. 'Something new?'

'It's more of an enhancement,' Thio replied, his attention still focused on his work. 'I studied Dalos' work on acoustic levitation. It seems limited in practice yet may have far greater potential… in theory anyway.'

'What kind of potential?' Jaxon enquired.

Thio placed the coal pen down on the page, lifted his head and met Jaxon's stare.

'Take the carriers, for example,' he began, 'or even this train, the power input caps its acoustic output. Hence why they can only lift so far off the ground. Sure, the lighter the object, the higher it can rise. But if the energy source is increased, we may be able to craft a vehicle that can navigate the skies.'

'The skies?' Jaxon's eyes ignited, thrilled at the possibility.

Thio nodded. 'Difficult terrain would no longer be a factor in navigation. With the right energy source, one could cross over oceans, deserts, even mountains.'

'An energy source like that?' Jaxon pointed at Thio's humming contraption towards the nose of the carriage.

'Potentially,' Thio said. 'It still needs a lot of refining. Again… just a theory.'

Jaxon imagined himself soaring high above the natural world. The endless opportunities for exploration kindled a wanderlust within him. As his mind explored the concept, it led him to think of his future post as Imperial Commander and its promising advantages in conflict.

'Thio,' he said, 'have you ever thought of the potential military uses for your ideas? I mean, should the Capital be attacked by a sizeable force, any form of counter-weapon would…'

'Forgive me, My Prince,' Thio said, cutting him short, 'but we do not make weapons. It is forbidden. Even if it were allowed, I want my work to help people live, not aid in their death.'

'Of course,' Jaxon said, a hint of defeat in his voice. He admired Thio's respect for the laws and his desire for good. Yet the fear of failing to uphold the safety of the realm stood prominent in his mind. He fidgeted with the small leather pouch that had previously contained the lump of mountain salt. Noticing this, Thio placed a soft hand atop the Prince's.

'You will make a fine Imperial Commander,' he offered.

'What if I don't?' Jaxon questioned. 'What if I fail the people? What if I fail my sister?'

'You won't,' Thio assured. 'It's in your nature to protect. Look at me, a mere stranger to you, yet you risk your safety to help me.'

'You've saved my life, Thio, more than once. I owe a great debt to you. It's just… the protection of a few does not compare to the protection of an entire realm,' Jaxon returned.

Thio caressed the back of Jaxon's hand with his thumb.

'You are under the guidance of Cyrus Thenta,' Thio stated. 'I've heard it said that he is the finest Imperial Commander this world has seen. You are in good hands. You only need to believe in yourself, My Prince… as Alysse, Dalos, and Mia believe in you.' He paused. 'As I believe in you.'

The Prince offered a soft smile as he looked down at Thio's gentle touch. The tender rubs soothed his angst as he turned his hand upright. Their fingers danced delicately around each other before interlocking. Jaxon looked up at Thio, who had not parted his stare from the young Prince. Thio reached up to remove his spectacles, fumbling awkwardly as he struggled to grip them with his injured hand.

Jaxon offered assistance, sliding them delicately off the apprentice's face as he leaned in closer. A medley of emotions surged within the two as their lips drew near. Nerves. Excitement. Lust.

Their lips had nearly paired when a low-key tone

sounded throughout the cabin, startling both men. The chime indicated their approaching destination. Thio's mind was instantly filled with images of Latyth, the city he had once called home, fearing the sight of ravenous flames engulfing its people. He sprang to his feet and raced to the nose of the train. Jaxon followed after him.

Pressing themselves against the wall of glass, they peered ahead as the tracks curved out of the obscuring valley. As the final wall of cliffside receded, the port city came into view.

Despite Thio's fear of ferocious blue flames, the sprawling coastal burg sat peacefully in the late afternoon sun. His legs wavered as relief consumed him.

The city of Latyth was renowned for its beauty. The natural undulating terrain on which the city sat atop encircled a sizeable bay. On one side, long stretches of quay walls lined the seaside port, alive with a multitude of trading posts and storage yards. Opposite, atop a high-rising spit that curved out into the sea, was the fort. It was an intimidating, solid structure seldom adorned with windows or access points. Its scout deck wrapped the entirety of its rooftop, offering all-encompassing views of the city and sea alike.

As the train slowed its approach towards the station, Thio spotted the signature blue dome of the Athenaeum where he had spent his teenage years learning his craft. Beyond that, nearer to the bay, was a large, pale red-stone complex. *The infirmary,* Thio thought to himself.

The train entered the station through a broad archway, then came to a stop beside one of the six platforms within. With a hiss, the doors to the carriage peeled open. Both Jaxon and Thio scouted the empty station for any sign of city folk. There were none with the exception of a station steward asleep at her post by the building's main terminal.

Perfect, Jaxon thought. He reached for his rucksack and shouldered it, Thio following suit.

'The tunnel entrance is through there,' Jaxon said, pointing towards the administrative office. 'Do you know the way to the infirmary?'

Thio nodded.

'Good. We will meet back here by dusk,' Jaxon said, placing a hand on Thio's arm. 'If anything happens, get your sister and seek shelter.'

Thio was filled with trepidation at the thought of an imminent attack. He worried not only for his sister's safety, but also that of the Prince's. The hazel eyes staring back at him fuelled his sudden motives. Without a second thought, he lunged forward and planted his lips on Jaxon's. The two men embraced with passion, expressing their newfound desire for one another. The taste of the young Prince's lips sent Thio's mind into ecstasy, the world around him momentarily fading out of thought.

Pulling away from each other, they exchanged adoring stares. Jaxon smiled as he pulled his tunic's hood over his soft curls, subtly licking the remnants of the young apprentice from his lips. Then, he was off.

Thio watched for a moment as Jaxon stealthily manoeuvred through the station and past the sleeping guard. Once out of sight, Thio turned his attention to the main entrance.

The street leading away from the station was unexpectedly calm, disturbed only by the young man darting across the pavement as he hurried towards the infirmary. *Do they not know?* he thought to himself as curious onlookers shot inquisitive stares.

Arriving at the rose-coloured complex, Thio entered and approached the desk clerk.

'The senior physician, Y'mara. Where is she?' Thio managed through his heavy breaths.

The young girl behind the desk stared up at him, unimpressed by his assertive tone.

'And you are?' she said, raising an eyebrow.

'Her brother,' he shot back, losing patience.

'Thio! I hardly recognised you without your long hair,' she said as a wide smile lit up her face. 'How are you?'

'I don't have time for small talk! Please, where is she?'

The young girl sensed the panic in his voice. She hastened over to a small chart and scanned the list of names.

'She is in the children's ward, through that hallway, then up the…'

Before she could finish giving the directions, Thio shot off down the corridor and leaped up a broad flight of stairs. Each floor donned plaques of their occupying wards. Scanning each as he ascended, his heart raced at the thought of seeing his younger sister again.

Elder's Ward, one read.

Birthing Ward, read another.

Dispensary.

Reaching the fourth floor, he read the next plaque. *Children's Ward.* He exited the stairwell and scanned the corridors.

'Y'mara?!' he called out as he passed each room. One by one he scanned the many faces of the ward's startled occupants.

'Y'mara?!'

'Thio?' A soft voice called out from a large patient room ahead.

Thio's head whipped around towards the call. At the end of the corridor stood his sister. A combination of confusion and excitement painted her youthful face. Her sleek build and long sandy hair appeared unchanged since he had seen her last, some eighteen months ago. The sight of her brought tears to his eyes as he ran up to her. With force, he flung his arms around her, almost knocking the two over.

'What are you doing here, big brother?' she said with glee as she embraced him, a broad smile pinned to her face.

Thio struggled to produce words through his sobs of relief at their reunion. He held her tight, wishing not to let go.

Prying herself from his grip, Y'mara looked up at her brother, running a playful hand over his newly styled hair.

'It's so good to see you!'

Thio tried his best to compose himself.

'I have to speak to you,' he managed, scouting the ward for an empty room. Spotting one, he clutched her hand and drew her into it.

'What's going on?' she said, her tone shifting to one of concern.

'Y'mara, we have to leave,' he insisted. 'Latyth is not safe.'

The panic in his voice worried the young physician, leaving her puzzled by his statement.

'Not safe? What do you mean?' she pressed.

'A band of rebels is approaching the city,' he said. 'They have already laid waste to Ton-Basin. Latyth is next.'

'What?!' she exclaimed. 'How do you know this?'

'I heard it from the Imperial Commander himself. I've come straight from the Capital to get you.' Thio continued to explain the recent happenings to his sister.

As Y'mara's mind sifted through the information she was receiving, all joy slowly drained from her face.

'If this is true, Thio, and Latyth is next, I cannot leave,' she said with concernment. 'I am in charge of the infirmary. Many will be injured. I have a duty to uphold here.'

The words crushed Thio's spirit instantly.

'Latyth is home to Qymathor's second-largest fort,' she continued, pointing towards a nearby window, the barracks standing visibly valiant across the bay. 'We are well protected.'

'Most of the troops are abroad!' he contested. 'I understand that you feel it's your duty to stay, Y'-mara, but I cannot risk losing you too.'

Thio wept again, a sudden resurgence of memories

of his late mother's death consumed him. Y'mara pulled her brother into a firm embrace, attempting to ease his pain. She held him for several minutes before speaking again.

'Big brother,' she said softly, 'I know what you did for me, all those years ago. You gave me a chance at life, and for that I thank you. I will never forget it.' She pulled away from him and stared deep into his flooded blue eyes. 'Now I have the ability to give others that chance. I'm so sorry, Thio, my place is here.'

Thio hung his head. He made sense of her reasoning, yet he struggled to accept it.

'Come, let's go for a walk,' she said, ushering her brother out of the room.

—

Navigating through the tunnels below Latyth came as second nature to Jaxon. Although he had only traversed them a few times, he felt confident in his route. Faintly recalling an old map his father once showed him, Jaxon surmised his current position to be below the immense body of water—somewhere in the middle of the bay. The petite handheld light he had produced from his rucksack mockingly illuminated a tiny sliver of the path before him.

Nonetheless, his hurried pace delivered him to the fort's concealed entrance in little time. Shining the light on a series of well-camouflaged buttons, he pressed in a combination. The door cracked open and light flooded his eyes.

Through the door was a simple study. On the wall to his right hung a collection of blades, a display of the historical development of military arms. On the opposing wall was a bookshelf lined with documented accounts of past wars and skirmishes. Ahead of him was a solid stone door, common throughout the building. Jaxon knew that this room was attached to the commanding officer's quarters.

Approaching the door, he pulled at its handle. Before he could pass through, he felt himself hauled backwards. The arm around his neck constricted tight, while another held a short blade to his throat.

'Who are you?! State your business here!' a man's voice blared in his ear.

Struggling to speak, Jaxon reached for his hood and drew it back.

'Your Grace!' the voice cracked in fear as he released his hold on the Royal Prince.

Inhaling sharply, Jaxon turned to identify his terrified assailant. Commander Rodyn stood frozen, his wide brown eyes stared in shock and his narrow mouth hung open, further lengthening his already lengthy beard. The man was shorter than most, yet sturdy. His off-duty purple robe was half illuminated by the warm glow of lamps in the windowless room.

'Commander,' Jaxon managed to say through the throbbing pain in his throat.

'I do beg pardon, Your Grace. I was unaware of your advent,' Rodyn said as he sharply bowed to the Prince.

'I am here in confidence,' Jaxon stated, moving quickly to discuss the impending insurgence. 'Commander, what measures have you made to secure the city?'

'Your Grace?' Rodyn said in confusion.

'The rebels! They may be here at any moment!' Jaxon exclaimed.

The puzzled look on the commander's face brought unease to Jaxon.

'Last report stated they had settled in Ton-Basin,' the commander said. 'There has been no word to say otherwise.'

Jaxon struggled to believe that the stout man was uninformed. Fearing its truth, he began to strategise.

'The troops sent to Aankathor,' he pressed, 'when are you expecting their return?'

'Well… yesterday, Your Grace,' Rodyn stated. 'They departed some six days ago from Aankathor, but we have not received an update since.'

'Send a scout ship,' Jaxon ordered, fearing an interception may have claimed the vessel.

'We have, Your Grace. They cannot seem to locate the transporter.'

'And you failed to report this to the Capital?' Jaxon asked, incredulous.

'I sent report, along with…'

'How many troops were on board?' Jaxon interrupted, the young Prince gripped by bewilderment.

'Five thousand, Your Grace.'

'Five thousand?! The feud in Aankathor did not require such a force! Why were so many sent?!' The outburst rocked the quivering commander.

'I was merely following orders, Your Grace,' he stuttered.

'Whose orders?'

'The Imperial Commander, Your Grace... Your uncle.'

A knot tightened instantly in Jaxon's stomach. A flood of revelation washed over him as he pieced together the deceit. *The rebels were never advancing on Latyth,* he thought. Without a word, Jaxon barged past the commander and rushed back towards the concealed door. Within seconds, he had descended into the darkness.

—

Thio and Y'mara walked arm in arm down the market street that ran adjacent to the infirmary. The wide avenue was lined with lively stalls. Aromas of fresh produce and spices hung in the air. The reminiscent scent of sweet candy drew Thio's attention to the brightly coloured cart in the approaching distance. He and many of the students of the Athenaeum had often chased down this slow-moving wagon to purchase a variety of candied fruits during their breaks.

The two continued down the street, taking in the warm coastal air.

'I forgot how peaceful it was here, despite the city's size,' Thio said.

Y'mara smiled as she looked up at him. 'I wish you could stay, big brother,' she said.

'Me too, but Dalos needs me.'

He looked around at the city folk as they went about their business, gathering provisions for their evening meals. The fear of an impending attack still lingered in his mind. Ahead he saw the ruby dome atop the station and wondered about Jaxon. Suddenly a commotion caught his eye. He adjusted his spectacles and focused on the stirring crowd.

Plowing down the street was a figure dressed in a hooded beige tunic. Thio instantly recognised the Prince.

'Thio!' Jaxon called out as he spotted the duo, advancing at speed.

'Is that…' Y'mara stopped in place.

Jaxon reached the pair within seconds, panic abundant in his eyes.

'What's going on?' Thio asked instantly.

'We need to go to the Athenaeum now!' Jaxon panted.

'Why?'

'They have a sonic transmitter. I need to get a message to Alysse.'

'The rebels?' Thio pressed.

'There's no time to explain. Come!'

Before Thio could say anything more, Jaxon yanked at his arm and they began their sprint towards the sapphire dome. Y'mara stood immobilised, watching the two men race away from her and up the hill.

Manoeuvring past a throng of students within the Athenaeum's main atrium, Thio took the lead and guided Jaxon through the western corridors that led to the administrative quarters. Reaching the faculty lounge, he scanned the room for the head Architect. Spotting him, he called out.

'Sir!'

The scrawny old man turned, instantly recognising his former student.

'Ah, look who it is… the chosen one,' he joked as Thio approached with Jaxon by his side, his hood still concealing his identity.

'We need your sonic transmitter, now!' Thio demanded.

The old man shot Thio a look of disdain at the command.

'How do you know about the sonic transmitters?'

'There's no time, sir! Please!'

Before the Architect could refuse, Jaxon pulled back his hood.

'Your Grace!' The old man bowed deeply.

'The transmitter,' Jaxon said sternly.

'Of course. Right this way.'

The frail man led the duo into his quarters, produced a sonic transmitter from an oak cabinet, and placed it on his study desk.

'Do you know how to use it?' Thio asked the old man.

'No,' he said, 'It was a gift from Dalos. He delivered it the day he collected you. He said he would send his daughter to teach me but…'

'I've been learning the language,' Jaxon stated, cutting the old man off. 'Since the day we needed it in the Grand Athenaeum, but I do not know the method of inputting it.'

'Can you mark the tones?' Thio asked, sliding a blank paper and pen to Jaxon. The prince nodded as he began scoring a series of dashes on the page. Without delay, Thio wrapped his hands around the wooden transmitter, placing a finger on each of the marble buttons. Slowly, he began to press in accordance with Jaxon's score. Smooth tones began to emanate from the box. The message was short. Thio looked to Jaxon for instruction. Confirming the message was correct, he gave a nod. Thio hit the large stud on its front face as the indicator light pulsed.

Jaxon placed his head in his hands then paced the room.

'Jaxon?' Thio said. 'What's going on? What did the message say?'

Jaxon, clearly fatigued, moved back to the desk. He picked up the pen and began writing. Thio looked down at three simple words. *Cyrus is Reclamation.*

—

The sonic transmitter atop the table in Alysse's room radiated harmonic tones. A sly figure standing in her room gently caressed the portrait of Lady Palymma, then strode leisurely over to the box, translating the words as he drew closer. Picking it up from the table, he listened to the three words once more and sneered. Eying the open door across the room, he moved towards the sheer drapes that framed the opening to the sky-high balcony.

Stepping through, the deep purple of his military suit turned an ugly brown in the setting sun.

He peered out across the Path of Peace to the gathered city folk by the Sanctuary of Qyma. He wondered how Alysse was faring against Kalax, knowing full well The Ancients played no part in this reclamation. A sinister smile emerged through the man's silver beard.

Cyrus Thenta looked down at the contraption in his hand, his long-held hatred ever-growing. Approaching the balustrade, he extended his hand over the balcony's edge, paused a moment, then released his grip. He watched as the tone-emanating transmitter plummeted some 600 metres to the stone path below.

CHAPTER 26

Alysse surveyed the congregation within the Sanctuary. Pockets of city folk whispered amongst themselves, occasionally looking over and pointing at the Princess. Others, she saw, hung their heads low, the murmuring of prayers evident from their chattering mouths. A small group of devout advocates of the Faith approached Reverend Kalax, respectfully genuflecting at his feet. Holding a small chalice, he dipped his thumb into it and smeared pale-orange oil across their foreheads. Others filed out of the bronze-arched doors.

Her heart raced. *What have I done?*

Mia approached the visibly tense Princess and reached for her hand, before gently pulling Alysse in close.

'My girl, I think it's best we leave,' she whispered in her ear.

Dalos guided his chair silently towards the two

women, keeping a keen eye on the disgruntled horde. The imperial guards had formed a tight circle around the company, their sheathed short swords at the ready.

'Mia is right,' he said softly. 'We should take the tunnels.'

Alysse stood in place with heavy breath as she eyed the group accumulating around the five High Priests. She fondled her gold pendant, longing for her father's guidance and her brother back by her side. A deluge of doubt bore down on her as she attempted to calculate her next move.

'No,' she said after some thought, 'I will not cower. We will return via the Path.'

Alysse gave a nod to the lone guard facing her. With a sharp turn, the other guards acknowledged his silent command and adjusted their formation. The audible shift drew Reverend Kalax's attention to the party, casually turning his head towards Alysse. He shot a foreboding glare across the sanctum. The priest's radiant orange eyes pierced the Princess as a gradual smirk twisted his wiry mouth.

The small entourage exited into the warm hues of the setting sun. Double the number of spectators had flocked to the marble thoroughfare outside the temple. A collective reticence fell upon the crowd as the guards parted a path through them. The adoring glances from her people had shifted into ones of scorn as Alysse passed through them silently.

'Blasphemer!' She heard emit from the throngs, whipping her head around in an attempt to identify the faceless protester.

'Seek forgiveness!' Another voice rang out from the opposite section of the crowd.

'Atone!' One more called out.

Alysse slowed her pace as she timidly scanned the faces surrounding her. Dalos shifted his suspender chair closer to the Princess, the escorting guards shrinking in around them.

'Alysse, we mustn't waver,' he said to her, fearing a sinister turn in the people.

Alysse looked ahead at the distant soaring bastion transcending into the sky. She wished to simply close her eyes and be instantly present within its security. The path ahead appeared to endlessly elongate before her eyes, drawing her comforts further and further away despite their advancement.

She quickened her steps, doing all in her power to silence the echoing jeers in her mind. Mia clutched her arm and encouraged the hastening of her stride. Alysse's flowing silk gown now swayed behind her in the turbulent wind. Her eyes were fixed on her destination. The guards kept pace as their purple horse-haired crests waved atop their helms. The cadenced clattering of their armour plates set a rapid rhythm for their return.

As the sun continued to drop behind the Drom Mountains, purple hues blanketed the city. The swarm of people thinned as Alysse and her company moved further away from the Sanctuary, her eyes never parting from the entrance to the Citadel. Mia turned her gaze rearward as the distracted crowd focused on the emerging High Priests. Little could be heard of Kalax's preachings from their position midway down the Path. She turned ahead and gazed skyward at the approaching tower. The tip of the monument gleamed with the last of the day's sunlight. With her acute vision, she spotted faint movement atop the Princess's balcony. She squinted.

Dalos, noticing her shift in attention, followed her gaze. His shaded spectacles did little to help his aged eyesight.

'What is it?' he asked.

'I thought I saw... never mind,' she replied, dismissing the possibility. 'A trick of the light, I'm sure.'

Alysse felt a pressing tire in her legs, finding relief as they finally reached the tiered incline of the Citadel's entrance. The day's light had faded into the west, revealing the cosmic cloak of stars that sparkled down from the heavens. Her footsteps, and those of her company, produced sporadic crunches as they ascended the ramped walkway.

Amidst her exhaustion, Alysse noted a sprawl of tiny shards of wood, copper, and marble scattered across the ground. Her mind, clouded with disarray, allowed no effort to discern their origin. Mia also acknowledged the peculiar presence of debris under her steps. At the base of the towering doors, she spotted a circular golden disk. As the doors parted and the group entered into the hall, Mia bent to retrieve the shiny object. Holding it in her hand, she identified the finely etched drawing of two golden-crowned wrens atop the twisted piece of metal. Pursuing its familiarity in her memory, she landed on the sonic transmitter she had gifted the Princess a year prior. Before she could engage Alysse's attention, a voice sounded in the entrance hall.

'Alysse?' Cyrus Thenta called out as he descended the grand staircase. 'You seemed troubled. What happened?'

Cyrus, feigning concern, motioned for the guards to disband as he approached his niece. Alysse welcomed his presence with an exhausted hug.

'Oh, Uncle,' she said, her legs weak. 'I may have misjudged. Kalax… The people…'

'Fear not, Your Grace,' he offered. 'All will be right soon.'

'Any word from Jaxon?' Alysse spoke softly in his ear.

Cyrus pulled back from the young woman's hold and shook his head.

'And the rebels? Any news on that front?' she asked.

'Nothing.'

Alysse's mind whirled, the cloud of doubt and worry ever thickening. Her body swayed as her strength declined.

'Come, my girl,' Mia said, taking hold of her. 'You need to rest.'

Cyrus turned to the two Chief Architects. 'Perhaps it is best that we accommodate you two in the Citadel for now,' he suggested to them.

Alysse nodded silently in agreement.

'Tend to Alysse,' he continued, 'I will arrange your chambers.'

CHAPTER 27

The sky above the horizon was illuminated with deep blue hues as the last light dwindled beyond the visibly limitless ocean. Thio and Y'mara sat idle at the station awaiting word from Jaxon. The platform sat at the edge of a steep, sloped ridge, high up in the city's southeastern elevation. The sprawl below twinkled as its residents kindled light within their dwellings.

The air was still. Only faint chatter could be heard as the day's liveliness faded. Thio rolled a small piece of candied fruit around his palate, savouring the nostalgic sweetness. Y'mara did the same. They sat in silence for some time, simply enjoying each other's company before Thio's approaching departure.

Reaching into his tunic, Thio withdrew the silver locket that hung around his neck and opened it. The two drawings of his mother and sister brought its familiar warmth to him. Y'mara, catching a glimmer of light reflecting off the silver keepsake, instantly recognised it. She smiled, then produced her own from a pocket in her coat. Unlocking it, she too looked down at the coal drawings within. Both lockets shared the same image of their mother on one side. Opposite, in place of her own portrait, was one of Thio, a young eight-year-old boy, his scruffy hair twirling playfully atop his head. His wide smile and oversized spectacles covered most of his little face. Held close to his chest was a single rose.

'My two favourite things,' Y'mara said, smiling at the drawing of her brother and the white rose that grew in abundance around their hometown.

'I'm sorry I missed the last bloom. Did you go?' Thio asked.

Y'mara shook her head.

Each year at summer's end, she and Thio would embark on the three-hour journey from Latyth, through the northern skirts of the Fenniq Belt, to their small home village of Syka. The white roses held deep significance for them, blooming each year in time with the anniversary of their mother's passing. With each bloom, they would scour the meadows for the largest rose, pluck it, and venture deep into the forest to Syka Falls, where they would lay it upon a solitary rock jutting over the lagoon in memory of their mother.

'The bloom will start in a month,' Thio stated, meeting her eyes. 'I will come back for it. I promise.'

Y'mara smiled at the thought. The previous year's bloom had been the first since their mother's passing that they had not made the journey. Thio's sudden departure from Latyth following Dalos' recruitment had made returning nearly impossible—a fact he had resented for some time.

Distant echoing footsteps broke the tranquility as the main doors to the station cracked open. Through them strode Jaxon, his common beige garments now replaced with a deep purple military suit and a muted green sash draped over one shoulder. A broad belt, now proudly holding his golden short sword, circled his knee-length coat. In that moment, Thio saw Jaxon as he truly was—a noble commander of the highest rank, powerful, and untouchable to the common folk. Despite knowing he was the Prince, Thio had not, until that moment, fully grasped Jaxon's role in this world—a role now thrust upon him. Trailing him was a handful of people. One, Thio recognised as the Head Architect. Y'mara spotted the city's governor. The other faces were unknown to them.

As the small convoy approached the platform, Jaxon saw Thio and Y'mara on the viewing bench overlooking the city. The spectacular vista beyond framed the young apprentice and his sister as they stood. Thio's broad shoulders and lean frame stood in stark contrast against their backdrop. The overwhelming beauty of the scene, paired with Thio's striking looks, brought a coy smile to Jaxon's face. The voices of the surrounding officers dulled in Jaxon's mind as his fixation on Thio intensified. One of the men accompanying him strove to regain the Prince's fleeting attention, halting him to discuss important arrangements.

Y'mara, noticing the exchange of stares, looked up at her brother, whose eyes were fixed on the young

Prince.

'So, the Prince—how did you manage to sway him to your cause?' she asked playfully.

'I didn't,' Thio stated, eyeing his newly dressed companion. 'He came of his own will.'

'Jaxon Aprya, Prince of the Imperium, simply volunteered to escort you across the country?' Y'mara responded quizzically.

'He learnt of my *cure*. You weren't the only person of importance I saved,' Thio said, smiling down at his sister.

Y'mara recalled the news of the Dusk within the Capital and its failed claim on the young Prince. An outpouring of pride filled her heart at the knowledge that her brother had saved the lives of many during that dark time. She understood why Jaxon would help him now.

'I see the way he looks at you,' she said, giving Thio a lighthearted nudge. 'I'm happy for you, big brother.'

Thio eyed Jaxon from across the platform. The young man stood proud amongst his company as the soft lights of the station caressed his figure. Then, a saddening realisation fell upon Thio.

'But he is the Prince—noble to nobles,' he began, 'and I am far from that. I could never rise to his stature. Pursuing him would be foolish on my part. Besides, his duty lies with the Imperium and the continuation of his family name. There are rules, Y'mara.'

'Fuck the rules,' she blurted. 'One should be free to pursue whomever they desire.' She placed a soft hand on his arm. 'Don't shy away from him, Thio, or you'll spend your days regretting what could have been.'

Thio swiftly dismissed the thought, settling instead on a logical outcome devoid of desire. While relationships of this nature were widely accepted across most societies, he could not shake the notion that pursuing this one would bring disappointment to the Great Houses of Eviiri and their traditions. He shifted uncomfortably, then turned to his sister.

'And what about you? Has love found you here?' he asked.

Y'mara opened her mouth, then closed it without speaking. She produced a bashful smile and lowered her head as she smoothed her hands over her belly.

Thio's eyes widened in a surge of shock, confusion, and excitement. 'Y'mara?'

Her bashful smile erupted into a widening grin as she nodded.

'I'm only a few months along. I was planning on writing to you soon, but…'

Before she could finish, Thio flung his arms around her, elation consuming him. He felt Y'mara welcome the embrace. He wished never to let go, the world all but slipped away in that moment.

Y'mara pressed her toes against the stone platform, lifted herself closer to Thio's ear, and whispered. 'If it's a girl, I will name her Patrya, after Mother,' she said excitedly. 'And if it's a boy… Thio.'

The honour of the gesture caused Thio to well up instantly. Struggling to find words, he squeezed his sister tighter.

From afar, Jaxon observed the embrace—their conversation inaudible. The sight brought upon vicarious joy at first, then shifted to thoughts of his own sister. All joy instantly stripped away as he refocused on the dangers she faced, rendering him unable to delight in the love before him.

'Your Grace!' Commander Rodyn called out from across the station, announcing his arrival as he strode towards Jaxon. 'If it pleases,' he said, outstretching his hand toward the viewing deck where Thio and Y'mara stood.

Jaxon followed the stocky commander as they crossed an overpass that bridged the platforms. The others trailed behind. As they reached the expansive view, both Thio and Y'mara offered respectful bows to the Prince—his self-appointed role as Imperial Commander evident in his illustrious demeanour. Jaxon eyed Thio, and Thio eyed Jaxon. An unspoken exchange of sensual intensity filled the air between them.

'Another scout ship, as requested, Your Grace,' Rodyn said, pointing to a small vessel faintly visible as it departed the fort's docks. Jaxon readjusted his focus on the bay. The speedy, slimline vessel curved around the spit and accelerated out into the vast northern sea.

'Good,' he said. 'Any findings must be sent to me directly.'

'Yes, Your Grace,' Rodyn said with a sharp nod.

'Should you locate the transport ship, redirect it immediately to the Bay of Zenithal. As for your remaining troops,' Jaxon continued, 'ready them. They will travel with us to the Capital.'

'At once, Your Grace.' Rodyn nodded a salute, turned in place, then marched towards the exit.

Jaxon shifted his attention to the station steward—a frail, hunched woman whose clouded eyes held decades of life's wisdom as they stared back at him.

'My Lady, the central route is obstructed. We had to abandon a carriage in the Kordas Desert. We will make via the western line instead. Notify the stations and commanders at The Westwall and Bryll. We will collect their troops as we pass through. Couple every carriage available and make sure they are adequately stocked.'

'Yes, Your Grace.' The old station steward complied with a rich timbre, unbefitting her feeble appearance. Her gait also contrasted her age as she paced off with haste at the Prince's command.

'And you, sir,' Jaxon spoke now to the Head Architect, 'do all you can to get word to the survivors in Ton-Basin. The western line passes through the Ton-Plains. We will reserve a carriage to deliver them here. Governor, allow them refuge where available.'

Saying nothing, the Head Architect and the city's governor confirmed with a nod and followed suit of the dismissed members.

Hearing this, Y'mara stepped forward and spoke. 'I will prepare the infirmary for the injured, Your Grace.'

Jaxon turned to the youthful physician, her eyes carrying the same ocean-blue depth as her brother's. Their sibling likeness was painted clear in her features.

'Thank you, Y'mara,' he said sincerely.

Y'mara acknowledged with a soft smile, then turned to Thio.

'Be safe, big brother. I will see you come the bloom,' she said as she wrapped her arms around him once again, his return embrace silent.

Jaxon stared at Thio as the apprentice watched his sister exit the lofty station. A single tear dropped from his sweeping sandy eyelashes, rolling over the structured form of his cheek.

Thio, fixed on his sister, barely noticed Jaxon's tender thumb wiping away that single tear.

'Are you okay?' Jaxon asked, dispersing the salty drop between his fingers.

'She's pregnant,' Thio said softly, a wholehearted glee prominent in his tone.

'I'm happy for you,' Jaxon said as he rubbed a gentle hand across Thio's back.

Rapture coursed through Thio's body. He quivered at the sensation as his eyes wavered in desire. Yet his mind fought against it. *He is the Prince of the Imperium and I am... nobody,* he thought. He turned to face Jaxon, taking half a step back from the elegant nobleman.

'What duty do you require of me, My Prince?' he asked, shifting into a formal tone.

Sensing the shift, Jaxon crawled his mind for a reason for this sudden change. *Does he wish to remain here with his sister?* he wondered.

'Arrangements have been made to bring a force to the Capital. We were all deceived. Latyth was never at risk. My uncle clearly orchestrated this lie to lure you out of the Capital. And in my own faults, he knew I would rush to your aid,' Jaxon stated, pausing in thought then taking a step closer to the apprentice. 'Thio, if your wish is to remain here with Y'mara, it will not lessen my regard for you. You are free to do so.'

Thio turned back and stared at the exit, then out at the dazzling city yonder the station's platform. The sapphire dome of the Athenaeum gleamed against the encroaching darkness of nightfall. Thio recalled seeing it from this very vantage on the night he and Dalos had embarked on their eighteen-month tour of the western regions of Qymathor. The abrupt and unforeseen shift in his once-ordinary life had left him unsettled then, yet the boundless dream of innovation had ignited an excitement beyond measure.

Tonight, however, that same thirst for adventure had been eclipsed by an even stronger desire to remain. He sifted through everything he had learned—his mission to rescue his sister had become obsolete, yet seeing her again, knowing of her pregnancy, awakened in him a far greater need to protect.

His thoughts drifted beyond Latyth, to the life he had built outside its borders and the ever-deepening bond with his mentor. It was an unforeseen partnership—one that many would sacrifice greatly to cultivate. Dalos had become a father to him, filling the void left by a man whose memory had long faded to time.

And then there was Mia. Though their acquaintance was young, she carried the same warmth his mother once had—a quiet, unwavering love, unbound by blood or nobility.

They are my family too, he thought, shifting his focus back to Jaxon. Behind the Prince's rich hazel eyes, he recognised the same fear that had seized him at the thought of his sister in peril. He made a decision in that instant and spoke it.

'I'm sorry, My Prince. Were it not for me, you would be at your sister's side right now.' Jaxon met his gaze as Thio pressed on. 'My sister is safe. Alysse is not—nor Dalos, nor Mia. You came here for me. Now, I will stand with you, My Prince… if it pleases.'

Jaxon stepped closer, his gaze steady. Lifting a hand, he cupped the back of Thio's neck, his thumb tracing the sharp line of his jaw. The past days had allowed a fine layer of sandy stubble to soften the edges of Thio's youthful face. In the quiet seclusion of the station, Jaxon leaned in, closing the space between them.

'It pleases,' he whispered before bringing his lips to Thio's.

Thio relished in the connection. His surroundings faded as his eyes closed. The firm grip of the Prince's hand upon the back of his neck exerted a tender yet intentional force. Then, a dissuading thought arose. *You are not worthy.*

Thio pulled back. 'My Prince, I…'

Delicate chimes vented from the station's audio ducts as the two whipped their attention to the centre of the space. The convoy of eight carriages before them shifted sequentially out of the main atrium and into the vast rail yard nestled behind the building. Thio and Jaxon watched on as the train systematically grew in length over the sprawl of twisted tracks. The synchronous dance of terrain-liners impressed the pair with every clasp of a joining carriage. After a few moments, the far-reaching iron and glass serpent re-entered the station, less than half of it spanning the entirety of the platform while the rest remained out in the yard.

In that same moment, a symphony of horns sounded from the city below, drawing Jaxon to the familiar call. He moved to the edge of the viewing deck and peered down to the main boulevard. Surging up the wide thoroughfare was a brigade of troops marching in precise formation. The green and purple river of approximately five hundred men and women waved in unison with every rhythmic stomp. Large banners bearing the sigil of House Aprya drooped in the stillness of the coastal air.

Thio, now by Jaxon's side, looked on in awe. Despite this being a fraction of the troop's true size, the Qymathorian force commanded a strength never before witnessed by the young apprentice. A new set of thoughts weighed in. He looked over to Jaxon, who now held command over this mighty infantry—a command stripped from Cyrus Thenta's deceitful grip.

'My Prince… your uncle—why would he turn against your family?' he asked carefully, cautious not to overstep.

The question had been weighing on Jaxon ever since he unfurled his uncle's deceit.

'I don't know,' he answered plainly. 'Our family has always kept faith with House Thenta. My father appointed Cyrus as Imperial Commander as a gesture of loyalty and unity between our Houses. Traditionally, the second sons of the Imperial family command its forces, but my father was an only child. After his marriage to my mother, he declared that Cyrus would hold the post—the first time in the Imperium's history that someone outside the ruling family had assumed the position.' He paused. 'I did all in my power to follow in his footsteps, but was constantly met with his disapproval. Despite all that, I respected him. His care for my mother was unmatched.'

'Perhaps her death caused him to sour?' Thio suggested.

'It is possible,' Jaxon said, reflecting on the notion. 'I remember seeing a changed man stand before me when I awoke from the Dusk. His eyes held none of the love or warmth they once had.' He paused, exploring the thought further. 'Surely, he does not hold my family accountable for his sister's death? In any case, his motives are the least of my concerns at present. Alysse is not safe.'

Thio heard the tremble in Jaxon's voice as his last words were spoken. He noted his fondling of the intricate gold handle of his short sword upon his belt. The dim night lights grew and shrunk on Jaxon's deep purple coat as long draws of breath fought to soothe his angst. Thio moved to comfort him, unsure of which act to take. Before he could place a hand on his Prince, the infantry horns sounded once more.

Through the wide-open main gates of the station, the ocean of troops filed in. The pounding of their steps shook the air within the cavernous space. On every fourth footfall, the legion delivered a drumming chant, quiet yet direct: *Qy-ma-thor*. Thio peered at the growing mass through the glass walls of the train which separated them from this side of the station. The tint of turquoise dulled the sea of purple and green. Flickers of light mirrored off their gold breast plates. Distracted by the flood of soldiers, Thio did not notice that Jaxon was no longer by his side.

The young Prince ascended the footbridge that crossed over the train at the far end of the platform. Once at its apex, he scanned the collection of loyal swordsmen and women, their faces staring straight ahead, emotionless and stern. Like a lattice of trees in a plantation, each stood in perfectly spaced formation, one abreast of the other. With the last grunt of their chant, the troop concluded their march with a forcible stomp that rumbled through the thick stone floor. Then, silence.

Jaxon stepped forward, continuing to examine his people. From a distance, a voice shouted from the ranks:

'To His Grace!'

As if tethered by an invisible rope, every man and woman whipped their gaze towards him. No matter where his eyes landed, Jaxon saw a pair staring back in direct line with his.

This is my time, he thought to himself. *Command.*

With a surge of strength, he leapt over the side rail of the footbridge, his nimbleness landing him gingerly atop the glass ceiling of the terrain-liner. He paced slowly towards the centre of the station, each step silent as it treaded his transparent platform.

'Defenders of Qymathor!' he commanded with intense projection. 'I call on your aid. Your Crown-Princess needs you now. Will you honour your duty to safeguard Qymathor?'

In unison, the crowd erupted: 'Qymathor!'

'Tonight we make for the Capital. A threat advances from the west and within. Let us cut it down before its roots take hold. Are you with me?'

'Qymathor!'

'For peace! For Eviiri! For Qymathor!'

'Qymathor!'

The final eruption of chants roared through Thio's very being as he stood enthralled by Jaxon's commanding presence, his new light dousing all fear—his purpose now clear.

The doors to each carriage hissed open.

'Forward!' shouted the same general. A rich-tonal blast sounded from the scattered horn bearers. With a grunt, the assembly shifted and began filing into the string of carriages.

Jaxon, still atop the train, turned to Thio on the opposite platform below. Their stares conveyed distinct emotions. The Prince displayed strength. The apprentice displayed admiration. Both displayed confidence as faint smiles curled their mouths.

CHAPTER 28

The chilled depths of the cavernous tunnels of Zenithal spread their dormant fingers wide beneath the active world above. The familiar sound of absolute quietude rang in Cyrus Thenta's ears. The abundant silence was deep enough for him to hear his rage throb with every heartbeat.

The stillness of the air began to stir as a growing wind advanced up the southern passage, carrying a faint scent of rust within its flow. Driving the wind was an approaching carrier. Onboard, the buttery blond ponytail of Britt Pensyr welcomed the murky glows of the trail lights as she neared.

The carrier came to a stop before Cyrus. Its headlamps illuminated his deep purple suit and the abundant disdain on his face. Paying no mind to his facial cues, Britt Pensyr strode confidently towards him, arrived, then greeted him with a passionate kiss. His lips, although familiar to her, were cold and indifferent. She pulled back with concern and studied his unchanged expression.

'What is it, my love?' she asked.

His nostrils flared, the edges curling in a momentary snarl. His mouth remained still until he spoke.

'Jaxon and the apprentice are still alive,' he said with sternness in tone, one eyebrow raised in inquiry.

'What?! I cut the power to the train. How did they survive the desert?' she asked.

'I had hoped you would explain that,' he returned.

Britt stood, eyes still wide with shock as she learnt the outcome of her ill intent. She scoured her mind to find possible ways of escaping such an unforgiving land. Trekking the sands would prove futile—no piece of technology could maintain regulated body temperature long enough to survive its heat. Her plan had hinged on disabling the train's power during the most isolated stretch of its journey, the farthest point from any city or town. *If abandoning the train was not the solution,* she thought, *then what?* Suddenly it became clear.

'Thio… The salt… He managed to harness its energy,' she whispered aloud to herself, then looked up at Cyrus. 'I should have taken the whole piece.'

Before Britt had time to react, Cyrus whipped his open hand across her face. She pressed her palm over the throbbing sting of her cheek as he advanced on her. With his other arm, he wrapped it around her head, clutched at her ponytail, and wrenched it backward. A reactive yelp escaped her mouth as his presence loomed over her. Mere inches from her face, she saw his eyes burning with a rage that cut through the dim trail-lights of their surroundings.

'I ought to sink your body into the bay,' he snarled, his breath hot.

'My love... I'm sorry!' she pleaded, shrieks of pain underlining her words.

With another forceful yank of her hair, he threw her to the ground. A sharp pang struck her left hip as the clasp on her utility belt punctured her skin, opening a small wound in her side.

'Have you any idea of the risks your failures pose to our cause?' Cyrus exploded. The cracks in his aged voice ricocheted off the frigid cavern walls. He closed his eyes to calm himself.

Britt stared up at him, confusion now paired with her distress.

'Failures?' she questioned. *What else have I done?*

Cyrus paced the area with his hand pressed firmly against his forehead.

'Dalos is also alive,' he stated.

'He can't be!' Britt exclaimed. 'He drank the poison. I saw it with my own eyes.'

Rage resurfaced as Cyrus spoke, 'You're lucky I don't remove those eyes.'

He took a series of deep breaths as he continued to circle the young beauty who lay stricken on the floor, his mind calculating his next move.

'Luck would have it,' he began, 'that both Dalos and Mia reside here in the Citadel. You will deal with them tonight.'

'I will, sire. I swear it,' Britt said as she struggled onto her knees, the gash on her hip producing a slender stream of blood. 'What of Alysse?'

'She will be her own undoing, but we need her alive,' he said, ignoring her struggle.

'And Jaxon?'

Cyrus halted. His hatred towards the young Prince was expressed in his tight fists.

'I will deal with him,' he said in a low voice. 'Our spies say he is gathering a force to bear on the Capital.'

Britt, realising the consequences of her failed attempts, dropped her head and let out a sigh.

'Had all gone to plan,' Cyrus continued, 'House Aprya would have died in the dark. Thanks to your incompetence, we now face exposure. Jaxon knows of my deception and it won't be long until word spreads. We must act fast.'

'Have you informed House…'

'Shut up! Do not question me on such matters!' Cyrus scolded. 'My dealings with them are my own. If the other Great Houses learn of our alliance, there will be war.'

He paced closer to the injured girl, smoothing a faint wrinkle in his coat and adjusting the Imperial insignia on his breast. Standing over her, he looked down at her striking face, her beauty radiating even in distress. Vivid blue eyes stared back at him, wet creases spilling out from the corners of those vivid blue eyes. A speck of blood sat pinched between the folds of her plump lips. He knelt down in front of her.

'Now prepare yourself,' he said, wiping the blood with a tender thumb.

Taking her hand, he lifted her to her feet. She stood, head lowered, before he eased it up with a hooked finger. They met each other's gaze once again. His rage curdled into lust, driving him to force his passion upon her. The subtle taste of iron swept over his tongue with every desirous glossing of her lips. He moved his tongue to her cheek, then across to her neck, then up to her ear. Her eyes rolled back with craving.

'Fail me again,' he whispered sternly, 'and it will be the last time you fail me.'

She gently pulled back, revealing an apologetic acceptance of his threat.

'Yes, my love.'

—

It was not the first time that Dalos had slept within the city's towering monolith. A decade prior to tonight, the Grand Athenaeum had battled with a barrage of bed mites, rendering his sleeping quarters un-sleepable. He was offered this very same room at the time, one he was privileged to select from the countless on the visitor floors. It had no balcony, nor large sweeping glass walls, only three narrow slit-windows carved through the thick white exterior. It sat almost centre of the southern facade of the Citadel, no higher than five floors above the Grand Entrance Hall. He prized it for its low angular view. Through the deep-set apertures was a clear scene of the bay, the Shrine, and the Athenaeum, each seemingly stacked one atop the other. The triad held great significance to him—his life's work at the Athenaeum, his love and bond with House Aprya and their ancestry, and a love of the water, instilled in him by his late wife, Myra.

Almost every night he would dream of her—the same dream. He had no desire to explore other memories of her, simply settling for this one experience life had gifted them. In this dream, they walked the shores of the White Isles, her hand in his, the undulant ivory hills painting their backdrop. Tonight, the memory was more clear than it had ever been, enhanced by the Fire Orchid essence coursing through his veins.

He could feel the sand beneath his feet, the sun warming his back, and the delicate scent of Myra carried by the sea breeze. She was radiant that day. Her long, honey-brown curls cascaded effortlessly from a loose bun. Her light summer frock fluttered gently over her graceful form. In the dream, a joyful smile revealed the deep dimples that charmed him so. She was his muse, his everything. And it was on that day, amidst the serene beauty of the White Isles, that Myra had revealed her pregnancy to him.

Outside of his dream, the room was dark. A sliver of moonlight slipped in through the narrow windows, casting a cool blue tint across the space. The room was silent, broken only by the rhythmic breaths of his slumber. Not even the approaching footsteps could be heard.

Britt Pensyr drifted soundlessly across the room, her bare feet absorbing the frigid coldness of the stone as she left a dewy trail of perspiration. Seeing the rotund figure peacefully asleep before her stirred reproach and angered her.

Arriving at his bed, she loomed over him and whispered.

'Why won't you die, old man?'

She ran a hand over his receding silver curls.

Dalos felt the touch in his dream, but it was the hand of Myra caressing him. He lingered in the sensation for a moment, until the realisation struck—this was not a part of his memory. The scene in his mind began collapsing in around him as Myra faded from sight. In a panic, his eyes shot open, his astral mind snapping back into the material world. And there, brewing above him, stood the young apprentice tall and blonde.

'Britt?!' he gasped. 'What in Korpys are you…'

Before his words concluded, the agile beauty leaped up and mounted his chest, her weight expelling the air from his lungs, her legs pinning both arms to the bed. Dalos fought to free himself to no avail.

Britt pressed her tongue between her teeth and smiled down at the struggling Chief. An aura of arrogance surrounded her.

'You would have to be my most infuriating victim, do you know that?' she said playfully, relishing in her control. 'You were first meant to die in Ton-Basin. My glorious Blue Flame would have made quick work of you if that panicked bitch hadn't called her little gathering.'

Rage exploded from Dalos. 'You treacherous cunt!'

'That was attempt number one,' she continued.

'Then I poisoned your treasured tea. Yet here you are.'

Britt leaned in close and stared directly into his beady eyes. Something odd caught her attention—a fiery orange glow within them.

'Ah,' she said in revelation, 'so that's your secret. Very clever. How did you manage to get your fat hands on Fire Orchid essence? I thought the flowers were lost.'

Dalos continued his struggle, the smug face of his assailant boiling his blood.

'You killed Gorryn,' he accused.

'I did,' she said proudly. 'Even a man with such intellect cannot control his primal drivers. And drive he did.'

She gyrated her pelvis on Dalos' chest, mocking the late Chief Architect's ferocious lust.

'Why, Britt? He gave you everything.'

She chuckled. 'My real mentors have bigger plans for me in their new world. But in order for a new world to come, we must rid ourselves of the old.'

Dalos squirmed, then something caught his attention. Her blouse was blood-soaked on one side. It was mostly dried, yet the silver moonlight revealed wetness in the centre, hinting at a fresh wound. *She's injured*, he surmised.

'I've imagined many ways to kill you, Chief,' she taunted. 'I thought my poison was a sure thing. No one would have detected it; I crafted it so. But I've grown tired of chance. Your essence cannot stop a knife to the heart.'

She reached around to a leather sheath on her belt

and slid out a small dagger. Dalos felt the backwards shift of her weight and seized the opportunity. He slipped his left arm out from under her leg and drove his fist into the patch of blood.

Britt shrieked in pain. Her agony jolted her body, allowing Dalos to free his other arm. As swiftly as the old man could move, he pressed the small disk on his leather wrist strap. In the same movement, he heaved himself up and thrust Britt off him. She tumbled off the end of the bed, still gripping the gash in her side. Pushing through the pain, she stood to face her target. Anger twisted her expression as she spoke.

'Give up, old man. You should welcome my blade,' she snarled, circling the bed. 'And don't worry, I will take great care of Thio.'

Britt lunged forward, dagger held high above her head. She thrust her arm downwards in line with her prey's bare chest. Dalos raised a defensive hand that interrupted her blow. A battle of strength ensued, Britt's slender figure matching the force of Dalos' aged muscles.

The tip of the knife crept closer to his skin. Then closer. Then closer. Dalos stared down at the slow-approaching lethal point. Closer. Closer. His strength waned. He watched as the knife made contact with his chest, then lower, and lower, the dull point pushing a divot into his flesh. Lower. The small pocket of skin ruptured, accepting the blade. A centimetre of metal now sat below the surface. Deeper. Deeper. A manic grin warped Britt's face as she delighted in the tentacles of blood that oozed out of the lesion. Another centimetre deeper. She revelled in his pain. Then, instant darkness consumed her sight and mind.

Britt's limp body flung sideways as the golden tip of a wooden cane connected with her temple. Mia's fear-driven breaths were momentarily silenced by the thud of Britt's body hitting the floor. She threw down her father's cane and rushed to his aid.

'Pa!' she wailed, terror-notes in her voice.

'I'm alright. I'm alright,' he said, inspecting his infliction. 'Just a scratch.'

Mia looked down at the open wound, his body's canvas brushed with crimson paint. She tore at the linen sheet that covered him and pressed a clump of it against his chest. He squirmed in pain.

From the floor beside Mia, a faint moan escaped the incapacitated blonde as she writhed in a haze of disorientation.

'Quick, bind her,' Dalos urged.

CHAPTER 29

Alysse fidgeted with her golden pendant in the private elevator as it descended the tower, Queen Marcia Iibryn standing by her side. Alysse and Marcia had taken the morning to discuss her coronation arrangements. The news of the tower's intruder had disrupted their early meal.

The peach-draped monarch had earlier expressed her apologies to Alysse for misdirecting her suspicions to the Faith. Her well-calculated mind had produced thin threads of reason and logic, with the one sewn to the Faith appearing thickest and strongest. Alysse too had found confidence in the accusal, only to be shamed publicly by the sworn denial of Reverend Kalax. But now she had someone—a direct link to the rebellion.

The elevator slowed to a stop on the floor of the Session Hall. Awaiting the arrival of the Princess in the foyer were four of her Imperial guards, rigid and armed. Without delay, Alysse issued a silent command with her eyes, prompting two guards to heave open the solid doors.

'Where is she?' Alysse asserted as she barged into the room.

Standing at the opposite end of the spacious hall was Mia, arms folded, a sneer prominently fixed to her face. Across from her sat Dalos in his suspender chair. His back faced the entrance but his glare was turned to the southern window. And sitting before that window was Britt Pensyr, her arms bound behind the backrest of another suspender chair. She turned her head to Alysse and spoke.

'Your Grace,' she said with patronising formality.

'Did you kill my father?' Alysse returned as she swiftly approached, her gait almost at a jog. Britt said nothing, her grin toying with the incensed Princess.

'Did you kill my father?!' she exploded, thrusting a tight grip around the buttery blonde's throat. The crushing grit of flesh and cartilage could be heard across the room. Britt stared up at her. The blood from her head wound had dried into sinuous strings that ran down the side of her face. Her eyes swelled as pressure expanded behind them.

'Alysse,' Mia said, stepping forward with concern in her tone. 'I implore restraint. We need her information.'

Alysse, although enraged, knew she had much to learn from this killer. She released her grip. In that same moment, Cyrus Thenta rushed into the room. He eyed its occupants, then spotted his subordinate, captured and exposed. A pit grew within him. He chose his moment, void of any onlookers, then delivered a threatening stare towards Britt. Between her violent coughs, her return gaze spoke of reassurance. She would not expose him.

'Your father's own righteousness killed him,' Britt said, strain in her voice, the hint of arrogance carried amongst her sporadic bursts of laughter.

'My father cared greatly for his people. He sacrificed much for them,' Alysse shot back.

'His choices clinched his early rest in that altar,' Britt played.

'What choices?' Alysse asked.

'You truly are blind,' Britt returned.

'Speak them then,' Dalos commanded, wincing as his chest throbbed.

'You will come to know them in time. Once the Reclamation is executed, all of your questions will find their answers,' Britt said.

Cyrus, fearing the young captive's words, moved to Alysse and ushered her across the room.

'This is pointless, Your Grace,' he whispered to her. 'We should kill her immediately and be done with it.'

'She is not working alone,' Alysse asserted. 'She is but one player in a larger game.'

Cyrus stood gripped with fear as Alysse moved back to the detainee. She commanded a suspender chair from the opulent meeting table and sat face to face with her opponent.

'Who are The Reclamation?' she asked, all rage now subdued behind steely eyes.

Britt turned towards her with a smile. 'Those who will lead us into a better world,' she said, rolling her head to admire the view beyond the turquoise-tinted windows.

'What is wrong with the one we live in now?' Alysse probed.

'Those mountains out there obstruct your vision,' Britt said, tracing the sun-soaked ridges of the distant Drom Mountains with her eyes. 'You were born in a golden cradle. You have no view of the real world beyond. There are many that sneer up at you—many that wish to see this erroneous tower crumble and fall.'

Erroneous tower? Alysse repeated in her mind, re-calling the precise words of Lex Frailyn during the Qyx-Iriyan. She pressed back in her chair, then glanced over at Marcia Iibryn, who watched on with intensity.

'I was wrong to accuse the Faith, I see that now,' Alysse began. 'It is clear this contest stems from with-in the Imperium. It is House Frailyn that challenges my rule. Queen Marcia, you said it yourself, should House Aprya fail, Lex Frailyn ascends as Emperor.'

Marcia Iibryn adjusted her posture. 'Rest assured, Your Grace, I will not back his claim. Nor will the others,' she said with conviction.

Britt broke into a series of laughs at the exchange.

'Something amuses you?' Alysse asked, frustration resurfacing.

'House Aprya. House Frailyn,' Britt spoke as she tilted her head from one side to another, 'you are all just more of the same.'

Alysse stood. 'The Great Houses freed this world from treachery. My family's rule has kept it from slipping back into chaos.'

Again, Britt laughed, this time staring directly into Alysse's eyes.

'Your family's rule has laid paths for many to stray. You gifted them the greatest weapon of all: freedom.' She paused, craning her neck towards the young Princess. 'And too much freedom breeds chaos.'

The words sat uneasily with Alysse. Could the world her father and forebears had built truly create pathways to chaos? The idea had no place to settle in her mind. The lessons taught to her spoke of prosperity, not chaos, being born of freedom. The controlling nature of the religious reign stood as proof. It had caged the people's minds and allowed only those with self-acclaimed divinity to have control over their own lives.

Dalos noticed the shift within Alysse and moved quickly to rid her of her own doubts. 'Don't listen to this traitorous strain. Even her words are poison.'

Cyrus approached the young Princess once more. 'Your Grace, what is to be done with her?'

Alysse remained silent. The words of this serpent rang in her mind. *Too much freedom breeds chaos.*

'If I may suggest,' Mia spoke, 'some time in the cells may loosen her tongue.'

Britt moved her stare to the soft Architect, rolled out said tongue, and clenched it firmly between her teeth.

'Perhaps I just bite it off,' she snickered. 'What then?'

'Then we will have no further need for you,' Alysse finally spoke. 'Uncle, prepare for her execution.'

The threat remained a loose thread in Alysse's mind, meant only to instil fear in the former apprentice. But Britt remained fearless. Alysse waited a moment, giving Britt the chance for a final plea. Nothing. She let out a faint sigh, straightened her posture, then headed for the door.

'I am with child,' Britt called out.

There it is, Alysse thought to herself as she halted. *And a clever plea at that.* The laws that govern this world state that no woman carrying a child may be put to death for their crimes, no matter how vile, until that child has been born into this world.

Dalos and Mia both gawked, confounded by the sudden revelation.

'It's Gorryn's child,' Britt stated, now addressing the two Chief Architects. 'Would you dare deny his lineage?'

'I don't believe you,' Alysse said.

Britt, too, harboured doubts. Her bold assertion would only be verified should her final confrontation with Chief Gorryn have proven triumphant—a plot set in motion too prematurely to discern its outcome yet.

'Then have me examined,' she said, confidently.

Alysse considered the idea; however, it did not sit foremost among her present concerns.

'Even if it were true, the child would be born of your hate. The Gods will curse it for your sins,' she said.

'The Gods?' Britt chuckled. 'You get too entangled with tales, Princess. Gods do not gift or smite. We do. We are in control of our world, not the Gods. The

Faith is simply control. Tell the people that their actions have divine consequences, and they will obey. You have misplaced your faith.'

'And where should I place it?' Alysse spat. 'In you? In The Reclamation?'

'In change,' Britt responded passionately. 'Change, whether gradual or sudden, sparks growth. It sparks progress. Change is inevitable *and* uncertain. But a willingness to embrace its uncertainty will lead you into true paradise.'

Dalos snarled. Mia scoffed. Yet Marcia Iibryn sat silent, her expression hinting at an unwanted respect for this young girl. Alysse, too, felt a conflicting set of thoughts. *She is dangerous, but more valuable to us alive.*

'Guards,' she called out, 'take her to the cells. I want her under constant watch. No one is to engage with her without my direct consent, understood?'

Two of the four guards moved towards the captive. Releasing her bonds, they heaved her up and carried her towards the exit.

Cyrus approached Alysse.

'Your Grace, I will secure her cell,' he said to her.

'No, Uncle,' she responded, a sternness in her tone, 'I need you to find Jaxon. We have had no word from him in days. Nor any report of the rebel's movements. Something isn't right.'

'Your Grace, it is safe to assume…'

'I don't need you to assume!' Alysse shot out. 'I need you to send word, send scouts, send yourself if bloody necessary. Just find him and bring him home.'

The unexpected request intrigued her audience.

'Bring him home?' Dalos questioned. 'Jaxon isn't in

the Capital?'

'No,' Alysse sighed, 'he volunteered himself as escort to your apprentice.'

'But Thio said he was travelling alone,' Mia inserted.

'He said so at my request. I hope you understand. I couldn't risk word spreading of the Prince's absence.'

'Let me send word to the Athenaeums. Surely someone has spotted them,' Dalos said, then turned to his daughter. 'Mia, m'girl, contact every station from here to Latyth.'

'I don't think that wise. This would render him vulnerable,' Cyrus Thenta interjected. 'Who knows what dangers he would face if exposed.'

Frustration built within Dalos as he spoke. 'Then we inquire only of Thio's whereabouts, Gods be good. Either way, we will find them.'

'Good idea,' Alysse said. 'Make no mention of Jaxon.'

Cyrus felt his world begin to crush in on him. It was only a matter of time before all fingers would point to him. *I have to flee,* he thought in a panic.

'Alysse,' Mia said softly as she approached with a warm touch, 'he is a smart boy. Thio will be protecting Jaxon just as heartily as Jaxon will Thio. If something was wrong, they would have found a way of notifying us.'

Her words delivered temporary comfort to the Princess.

'Your Grace,' Cyrus said, 'I *will* locate them.'

A lie.

'Thank you, Uncle.'

With a nod, Cyrus left the room as fast as he could without drawing suspicion. Mia and Dalos followed shortly after, leaving only Alysse and Marcia Iibryn in the lofty Session Hall.

Alysse massaged her forehead to relieve her growing headache. The morning's events had all but drained her to exhaustion. She moved to a suspender chair and slumped into it. Marcia allowed her a moment to regain her thoughts before speaking.

'My dear, what is your next move?'

Alysse looked up at the kind-eyed queen. Her face, softened by the morning light, was marked by a quiet abundance of curiosity. She probed her mind for an answer but found none.

'I am powerless to command the Great Houses until my coronation,' she said. 'We must proceed with the ceremony as quickly as possible.'

'And what of Lex Frailyn?' Marcia asked.

'You know him well,' Alysse said. 'What would you do?'

Marcia stood from her chair and approached the southern window, fixing her gaze upon the Shrine in the bay.

'Mention none of this until you wear the crown,' she began. 'The ceremony concludes at the Shrine of Old. Only you and the monarchs stand upon the island, in the presence of our former rulers, to confirm your ascendancy. That will be your time.'

'My time for what?' Alysse questioned.

'To decide the future of your reign, my dear.'

Alysse pondered Marcia's words deeply. She understood that once on the island, they would be free from outside influence. It would be her chance to expose her adversary in the presence of those with the power to halt their plans.

'Very well,' she concluded.

CHAPTER 30

Thio threaded his way through the assemblage of Qymathorian troops aboard the train. As he returned from the galley with food for his Prince, he couldn't help but ponder as to the lives and experiences of these soldiers. Most were stern-faced, rigid, almost mechanical. But all were silent. What powers compelled them to follow their commands so loyally? To fight another who also swore to follow commands? Their faces had seemingly lost all individuality, instead adopting a hive-minded unity serving a greater power.

He spotted a few peering out at the vast lands outside as the train navigated the tracks at full speed. The rest gazed blankly ahead. In their line of sight, sat at the nose of the train, was Jaxon, his focus locked on the apparatus in his hands.

Reaching the circular table, Thio placed the tray of food next to his Prince while Jaxon remained still, staring at the sonic transmitter's indicator light.

'Anything?' Thio asked.

Jaxon shook his head in silence, pointing to the rapid red-orange pulses of the indicator light. Thio could only speculate that the colour hinted at an error of sorts, that the latest message had failed to be delivered.

'Perhaps we are out of range,' he said, offering the comfort of logic, 'or the Drom Mountains are interfering with the sonics.'

Plausible reasoning, Jaxon thought. Yet it could not sway the dread devouring him.

'Here, you need to eat,' Thio said, sliding the tray closer. 'Judging by the frequency of those rifts, we should be at The Westwall soon.'

Jaxon lifted his gaze to the scenery through the tinted glass walls of the train. The waves of raised and sunken fault blocks created rows of rocky walls that spread out wide, receding kilometres into the continent from the western coast. He recalled the Holy Book describing these gargantuan tracts of land as rips, formed when Kapry pulled the lands of Qymathor towards him, hungering for destruction. Thio, however, having spent some months studying these formations alongside Dalos, had concluded that these rifts were simply a result of the continental lands pulling away from one another over millennia.

Jaxon refocused on his objective of collecting troops from the approaching city.

The Westwall had earned its name from its position and purpose. Situated atop the final band of terrain, it served as a defensive perimeter against adversaries from the west. Its sheer cliff walls rendered landing impossible, enabling the city's defences to assail any opposition from above. The city's infrastructure extended right up to the precipice where it sat, precariously awaiting its inevitable descent into the tumultuous Q'Tenka Sea.

Their stop at The Westwall was brief. Additional carriages were rapidly added to accommodate the transportation of the city's infantry, expanding the train's segments by four lengths. Thio remained onboard, observing the homogeneous motions of the embarking troops. With the added space, a thousand more men and women now traversed south under Jaxon's command. The Prince re-entered the front carriage, his expression bearing the same authoritative air that Thio had observed in Latyth.

'Bryll is next,' Jaxon said. 'They don't have much, but we need every soldier.'

Thio noted confidence in the Prince's delivery.

'What is your plan for the Capital?' he asked.

Jaxon turned to the mass of green and purple within the carriage. Flickers of gold danced across the armour plates of his troops as sunlight broke through the passing tree line.

'We will show our force and make safe the city,' he began, 'then I will have my uncle answer for his crimes.'

Show our force, Thio thought to himself. Who knows how many men Cyrus Thenta had twisted to his will within the Capital. Two hundred at least, ordered to torch the gallant palms along the Path of Peace. *Will there be combat?*

'My prince… I must admit,' Thio began softly, 'my life has been spent buried in books. Should we face combat, I want to be prepared. Will you teach me?'

Jaxon smiled. It was never the place of the Architects' guild to fight in warfare, yet to hear the willingness of one of its members to aid inspired great respect. He moved to a nearby officer and requested his blade. The surrounding soldiers cleared a space in the centre of the wide carriage.

Jaxon handed the sheathed blade to Thio. It was short, no longer than half an arm's length, yet had significant weight to it. Its golden pommel displayed an intricate sigil of House Aprya atop the pale leather cord-wrapped handle. Its straight sandy sheath was tipped by another gold cap with a depiction of the Citadel running up its length. The object felt foreign to Thio.

'First,' Jaxon began, 'your stance. Be sure it is stable.'

Thio shuffled his feet wide, placing one ahead of the other. 'Like this?'

'Good.' Jaxon commended. 'Now, feel the blade in your hand. Think of it not as an independent object, but an extension of your arm. Feel it move with you. Feel its weight. Always know where it is and where it is going.'

Thio closed his eyes and swept the blade through the space around him. He felt its balanced weight shift with every roll of his wrist, tuning into its movements.

'It will also serve as your greatest defence,' Jaxon continued. 'Remember, your body is the weapon. The blade is just a part of it. Move as one.'

The young Prince approached Thio and removed the sheath. The striking warm-silver blade caught the sunlight, its one-sided edge honed to a razor-sharpness.

'Now, attack me.'

'My Prince?' Thio said quizzically.

'Go ahead. Don't hold back,' Jaxon said as he produced his own blade and took his stance.

Thio stood still, eyeing the curious onlookers around him. Nerves grew at the thought of harming the Prince unwittingly. Jaxon's stare was locked on his opponent.

'Attack!' Jaxon exclaimed, then lunged forward.

Thio instinctively raised his arm, blocking the inbound attack with the thick edge of his sword. Jaxon smiled at the wide-eyed apprentice, then spun his body and attacked again. This time, Thio reached up with his other hand and blocked the swinging arm. The two stood interlocked for a moment before Jaxon dropped low and swept his leg, catching Thio off guard and sending him tumbling to the floor.

'You must be aware of every muscle in your body,' Jaxon said as he extended his hand to Thio, hauling him back to his feet.

Thio brushed himself off, embarrassed by the faint smiles of the surrounding soldiers.

'Now, attack me,' Jaxon said again.

Thio regained his composure, adjusted his stance, and took a deep breath. Once focused, he lunged towards the Prince. Jaxon swiftly redirected the approaching blade, causing Thio's body to spin off centre. In a blink, the flat edge of Jaxon's blade was pressed gently against Thio's throat.

'Strike with purpose,' Jaxon said. 'Envision their counter and counter it.'

Thio stepped back, then lunged again, this time jousting at Jaxon's right.

The Prince struck his arm with his bare hand, spun, and wrapped his arm around Thio's neck.

The counter caused Thio to grunt in frustration.

'Yes, get angry,' Jaxon pressed, their faces inches away from one another, 'but don't let it control you. Focus it.'

Jaxon released his grip. Thio turned to face his opponent. The sword in his hand moved with fluidity as he adjusted his posture and repositioned his stance. His mind searched for purpose, a reason to slay an opponent. The thought of taking a life was a dispiriting prospect. *For duty? For the Imperium? No, for love.* His sister's face appeared in his mind's eye.

Thio stared directly into Jaxon's eyes yet looked upon his whole body. His surroundings faded as his focus intensified. *Know their counter and counter it,* he repeated in thought. He executed his moves in his mind. Left. Right. Right again. No, left.

He lunged. His blade passed Jaxon on his left. It was countered. Thio shifted his body and charged right. Countered. He held back for a moment then feigned left. Jaxon veered right to counter but was met by an unexpected shift of Thio's bare hand. The hand forced away the Prince's blade as Thio's honed in on his target. Before Jaxon could counter, he felt the cold sting of steel on his neck.

'I have you!' Thio exclaimed, adrenaline fuelling his outburst.

One side of Jaxon's mouth turned up in a smile.

'I could have you imprisoned for attacking a member of the ruling family,' he said playfully.

Thio released the Prince and eyed the carriage's occupants. Collective nods of commendation moved around the train.

'It seems combat is in you,' Jaxon commended. 'Well done.'

Thio detested the notion. He was not a fighter, yet knowing he possessed the ability to protect by these means brought comfort.

'Ok, again,' Jaxon instructed, taking his stance.

CHAPTER 31

Cyrus clutched his sonic transmitter, awaiting a response. A steady breeze blew in from the towering balcony doors of his quarters. He peered out to the southern ocean in the distance, his mind clouded with vexation.

Hurry, he urged the receiver in his mind, beads of sweat forming on his brow.

As if by prediction, the cube in his hands began to sing.

'You ensured me Jaxon would be dealt with,' the message spoke.

'There was an oversight,' Cyrus responded.

'If you can no longer do your part, I will take alternate measures and you will lose your prize.'

Cyrus could feel the umbrage woven through the melodics, though the tones themselves were simple and void of emotion.

'No need,' he inputted, 'thanks to Britt, we have set

new traps. Jaxon will not make it through the West Passage into Zenithal. Our new crumblers are in place.'

'Be sure he is buried,' the incoming harmonics translated.

'Yes, my liege.'

Across the room, Cyrus' wife, Fayh, entered through the door carelessly left ajar in her husband's hurry. The gentle woman stood there, silent, curious as to the panic in her husband's movements.

Having been married to the Imperial Commander for thirty-four years, Fayh had often seen her husband in these states. She had at times moved to calm him, yet had always feared his volatility. This time, however, she sensed fear in his demeanour, an emotion she had not seen in him since the death of his sister. Remaining unnoticed, she listened in on the exchange.

'Our plan moves ahead,' she translated from the tones. 'My troops will arrive in the Capital on the day of the coronation.'

'And Alysse?' Cyrus inputted.

The question peaked Fayh's curiosity.

'Once she has renounced her seat and named me in her stead, she is yours to do with as you please,' the transmitter rang.

Dread struck the fragile woman, her breaths quickening into soft, shallow pants.

'And the other Houses?' Cyrus questioned.

'They will accept, or suffer the same fate as their Emperor.'

'Understood.'

'In the meantime, my forces draw closer to Latyth. Once there, they will lay waste to the port city.'

The report horrified Fayh. Her legs buckled and she stumbled sideways, knocking a small glass vase from its ledge. She did all that she could to catch it, but failed.

The shatter of glass caught Cyrus' attention, his head whipping around to meet his wife's gaze. Panic flooded her eyes as he advanced. She had no time to exit before his grasp was upon her.

'What did you hear?' he asked forcefully, his grip tightening around her arms.

'Nothing, husband,' she said, attempting to dissuade her aggressor with a fleeting smile.

'Don't lie to me, woman!' he yelled.

'I swear it. I don't even know the language,' Fayh cowered.

'You know the language. But it matters not,' he sneered, his grip tightening as she shrieked in fear.

'Cyrus… please…'

Cyrus shifted a hand from her arm to her neck, steering his wife into the room and towards the open balcony door.

'You useless, barren woman,' he growled. 'Too long have I yearned to rid myself of you. You were never worthy of my name, nor my offspring. That is why the Gods cursed your womb.'

'Guards!' She struggled, her attempt to scream silenced by her husband's constricting grip on her throat.

He edged her out onto the balcony where her gasps for air were muted by the four-hundred-metre-high winds. A sharp pain shot through her back as he thrust her against the balustrade.

'Let us hope the Gods show you mercy,' he whispered as he lifted the thin woman over the edge, then released her. Her screams faded as she plummeted to her death.

Cyrus reentered the room in a hurry, collected a pre-packed rucksack and the transmitter on the table, then moved for the exit. Ensuring the hallways were clear, he made his way to the elevator and summoned it, the short sword hanging from his waist in constant reach.

Below the Citadel, he navigated through the tunnels towards the Imperial holding cells. These cells were reserved for those whose crimes far exceeded the common laws. They were all empty except one— one in which his mistress, subordinate, and next victim occupied.

He placed his rucksack in a dark nook, then rounded a corner, shaking off any visible signs of his rush. At the entrance to the cells were two Imperial Guards standing stoically and armed.

'I am here to question the prisoner,' Cyrus said confidently, approaching the guards. 'Step aside.'

'We cannot, Commander. The Crown Princess herself must...'

'The *Crown Princess* has ordered me to question the prisoner. Step aside,' he said, his tone sharp.

The two guards remained still.

'Your Imperial Commander commands you. Stand aside!'

Cyrus moved to part the two guards but was met

with drawn blades, one of which sat idle at his throat. He knew he would not succeed in a challenge. His age had steered him greatly from the formidable fighter of his youth. He conceded and stepped back, saying nothing, then retreated into the darkness.

CHAPTER 32

'Gods have mercy,' Jaxon whispered as he stood at the front window of the slowing train, Thio by his side.

In the near distance soared the impressive Ton Ranges. From within the wedge of the two great mountain forms, black smoke twisted its way skyward. Licks of blue flame shimmered from small pockets of deformed rubble. The modest buildings that had once snaked up the valley were unrecognisable. In their place sat blistered globs of melted stone, steel, and glass.

Thio fought to hold back his emotions upon seeing the carnage. The once-curious burg was no more, its desolation beyond comprehension. *What kind of flame can melt a city?* he thought.

The train eased to a stop mid-track by the foothills of the wrecked town. Outside, makeshift shelters had been erected from what little could be salvaged after the calamitous inferno. Men, women, and children emerged from their squalid dwellings as the train released a long, echoing chime.

Jaxon moved to the carriage doors that hissed open to welcome the cold air sweeping down from the mountains. Soft rain accompanied the chill, brushing over the Prince's sharp face and Thio's alike. Leaping down from the high stage of the carriage, Jaxon found himself surrounded by a mass of broken souls. Some bowed as he passed. Others glared. More wept. The backdrop of their town stood as a reminder of their horrors. To his right, a burly civilian approached. His attire marked him as an ore miner. The soot upon his face serving as further proof of the fact.

'Your Grace,' he said, standing before his Prince, a sneer twisting his face, 'have you come to explain why my wife and daughter are ash?'

The words were delivered with a brew of animus and pain. The man's eyes swelled with grief.

'Sir, I…'

'How could you let this happen?' a feminine voice called out, halting Jaxon's words. He turned towards the voice but failed to locate its source.

'You have failed us!' another voice cried out.

The sombre surroundings ruptured with rebuke as more and more voices asserted their anger, drowning out the calming rain.

Jaxon became overwhelmed by the barrage of hostility. 'You're right!' he expelled, silencing the crowd. 'We failed you. For that, I will forever feel the deepest regret. I know there is no redress that will replace your loved ones.'

Thio could hear the struggle in Jaxon's voice, a subtle tremor betraying the weight of his burden. He knew the Prince could not have foreseen such an act. It was his uncle, the Imperial Commander, who bore the true blame. Yet, it seemed that Jaxon had unwillingly assumed the mantle of responsibility.

'Who is to blame?' asked a mother holding her infant child.

Before Jaxon could speak, a young man stepped forward. Garbed in a black robe, he wore a golden Fire Orchid pendant that hung proudly around his neck, proclaiming his devotion to the Faith.

'I know who is to blame,' he said with conviction. 'I have read all about the *Blue Flame* in the history books. It was The Architects! They designed it. They were the only ones who knew its craft. It was their weapon against the Faith. And now it's their weapon against us!'

'Preposterous!' an elderly gentleman rang out, his deep blue coat signalling his membership within the Architects' guild. 'That technology is long gone. It can't be replicated.'

'If you conjured it once, you can conjure it again,' the young man of the Faith challenged.

'Our laws forbid the design and creation of weapons. Every member is sworn to this oath,' the guildsman countered. 'Our guild holds our vows above all.'

'If not you, then who?' the young man asked.

'Ask your Gods for answers,' spat the guildsman. 'Where were they in our time of need? Where were they when our families burned?!'

'The Gods do not intervene!'

'Then why do we need them?' Rage exploded from the guildsman.

'Blasphemy!' yelled a voice from within the crowd.

The jeer was swiftly followed by tense discord between the guildspeople and the Faith's devout followers. Chaos erupted.

Thio eyed Jaxon. The turbulence in his eyes grew with every howl from the swarm. Sensing the Prince's dismay, he decided to act. Barging through the brawl, he squeezed his way into the centre of the crowd and projected his voice as loud as he could.

'People! People!' he shouted. 'You have lost enough already! Do not now lose regard for one another. What happened here was evil in its purest form. As the Prince said, no words can bring back the dead. I know you're angry, but now is not the time to fight each other. We should be banding together if we wish to rebuild.'

The crowd grew silent at the young man's words.

Jaxon cast Thio a glance of gratitude for restoring order amidst the unrest. He wove through the crowd and stood by his side.

The guildsman, standing at the forefront, instantly recognised Thio, having observed him wandering the halls of Ton-Basin's Athenaeum over the past months.

'I know you,' he said. 'I saw you and Dalos leaving the city on the eve of the carnage. Do you expect us to believe that was mere chance? Maybe it was part of a deliberate design!'

The guildsman's enquiry stirred something within

Jaxon that he had not anticipated. Never had he thought to question Thio. The allure of the young man had so completely captivated him that he had neglected his duties, failing to assess Thio as an Imperial Commander would. He recalled his uncle's words: *You must not only see what is within your view, but also anticipate what lies beyond your sight.* Despite his growing hatred for his uncle, the words still held weight. For all his life, Jaxon had been warned of his own impulsiveness, and the dangers of acting without proper consideration. *Have I been too hasty in placing trust in this boy?* he wondered. He had always trusted his uncle—idolised him—only for that trust to be shattered in an instant. Who, then, could he truly trust? He turned to Thio and awaited his response.

'Dalos had urgent business in the Capital,' Thio stated. 'That was the reason for our abrupt departure. Nothing more.'

Jaxon knew this to be true. He knew it had been Alysse's impromptu calling of the Qyx-Iriyan that had drawn Dalos, and by extension, Thio, from Ton-Basin. Yet a seed of doubt still lingered.

'There are greater forces at work here,' Thio continued, 'forces that threaten all of Qymathor, if not all of Eviiri. We, the people, must continue to support those who have supported us.'

'He's right,' Jaxon interjected after consideration. 'We are here to help. We have arranged your refuge in Latyth. There, you will be housed and fed, and the injured will receive the care they need. The last carriage over there will transport you. Take only what you need.' He paused, refocusing on his purpose here. 'Please, allow us to do what we can with the time we have now. Once this malice has been dealt with, House Aprya will see to it that your homes and livelihoods are restored. That, I promise you.'

He stepped forward towards the enraged crowd.

'Forgive our failures, if you can. Our hearts bleed alongside yours. House Aprya will honour the fallen in accordance with the traditions of our Faith. I ask that you hold fast to your own. Believe that Qymathor will regain its footing—and that we shall prosper once more.'

'Thank you, Your Grace,' an elderly woman said, reaching for the Prince's hand.

Jaxon acknowledged the frail woman's gratitude with a smile. Noticing her limp, he summoned a nearby soldier to assist her to the far carriage. Others followed, collecting what little they had, and boarded the section of train. Soon after, the entire mass of refugees were aboard their iron and glass salvation.

Exhausted, Jaxon made for the front carriage, saying nothing to Thio as he passed.

The coldness of Jaxon's manner struck Thio as odd. *Did I overstep?* he wondered, already beginning to punish himself. He anxiously followed the Prince aboard the train.

Thio observed Jaxon move to the front table within the carriage and begin tidying the scattered papers and maps, seemingly reshuffling them into no particular order. An hour had passed and the Prince had not once met Thio's gaze since the turmoil outside had subsided. Thio approached with caution and spoke hesitantly.

'Is everything okay, My Prince?' he asked.

'Fine, all things considered,' Jaxon responded sharply. 'We must press on.'

'My Prince...'

'Stop calling me...' Jaxon halted, uncertain whether his anger was justly aimed at the person before him. He wished to question Thio in that very moment, yet feared hearing anything that might alter his feelings toward the one he had come to care for. He sought desperately not to water the seed of doubt that threatened to take root in his mind.

Thio dropped his head, his earlier doubts of ever measuring up to one as esteemed as Jaxon Aprya resurfacing in an instant. He remained silent and began heading towards the rear of the carriage.

'I'm sorry,' Jaxon called out. 'Nothing is as it should be. I find myself at odds with...'

Suddenly, the sonic transmitter atop the table began to resonate.

'Alysse?!' Jaxon exclaimed, thrusting himself towards the emanating tones. He forced his attention onto the song, struggling to interpret its meaning with any speed.

'This is... we... respond...'

At its first sounding, those were the only words he could grasp.

'What does it say?' Thio pressed.

Jaxon raised a hand to quiet the inquisitive apprentice, sharpening his focus further on the tones. Bit by bit, word by word, the message became clear.

This is Chief Mia Okombuur. We are urgently searching

for Thio, apprentice to Dalos. Respond if you know of his whereabouts, Jaxon spoke the message in his mind.

'It's Mia,' he said aloud.

'Is she okay?' Thio asked. 'What about Alysse? And Dalos?'

Jaxon recited the message to himself again. It was impossible to grasp the sender's nuance, as though it were silent words on a page. Much like a written letter, its meaning could be shaped by the reader's own state of mind, often leading to misinterpretation. In his haste, Jaxon felt the seed of doubt take root, rashly concluding that those within the Capital had uncovered Thio's possible involvement and were striving to apprehend him. He paused, weighing his thoughts, then spoke.

'They're looking for us,' he said, intentionally omitting the mention of only Thio. With caution in mind, he ushered the young apprentice to the table. 'Come, help me respond.'

CHAPTER 33

The petite seamstress wove fine silk threads through the hem of Alysse's long gown. Phthalo green fabric encrusted with jewels snaked up the form-fitting silhouette of the slender Princess. Beige detailing shaped her bodice with geometric patterns. Low-hanging, deep sleeves weighed down her arms as she stood rigid atop a short podium that had been placed in her room. This final dress fitting served as a reminder of her approaching ascendancy as Empress and the dawn of a new epoch in Eviiri.

Queen Marcia Iibryn paced the bed chambers, admiring the Crown Princess's fineries. A music box filled the room with a soft, calming tune atop the silence, while two armed Imperial guards stood rigid by the door. Marcia strode past a dressmaking mannequin in the corner of the room, its simple hourglass form catching her eye and twisting her head as she traced its lines.

Arriving before an ornate dresser, the visiting queen noticed Alysse's pendant. Its fine etchings displayed flawless precision to the eye.

'What a gorgeous pendant,' Marcia said, lifting the golden drop and turning it gently between her fingers. 'Impeccable craftsmanship.'

'It was handed down to me by my father,' Alysse said, 'and his father handed it to him. Its provenance can be traced back to Emperor Jannon the First, who had it made for his son.'

'Marq?' Marcia asked.

'No, his first son, Jarrys.'

'Ah, the Lost Prince,' Marcia recalled. 'Such a tragic accident.'

'It was no accident,' Alysse asserted. 'His life wasn't lost; it was taken.'

'My apologies, Your Grace. I'm afraid the early histories of your House have been lost to my aging mind.'

Alysse offered a simple smile. The true events of the young Prince's death were not widely known in the present day. The truth had quickly turned to rumour, and rumour to forgotten memory.

'But the recent histories are still very much there,' Marcia said, moving towards the hung portrait of Jannon III. The lifelike details of the painting captured the essence of the gentle ruler. His soft eyes peered directly at his admirer.

'I knew your father since he was a boy,' Marcia said. 'Even then, he was as kind as they come. I'm sure you know... well, perhaps you don't.'

'Know what?' Alysse asked, turning with curiosity.

'There were plans for our betrothal,' Marcia said with a raised eyebrow.

'You and my father?' Alysse said, intrigued by the account.

Marcia nodded and chuckled quietly to herself.

'I remember his 16th birthday. It was an extravagant affair,' Marcia recalled. 'My father spent an outrageous sum on my gown. Fabric upon fabric. Jewels between jewels. I looked like a fool. It was around that time your father was to choose his bride.'

Alysse giggled. 'Do you think your gown swayed his choice?'

'Oh, my dear, I stood no chance,' Marcia said playfully. 'My House was accompanied by another noble family—one with a daughter more beautiful than a tender sunset.'

Alysse stood motionless, her gaze fixed on the old woman, curiosity piqued as Marcia slowly raised a hand and pointed to the portrait hung opposite the late Emperor's.

'Palymma Thenta,' she said with admiration, 'your mother. What a vision she was. A true beauty, inside and out. She was a perfect choice for him. Gentle, sweet, compassionate. She was my closest friend in Aankathor, you know.'

'You and my mother were friends?' Alysse pried with a smile of surprise.

'Oh yes, I loved her dearly,' Marcia said, walking over to the portrait. 'Despite our differences in age, she was mature. She always knew how to put things into perspective. I was to be Queen of Aankathor. My life was charted out for me, as you well know. But your mother saw me for me, irrespective of status or title.'

'I didn't know this,' Alysse said, a growing warmth rising within her.

'Mm, and I knew the moment she laid eyes on your father, she would seek no other. He was, after all, cruelly handsome.'

Alysse smiled tenderly, recalling the love her parents exuded towards one another.

Marcia moved to Alysse and stood before her. She reached up and adjusted a ringlet of hair that had dropped in front of the young Princess's face.

'I see her in you, very much so. Especially here.' Marcia reached up to place a gentle hand over Alysse's heart. The words and touch conjured a swell of emotion.

'I miss her,' Alysse said softly.

'Me too.' Marcia said. 'When she left Aankathor, I was beside myself. I not only felt alone, I feared for her. What paths would she tread in this foreign land? Who would turn sour towards her, now that she sat so high in this tower? But I took comfort in knowing her brother was by her side.'

'Uncle Cyrus?'

'His love for her was boundless,' Marcia continued, 'borderline obsessive, now that I think about it. Anyway, no person would have dared make any attempt on his sister while Cyrus Thenta was present. Your father respected that greatly.'

'I guess that's why he named him Imperial Commander,' Alysse said, then sighed. 'Yet it wasn't a person that claimed her life.'

'You're right,' Marcia agreed. 'The Dusk bled through the realm like ink across parchment, staining all it touched. I couldn't begin to count the lives lost in my very own country, let alone the world. When news arrived that your mother and brother had succumbed to its grasp, I prayed steadily for three days. It was by the Gods' will that you and your father were spared. The outcome could have been catastrophic for your House.'

Alysse recalled the panic-driven chaos that had ensued once word had reached her father. Their visit to the White Isles for diplomatic talks had been quickly dissolved as they made rushed plans to return to the Capital.

'Then word came of this *cure* that had delivered your brother from peril,' Marcia continued. 'The world could breathe again.'

'But it was too late for her,' Alysse said, defeat in her tone.

'Yes, it was too late for her.'

A ruckus at the door commanded both Alysse and Marcia's attention. Beyond, Mia Okombuur pleaded with the guards for entry.

'Alysse!' she called out through the barricade of bodies.

'Mia?' Alysse motioned to the guards to allow her to pass.

She entered. Following closely behind her was Dalos atop his suspender chair.

'Alysse, thank the Gods. Where is your uncle?' she managed through her panic.

'My uncle? He's... what's going on?' Alysse said,

suddenly stricken with concern.

'We received word from Jaxon,' Dalos spoke, an unusual rasp enveloping his words.

Alysse struggled with her emotions. Elation? Dread? Confusion?

'Where is he?' she exclaimed. 'Is he okay?'

'He's fine, Your Grace, but you may not be,' Mia said.

'What are you saying, girl?' Marcia whipped. 'Spit it out.'

Mia approached the Princess, revelation flashing in her eyes through her bronze-framed spectacles.

'It makes sense now,' she began. 'When we returned from the Sanctuary, I spotted this by the entrance.'

She reached into a pocket in her trousers and produced a small etched disk, two golden-crown wrens still distinct on its twisted face.

'Jaxon tried to send a message to you, and only you,' she said, handing the disk to Alysse.

Alysse inspected the warped object, the drawings familiar in her mind.

'This is from my transmitter,' she said, scanning the room for the now-missing box.

'It seems the message fell upon ears it was not intended for,' Dalos stated, his rasp producing a spluttering cough.

'What message?' Alysse said, wide-eyed.

Mia leaned in close to the Princess and spoke at a low volume.

'Cyrus is Reclamation.'

The words shattered her composure, slicing

through her like glass. She played the recent events back in her mind, outlining their connections. At the centre of them all was the face of her uncle, Cyrus Thenta. She stumbled, almost falling from the podium. Catching herself, she met Dalos' gaze, his eyes projecting a fear uncharacteristic of his persona.

'M'girl, there's more,' he managed through a deep sigh. 'Just now, a body was found at the base of the tower, cloaked in purple silk. We believe it to be your aunt.'

Alysse felt numb.

'Aunt Fayh...' she whispered. The room around her began to spin. The faces of Mia, Dalos, and Marcia warped before her waking eyes. A mind-splitting ring reverberated through her senses as she wrestled with the news. The only thing clear to her was her uncle's face. She fought to reclaim her clarity, then found her voice.

'Guards, find my uncle,' she asserted, moving towards her bed and slumping down atop it. She took a series of deep breaths to calm herself. Despite the unsought revelation, positive news prevailed as she remembered who delivered this message.

'Where is Jaxon?' she asked.

'He is on his way back to the Capital, with Thio and an army of three thousand,' Mia stated. 'They should arrive by nightfall.'

'Good.'

'Alysse,' Dalos spoke, short of breath, 'your coronation is the day after next. May I suggest you postpone?'

'I don't think that wise, Your Grace,' Marcia Iibryn

interjected. 'Remember, your uncle holds the realm until you are crowned.'

Alysse weighed both options.

'No army or civilian will support his authority once word of his treason spreads.' She paused. 'But you're right, Queen Marcia, the coronation must continue as planned.'

Dalos shifted in his chair, rubbing a hand over his chest and wincing in pain. He erupted into violent coughs. Alysse and Mia both turned their attention to the ailing man.

'Pa? What is it?' Mia asked, crouching beside her father.

Through his splutter, Dalos managed a few quiet words. 'Not here. Not now,' he whispered to her, fighting his body's urge to convulse.

'Dalos?' Alysse said, inching closer to the trembling man.

'I'm fine, m'girl. Don't...' Another bout of coughs severed his words. He lifted his pocket cloth over his mouth and expelled his agony into it. Traces of blood soaked through the thin fabric, exposing themselves to his concerned onlookers. He grasped at his chest again.

'Pa?!' Mia exclaimed, shoving his arm aside. She tore at his shirt to reveal festering fingers of deep blue and purple veins radiating from his knife wound.

'By the Gods...' she expelled.

Alysse looked down in horror at the threads of rotting flesh.

'What is happening?' she asked.

'The blade was poisoned,' Mia concluded, a well of

fear in her tone.

'What can be done? Call the physicians!' Alysse panicked.

'No!' Dalos ruptured. 'Both of you, listen to me. Your efforts will be for naught. These kinds of poisons have no remedy.'

'Do not say such things,' Alysse forced herself to say, tears threatening to fall. 'Perhaps Thio can…'

'Alysse, please,' Dalos pleaded. 'I will not be a burden to any of you, not anymore.'

'Then what?' Alysse questioned. 'We stand idle while you die?'

'Yes,' Dalos said calmly.

The response silenced the room.

'You cannot mean that,' Mia said, her voice breaking.

'I can, and I do.' Dalos took a wheezing breath. 'I am no longer able to protect you—any of you. And I will not have your time wasted on me. Seek a remedy for the matters at hand. I will continue to do what I can, while I can.'

'I will not allow it,' Alysse muttered through the flow of tears now cascading down her face.

'I'm afraid that is out of your control, m'girl,' Dalos said softly, smiling in an attempt to calm the Princess.

Mia held her father's hand. She too knew of such poisons without a cure. The thought of losing her father, of being left without family in this world, threatened every pillar of strength holding her up. Yet she knew there was nothing that could be done, only to ease his inevitable passing. She knew his fate in that moment, stood, and wiped the tears from her face.

'Come, Pa, let me take you home.'

CHAPTER 34

The entire train sat in silence. Nothing but the transmitter's songs carried through the stale air.

Thio gripped the wooden cube in his hands, awaiting further input commands, his damp fingers coating the marble buttons in a thin glaze of sweat. He focused solely on Jaxon as the Prince mouthed the message hidden within the emanating tones. Having spent most of the day conversing with Mia through this songwriting contraption on Jaxon's behalf, Thio had begun to understand the principles of the melodic-based language. Each phonetic sound was assigned a note, and the combinations of those phonetics, when played in harmony, produced complete words within a single chord. A short dance of melody could convey full and lengthy sentences, yet sound audibly brief to any naïve listener. Using this understanding, Thio had begun to construct fleeting words amidst the array of sounds—not enough, however, to fully grasp their meaning.

Jaxon observed Thio input his last message, then noticed the indicator light flicker and fade. The circular table at the front of the train lay buried beneath a sprawl of scores, some inked with precision, others hastily marked. The familiar hum of the train's resonators became prominent once again as it snaked through the Besti-Qa farming plains on approach to the Capital. In the silence, Jaxon drew a long breath, a faint shimmer veiling in his eyes.

'What did she say?' Thio asked.

Jaxon considered his response. Certain details from Mia's report had only deepened the suspicions stirring within him. He paused a moment longer, then opted instead to pose a question of his own.

'Do you know Britt Pensyr?' he asked.

'Chief Gorryn's apprentice?' Thio responded, a furrowed brow creasing his face.

'So you know her?'

'Well… yes. I met her not long after arriving in the Capital. Why?'

Jaxon frowned, turning his gaze away from his newly found companion.

'Why, Jaxon?' Thio pressed.

'She's been doing my uncle's bidding,' he began, a temper rising in his voice. 'She killed Chief Gorryn.'

'What?!'

'My Aunt Fayh,' Jaxon continued through the lump in his throat, 'was found dead at the base of the tower —thrown from her balcony.'

'Jaxon… I…'

'How well did you know this apprentice?' the

Prince interrupted.

'Not well at all,' Thio replied confidently. 'I met her once, the day Alysse summoned me to the Citadel. She showed me around the geology sector. She seemed quite interested in me and my work, but that's all. Any regard for her was lost after she stole my...'

Thio suddenly whipped his head up with a look of dread, and stared at the approaching Drom Mountains. He traced the rail lines to the opening at its base, his mind considering the possibility that Britt Pensyr had used his research to harness its destructive capabilities. He recalled Dalos' description of the Western Passage: *Sturdy and true, not even the Gods could buckle them.* But the Gods had not intended for man to destabilise mountain salt. He leapt up from his seat and swiftly moved to the hidden control unit at the train's nose.

'What are you doing?' Jaxon exclaimed.

'We need to stop the train!' Thio yelled, frantically trying to unlatch the control unit.

'Stop!' Jaxon returned, rushing towards the panicked apprentice. With all his might, he clutched at Thio's tunic and heaved him backwards.

Thio skidded across the floor of the train, landing at the feet of the troops now standing in defence of their Prince. As if unfazed by their mighty presence, Thio persisted in his attempts to gain access to the controls. Regaining his footing, he hurled himself forward. Before he could take another step, Jaxon unsheathed his golden short sword, darted around the charging boy, and secured him in a standing headlock, pressing the blade to his throat.

'One more step, and it'll be your last!' Jaxon roared.

The entire cabin's staunch occupants drew their swords and pointed them towards Thio, a communal grunt echoing through the carriage.

'You need to listen to me!' Thio pleaded, seeing the entrance fast approaching. 'She's going to collapse the Passage!'

'That's impossible,' Jaxon retorted, 'there is no force that can bring down these tunnels.'

'There is now!'

Jaxon caught the panic notes in Thio's voice. He knew not of any tool or weapon that could crumble such a fortified structure, yet a part of him wanted to believe the apprentice. Though his mind brimmed with fresh suspicions, his heart yearned for things to return as they once were. He looked down at his captive, then up at the fast-approaching black hole. Their surroundings were stripped of light in an instant as the train pierced the tunnel's entrance. Ahead was pure darkness.

'Please, Jaxon,' Thio appealed, pressing his weight against the Prince, as if it were a tender embrace.

Jaxon felt the weight of Thio's body in his grip, torn between the urge to trust him and the growing doubt gnawing at his heart. Love and logic clashed within him, leaving him unsure of how to act. *Stopping the train now would prove futile,* he thought, *we're already in the tunnel.* In that moment, he relaxed his grip on the young apprentice and turned his gaze to the control unit.

Thio staggered to the floor as Jaxon's body slipped

out from behind him. He watched as the Prince un-latched the control panel and dialled in his com-mands. Bracing himself for the sudden deceleration, Thio gripped the secured table. Yet, instead of slow-ing, he was forcefully thrown back as the train accel-erated with startling intensity.

The standing soldiers toppled backwards in unison. A deep rumble surged as the train's res-onators outputted maximum acoustic thrust. The lightless exterior offered no reference to the accelerat-ing speed of the fourteen-carriage serpent.

Thio struggled to his feet, battling the forces pulling him backward. He trudged towards the glass nose of the train until he stood by Jaxon's side. He scanned the darkness for any points of light—those that might reveal the steady glow of a new and more powerful crumbler.

In the far distance, Jaxon spotted light, light he had seen many times—the end of the Passage. He drew his first breath since throttling the engines, more eager than ever to escape the mountain pass. Turning back to his troops, he surveyed the full stretch of the train—fourteen carriages trailing endlessly into the tunnel's dark maw. Some three thousand men and women stared back at him.

As the tunnel's exit drew nearer, Thio began to discern the rocky walls in the growing light, and was now able to observe the true speed of the train. His eyes strained to catch any detail as the cavernous interior rushed by. He focused on the opening rapidly approaching. It was then that he saw it. Attached to either side of the tunnel walls were sizeable contraptions—flat panels and twisted piping encased glowing red orbs.

'Jaxon! Get down!'

—

From his vantage point atop the roof of a commonplace city dwelling, Cyrus Thenta peered across the Bay of Zenithal towards the Western Passage. The tiny black dot marking the tunnel's entrance was near invisible from this distance, discernible only by the line of tracks exiting from it. He waited patiently, alone, a remote detonator clenched in his hands. He peered down at his wristwatch and began counting down in his head. *Ten. Nine. Eight.* He returned his gaze to the mountain. *Seven. Six.*

To his surprise, the train's front carriage suddenly shot out from the tunnel's exit. In a panic, he slammed the detonation button on the remote. A heartbeat later, a blinding white light erupted from the Passage. He stood and watched the growing length of the train spit out over the water. Two carriages. Three. Four. A thick plume of black smoke followed closely after. Large chunks of mountain rock soared high over the turquoise waters. Five carriages. Six. Then nothing more.

'Fuck!' he grunted.

Readying his escape, Cyrus pulled a large hood over his head and exited the dwelling. Stepping out onto the lively street of the Capital's south-western island, he kept his head low as he navigated to the outer rim of the quay wall. Ahead of him was a small dock with three fingers of stone piers that jutted out over the bay. Resting by one of the fingers was a water cruiser, unmarked and empty. He heaved his rucksack onto its flat deck and climbed onboard. Engaging the vessel's power, Cyrus pulled away from the dock, turned south towards the vast sea, then ignited the throttle.

—

Having thrown himself over the Prince, Thio struggled to shield Jaxon from the forceful turbulence of the blast. Both men were hurled across the carriage floor, along with many of the surrounding troops.

Jaxon peered up to see sunlight, the glorious Capital capturing its rays. He wondered if he was alive, turning to his human shield for confirmation. Regaining his orientation, he took Thio's hand and was heaved up off the floor. The view of his home overwhelmed him. The two men stood in silence for a moment, relieved to be alive. It wasn't until Jaxon turned his gaze towards the rear end of the train that he saw the true extent of the carnage.

Where fourteen carriages had once trailed, only six remained. Jaxon's shoulders slumped as he moved down the train, the thought of thousands of trapped or fallen troops within the Passage pressing heavily upon him.

'Are you hurt, My Prince?' Thio asked, noting the young man's limp.

Jaxon said nothing, halting halfway down the carriage to assist a wounded soldier. Though the fog clouding his thoughts, his mind still churned—suspicions resurfacing, rage mounting with every step.

'Explain it to me,' he finally spoke, a sharpness in his voice.

'My Prince?' Thio said quizzically, sensing contempt.

'How did you know about the tunnel?'

'I…' The question threw him.

'How did your technology find its way into the Passage?' Jaxon demanded.

Thio felt instantly responsible. He had seen only the potential for energy, and had been blind to its other capabilities. What had he really created?

'It was Britt,' he said. 'She read my notes. She stole my salt. How was I to know she would turn it into a weapon? Upon our acceptance into the guild, we swear an oath never to create with the intent to harm. Dalos stood at the very forefront of that vow, holding each of us to its words. I would never betray it—I would never betray him!'

Jaxon sneered, the weight of the fallen soldiers pressing heavily upon his young shoulders. He looked at Thio, struggling to reconcile the grim facts with the innocence written across his face.

'Once we are back,' Jaxon began, 'I think it best you return to the Athenaeum immediately. I will confer with Dalos and insist he put an end to this research.'

'Jaxon…'

'That will be all, Thio,' Jaxon said sternly.

Thio took a step back, his defeat expressed in the curl of his shoulders. He shifted to draw the gaze of his Prince, but the gaze was not returned. Accepting the silent command, Thio made his way down the carriage.

Jaxon watched the young man pass into the next section of the train, where soldiers still reeled from the havoc they had just endured. Despite Thio's clear deflation, he began assisting them.

—

Alysse stood at the entrance to the Citadel grounds, the Path of Peace stretching out across the city before her. The distant Sanctuary of Qyma shone bright in the late afternoon sun. Surging down the path was a sea of green and purple, her brother leading the wave of troops.

Horns sounded from the mass of warriors echoed across the rigid structures of the city. The blasts were shadowed by the rupture of the four Citadel horns, beckoning the arrival of this military force.

The march felt never-ending to Alysse, who waited with anticipation. The excitement and relief of seeing her brother were written in the tearful smile on her face. As the brigade reached the entrance, Alysse wasted no time. Breaking formality, she took flight, sprinting at full speed and plowing into the arms of her brother.

Mia watched on from the wings of the ramped walkway, delighted at their reunion. To the left of the great mass, she spotted a solitary figure, disconnected from the rest. His common garbs and short buzz cut were instantly recognisable to her. She approached him, noting a sunkenness in his stance before wrapping her arms around him.

'Welcome back, my boy,' she whispered to Thio, squeezing him tight.

'I'm glad to see you, Mia,' he responded, a flatness in his tone.

'What's wrong?' she asked with concern, releasing her grip and studying the young apprentice's face. 'Thio? Your sister?'

She scanned the surrounding figures. A pit grew as she suspected the worst.

'She's fine,' he assured. 'She chose to stay in Latyth.'

'Thank the Gods she's alright. How are you doing?'

'I'm fine. I...' Thio paused, peering over Mia's shoulder, searching for his mentor. The round man was nowhere to be seen. He focused back on Mia then spoke.

'Where is Dalos?'

CHAPTER 35

The warm glow of the wall-lamps kept the deep blue ambience of the evening at bay as Dalos struggled to sip his cup of tea. He peered around his chambers at the collection of memories that filled the shelves. A vast painting of the White Isles hung on the western wall. A small-scale wooden explorer vessel sat atop a chest at the foot of his bed. The portrait of his wife, Myra, stared lovingly at him from across the room.

He pictured the iron safe nestled behind that wall and the vials of Fire Orchid essence that had once sat securely within. He recalled the sound of the last vial shattering on the floor—the vial that could have been his saviour now.

The torturous throb in his chest had grown worse throughout the day as his mind flowed in and out of clarity. His efforts to shift his body had become cumbersome, and his desire to eat had all but vanished. But not his tea—his treasured tea. Propped up in his bed, he took a sip then recited a passage from The Unsettled Sea.

'Come, creature—take my fear. Take it all. I have no use for it. The sea is yours, and the land is mine. Let us share them. Do you not see? You yearn for my land, but you cannot walk. I yearn for your sea, but I cannot swim. So here—take it. Take it all.'

His eyes grew heavy. Awareness slipped in and out, consuming him in waves, until a gentle voice parted the fog and returned him to the now.

'Sir?'

Dalos recognised the voice yet could not place its maker.

'Who's that?' he said, letting his head drop sideways.

A slender figure approached slowly. A streak of reflected lamp-light glinted across a pair of spectacles. A sandy-coloured buzz cut slipped into the light. It was Thio.

'Ah, m'boy!' Dalos said excitedly, fighting against every ache.

Trailing Thio was Mia. She stood to the side as Thio arrived beside his mentor and peered down at the bed-stricken man. Slender purple veins coursed up the folds in his neck before disappearing under his silver beard. His eyes sat deeper than usual, framed by dark pockets of bulging skin. Thio would not have recognised him if it weren't for the cheerful grin stretched across his face.

'I'm here, sir,' he said before hurling his arms around the fragile man.

Dalos ignored the pain for the sake of the embrace.

'I'm so glad to see you, m'boy,' he said as his eyes filled with tears of his own. 'You look well.'

'You don't,' Thio said playfully as he pulled back from the hug and studied his mentor again.

'What do you mean? I've never looked better,' Dalos joked.

Thio let out a short laugh as he wiped a tear from his face.

'What happened, sir?'

'Ah, a careless snakebite,' Dalos said.

'Don't we have antidotes for that?' Thio said, playing along with the lie.

'Not for this kind of snake, m'boy,' Dalos said with a sweet smile.

'Sir…'

Dalos moved to shift the conversation. 'Anyway, Y'mara, how is she?'

'She's safe,' Thio said, 'and with child.'

'Gods be good! How wonderful.'

The cheer in the old man's voice had almost fooled his onlookers as Mia and Thio smiled along with him.

'Sir…' Thio began, hesitant to turn the mood of his mentor, 'my research… it's been used as a weapon. I failed you, I'm sorry.'

'Listen to me, m'boy.' Dalos heaved a hand to cover Thio's. 'What that girl has done is inexcusable and she will face the Gods' judgement when her time comes. But you, brilliant Thio, you will steer this world towards a brighter future. You have the right heart for it. I have never doubted you, not once. There is greatness in you, m'boy.'

Thio appreciated the words but could not rid his

mind of the disappointment he had seen growing in Jaxon's eyes.

'I fear the Prince disagrees,' he said sombrely.

'Jaxon is still growing into his role,' Mia interjected. 'With everything that has happened, his caution is warranted. Be patient with him. He will come to see you as the asset you are to him, and to Eviiri.'

'How can you all see what I cannot?' Thio asked, dropping his head.

'M'boy,' Dalos said as he squeezed his hand, 'you have forever doubted yourself. It's time to put those doubts to rest. Grab the opportunities presented to you and fly.'

'But...'

'No buts!' Dalos exclaimed, setting off a bout of rumbling coughs. 'By the Gods, I ought to shake some sense into you.'

'I'd like to see you try,' Thio joked.

'Cheeky shit,' Dalos said, his laugh swiftly interrupted by a wince of pain.

Thio feigned a smile, but the tears forming in his eyes spoke of his true emotions. He grasped Dalos' hand, then spoke his truth.

'I want to thank you, sir, for everything,' he said, his words trembling through his quivering lips.

'No, m'boy, it is I who want to thank you,' Dalos returned. 'You are an exultant vision into my past. Seeing you discover the wonders of this world has brought me joy beyond measure. I'm only sorry that I won't get to see you truly flourish in it.'

'What will happen to me?' Thio asked through his tears.

'Your work will continue,' Dalos said strongly. 'There will come a day when you will stand in my stead as Chief Architect. I believe that for you. I just need you to believe it too.'

Thio wiped his face. 'I will try, sir.'

Mia approached Thio and placed a hand on his shoulder.

'You will have me to guide you,' she said. 'I will mentor you—show you the ropes. That doesn't sound too bad, does it?'

'Not at all.' Thio smiled up at her. 'It would be my honour.'

'See! It's settled. You don't need me. I would only slow you down,' Dalos chuckled.

The three sat in silence, each laying a tender hand on the other. Dalos' wheezing breaths grew louder in the stillness before the sound of footsteps became apparent from the adjoining hallway. Through the bedroom door, Jaxon and Alysse strode into the room.

'Dalos?' the Prince said, approaching the dying man.

'Jaxon, m'boy!'

'How are you feeling?' Alysse asked in a soft voice.

'Ready for my next adventure,' Dalos said with calmness. 'Thank you for coming. I know you have much to deal with, so I will keep this brief.'

'Keep what brief?' Jaxon asked.

'Mia, m'girl, the portrait of your mother,' Dalos said, lifting a sluggish finger towards the painting.

Mia turned a confused look at her father.

'Behind it is a safe,' he continued.

Mia shot a puzzled look at the wall before walking over to the portrait. She examined the section of wall on which it hung and noted a fine seam between the carved wooden details. With both hands, she grasped the framework and pulled. The section of wall clicked, then swung open to reveal a large black-iron box. She studied the metal ornaments encrusted around its surface. A seascape spectacle danced around each face of the robust cube. It was a setting she instantly recognised.

'Do you remember my favourite scene from your mother's book?' Dalos asked.

'I do.'

'Follow the wind, tend to the sea,' Dalos instructed.

Mia placed hesitant hands upon the box. She traced her fingers along the flows of clouds with one hand and gently caressed the wild sea with her other. Each flick of wave and curl of cloud clicked as her touch circled the box. Arriving back at the front-facing side, she pressed the small boat with one thumb. Opposing the boat was a fantastical sea creature. Following the same motion, she pressed it with her other. The box hissed then cracked open.

Within the deep hollow of metal was an empty oak vial-rack. Taking up most of the space at its rear was an accumulation of journals.

'Second pile. Third from the top,' Dalos said. 'Hand it to Alysse.'

Mia collected the precise book and passed it to her Princess.

'What are these?' Alysse asked, studying the leather-bound collection of pages.

'These are your father's journals. They date all the way back to his childhood,' Dalos stated.

Alysse felt an overwhelming connection to her father in that moment. Despite his physical absence, his memory lived on within these pages. She fanned through it, taking account of the childlike disorder of the handwriting. Spotting a name, she stopped and read the entry aloud.

Today I met a boy named Dalos. He is a student at the Athenaeum. He is quite odd. I could swear his eyes were orange. We played in the gardens, and he taught me about all the different flowers that grew there. He is very smart.

The room smiled in unison as Alysse turned a few pages.

Dalos came to visit today. He brought me a gift from the Athenaeum. It was a strange tool that used sound to carve stone. We wrote our names on one of the planters in the garden. I hope Father doesn't find out.

Mia chuckled, throwing a playful side-eye towards her father. Alysse read on.

Today is Dalos' birthday. Father has allowed me the after-noon to celebrate with him.

What a day! We took a rowboat across the bay to the Shrine. Dalos had never seen it. I had to do most of the rowing, though. He is still so small. Since knowing him, I have grown at least half a head taller, yet he appears un-

*changed, as though time passed him by.
I think he had fun, although he did wander off alone to look
at the altars. I think he was crying.*

Thio studied the room's occupants. Smiles softened by dewy eyes marked each of their faces. Alysse advanced a few pages then continued.

*I hoped to play with Dalos today, but Father told me he is
quite ill. Reverend Kalax is tending to him. I pray he will
be okay.*

Dalos motioned to Mia, pointing at the safe. 'That one, second from the top.'

Mia picked up the journal and exchanged it with Alysse. She opened it to the marked page and began to read.

*Tomorrow is my 16th birthday. Father has arranged a
party. Many will attend. He says that House Frailyn,
House Iibryn, and House Thenta are attending. He said I
am to marry Marcia Iibryn, but I hear Lord Brata Thenta's
daughter is quite beautiful. I wonder if she will like me.*

Alysse smiled at the account, for this was the day her father and mother had met.

*I had a great birthday. It is true, Palymma Thenta's beauty
is unmatched. I know I am promised to Marcia, but I cannot rid Lady Palymma from my mind. We all played a
game of hide-and-seek. Palymma slipped out of a tree and
grazed her knee. Her brother Cyrus was quick to her aid. It*

is clear he cares for her greatly. I can foresee a strong friendship with him.

The utterance of his uncle's name ignited an instant rage within Jaxon. He fought to control it as Alysse shuffled through more pages.

Dalos just announced he has been chosen as Chief Hyllan's apprentice. I am so proud of my dear friend. The title is well deserved. His knowledge and wisdom seem to stretch far beyond his years.

'Now the top one. Read the last page,' Dalos said, his voice cracking through a series of coughs.

Alysse turned the journal and opened the last page. The handwriting was clean and formal. In the top corner was a date that drew the blood from her face.

'This is from the day of his death,' she said, her heart racing.

Dalos gave a soft nod, encouraging her to read on.

I fear this may be my last entry. I received a letter a short while ago. I am unsure of its origin, but it would seem my departure from this world is nearing.

Jarrys, I speak directly to you now. You must protect Alysse and Jaxon. They are your blood as much as they are mine. I thank you, old friend, for everything. Your sacrifice can never be repaid.

Thio turned a quizzical gaze on Dalos.

'Jarrys? Who is Jarrys?' he asked.

'Jarrys was the name of Emperor Jannon's firstborn

son,' Alysse stated.

'Why would he be addressing the Lost Prince?' Jaxon enquired. 'He was killed 200 years ago, was he not?'

'He was not,' Dalos spoke softly.

Alysse shot the old man a look of confusion.

'Dalos, what are you saying?' she asked.

The afflicted Architect expelled a soft sigh, then spoke.

'I have gone by many names in my time. Arlo… Rixyn… Dalos… but my first… my very first name was Jarrys Aprya.'

Alysse lost her grip on the journal in her hand and let it fall to the ground.

'Alysse,' Dalos said, staring directly at the Princess, 'it is time you learn of the truce between the Faith and the Imperium.'

Jaxon took a step forward and stood by his sister's side, eager to hear what was about to be told.

'To end the Thousand Year War,' he began, 'the High Priests requisitioned the Emperor's firstborn son as reparation for his crimes against the Gods. That son, as it happens, was me.'

The room was completely silent. Mia moved to her father and placed a comforting hand on his shoulder. She had learnt this truth some days prior when she had visited the Shrine of Old with her father.

'They staged my death in the Sanctuary of Qyma before the eyes of the people,' Dalos continued. 'After that, I lived amongst The Ancients for a time, consuming Fire Orchid essence to preserve my youth. I was moved from city to city, continent to continent, to avoid recognition. Once all memory of me had faded, I returned to the Capital to study at the Grand Athenaeum. I was raised to be the bridge between the Faith and The Architects. My duty was to ensure that no technologies would be crafted for use as weapons against the Faith. That was when I met your father—the final link between all three factions. The Ancients had poisoned my mind and convinced me that the Imperium was a force of evil upon this world. I was set the task of gaining your father's trust in order to acquire knowledge of the Imperium's inner workings.'

Alysse trembled, fearing that Dalos had ushered in the demise of her father.

'But I could not,' Dalos continued, a flow of tears streaking his face. 'What I saw in your father was his true desire for good. There was no evil in him. I could not betray my own blood. He taught me the value of life—a full life. So I decided to live. From then on I refused the essence from the High Priests and chose to age alongside my closest friend.'

'And The Ancients just allowed this?' Thio asked.

'They were wise not to risk the exposure of their design,' Dalos responded.

Alysse turned and paced towards the slender windows. In the silver light of the two moons, she traced the outline of the Shrine of Old.

'M'girl,' Dalos struggled to project his voice, 'I am sorry I have not spoken of this sooner.'

'Who else knows of this?' she asked, a calm in her voice.

'Your father, of course. And your uncle.' Dalos

sighed. 'He overheard your father speak my true name. I begged him not to reveal this truth, but your father placed too much trust in Cyrus.'

'That is why he wants you dead,' Thio stated. 'You are an Aprya.'

'I guess he succeeded,' Dalos said. 'No essence to save me this time.'

Mia shuffled through the information she had just heard from these journals. Her father had sacrificed his life for friendship.

'Pa… you had a chance to live forever,' she said.

'My dear daughter, if I had chosen that path, I would never have met your mother, and you would not be in this world.' He paused to expel his agony into his pocket cloth. 'I am so proud of you. All of you. I would give up a thousand lifetimes to relive this one.'

Dalos felt his eyes failing as his vision wavered. The soft lights around him seemed to dim. His grip on Thio's hand weakened. Feeling this, Thio leaned in close.

'Sir?' he managed through a growing swell of tears.

'Do not weep for me,' Dalos whispered. 'I have lived a full life. Now I can rest.'

He mustered enough energy to turn his head towards the portrait of his wife. With his last breath, he spoke directly to her.

'See you soon, my love.'

His eyes closed for the last time.

'Sir?' Thio pressed. 'Sir?!'

The young apprentice dropped his head and wept atop the still chest of his mentor.

CHAPTER 36

A delicate chime sounded in the station above Latyth. Under the dim night lights, Y'mara stood surrounded by a collection of medics, patiently awaiting the arrival of the survivors from Ton-Basin. The night was cooler than most, a turn from the familiar balmy evenings of summer. A mellow sea breeze carried with it a salty dew that lingered in her nostrils as she gently caressed her stomach.

From the station's southern entrance, the single train carriage eased soundlessly to a stop before the doors hissed open. A timid crowd began filing out onto the platform.

'Over there, care to his burns,' Y'mara ordered a handful of medics. 'Tend to her cut,' she ordered another. 'Bring a chair for this woman.'

Towards the station's main entrance, Latyth's governor ushered the able to a series of carriers, welcoming them and assuring their safety. He expressed his condolences and offered details of their accommodation within the city. A caravan of food carts provided wrapped meals for the hungry. Others offered clothing and essentials to those who had lost everything.

As Y'mara completed her preliminary count of the injured, she noticed a boy no older than six standing alone, his eyes searching the crowd.

'Hello,' she said, kneeling down beside him, 'my name is Y'mara. What's yours?'

'Sevy,' the frightened boy answered, his voice barely audible as he shivered.

'It's nice to meet you, Sevy. Are you okay?' she asked.

'Have you seen Mama?' the boy managed through trembling lips, his eyes swollen with fear.

'Did she come with you on the train?' Y'mara inquired.

'I don't know,' he answered, still scanning the crowd.

'Did you see her before you boarded?'

'No.'

'When did you see her last?' Y'mara asked, fearing the worst.

'Days ago. She went to the markets. She said she would be back soon.'

His glazed eyes welled with tears as he continued to shiver in the cold. Y'mara's heart wept for the boy. He was frightened and alone. His mother must have been one of the many that had perished in the attack.

'What about your father?' she asked, wiping the tears from his face.

'He worked in the mines,' he explained. 'Mama

said there was an accident, and Papa was hurt. She was crying. The Emperor came to our house and spoke to her. But I haven't seen Papa since.'

Y'mara called her mind back to the news of the collapsed mines in Ton-Basin only a month ago. She and her colleagues had held a vigil to honour the souls trapped within the mountain, one of whom, she concluded, was the father of this now parentless child.

'Sevy…' She paused, unsure whether to speak the truth or hold her words. *The child has suffered enough,* she thought to herself, *let him rest.*

'I am going to take care of you, is that okay?' she continued.

Sevy returned a shy nod.

'A lot of these people are hurt. Perhaps you can help me care for them, what do you say?' she offered with a smile.

The small boy nodded his head again, twisting his sleeve between his fingers.

'What a brave boy you are,' she said, gently caressing his scruffy hair. 'Come, you must be hungry.'

Y'mara took hold of his hand and guided him through the mass of people on the platform. His grip was tight and cold. He pressed his body against hers as they squeezed past city folk and medics alike. Still paying mind to the victims around her, Y'mara peered over at a group gathered around an old man. The fatigued figure was slumped on a chair, his right arm missing below the elbow. She called out a list of procedures to the medics who responded with affirming nods.

By the entrance, Y'mara collected a bowl of rice and seasoned vegetables for the young boy. His face gleamed at the portion of warm food as he began devouring it. Searching for a quiet place to seat the boy, Y'mara spotted the bench on which she and Thio had sat the previous evening. Out beyond the station, she saw something that caught her attention. *A ship.* She immediately ushered over a young medic.

'The transport ship has returned,' she said with excitement. 'Go to the fort. Ask Commander Rodyn if he can spare some men to aid in moving these people. Be as quick as you can.'

'Yes, Y'mara,' the young medic confirmed, rushing out through the main entrance.

Y'mara knelt down beside her small companion and smiled.

'Sevy, I have to speak to a few people. Why don't you sit on that seat over there and wait for me. There's a big ship coming into port full of brave people, just like you.'

'Ok!' the boy said, his excited smile dotted with grains of rice.

'Be sure to wave at them as they arrive,' Y'mara encouraged, wrapping the boy in a wool blanket and sending him towards the far platform.

—

Striding heavily down the fort's pier, Commander Rodyn studied the mooring vessel. The waters surrounding the one-hundred-metre-long transporter churned as its thrusters manoeuvred it into position. Once secure in its place alongside the pier, an autonomous gangway extended out from a section of open hull. Stepping onto the wide bridge, Commander Rodyn stared up at the floating agglomerate of iron.

'Officers! Where in Korpys have you been?' he spat. 'Open these doors immediately.'

His echoing voice was met with silence, which only fuelled his anger further. The iron doors remained sealed.

'This is your commander. Open the doors now!'

From equidistant portholes along the transporter's exterior, deep clunks rattled as each opened. From the open ports emerged the ship's array of cannons. Solid shafts of wrought iron protruded out over the water, then turned their aim skyward. The unauthorised display of artillery did little to ease Commander Rodyn's mounting concerns, prompting a stern and immediate rebuke.

'Stand down!' he yelled.

In that moment, the robust doors in front of him hissed, then rolled open. Beyond the threshold of the hull was pure darkness. Confused, Commander Rodyn surveyed the depths from his position midway atop the bridge. His heavy breath paired with his thumping heart as the frosty interior air flowed out around him. The ship was completely silent.

Cautious, he took a step towards the black void, then another, craning his head from side to side, searching for movement within the iron beast. From his left, the nearest cannon panned a degree eastward. Another, slightly west. The sound of soft, turbulent waves lapped at the hull some metres below him. Then, a battle horn ruptured the air.

In unison, each cannon violently recoiled as they ejected their payloads across the bay. The thrust of the blasts shifted the entire vessel. Commander Rodyn fought to steady himself as the gangway quaked beneath his feet. Twisting his view towards the city, he watched on in horror as the fired shells hit their marks. Upon impact, monstrous plumes of blue flame erupted, illuminating the night sky.

The commander staggered to his feet, aghast at the events unfolding in his city. Finding his footing, he surged forward towards the darkness as another wave of cannon blasts exploded through the air. Before he could reach the threshold, a swarm of black-armoured figures poured out onto the gangway, their short swords reflecting the blue hellfire across the bay. Rodyn reached for his sword, clutched it, withdrew it, then froze. The sting of metal across his throat was the last thing he felt as his body plunged into the depths of the bay.

—

Sevy dropped his bowl of rice as he bore witness to the calamity consuming the city below. The sight of the blue flames brought with it a rebirth of the fear that had gripped him in Ton-Basin. Distant screams echoed across the bay as buildings collapsed and trees burnt.

Men, women, and children scrambled through the main gates of the station. Explosions rumbled the foundation of the crimson dome as it rattled overhead.

Sprinting across the platform, Y'mara shouted commands to the terrified crowd.

'Stay calm! Evacuate the station! Head for the road! Seek shelter in the valleys!'

As she leapt up the footbridge, the city's downfall came into view. Blue and amber flames engulfed large pockets of heavily populated areas. By the fort, she witnessed the inky tendrils of a black fog spreading across the docks. The fog, however, was the swarm of obsidian-clad soldiers permeating out from the transporter—thousands of them. The gold and green ship in the bay rocked as its cannons fired another round of death upon the city. She traced a shell hurling west towards the hill where the Athenaeum sat. Its blazing trail arched over the infirmary and pierced the sapphire dome, exploding glass and stone across its surroundings.

Wasting no more time, Y'mara shot down the footbridge and ran to the young boy.

'Sevy, it's okay, I'm here,' she said, crouching down in front of him, his fair face saturated in fear.

'Where's Mama?' he cried.

'I will protect you, okay? Come with me.'

Y'mara picked up the boy and scanned the station. The flurry of panicked refugees had impeded all exits. She eyed the steep drop at the edge of the platform. The hillside below was thick with foliage. It was a dangerous path, one she hoped she would not have to tread.

'The train!' a voice screamed out from the crowd. 'Open the doors! Let us in!'

A huddle of fear-stricken folk rushed the idle carriage, their fists hammering the glass doors.

Within the control room perched above the platforms, the station steward laboured to gauge the chaos through her aged, clouded eyes. The muted pleas from below were enough to describe the desperation of the station's occupants. Fumbling with the controls, she activated the train's power and opened the doors. A stampede ensued as the crowd flooded towards the empty carriage.

Y'mara readied herself to board the train as Sevy clung to her. She felt moisture on her chest, a result of the boy's streams of tears. His erratic sobs produced sharp convulsions. His thin body trembled with fear. Y'mara's primary focus now was the safety of this boy and that of her unborn child.

The mob's flow into the train slowed as they bottlenecked at the doors. Issuing words of calm, Y'mara turned her gaze toward a fresh burst of blue fire in the city below. The transport ship showed no sign of a ceasefire. One after another, the cannons fired. Explosion after explosion quaked the city as another round of wrathful payloads webbed out. With each discharge of artillery, blazing trails streaked through the darkness. It was in that moment Y'mara spotted the incoming terror.

A blazing blue orb shot up over the bay, coursing

in a direct line toward the station. Rising higher and higher, it arched over the city. As it drew closer, Y'-mara took the only feasible measure she could.

'Sevy, hold on tight,' she whispered to him.

Her grasp around the boy tightened. She forced her way through the crowd to the open side of the platform. Calculating the angle of the approaching doom, she ran at full speed towards the edge. The whistling sound of the projectile grew louder as she approached the steep slope. Without hesitation, she leapt off the edge of the platform and plummeted into the dense foliage below. From above, a thunderous blue inferno engulfed the air.

Sevy cried out in pain as they plowed through wild shrubs and tree branches, rolling uncontrollably down the steep embankment.

Finally coming to a stop near a slow-churning river, Y'mara jerked back in pain, her breath caught in her throat. Sharp cramps in her stomach drew her attention to her groin. Moisture covered her hands as she dabbed the exterior of her trousers. Fearing the worst, she peered at them but saw nothing in the darkness. As another rupture of blue flame illuminated the sky, she saw that the moisture was, indeed, blood.

CHAPTER 37

'Your life in this world has ended. Your journey to the next shall now begin.'

Reverend Kalax spoke to the small group gathered at the Shrine of Old as Hithema and Siiva dabbed pale-orange oil across Dalos' lifeless skin. The rings of trail-lights encircling the island warmed the faces of the attending mourners as night engulfed the city.

Thio held Mia as she wept, fighting to hold together his own grief. He fixed his gaze on the strange ritual unfolding before him, if only to avoid looking upon the body. He turned his gaze to Jaxon and Alysse, who stood arm in arm. Through his tear-glazed eyes, he saw the heartache in theirs. He thought of their bond with the jovial Architect—for they had known Dalos all their lives. For Thio, not even two years had passed since their first meeting, and it seemed almost presumptuous to lay claim to grief so profound.

Mia could feel the sporadic quivers of grief that Thio fought to mask. She squeezed his arm and looked up at him. He returned her gaze. Without words, she encouraged him to mourn, affirming that his grief was no less valid than that of those around him.

'Go now, Jarrys Aprya. The Five await your return,' Kalax said, breaking the silence. The trail-lights dimmed into darkness.

Alysse wept at the mention of that name, Jarrys Aprya. It became clear to her in that moment. The devotion and love that Dalos had shown her and her family was instilled in his blood—the same blood that had bound them through life, the blood shared by kin. For generations, Dalos had watched over the well-being of his family from the shadows, only stepping into the light after meeting her father. She wished she had known this sooner. For too long, she had harboured a hatred toward the High Priests and the false account of their actions some two hundred years ago. Now, she could find peace knowing that the Lost Prince, Jarrys, had always been there protecting her.

In the silence, Thio reflected. Despite Dalos' pursuit of worldly knowledge, Thio knew that the Faith and its traditions were held close within his mentor's heart. He knew that his closest friend deserved a proper send-off. In that instant, he mustered his courage and began to sing the Soul's Hymn aloud. His voice was timid and broken, carrying cracks of emotion—yet his tone was true and pure.

Jaxon turned his gaze toward the quiet chanter, a

profound respect washing over him. The tender melody rising from the young man stirred something within—urging his own heart to offer tribute. Clearing his throat, he began to harmonise alongside Thio.

Mia's legs weakened as grief settled over her like a heavy weight. The echoes of the two young men resonated through the very heart of her. She could do nothing but hold tightly to Thio.

Alysse stared at the stack of eight marble altars, her attention drawn particularly to the bottom-most stone coffin. She thought of the Emperor that lay inside—Jannon the First, father to Dalos. The idea of sacrificing a child could never sit peacefully within her conscience. *How could any father give up his son?* But then, another thought crossed her mind, one that painted a much grander image. *Was it truly a sacrifice?* she asked herself. *The Emperor had done what was necessary to secure the realm's safety.* She recited the letter her father had received. Having read it countless times, the words were etched in her mind. It spoke of kneeling to the enemy, or facing death as the consequence of refusal. *Was his own death a sign of his sacrifice to maintain peace? And if so, what choices will I face?* She closed her eyes, the weight of her future bearing down on her.

Once Thio and Jaxon had concluded the hymn, the trail-lights on the sacred island stirred to life again, casting light upon the tears that had flowed throughout the service. The gathered crowd began moving to the water crafts nestled at the pier. Alysse remained in place for a moment.

'Come, my girl,' Mia ushered, offering a hand to

the Princess.

Alysse turned her attention to the three attending High Priests, a sorrowful rage in her glare.

'I'll catch up,' she said, encouraging Mia to continue to the pier.

Alysse waited until her companions were at a suitable distance before approaching Reverend Kalax.

'Alefre'a,' he said, bowing as she neared.

'You had Dalos spy on my father,' she spat, her voice thick with contempt.

Kalax scoffed, returning his focus to the final stages of embalming his once-captive.

'Do not turn your back on me!' Alysse erupted.

Slowly, almost methodically, Kalax turned to meet the enraged Princess' gaze, tilting his head as he examined her from head to toe.

'We are tasked with rendering the Gods' will,' he began, condescension rife in his tone. 'We must observe those who stray too far.'

'And how exactly did my father stray too far?'

Kalax chuckled quietly to himself, turning back to find the two other High Priests sharing in his amusement.

'He didn't,' Kalax said plainly. 'Just like those before him, he stayed true to his path. However, caution is always necessary.'

'Surely you would have known that Dalos would never betray his own blood?' Alysse retorted. 'So why try to twist a child's mind to see hatred in those who strive to prevent it?'

'A child's mind?' Kalax laughed. 'When Dalos met your father, he had already lived for over a century.

He had witnessed both the good and evil of this world with his own eyes. He saw what his family's rule truly wrought—the stripping of the people's Faith. Only through our continued efforts were the people of Eviiri spared from the Gods' wrath.'

'So what happens now?' Alysse asked. 'Am I to be watched over?'

'You have always been in the Gods' sight, Alefre'a,' Kalax whispered. 'There are those who follow us, and there are those who follow you. We teach our followers how to respond to those who seek to strip the Gods from their hearts. What will you teach yours when your enemies seek to tear down your tower?'

'My enemies have already begun dismantling the very foundations of the Imperium,' Alysse exclaimed. 'Do not forget, Reverend, that the Faith is one pillar of a triad that holds this world together. If one of the three falls, all will collapse. My role is to prevent that. I am not your enemy.'

'And I am not yours,' Kalax asserted, his tone sharp and direct.

—

'I didn't know you could sing,' Mia said as she strolled arm in arm with Thio.

'I'm surprised I remembered the words,' Thio said, shaking off the cloud of embarrassment. 'The last time I sang the hymn was for my mother. I barely remember songs in the common tongue, let alone the ancient language.'

'Dalos would have loved it,' she said, squeezing his arm.

Thio smiled, the boisterous cadence of his mentor's voice echoing in his mind. He could hear the sharp quips Dalos would have woven into his praises—his way of filling the air with joy. Those quips had always expressed more love and appreciation than any earnest compliment, and Thio missed them, now more than ever.

'You and Jaxon compliment each other,' Mia expressed, 'and not only in song.'

'I doubt that,' Thio said, dropping his head, defeated by the Prince's recent distrust.

'Hey!' Mia exclaimed, halting the young apprentice. 'What did Dalos say? It's time to put those doubts to rest. Self-doubt is a chasm between you and the heights you seek; only by leaping across can you taste the air of the summit.'

'And what if the chasm is too wide?' Thio argued. 'Say, between a poor boy, full of failures, and the untouchable Commander of the Imperium?'

Mia expelled a frustrated huff, shaking her head at the boy's self-assessment.

'You're a smart boy, Thio,' she said, staring directly into his eyes, 'teach yourself how to fly. Then no gap will be too great.'

Thio gazed upward. With the city's glow withheld during the ceremony, the heavens had revealed themselves in their full brilliance. Countless stars twinkled back at him from the darkness. The boundless expanse of sky spoke to him in that moment. Perhaps it was Dalos, offering his wisdom from beyond; perhaps it was his mother. Or perhaps it was nothing but the stirring of his own subconscious. Either way, Thio found himself contemplating the limitless possibilities his future held. His recent work was but the merest glimpse of what might be—harnessing its energy could unlock technologies the world had yet to imagine. In the depths of his thoughts, confidence began to blossom for the first time.

'Come on,' Mia said, snatching Thio's attention, 'let's go.'

Thio turned back toward his mentor's body, offering his final goodbyes in the silence of his mind. Moving from the altar, Alysse paced steadily towards them, her expression shrouded in the dim light. A range of concerns now pressed him.

'Wait,' he said to Mia as she began continuing towards the watercraft moored at the pier. Stepping forward to intercept the approaching Princess, he voiced his concerns, 'Your Grace, I request an audience with your prisoner.'

'For what purpose?' Alysse responded, her voice carrying a chill as her stride remained unbroken.

'I want her to answer for Dalos and Gorryn,' he said, moving to keep pace with the vexed Princess. 'Plus, she stole something of mine—something she has wielded to devastating effect. We need to…'

'Your new energy source?' Alysse interjected, her words cutting him short as she came to an abrupt halt. 'I am aware. You are hereby prohibited from any further work on it. Should you disobey, it will be deemed treason, and will result in heavy penalty.'

'But Your Grace…'

'Enough, Thio!' she erupted, massaging her forehead in frustration. 'Do you recall what you swore to me up there?' She gestured towards the Skyhold at the Citadel's apex. 'You gave me your word that you would protect Dalos, no matter the cost. And then you left, taking my brother with you. For what? Your sister? Forgive me, but I see no sign of her here with you.'

Her words ignited a sudden fury within Thio.

'I didn't ask Jaxon to come with me!' he snapped. 'But you should be grateful that he did. If it weren't for his efforts in Latyth, your uncle would still be by your side, ready to drive his knife into your back. Jaxon is alive because of me. You are alive because of me.'

Alysse tensed, the young apprentice's words reverberating across the Shrine of Old.

'But that will soon change if the girl in your custody has shared my research with others who will use it against you.' Thio pressed on, pausing only to steady his breath. 'Alysse, let me right my wrongs. You said it yourself—our world depends on the structural integrity of all three factions. The cracks are deepening. Do not stand by and watch them explode.'

Jaxon, having heard the commotion, rushed to his sister's side, his hand firmly grasped around his short sword.

'Thio, back off!' he grunted.

Alysse raised a hand to subdue her brother. She stared into Thio's eyes and found a tumultuous stew of fury, sorrow, and concern staring back at her. She wondered what he would say, or how he might respond to Britt's words. Though Jaxon had his doubts about the young apprentice, Alysse had her own reasons for wanting the truth laid bare—whether to clear Thio of suspicion or to watch his mask fall away.

'Very well,' she said softly. 'We'll go together.'

CHAPTER 38

Thio felt the cold embrace of the cavernous sprawl of underground tunnels, the scent of rust heavy in the air. The only sound was the steady echoes of his companions' footsteps. He caught fleeting glimpses of Alysse's intricately detailed black gown as it caught the light of each passing wall lamp. Behind him, the stern presence of the new Imperial Commander pressed upon him. Thio longed for his touch. He desired so strongly to settle the doubts that had festered in the Prince's mind. And, from his chaperon, he sensed a reciprocated yearning—one that strained against the chains of duty and caution.

Rounding the final corner, Alysse motioned for the two Imperial guards posted at the cell's entrance to stand down as they passed the threshold into the Citadel's fortified prison. As they neared the only occupied cell, Alysse spotted her captive, the buttery blonde's gaze drawn by the approaching trio.

'Your Grace,' Britt chirped, 'I see you brought me a gift. Hello, Thio.'

Jaxon quickly trained his eyes on the young girl, carefully observing the subtle cues in her interaction. He watched as Thio approached the bars and stared directly into her vivid blue eyes.

Thio seethed at the sight of her as she produced a wide grin, winking seductively at her fellow guildsman. With a surge of disgust, Thio expelled a hefty wad of spit, striking the young blonde square in the face. Britt recoiled before laughing, wiping the thick glob from her eye, then enveloping her entire thumb in her mouth.

'Why?' Thio sneered.

'Why what?' Britt countered, savouring the taste of Thio's saliva.

'Let's start with Chief Gorryn,' Thio snarled.

'That lumbering beast,' she chuckled. 'He served his purpose. I had no further need for him.'

'You were his apprentice. He taught you everything.'

'Tell me, Thio, what is the point of having an apprentice?' she began. 'No, wait—let me answer that for you. An apprentice is the chosen successor of a Chief Architect.'

'That isn't a certainty, and you know it,' Thio rebutted. 'Being an apprentice simply grants an advantage in the election.'

Britt slumped her shoulders playfully.

'Alright, fine. You're right,' she said, rolling her eyes. 'However, a Chief Architect is also elected based on their work. Dalos had his resonance. Gorryn had his nanotechnology. Mia had… well, I'm not exactly sure what Mia had, aside from her father's name.'

'So you thought by killing Gorryn, you would simply step into his place?'

'Tharpys, no,' Britt laughed. 'I have no major discoveries to my name. The geology sector has been quite stagnant—at least, until you showed your pretty face.'

'So stealing my work was your ticket up?' Thio said, his fists tightening.

'*Your* work?' Britt scoffed. 'Don't you mean *our* work?'

Her words rippled through the cell and out to those gathered beyond the bars, settling uncomfortably within the already prominent doubts clouding Jaxon's mind.

'What do you mean?' he asked, leaning forward, eager to hear more from this blonde beauty.

Britt knew she had captured their full attention with her lie. Her plot to drive a wedge between Thio and the royal House had reached its apex.

'We worked on this together, Your Grace, as partners,' she continued. 'Don't you remember, Thio? All those long nights together? We would work for hours, then fuck for hours more.'

'Liar!' Thio erupted.

'Don't be shy now, my love,' Britt pressed, 'just because you're in the presence of royalty. We are such a good team. Tell them.'

Alysse absorbed every word of their interaction before speaking.

'Thio? Is this true?' she asked.

'Not one bit of it!' Thio responded sharply, his eyes never parting from his adversary. 'I barely know this girl. Before arriving in the Capital, I had no knowledge of her.'

'Is that so?' Britt giggled. 'Our time in Ton-Basin would beg to differ. Come now, you remember. Oh, and your help with the Blue Flame—thanks for that. It's a shame Dalos wasn't there to witness its beauty.'

'You will not speak his name!' Thio exploded, slamming his hand on the iron bars.

'Why not?' Britt asked, her tone laced with elation, pleased that her falsehoods were unfolding as planned. 'Killing him was your idea, after all. We promised each other that we would rid ourselves of our incompetent mentors and carve our own path to greater things.'

'You lying cunt!'

'Enough!' Alysse shouted, silencing the cavern, then turning to her brother. 'Jaxon, escort Thio to a cell.'

Jaxon moved swiftly to apprehend the enraged apprentice.

'Alysse!' Thio pleaded, his voice desperate. 'You cannot honestly believe her. Dalos was like a father to me. I would never do this!'

'Perhaps,' Alysse said sternly. 'But caution is necessary. You will remain under our watch until I deem otherwise.'

Britt smirked as she watched the young Prince seize the struggling apprentice. Shifting her gaze to Alysse, she saw her give her brother a subtle nod before she turned and exited the dank prison.

Jaxon lugged Thio towards the vacant cell directly opposite Britt's, a veil of sadness now drooping over him. *Have I been played this whole time?* he thought. *Did he at all care for me?*

As they neared the cold cell, Thio turned pleading eyes to his Prince.

'Jaxon, please.'

'You will address me as Your Grace or Commander,' Jaxon said, his voice cracking with sorrow as they arrived at the grim chamber.

'Jaxon! Listen to me!'

The Prince shoved the young apprentice into the cell, slamming the gate shut and securing its lock with fury. Desperate appeals echoed louder in Jaxon's mind as he reflected on their newfound bond. He remembered the taste of Thio's lips, the gentle touch of his hand, and the innocence in those ocean-blue eyes. His heart raced faster with every plea until the weight of it became unbearable. With a sudden motion, he slammed his hand against the bars, silencing the boy in an instant.

'Was any of it real, Thio?!' he exclaimed, peering deep into those ocean-blue eyes.

'She made it up. All of it. I swear.'

Jaxon clenched his jaw.

'Not that—us. Was any of *us* real?'

The question caught Thio off guard. The pain he witnessed in the Prince's eyes spoke not of his suspected betrayal, but of his fear that their bond had been nothing more than an illusion or ploy. In that moment, he realised their passion was as deeply felt by Jaxon as it had been in his own heart.

'Of course it was,' he answered with conviction.

'Then why did I feel your persistent hesitation?' Jaxon asked, his throat tight as he swallowed a lump that formed there.

Thio approached the bars, his face twisted with heartache.

'You are the Prince of the Imperium, the Imperial Commander of the Emperor's forces. I am nobody. I am not of any noble House. I possess neither wealth, nor lands, nor titles. In what world could I ever be worthy of you?'

'In this one!' Jaxon cried. 'Do you think I care whether you are noble-born, or how much wealth you hold? I saw beyond the picture you have painted for yourself. I saw your true riches—your desire to create beauty in this world, not just for yourself, but for the betterment of all.' He paused. 'At least, I thought I did.'

'Jaxon…'

The Prince said no more, rechecking the lock before striding off down the dim hallway.

Thio pressed his face against the cold iron bars. In a single night, his world had been all but stripped away. He had lost everything—his closest friend and mentor, his work, and now his love. Was it by the Gods' design? No. He didn't believe in the Gods. This was the work of The Reclamation. His sorrow twisted into anger as he lifted his gaze to the peppy blonde in the cell across the room. Her eyes had never left his.

'I see now why my advances were lost on you. I didn't have the right parts,' she giggled. 'But the

Prince, eh? He's quite a catch. Well… *was.*'

Thio's exhaustion left little room for anything but his hatred to spill out in words, his eyes seething with anger.

'Britt,' he began, teeth clenched, 'I swear on my mother's memory, when I am out of this cell, I will kill you.'

Britt laughed. 'You're never getting out of this cell, dummy. They believed every word. Plus, The Reclamation will soon take control of this city, and once I am out of this cell, *I* will kill *you.*'

CHAPTER 39

Alysse had barely slept the night before. The recent accusations regarding Thio's involvement echoed loudly in her mind, stirring doubts she struggled to quell. She found it difficult to believe that Dalos would have remained blind to such betrayals. She also believed her brother would have sensed if something had been amiss in the young apprentice's actions. But either way, Thio was not her greatest concern today. She gazed out beyond the city, towards the Southern Sea. Anchored in the Bay of Zenithal were three imposing military vessels. One shimmered with gold and yellow hues, its sails proudly displaying the banner of House Tennyr. The second, a modest red ship, bore the bold and fierce sigil of House Peryx. The largest of them all, dwarfing the others, was painted with light blue streaks across its hull. From its towering masts hung the banners of House Frailyn. Alysse straightened her posture, adopting a defiant stance in the face of her suspected adversary.

'You've come so far, Little Wren,' her father's voice spoke softly from behind her, 'yet your confidence is still lacking.'

Alysse closed her eyes for a moment, savouring the comforting rhythm of his voice as she twirled her golden pendant between her fingers. His words echoed the very doubts she had been hiding.

'I know, Pa,' she said faintly. 'I need to trust in myself. I know where the threat lies. It is with Lex Frailyn and his Reclamation. But I am uncertain of what action to take.'

'Lex Frailyn?' Jannon asked. 'Are you certain of this? Or have you allowed your fear of him to lead you to this conclusion?'

'My only fear is the uncertain,' she answered. 'But I know the histories. It was his ancestor that lost the vote at the Coalition of Crowns. House Frailyn was so close to ruling over the Imperium. This is their reclamation. I have to act before it's too late.'

Alysse caught the silhouette of her father step into view, his muted green suit framed by the midday sun.

'Act, yes,' he said, peering deep into her hazel eyes, 'but remember, Little Wren, there is no courage in a decision made from fear. A wren does not take flight because the winds roar, but because the sky calls it to soar. What is it you truly seek?'

Alysse turned her gaze back towards the ships in the bay.

'To make the right choices for the good of the realm,' she asserted.

'I faced many difficult choices in my life—ones that threatened the very good of the realm,' he began. 'But I knew, in my heart, that they were right, despite their repercussions. What price are you willing to pay for your choices? Will you clip your wings out of fear of the storm, allowing the very thing you fear to become your cage? Or will you stay true to what you know is right?'

Alysse stood still, the weight of her father's words sinking into the silence between them. Her fingers tightened around the pendant, its warmth a sharp contrast to the chill now settling over her heart.

'Tell me what to do, Pa,' she pleaded.

'I am not here to make your decisions for you. You must do that. I am only here to teach you how to fly. Once you have mastered control of your wings, you can weather any storm.'

A knock at the door startled Alysse. She whipped her head up to find herself alone once again.

'Come in,' she called out.

Marcia Iibryn stepped through the doors, her ceremonial peach gown more magnificent than any Alysse had ever seen, draping the silver-haired woman in regal splendour.

'Queen Marcia,' Alysse greeted with a brief, respectful bow.

'You look impeccable, my dear,' the peach-draped monarch exalted, admiring the extravagance of the Princess' royal vestment. Her gaze lingered on the finely stitched lace that adorned the muted green fabric, her slender figure poised with grace against the blue sky beyond.

'You're too kind, Your Grace,' Alysse replied. 'Though, I fear I am overshadowed by your elegance.'

'Oh, nonsense,' Marcia dismissed with a wave. 'Today is *your* day. Are you ready?'

'No,' Alysse answered bluntly as they both shared a light chuckle.

'You will be fine,' Marcia assured. 'Keep that chin up.'

'I wanted to thank you, Your Grace, for your generous guidance these past few days.' Alysse said sincerely. 'I know none of this is your burden to bear, but I want you to know you have been a great comfort amidst the turmoil. I do hope that after today, we will see the end of such strife.'

'I'm sure of it, Princess,' Marcia agreed with a smile. 'Your decision today will be written in the tales of Eviiri.'

'I doubt that,' Alysse laughed. 'Once Lex Frailyn has been dealt with, the realm will return to normalcy, and The Reclamation will be erased from history.'

Marcia gave a quiet smile, her eyes lingering on Alysse for a moment before she glanced away, as if savouring the idea.

'Alysse,' Jaxon's voice called out from the doorway, capturing the attention of both regal figures, 'it's time.'

Marcia turned back to Alysse and stretched out her hand. 'Come, my dear. Let us see that crown.'

—

The people of Zenithal gathered along the Path of Peace, the crowd once again filling the entirety of the five-kilometre-long stone boulevard. The sea of city folk stood patiently behind a blockade of green and purple troops, impeccably arranged just outside the Citadel gates. Within the gates stood a small crowd of nobles, most notably the four monarchs—now including Marcia Iibryn. Opposite them stood the five High Priests, dripping in onyx gems, their headdresses shimmering in the sunlight. And finally, standing apart from the assembly, was Mia, her expression a stark blend of pride and profound loneliness, both Dalos and Thio absent from her side.

Mia fought to hold back tears, striving to feel joy for Alysse in her moment of glory, though her heart ached with the longing for her father's cheerful presence. The news of Thio's imprisonment also weighed heavily on her heart. She knew Thio's nature, and the depth of his love and admiration for Dalos. She had no doubt of his innocence and was determined to seek his release once the day's formalities had concluded.

Suddenly, the four great horns of the Citadel rumbled across the city, summoning the colossal golden-arched doors to crack open. The crowds of city folk stood silent, each craning their necks in hope of catching a glimpse of the Princess as she stepped out of the towering stronghold, her brother by her side. The two royal heirs strode proudly down the tiered walkway and towards a temporary dais that had been erected for the ceremony. It stood some ten metres high. Assisting his sister with the climb, Jaxon turned to her.

'I can feel you trembling,' he said. 'Remember, I'm right here, I won't let anything happen to you.'

Alysse said nothing, her stomach twisting with nerves. Reaching the peak of the high platform, she gazed out at the hundreds of thousands of spectators on the Path. Most simply stared back at her, while others waved long dowels capped with muted green streamers. A few tossed white orchid petals into the air. But to Alysse, their actions were drowned in silence. A cloud of angst swelled over her. She feared that news of her accusations against the High Priests in the Sanctuary of Qyma had spread throughout the city, causing those once loyal to her to seek faith elsewhere. Despite having rehearsed her inaugural address countless times, the words had all but abandoned her in that moment.

Jaxon watched her intently from the dais' periphery, her facial cues revealing her confidence-deprived disposition. He scanned the many faces staring up at her, most lingering in anticipation. His gaze shifted to the High Priests. Kalax stood with his arms crossed behind his back, mindlessly inspecting the manicured foliage of the Citadel grounds, as though he were an impatient child, longing for any other form of stimulus. Jaxon glanced over at the leaders of the Great Houses. Lyro Tennyr stood rigid and proud of his Empress-in-waiting. The young king, Benin Peryx, kicked at the ground absently, his boots leaving faint marks on the marble pavement. Lex Frailyn wore the same stony expression he was well known for, his mouth curling into a scoff as his impatience grew. Jaxon noticed Marcia Iibryn shifting her body in an attempt to catch the attention of the frozen Princess. But Alysse was blind to it all. He returned his gaze to his sister, her eyes still fixed blankly ahead. Fearing her deepening dread, Jaxon approached her, his steps measured and deliberate, as if to offer her the silent support she so desperately needed.

'Alysse?' he whispered.

Alysse heard her brother's voice, yet felt powerless to move her muscles. The crowd lining the Path before her began to blur as day turned to night in her mind. All that remained was the pounding of her own heart, battering against her from within.

I cannot allow fear to guide me, she told herself. *The paths we take to avoid our fears often lead us directly to them.* Her father's words echoed endlessly in her mind as she fought to regain control of her psyche. It was not until two golden-crowned wrens fluttered and sang about the dais that Alysse's mind returned to the moment.

'Alysse?' Jaxon repeated, placing a gentle hand on her back.

She turned to him, dazed, her gaze falling on the concern etched in the furrow of his brow and the tightness of his jaw. She looked out at the crowd, once more clear before her, then down at the gathered nobles before turning back to her brother. She delivered him a reassuring nod, then cleared her throat.

'My dear people of Zenithal,' she began, a tremor in her voice, 'I... I stand before you today, not as the perfect ruler my father was, but as one who must strive to carry his legacy into the future.'

She paused, feeling the weight of every gaze upon her. Taking a deep breath, she continued. 'I will not lie to you. The task ahead is great, and I... I cannot pretend that fear plays no part in its fulfilment. I have spent years staring fear in the face, the same fear I see in many of you here. The path before us is fraught with uncertainty, and the decisions we make today will echo through generations. But I know we can continue to stand defiant in the face of our fears, together, as one people.'

Sporadic cheers of support erupted from the crowd, each call of admiration chipping away at her doubts. Although her heart continued to race and her palms were slick with sweat, Alysse felt a growing calm within her.

'I may not yet be the leader you all hope me to be,' she continued. 'But allow me to prove myself to you. Allow me to steer our path away from adversaries that seek to destroy what we hold dear. Allow me to be the peacekeeper my father was.'

More cheers rang out as Alysse looked over at Jaxon, his supportive gaze offering her the strength she needed. She then turned her attention down to the monarchs—to Lex Frailyn directly. Her voice, though still trembling, grew firmer. 'A storm looms over this city, its winds stirred by those seeking to weaken the strength of our united people. But should this storm make landfall, we will weather it, together.

They may try to destroy our buildings and burn our homes, but they cannot blacken our hearts. For every flame intended to scorch us, we shall douse with resolve.'

The cheers grew louder. Alysse dropped her head and closed her eyes, soaking in the warmth her people now displayed.

'I cannot do this alone,' she said. 'So I ask you, people of Zenithal, do not stand behind me—stand beside me. Together, we will protect the peace our forebears fought so vigorously to attain. And when the storm passes, and day breaks, Eviiri will thrive once again.'

Deep harmonic rumbles rolled from the great horns as the sea of people rippled with ovation, calming Alysse's nerves and ushering forth the confidence she had lost of late. She acknowledged her admirers with a gentle wave.

Jaxon applauded his sister proudly, admiring the courage and conviction she had found in her speech. He watched on as the air above the crowd filled with orchid petals and cheer. Amid the jubilant uproar, he had not yet noticed Reverend Kalax climbing the stairs of the dais. It wasn't until the priest's obsidian robes shimmered in his periphery that Jaxon acknowledged his presence.

'Alefre'am,' Kalax greeted him with a short bow, 'the crown?'

Jaxon had almost forgotten his next role in the ceremony: crowning Eviiri's new Empress. He gestured towards a hefty wooden box that had been placed atop the towering platform. Acknowledging its whereabouts, he ushered Kalax towards it, then approached Alysse.

'Good job,' he said to her. 'Father would be proud.'

Her smile said everything words could not as she hugged her brother. Peering over his shoulder, she watched Kalax approach the podium to make his address. She pulled away from Jaxon and turned her attention to the androgynous priest.

'Children of Eviiri,' Kalax began, silencing the crowd with his soothing voice, 'I stand before you, a humble servant of the Gods who have shaped this world and brought us to this pivotal moment. I speak as a representative for Qyma the Creator, who smiles upon the ascendance of her creation, guiding us toward the future she has envisioned. I speak for Kapry the Destroyer, who clears the past to make way for progress, unburdening us of what no longer serves our path. I speak for Shaavy the Preserver, who safeguards the flow of life, ensuring that what is vital endures through time, holding together the very fabric of our existence. I speak for Doma the Prosperous, who blesses us with abundance, guiding us toward growth and the flourishing of our people. And I speak for Aanka the Harmonious, who fosters balance and unity, ensuring that peace prevails and that you, the people of Eviiri, remain steadfast and whole in this ever-changing world.'

Another wave of applause spread across the city.

'With their favour,' he continued, 'I now bless the crown of our new Opre'a.'

Alysse recalled the male form of the word, *Opre'am*, meaning Emperor. She had heard Kalax address her father by this ancient title many times. And now, she was relieved to cast aside her former title of *Alefre'a*, for she was no longer a royal child.

Kalax lifted the wooden box, admiring the elaborate gold etching that adorned it, the sigil of House Aprya prominently displayed on its lid. He turned to Alysse and Jaxon, and offered a respectful bow before opening it.

Within sat a golden crown. The delicate diadem, commissioned by her predecessor as tradition dictated, was an intricate weave of lemon tree branches. Each fruit, a yellow gem, sparkled with beauty and depth. At its front were two golden-crowned wrens, their wings outstretched, framing the crested sigil of House Aprya.

Alysse was immediately overcome with emotion as her eyes traced the details her father had personally commissioned. She felt as though a part of him had been woven into it, the warmth and guidance he had always provided her now embodied within.

Jaxon briefly admired the crown before reaching into the box and lifting it from its silk cradle. Holding it up towards the people, he too felt his father's presence in that moment. He paused for a moment while the crowd cheered, then turned back to Alysse who had knelt to receive it. Delicately sliding it over her dark, slicked-back hair, Jaxon ushered her to her feet.

Alysse stepped forward, her hand interlocked with Jaxon's. Together they moved to the front of the dais, ushering forth a new age. With a raise of their hands, the gathered sea of people roared with glee.

'It's done, Jax,' she said to him.

'It's done,' he repeated, a wide smile producing proud dimples in his cheeks. 'Only one part remains… your Confirmation at the Shrine of Old.'

CHAPTER 40

'It stinks down here,' Britt said, inhaling a deep whiff of the rust-scented air. 'Do you know what that is?'

Thio remained silent, not having spoken a word since the previous night. His mind seethed with anger while his body shivered in the cold. The frigid stone bench on which he lay pressed against every curve of his body. The rhythmic tapping of his prison mate's foot against the stone floor only fuelled his rage.

'No?' Britt continued. 'Well, I certainly do. That's the smell of the blood of two hundred Faith Partisans —sorry, two hundred and ten. Do you know how long it takes to eviscerate that many bodies and pulverise what's left? A while. But it had to be done.'

The walls of the cavernous prison block suddenly rumbled as the resonating blasts of the Citadel's horns permeated the layers of thick ground above.

'Sounds like we have a new Empress,' Britt sang.

'May her rule be long and prosperous.'

She stood and walked to the bars that caged her.

'Come on, Thio,' she called out, a playful dance in her voice. 'Talk to me. It's lonely down here.'

'I have nothing to say to you,' Thio snapped back.

Britt folded her arms and frowned. 'You're no fun,' she complained. 'I know, let's play a game! Since you're going to die soon, how about you tell me a secret, and I'll tell one back?'

'I don't have any secrets,' Thio stated.

'Everyone has secrets,' the perky blonde argued, placing a thoughtful hand beneath her chin as one brow arched in contemplation. 'Let's see... you've stolen something from an Athenaeum before? Or... you were secretly jealous of your sister's success?' She paused, formulating a way to get under his skin. 'Oh, I know! Tell me how big the Prince is. I've seen his hands, so I can only imagine.'

Thio resisted her obvious attempts to surface the rage within him. Instead, he stared blankly at her.

'Why are you doing this, Britt?' he asked plainly. 'What did Cyrus promise you?'

Britt laughed. 'Cyrus promised me nothing more than security while I carried out my tasks. It was our leader that promised me my heart's desire.'

'And what is your heart's desire?' Thio asked.

Britt leant forward and pressed her head against the solid bars of her cell. 'The Grand Athenaeum,' she said, shifting into a serious tone. 'Gone will be the days of three Chief Architects, all pussyfooting around each other. The guild shall be led by a single, strong mind—one willing to probe deeper into our abilities to create things of true grandeur. One unburdened by centuries-old pacts and vows.'

Thio sneered. 'You want to create weapons, is that it?'

'You're the one creating weapons, my love,' Britt chuckled.

'My work was never intended to be used like that,' Thio bit back.

'Perhaps not by you,' she responded. 'But *I* saw its potential. So did Cyrus.'

'And what does the former Imperial Commander seek to gain from his treason?' Thio probed. 'He already had command of the Imperial forces.'

'He never wanted any of that,' she stated, pulling her face away from the bars and leaning back.

'What, then?'

'How shall I put this?' Britt pondered. 'Not long after the Commander and I began our... nocturnal activities, he had a wig made for me—a dark brown wig. He insisted I wear it every time we indulged in each other.'

'Why?' Thio asked, confused.

'I wasn't sure at first,' Britt continued. 'I thought he simply hated blondes. But then one day, he brought me one of Alysse's gowns and made me wear that too. That's when I unraveled his... unnatural obsessions.'

'What are you saying?' Thio asked, an uncomfortable image beginning to nest in his mind. 'That he dressed you up as the Princess—his niece?'

Britt shrugged, as if unsure, but her smile exposed the truth of her words.

'I'm sure you've heard of his *boundless love* for the Lady Palymma,' she implied. 'Well, it would seem he loved her as one would a wife, rather than a sister. Palymma, of course, felt nothing of the sort for him. She was blind to his lust for her entirely. When she married the Emperor, Cyrus insisted he, too, relocate to the Capital to *keep her safe*. Then, the one time he wasn't there to protect her, she died. He was away with the Emperor and Alysse on their visit to the White Isles.'

Thio's mind drifted from the last few details, his stomach still churning with disgust at the thought of someone lusting after a sibling.

'With his sister gone,' Britt pressed on, 'who was the next best thing? Alysse, after all, is a spitting image of her mother.'

'That's sick,' Thio recoiled. 'He's her uncle.'

'Hey, I agree,' Britt stated, raising both hands. 'But just like you, my love, the heart wants what the heart wants.'

Thio paid no mind to her comparison, for the two bore no resemblance. Instead, his thoughts shifted to concern for Alysse, her uncle now unaccounted for somewhere in the Capital.

'Anyway, as I was saying,' Britt continued, 'Cyrus blamed the Emperor for his sister's death—thanks to you, no less.'

'Me?' Thio quizzed. 'What did I do?'

'Your little cure, my love,' she said condescendingly. 'I'm sure you were told that the Empress died before it arrived. In actuality, there was only one dose, so the Emperor had to choose—his wife or his son.'

'So that's why Cyrus hates Jaxon,' Thio surmised.

'See, you *are* clever,' Britt applauded, her tone patronising. 'From then on, his hatred for House Aprya grew deeper and stronger—except for Alysse. It was then that he was approached by the leader of The Reclamation with an offer too great to refuse.'

Thio said nothing as he silently ingested the information the loose-lipped blonde was divulging.

'He was to do their bidding,' she went on, 'and in return, he would have Alysse to do with as he pleased, far away from the grip of the Imperium. That is one reason she is still alive.'

'What's the other?' Thio probed.

'Our leader needs her to wear the crown before she's shipped away to live out her life in endless torment.'

'Who is your leader?' Thio asked directly.

'Hey, that's not fair,' Britt whined. 'I've told you so many secrets, and you've yet to tell me one.'

Thio decided to play along, settling for a truth he had come to know since his imprisonment.

'You want to know a secret?' he began. 'I have spent every moment in this cell devising ways to kill you. I've imagined things I never thought I was capable of imagining.'

Britt raised her eyebrows and scoffed.

'Well, that's a bit rude, don't you think?' she argued. 'Although, I do appreciate your honesty. It is good to get everything off your chest before you die.'

'How can you be so certain their plan will work?' he countered.

'Do you know what the final act of the coronation entails?' she asked.

'No.'

'The five leaders of the Great Houses move to the Shrine of Old, where they affirm the ascendancy before the past rulers,' she explained. 'It's just the five of them—no crowds, no priests, no guards. Not even your lover boy, Jaxon, can attend.' She leant in closer. 'It is there that The Reclamation will occur, and finally put an end to the mighty House Aprya.'

Thio's heart began to race. 'I thought you said they weren't going to kill Alysse.'

'Well, I'm not entirely sure now that Cyrus has exposed himself,' she stated. 'They may, or they may not. That's for them to decide. Jaxon will die, though. That, I am sure of.'

Thio had heard enough. He shot up from the hard stone bench and began desperately jostling his cell's lock.

'Hah, don't even bother,' Britt chuckled as she watched his futile act. 'There's nothing slender enough to pick these locks. Trust me, I've tried.'

Thio began searching the entire cell, probing for anything he could use to break free from his cage. He thought of his own research, his mountain salt now long gone, and how it could have melted the bars. He shook the idea from his mind and returned to the stone bench, dropping to his knees and peering under the cold slab. He shifted his head back and forth, searching for any form of metal fixing or dowel.

In his frantic movements, his silver locket slipped out of his tunic and dangled from its silver chain. He halted immediately, clutching the cherished keepsake, its slender form cradled perfectly in the crease of his palm. He opened it, staring down at the drawings within, then to the lock on the bars. Every fibre of his body resisted the thought of destroying this prized heirloom that once belonged to his father. Yet he knew it would be the only chance he had to reach Jaxon before it was too late.

Slipping the chain over his head, he rushed to the door and blindly fumbled for the keyhole in its exterior. Once he found it, he carefully inserted one end of the locket. The narrow piece of silver slid in a few millimetres before jamming against the lock's tight enclosure. He pressed harder. The sound of metal scraping against his locket pierced his heart, but he persisted.

'That won't work, you fool,' Britt provoked. 'I hope that thing isn't important to you. It's as good as fucked now.'

Thio ignored her taunts, focusing on the feel of the mechanical components within the lock. Confident he had secured the correct pins, he began twisting the locket. Slowly. Gently. He could feel the inner workings begin to shift before it jammed, halting his progress. He manoeuvred the locket again. Gently. Slowly. Then more movement. He knew he was close. *Just a bit further,* he told himself. The locket twisted slightly before jamming once again. It was the final pin. Almost the entire locket now sat wedged inside the lock. He could feel the strain on the thin metal; any additional tension and it would break. *I have to,* he pressed himself, battling his urge to stop and save his father's gift.

He took a deep breath, then drove the locket deeper. A mixture of clicks, clangs, and snaps echoed throughout the frigid prison space as the barred door swung open.

Thio looked down at his hand to find only a tiny fragment of his locket remaining, the rest lost to the violent struggle of his escape. He cursed himself for it, then turned his gaze to Britt who stood wide-eyed across the hallway. He wanted nothing more than to wrap his hands around her slender neck, but now was not the time. He peered down the long, dark corridor that led towards the Citadel's entrance and made his escape. Before exiting the prison, he turned back to Britt and sneered.

'I'll be back for you,' he growled.

Britt stood frozen as she watched Thio disappear into the darkness.

CHAPTER 41

The brilliant turquoise waters of the Bay of Zenithal sparkled in front of Alysse as the single-occupied watercraft drifted steadily over its calm surface towards the Shrine of Old. Behind her, in a perfect V-formation, followed the three kings and one queen of the Great Houses, each occupying their own craft, seated poised and graceful, with the towering Citadel as their backdrop.

Alysse took the opportunity during the silent journey to reflect on what had been, and what was to come. The weight of her father's legacy loomed heavy on her, and the path ahead seemed both daunting and unclear. Yet, in this moment of solitude, a flicker of resolve stirred within her. She was no longer the child who had once shied from responsibility—today, she was Empress, and it was time to prove herself worthy of the title.

The vessel she sat upon drifted gently alongside

the dock of the solemn island. Steadying its thrusters, the vehicle came to a stop, securing itself to the stone pier as Alysse stepped off and began her walk towards the gleaming stack of marble altars. She hesitated to look up at it, the image of her father's body strung from its apex still vivid in her mind. Yet when she did, she saw nothing of the horrific scene. Instead, the monument stood in pristine solitude, each block of white stone silent and unmarked. It was the first time she had stood with a sound mind in the presence of her predecessors since that day. She took a moment to breathe in the salty air of her surroundings, absorbing the very spirit of those within their altars. She felt at one with them, her place among the rulers as firm as the stone path she trod.

As she moved closer, she turned her gaze to the peak of the monument—to her father's altar. She wished for nothing more than to have him there beside her, an anchor of familiarity in an unfamiliar time. In a sense, she knew he was there, in spirit, as he had been these past weeks. The sway of her pendant against her skin reminded her of that truth.

Arriving at the base of the altars, Alysse turned to see the four monarchs trailing close behind. As they positioned themselves in an arc around her, she glanced over at Marcia Iibryn and smiled. The smile was returned with a reassuring nod to proceed. Composing herself, she addressed her audience.

'As tradition demands,' she began, 'I stand before you, in the presence of those who came before, and ask that you confirm my position as your Empress, so that together, we may chart the path ahead and nurture the long-standing peace of Eviiri.'

Alysse circled her gaze over each of the four monarchs standing gallantly before her, each bowing in turn, affirming her ascendancy. In that moment, Alysse felt relief—not for her new power, nor the weight of the crown atop her head, but for the confidence she had found in not cowering to fear. Having the confirmation from those she was set to lead assured her that her role was more than just inherited. She turned to the stack of eight marble altars and began reciting her vows.

—

Jaxon hurried down to the Entrance Hall, summoned by one of the Imperial guards to an incident that had occurred below the Citadel. Once in the main foyer, he rushed down the flight of stairs to find a single guard with a struggling captive in his grasp —Thio.

'What's going on?' he said, puzzled.

'He escaped the cells, Commander,' the guard explained. 'He fought as best he could, but it wasn't enough.'

Jaxon, now standing before them, noted the swelling on the left side of the guard's face, a small cut splitting his skin. He turned his gaze to Thio and shot him a glare of frustration, tinged with a hint of admiration for landing a blow on an Imperial guard. *He remembered my training,* he thought.

'How did you…'

'There's no time, Jaxon!' Thio exclaimed, jolting the Prince's attention. 'They're going to kill Alysse. They're going to kill you!'

Jaxon noted the seriousness of Thio's tone, leaning in closer to inquire more. 'Who is?'

'I don't know,' Thio declared, the beats of his pounding heart disturbing the flow of his words. 'But you need to…'

Before Thio could complete his sentence, the guard shoved Thio to the ground and swiftly drew his short sword, aiming it directly at the Prince. He lunged, narrowly missing his target as Jaxon shifted sideways with remarkable speed. The guard's stumble allowed Jaxon enough time to draw his own blade, meeting his assailant face to face.

They engaged in a ferocious battle for survival, their razor-sharp steel slicing through the air around them.

Thio watched from the ground, unarmed and powerless to help, his eyes struggling to keep pace with the darting manoeuvres of the brawling couple. *I have to do something*, he thought, scouring his surroundings for anything he could wield.

Jaxon kept his focus on the guard's movements—left, right, right, and down—effortlessly avoiding each attempted strike. The opposing blade slipped dangerously close to his body, but each time it was deflected with a swift block of his own. His adrenaline had fully engaged his body's senses. He saw his attacker move as if time itself had slowed. And on they fought.

By now, Thio had hauled himself to his feet, awaiting the opportune moment to aid his Prince. The swirl of steel offered little opportunity to enter the fight without great risk of injury—or worse. He watched Jaxon dance around the guard's attacks, his movements graceful yet robust. With a solid thrust, the Prince knocked the aggressor backwards, disorienting him momentarily. That was Thio's window.

The young apprentice took flight, hurling himself towards the man clad in purple and green. With all the strength he could muster, he flung his arm around the guard's neck and heaved him backwards. The sudden jolt startled the guard, leaving him frozen and exposed—just enough time for Jaxon to drive his short sword deep into his guts.

The Prince withdrew his blade from his victim, seeing Thio's face come into view as the body collapsed to the ground. They both stood silent for a moment as they caught their breaths.

Jaxon started to speak his gratitude but was halted by the apprentice's words.

'Get to Alysse,' Thio urged.

Jaxon turned his gaze to the Citadel's southern exit, and the stretch of water that separated him from his sister. He knew not what dangers she faced there, only that Thio could be advantageous to have by his side. He turned back to the shaken boy.

'Come with me,' he said, offering his hand to Thio.

—

Lex Frailyn was the first to speak once Alysse had concluded her vows.

'Now that it's done, I request your leave to return home,' he said. 'I have grown tired of this city.'

Alysse shot him a direct stare, the power of her new title reflected clearly in her eyes.

'You seem rushed, Your Grace,' she said. 'But there is one more matter that I must address.'

Lex let out an audible groan, his eyes filled with annoyance. 'Fine. Get on with it.'

Alysse pulled her shoulders back and lifted her chin, adopting a defiant stance. 'Lex Frailyn, I hereby order you to stand down,' she asserted, noting the confusion that now accompanied his annoyance. 'This futile attempt to…'

'My dear,' the soft voice of Marcia Iibryn interrupted as the peach-draped monarch stepped forward, 'let us not waste any more time.'

Alysse turned to the approaching woman with a bewildered look. 'I am not *wasting time*. I am performing my duty as Empress. Lex *must* answer for his crimes.'

'Oh, sweet girl,' Marcia said, reaching for her hand. 'Lex may appear to be your enemy, but I assure you, he is not. The only futile thing here is your decision to accuse him.'

'But you said…' Alysse paused, her mind twisting in turmoil.

'What did I say?' Marcia asked, cocking her head to one side.

'You said my decision today will be written in the

histories.'

'And it will be.' Marcia smiled. 'But it has nothing to do with Lex Frailyn. The person you truly seek is the one who has diverted your attention and divided your supporters. All they have left to do now is ascend.'

Divert, divide, ascend, Alysse repeated in her mind. 'I don't understand.'

'Of course you don't,' Marcia said in a patronising tone. 'You're just as stupid as your father.'

King Lyro Tennyr took a forceful step forward. 'How dare you speak to your Empress with such contempt!'

Alysse stared deep into Marcia's eyes, for within them, she saw a darkness she had not noticed before. The twisted smile that now painted the monarch's face was clear.

'It was you,' Alysse gasped.

'It was me,' Marcia said proudly. 'I orchestrated the death of your father, the burning of the palms, the attacks—all of it.' She leant in closer to Alysse. 'My dear, this is *my* reclamation.'

The kings stood in stunned silence, rage forming only on Lyro Tennyr's face.

All of Alysse's assurances shattered in an instant. She clawed at every corner of her mind, desperately seeking reason, but it was either nonexistent or buried so deep that even years of searching might prove fruitless.

'But... why?' She trembled.

'Your father took something from me many years ago,' Marcia snarled. 'He took my future. *I* was his intended bride. *I* was to be Empress. *I* was meant to rule Eviiri by his side. But instead, he chose your disloyal, whore of a mother—my closest friend! Have you ever been burdened with such humiliation? Of course you haven't. House Aprya has always held themselves above all. But no more.'

'The brand on my father... it's your mark?' Alysse asked.

'Hah,' Marcia chuckled, 'a simple reminder of my humiliation—it has kept the fire burning all these years. You see, I had already begun creating the perfect wedding gown. It stood in my room, draped over a dressmaker's mannequin, just like yours. After my father told me that Jannon had chosen another, I tore that dress into an unrecognisable heap of fabric and jewels. All that was left was the bare mannequin. I stared at it for days, hating the very shape of it. And, well, it stuck.'

Alysse pictured the mannequin in her room, placing the mark of The Reclamation beside it. It became so simply obvious.

* * *

'Why haven't you killed me already?' Alysse questioned. 'You've had ample opportunity.'

'I'm afraid it's not that simple,' Marcia explained. 'As I told you, should House Aprya fail to meet their duties, the crown passes to House Frailyn.' She turned to the Kaprythorian King. 'I could never face an opponent as formidable as Lex.'

Lex Frailyn said nothing in return, seemingly enjoying the discord unfolding before him.

'So if you mean not to kill me, how do you intend to take my crown?' Alysse asked, her hands still trembling.

Marcia returned her gaze to the disheveled Empress. 'You will give it to me,' she said plainly. 'Only an Emperor or Empress has the power to pass on their crown. That is why I had to bide my time until it actually sat atop your pretty little head.'

Anger began to build within Alysse, the peach-draped queen's confidence fuelling her fire.

'And why would I hand it over to you after you killed my father?' she spat. 'After you killed Dalos, after you destroyed an entire city?'

'Because you don't want the blood of millions more on your hands,' Marcia said with conviction. 'Ton-Basin was just the beginning. By now, my troops will have laid waste to Latyth, with their targets set on every major city throughout Qymathor. Will you let your people die while you cling to something you are clearly unfit to hold?'

Alysse, shocked by the news of Latyth's downfall, turned to the three kings standing idle nearby, her eyes pleading for support.

'This is an outrage!' Lyro Tennyr proclaimed. 'House Tennyr has stood behind House Aprya since the beginning. We do not intend to break centuries of loyalty. Empress, you have my support.'

The young Benin Peryx stepped forward, adopting a proud stance behind Marcia Iibryn.

'Queen Marcia is right,' he spoke in the same re-hearsed tone Alysse had heard before. 'You are unfit to hold the title of Empress. Domathor will support Queen Marcia's ascendancy.'

Marcia smiled down at the naïve child, her manip-ulation of the recently orphaned king unfolding ex-actly as she had planned.

Alysse turned to the last king. 'Lex?'

Lex Frailyn took a moment to gather his thoughts,

then spoke.

'As I said at the Qyx-Iriyan, I will not bring peril to my country.' He straightened his posture and delivered his proclamation. 'I have thus decided that your squabbles are your own. I hereby proclaim that Kaprythor will extricate itself from Imperial rule and stand as an independent nation. We will not take up arms to defend any other than Kaprythor. We will have no say in your affairs, nor heed any from you.'

Marcia scoffed, unsurprised by Lex Frailyn's announcement.

He approached Alysse, cautiously peering over her shoulder toward Marcia before returning his focus to his now former Empress.

'I wish you good fortune, Alysse.'

The words were delivered with sincerity.

'Your Grace… please,' Alysse whispered.

Lex stared into her eyes, hesitating a moment, a sorrow reflected in his own. Saying no more, he lowered his head in what could only be considered a bow, then retreated to his watercraft. The gathered monarchs watched as he boarded his vessel and steered it south towards his ship.

'Benin,' Marcia called out, 'be a good lad and return to your ship. Lyro, I suggest you do the same. Let us women talk this out.'

'I will not abandon my Empress,' Lyro said sternly.

'It's okay,' Alysse returned. 'Go.'

'But Your Grace…'

'I can handle this,' she assured.

Lyro Tennyr shot Marcia a look of disdain, a silent threat carried alongside it. He conceded to the Empress' request and followed the young king who had already boarded his craft.

Alysse watched the two kings steer their boats southward.

Marcia commanded Alysse's attention once again. 'So, my dear, how shall we proceed?'

Alysse looked up at her father's altar. She waited for his warm words to guide her, but she did not hear them—not because he no longer wished to speak them, but because there was no need. In that moment, Alysse realised that her father's guidance lived on only in memory—his many lessons now a part of her. She knew, in her heart, that she already possessed the wisdom he had hoped to impart. She met Marcia's gaze with a stern expression.

'No,' she said simply.

'No?'

'No. I will not falter.'

'Don't be foolish, my dear.' Marcia laughed. 'Is your wish to rejoin your father that great?'

'If it meant not bowing to you,' Alysse challenged. 'Will you also place me atop this monument only to string me from my altar?'

Marcia laughed. 'That part was not my doing.'

Suddenly a deep voice spoke out. 'It was mine.'

From behind the marble shrine stepped Cyrus Thenta, his purple suit replaced by a beige hooded robe.

Alysse's eyes widened as she caught sight of her uncle approaching, his golden short sword in hand.

'Cyrus,' Marcia rejoiced, 'impeccable timing. Perhaps you can convince your niece to reconsider my terms.'

Alysse shot rage at the silver-bearded man. 'Why, Uncle?'

'For your mother, Your Grace,' he answered. 'For you.'

'My father loved you—he respected you, and you murdered him!'

'And he killed my sister!' he exploded. 'She was mine! I loved her more than anything in this damned world. He plotted her death and made certain I was absent while he executed it.'

'The Dusk killed her, not him,' Alysse tried to reason. 'Father did everything he could to save her.'

'No, he didn't,' Cyrus said, his voice thick with rage-filled grief. 'He planted the Dusk. He even had an opportunity to save her, but instead, he chose to save your reckless fool of a brother.'

'You're wrong, Uncle!' Alysse yelled, pointing a stern finger at Marcia. 'She is the one responsible. She killed Mother and convinced you it was my father. She has just confessed. Can't you see? You are nothing more than a tool in her grasp.'

Cyrus glanced at Marcia, seeking confirmation. The rage she had kindled in him a decade ago flared once more, as intense as when she had convinced him that Jannon was responsible for this act. But Marcia let none of her deceit show.

'Who are you to believe, Cyrus?' Marcia spoke, her voice smooth and controlled. 'This half-witted child or the only person who has shared your hatred for her House all these years? If it weren't for my support, Jannon would still be here, parading in light.'

Cyrus agreed with the convincing queen, moving to her side. He watched her shift her attention back to Alysse.

'It seems we are at an impasse,' Marcia announced. 'Should you insist on refusing, it will leave me no choice. Now that Lex has withdrawn from the Imperium, I will have no challengers. So, I ask you for the last time, will you hand me the crown?'

Alysse stood deep in thought, her choices tugging her from side to side. It was movement atop the turquoise water behind Marcia and her uncle that caught her attention—a boat. *Jaxon*, she thought. She felt secure in that moment, then spoke her final decision.

'I will not.'

'Very well,' Marcia sighed. 'Cyrus, eliminate her.'

Cyrus looked down at Marcia, his eyes filled with hesitation. He could not act, for Alysse was his prize —his reward for executing Marcia's plot. He had envisioned a life with his niece, distant and free from judgemental eyes, where he could finally explore his twisted love and lust for her.

Marcia snarled at the depraved man. She had always felt disgust toward him, having known of his secret yearnings since childhood. Yet, she had understood how to exploit his weaknesses to her advantage. It seemed, however, that this final task was beyond his capabilities.

'Fine,' she grumbled.

As fast as the aged queen could move, she produced a small dagger from her long sleeve and charged at the Empress.

Alysse stood frozen in fear as Marcia darted towards her. She closed her eyes, awaiting the blow that would surely take her life. The blow, however, did not come. Instead, a voice called out.

'No!' Cyrus exploded, trailing Marcia.

She had taken only a few strides before she recoiled backwards in pain. Her shriek jolted Alysse's eyes open. Standing just feet away, she saw Marcia frozen in place, her eyes wide and mouth agape. Her gaze followed the line of Marcia's peach gown, tracing the fine details before resting on the short sword protruding from her chest. The blade was coated in blood.

As swiftly as Cyrus had plunged his sword into her back, he withdrew it, panting with fury. He watched the woman's body collapse to the ground, lifeless and still. Calming his breath, he flicked his head up to meet Alysse's gaze, fear rife in her eyes. It was then that he advanced on her.

'Finally you will be mine!' he roared, clutching her arm.

Alysse screamed, struggling to escape his hold. In her frantic efforts, she stumbled and fell to the ground. But this did not stop her uncle. He tugged at her arm, dragging her across the stone path toward a hidden watercraft tucked behind the island. Advancing closer to his escape, he was halted by a voice in the distance.

'Alysse!' Jaxon belted as he sprinted at full speed towards his sister, Thio trailing close behind.

Cyrus released his grip and readied himself for combat, blood still dripping from his short sword.

Jaxon lunged forward, his sword raised, eyes locked on his target. Cyrus was quick, parrying the first strike with his own blade, the sharp clang of steel reverberating in the tense air. Jaxon's movements were fluid, his muscles coiling with controlled fury, every strike aimed with precision. Cyrus, however, having reignited the skills he thought lost, moved with ease, deflecting each blow. His eyes never left Jaxon's.

Their swords clashed again, sparks flying as metal met metal. Jaxon gritted his teeth, pushing with all his strength, forcing Cyrus back a step. The ground beneath their feet seemed to rumble with the force of their battle. Cyrus retaliated with a swift thrust, his short sword aimed for Jaxon's side, but Jaxon sidestepped, narrowly avoiding the strike. He retaliated immediately, aiming for Cyrus's arm, but the older man twisted away, his movements a blur.

Each blow, each parry, was a testament to years of training and raw power. Jaxon's breath became faster, his heart pounding in his chest, but he remained focused, his resolve unshaken. Cyrus, however, seemed almost calm, his eyes cold and calculating, waiting for the right moment to strike. The fight raged on, neither willing to give an inch, each determined to outlast the other.

Thio rushed to Alysse's side, helping her to her feet and ensuring she was unhurt. He urged her away from the brawling uncle and nephew, feeling her reluctance to leave her brother behind.

'Wait!' she pleaded, pulling away from Thio. She stood watching, her body trembling with panic, eyes fixed on the clashing blades.

Jaxon's movements grew more desperate as his uncle's skill seemed to match his own. But as they circled, a shift occurred—a subtle misstep from Cyrus. Jaxon saw it, an opening that would end the fight. With a surge of adrenaline, he lunged, his blade finding its mark. The sword plunged deep into Cyrus's side, and a sharp gasp escaped his uncle's lips.

For a brief moment, Cyrus stood still, staring down at the blood blooming on his tunic. His grip loosened on his sword, the blade falling uselessly to the ground. Jaxon watched him falter, the shock and disbelief on his face stark. The older man crumpled to his knees, his strength finally slipping away. His eyes met Jaxon's one last time, the weight of betrayal and anger lingering between them.

Cyrus slumped forward, lifeless, his body hitting the ground with a sickening thud. Jaxon stood over him, breath heavy, his chest tightening as the reality of what he had done settled in. The battle was over. His uncle was dead.

Alysse whimpered as she ran into the arms of her brother. The two held each other tightly, relief washing over them.

'It's done, Alysse,' he reassured. 'It's over.'

Alysse could not find words within her sobs.

Thio slowly approached the pair, his hands fidgeting with his tunic. He watched as they parted and turned to him.

'Your Grace?' he said, his tone soft with timid sentiment.

In an unexpected move, Alysse flung her arms around the apprentice, squeezing him.

'Forgive me,' she whispered.

'There's nothing to forgive, Your Grace,' Thio replied, his voice filled with sincerity.

Alysse met his gaze, sorrow reflected in her eyes. She had been wrong to imprison him. Britt's deceitful words had now been fully unveiled. There was more news to deliver, yet she struggled to summon the strength to speak it.

'Thio,' she began, 'they attacked Latyth. To what extent, I am unsure. I am so sorry.'

Thio's heart sank instantly. *Y'mara.* The urge to leave that very second stiffened his body.

'Jaxon,' Alysse said, turning to her brother, 'make arrangements for Thio's transport. Gather as much information as you can and send the necessary aid.'

'Yes, Empress,' he replied, moving toward Thio and placing a tender hand on his back.

'Do not let your hope falter,' he said softly. 'You cannot know for sure.'

Thio appreciated his Prince's words, yet silently feared the worst.

'I will understand if you choose not to return,' Alysse said, her voice steady but soft. 'That decision is yours to make. Dalos saw greatness in you. I now see that greatness with my own eyes. Please know there will always be a place for you here.'

'Thank you, Your Grace,' Thio replied, his efforts to mask his emotions failing. 'And you, My Prince.'

CHAPTER 42

A few days had passed since the coronation. The realm sat silently awaiting news from their new Empress. The uncertainty of the future had begun to spread amongst the people as each learnt of the events of that day.

Jaxon escorted Alysse through the gardens south of the Citadel. The skies were clear, and the air smelled clean. The previous night was the first that Alysse had slept without disturbance from worry or fear.

'Empress,' Jaxon said, his soft voice accompanying the slow rhythmic clops of his thick boots.

'I'm still your sister, Jax,' Alysse interjected. 'You don't have to call me Empress.'

'Well, I'm the Imperial Commander,' Jaxon responded, puffing his chest, 'and you will address me as such.'

They both laughed, allowing themselves a moment of joy as they idled their way along the garden path.

'So, Imperial Commander, what news?' Alysse asked, returning to formality.

Jaxon drew a long breath, his smile fading. 'I sent word to Arius Iibryn, Marcia's eldest son and heir, with a detailed account of what happened here. As per your request, I instructed him to sail for Zenithal to swear his fealty to you and denounce his mother's actions.'

'And?' Alysse probed, hoping for good news. 'What was his response?'

'He has refused,' Jaxon sighed. 'It was clear from his response that his mother has poisoned his mind against us.'

Alysse could feel the tension in his words. 'What is it, Jax?'

'He has made clear his intentions for war, Alysse,' Jaxon declared. 'He has the support of King Benin and the Domathorian armies. With Lex Frailyn seceding from the Imperium, we may not be able to defend ourselves.'

'We have Lyro's forces and our own,' Alysse reassured.

'Even with the Shaavythorian forces, it won't be enough,' Jaxon informed. 'The Reclamation has left us gravely weakened.'

Alysse knew her brother was right. After the might of Kaprythor, Domathor commanded the second-largest force—a force now led by a thirteen-year-old boy, who had fallen for Marcia's manipulative tricks.

'Then we will explore other paths to victory,' Alysse stated, moving to shift the topic. 'What news from Latyth?'

'The port has been destroyed, along with much else. All trade has been rerouted,' Jaxon said. 'Civilian casualties were high, though many were fortunate enough to escape.'

'And Thio?' Alysse asked.

'No word,' Jaxon sighed, lowering his head. 'He departed that night with the supply train.'

Alysse caught the sorrow in Jaxon's tone. Though she knew little of the bond that had formed between him and the apprentice, she could see its effects in the painful expression etched across his face.

'I'm sorry, Jax,' she offered.

'I was wrong to distrust him,' Jaxon said, his voice heavy with regret. 'Despite all my faults, he still came to my aid. He saved my life *again*, and I just… let him go.'

Alysse halted their stroll, turning to face her heartbroken brother. 'Thio has his own path to tread—we all do. And who knows, his may lead him back to you. This isn't the last we will see of him, of that I am certain.'

Jaxon turned his gaze south to the brilliant blue dome of the Grand Athenaeum, silently praying for the return of the one who had captured his heart so swiftly. He felt confident in Alysse's words. Taking a deep breath, he returned his attention to her.

'I have much to do. Will you be okay?'

Alysse offered him a comforting smile. 'Go. I'll stay a bit longer.'

Jaxon returned her smile and gave a nod, before turning back to the Citadel.

Alysse continued to meander down the garden

path, brushing her hand lightly over the hedges that flanked it. Towards the end of the stone planter in which they grew, she spotted something she had not seen before. She crouched down beside it and lifted the dangling leaves. There, behind the thick brush, were two names engraved in the stone.

Jannon and *Dalos.*

Alysse's breath caught in her throat. She imagined them then, young and carefree, unaware of the tumultuous lives they would lead. The image of her father, so strong and steadfast, now seemed softer, filled with the innocence of youth. A tear formed in the corner of her eye, though it did not fall. She smiled, bittersweet, as she whispered under her breath, 'cheeky shits.'

Tucking the names back beneath the leaves, she stood and carried on to the stone bench in the centre of the garden and sat under the sun's warmth. Her fingers traced the polished surface of the stone as she gazed out across the Bay of Zenithal. The weight of Jaxon's news settled heavily on her shoulders, but she knew she was prepared. Her father's lessons, each imparted with care and wisdom, had begun shaping her since childhood. He had never shielded her from hardship, never told her that the path ahead would be easy. Instead, he had taught her how to face it—how to rise with the strength of the generations that came before her.

Her eyes drifted towards the nearest lemon tree, its branches ripe with fruit, the leaves rustling gently in the breeze. Nestled among the branches was the nest of a resident golden-crowned wren. She watched as the wren flitted around, its small wings fluttering with purpose as it encouraged its young to take its first flight.

The wren hovered just beyond the nest, its small body bobbing in the air. Within the nest was a young fledgling. It chirped softly as its parent urged the young bird to take the leap. Then, with a sudden twist of its wings, the adult bird soared into the sky, leaving the baby perched at the edge of the nest. For a moment, the young wren hesitated, its small wings quivering with uncertainty. Alysse could see the fear in its eyes, the same fear that had plagued her in the past, the fear of taking that first step into the unknown.

But then, with a burst of courage, the tiny wren spread its wings. It hesitated no longer, and with a determined flap, it dove into the open air. Alysse's heart leapt in her chest as she watched the young bird catch the wind beneath its wings. It soared free from the nest, for the first time, gliding gracefully over the Bay of Zenithal.

The sight filled Alysse with a quiet understanding. The adult wren, like her father, had prepared its young for this moment, and now, as it flew off into the distance, the young wren was left to face the world alone. But it was ready. And so was she.

Alysse stood, her resolve firming like the roots of the trees around her. She was no longer just the girl who had feared the future—she was the Empress, and it was time for her to take her leap. She, too, would spread her wings and soar, carrying the wisdom of the past and the hope of the future with her.

CHAPTER 43

Thio had scoured Latyth for days in search of Y'mara. The port city was all but abandoned, with only pockets of builders remaining, attempting to restore what had been lost. The infirmary lay in ruins. The Athenaeum had been reduced to ash. The once-grand city had been brought to its knees. Yet he continued his search.

On the fourth day, Thio conceded his efforts and made ready for the trek through the mountain pass to Syka, his home village. He recalled the path as if he had walked it only one day prior. The familiar over-hang of great oak trees provided a shaded pathway through the thick flora.

Hours had passed since he set off. His unbroken journey was nearing its end as he rounded the last weathered groove etched through the Fenniq mountain range.

Before him lay the quiet village of Syka. Modest

cottages dotted the foothills, their simple forms nestled against the land. Steady streams carved thin channels through the village, winding between the homes of its inhabitants. The village was still, secluded, and peaceful. He was home.

Thio passed the village centre, spotting faces he knew from his childhood—faces now weathered with time. They stared back at him as if he were a stranger, lost on his journey. He offered a polite smile, his steps moving him with purpose as he made his way down the narrow road to his destination. It was then he saw it; his cottage.

It appeared unchanged in the two years since his last visit. Wild vines snaked up the terracotta walls, sprouting from the flower-filled gardens below. The vivid-blue door seemed to sparkle in the sunlight, almost beckoning him to enter. Thio felt an overwhelming sense of belonging. He approached the door and paused, his heart pounding within his chest. As his hand rose to knock, a soft voice called out from behind.

'Thio?' Y'mara called, strolling down the road with a basket of fresh produce in hand.

Thio turned at the sound of his sister's voice, his heart easing the moment his eyes met hers. He threw his rucksack down and rushed into her arms, the contents of her basket spilling across the uneven ground.

Y'mara clung to her brother as they silently embraced for what felt like minutes.

'Are you okay?' he whispered.

'I'm okay,' she replied, her elation tinged with a

hint of sadness.

Thio pulled back at her tone, looking deep into her ocean-blue eyes, noting the sadness that lingered there. He glanced down at her stomach, then back to her eyes.

Y'mara said nothing, offering only a pained smile and a soft shake of her head.

A profound sadness shattered Thio's heart in an instant, only to be swiftly replaced by seething hatred. He reflected on the losses he had suffered in such a short span of time—each one the consequence of Marcia Iibryn and her Reclamation.

Y'mara noticed the shift in his emotions and moved to regain his attention.

'It's okay, big brother,' she said softly, her hand resting gently on his arm. 'The baby is with Mother.'

'Tell me what happened,' he inquired softly.

Y'mara recounted the horrific events of that night, sparing no detail.

A short while later, a child's voice called out from further up the road.

'Y'mara!'

Both Y'mara and Thio turned to see a young boy, no older than six, casually strolling down the path. His scruffy hair bounced with every playful step.

Y'mara extended her hand to him, beckoning the little boy forward.

'Sevy, I'd like you to meet someone,' she said, a smile carefully masking her pain. 'This is my brother, Thio. Thio, this is Sevy.'

The child hesitated, his liveliness momentarily stilled by shyness.

Thio crouched to meet Sevy's gaze, offering a gentle smile.

'Hello, Sevy,' he said warmly, swallowing the sorrow that threatened to show. 'You must be the brave boy who protected my sister.'

Sevy said nothing, timidly fidgeting with a small stick he had found during his day's play.

'Thank you,' Thio said, playfully ruffling the child's wild mane.

'Come, let us eat,' Y'mara suggested. 'Then we will go to the rose fields.'

Both Thio and Sevy nodded in agreement, their smiles aligning in unison as the child's shyness gently slipped away. The young boy reached up and took the hand Thio had offered.

—

Sevy swung with glee from the arms of Thio and Y'mara as they trekked down the dirt road to the large open fields south of the village, his contagious giggles filling the air.

As they reached the crest of a grassy hill, the expansive fields beyond unfolded before them. An endless sea of roses painted the wide valley a brilliant white. The breathtaking sight filled Thio's eyes with awe. He had never seen a bloom more magnificent.

Y'mara knelt to meet the child's gaze.

'Sevy, I want you to find the biggest rose. Can you do that?'

The enthusiastic boy nodded eagerly, his eyes already scanning the vast field.

Thio and Y'mara followed Sevy into the thick sea of roses. The sweet aroma evoked nostalgic imagery in their minds.

'You know,' Thio said to his sister, 'it was the oil from these roses that became the key ingredient in the cure.'

'Really?' she asked, surprised that the simple addition of such a common flower could have brought the compound to full strength.

Thio confirmed it with a nod as the two continued their search.

An hour passed quicker than expected. The trio had scoured most of the field and settled on a rose as wide as the span of Thio's hand. But a single rose was not all they plucked—together, they picked three.

The journey through the forest took less time than it had when they were children. The calls of native birds echoed through the canopy. The churning of a narrow river led their way, and at its end, the Syka Falls cascaded into a crystal-clear lagoon.

A handful of children played in the pristine waters, their laughter resonating throughout the valley. Sevy spotted them and was eager to join in their fun. It wasn't until Y'mara gave him an encouraging nudge that he raced down the hill and leapt into the play.

Thio led the way up the rocky embankment to the peak of the falls, where a large boulder protruded out over the serene setting. Here was where they would lay their roses, for that was where their mother would sit for hours and watch them play in the water.

Y'mara was the first to lay a rose. It was the largest of the three, with broad white petals spread in full beauty.

'For Mother,' she said, placing it gently on the small rocky outcrop.

Thio reached into the deep pocket of his tunic and produced his own rose, placing it beside hers.

'For Dalos,' he said.

Y'mara then took the third rose—a tight, unopened bud—and nestled it between the two.

'For Thio the Unborn,' she announced.

Thio took her hand, and they stood in silent reflection, mourning their fallen loved ones.

'What will you do now?' Y'mara asked. 'Will you return to the Capital?'

Thio sighed, the weight of the past weeks pressing heavily on him.

'I'm done, Y'mara,' he said, finally meeting her gaze. 'I've lost Dalos. I've lost my work. I've lost the very drive that once fuelled my excitement for the future. There is nothing for me there.' He paused, his eyes drifting to the children playing in the lagoon, their innocence reflecting back at him.

'I only ever wanted to do good,' he continued, 'but no matter how hard I try, something always takes that away from me. And now, there's this void inside me. When I look into it, I see only darkness staring back. There's no light in there, and no escape should I fall in. It's terrifying. I don't feel like the same person I once was.'

'Hey, look at me,' Y'mara said gently, turning his

face towards hers with a soft hand. 'Everything you have done in your life has been good—great even, because that's who you are. I'm sorry to hear about Dalos. The world has truly lost one of its best. But his end is not yours. Are you just going to give up now—throw everything away? What would Dalos say to you if he heard you speak like this?'

Thio smiled, reminiscing on his playful relationship with his mentor. 'He wouldn't say anything. He'd probably just roll his eyes and whack me with his cane.'

In that moment, a steady gust swept through the valley, rattling the trees above. A thin branch released a wiry twig, which fell and struck Thio directly on his head.

Y'mara burst into laughter as Thio flinched at the sudden strike. 'See? Dalos disapproves.'

Thio looked up at the swaying tree, rubbing his head. 'That wasn't him. That branch is far too skinny.'

Y'mara chuckled before leaning in closer. 'You can't give up, big brother. The world is calling for you. Continue your work and show those in the Capital your true worth.'

Thio pondered his sister's words, knowing she was right. Yet, his desires had shifted in recent days. The pursuit of betterment no longer stood at the forefront of his ambitions. In its place now sat the ugly face of revenge—revenge against those who had stolen from him, those who had taken what he valued most.

'There is something else I've been working on,' he announced.

'See, there you go,' Y'mara said cheerfully. 'It's

settled. Get your ass up and get to work.'

'Fine,' Thio said, rolling his eyes. 'But let me stay a little longer.'

EPILOGUE

Arius Iibryn traced his fork through the medley of softened vegetables, shifting them from one edge of the plate to the other, only to return them once more. He had hoped the monotonous motion alone might stir his appetite—or, at the very least, offer a distraction from his ever-darkening thoughts. It was the light refracting through the impressive imperial topaz —cradled within the thick golden band upon his finger—that caught his wandering gaze. He released his grip on the fork and let it clatter against the plate as he raised the precious heirloom before his eyes, studying its finery.

The gem was its crowning feature. It was roughly the size of his burly knuckle, emanating warm peach hues and a clarity so pure it complemented any light that passed through it. A gem of such colour and purity could only be found in the remote depths of Aankathor's Perdys Valley—a valley as perilous as it was breathtaking.

The gold bands flanking the glimmering stone bore intricate reliefs—raised forms etched by Eviiri's master jeweller. Most prominent amongst them was the sigil of House Iibryn: a sharp-edged 'V', symbolising the valley that had bestowed unthinkable wealth upon its monarchs. Within its cradle sat a diamond-shaped form, a quiet tribute to House Iibryn's lands—small in reach, yet endlessly bountiful.

Arius turned his hand, inspecting the ring's underside. To an untrained eye, the band would have appeared seamless, its golden form unaltered since its forging. But under the bright midday sun, he could discern the subtle shift in hue where it had been resized. The slender insert used to widen its circumference gleamed with a cleaner, more recent lustre. It instantly conjured memories of his mother, Marcia Iibryn.

It had taken nearly two months for her body to be returned to Vin-Perda, seemingly held hostage by those within the Capital after the events of Alysse's coronation. He recalled looking down upon her grey and sunken face, remnants of salt-stiffened tears crusted in each corner of her eyes. Her peach gown bore a sprawling bloom of dried blood across the chest.

Her hands had been folded purposefully over her wound—where Cyrus Thenta's blade had passed clean through, and where her fierce heart had once beaten. He recalled holding those cold and frigid hands. Although he had not let a single tear form, he still ached behind his fixed snarl. Her skin had begun to warm within his hold, but the solid ring she wore remained ice-cold. He had gently slipped it off her finger and examined it, knowing it belonged to him, now that he was the new King of Aankathor.

Leaning down and placing a tender kiss on her forehead, he had whispered to her. 'I will see your will carried to its end, Mother. I will reclaim what they stole from us. House Aprya, and all the scum that rally behind them, will pay in blood. They will collapse, along with their tower. This, I swear to you.'

Bringing his mind back to the opulent courtyard of their hold, Arius glared down at his half-eaten meal before fiercely shoving the plate across the stone table. The motion sent his glass of red wine toppling, its shattering vessel spilling its deep crimson vintage across the setting. A young maid, pale with alarm, rushed forward to clear the ruin left in the wake of her King's fury.

He watched as the girl draped thick linen over the spill, then hastily collected the large shards of glass. In her frantic obedience, she unknowingly opened a small cut in her palm.

'Stop,' Arius called out. 'Come here.'

The girl halted immediately, her eyes widening as she realised her mishap. Frozen in place, she dared not look directly at her ruler. Fearing the consequence of her disobedience, she cowered and began taking slow steps towards him, her eyes darting around at random spots on the pavement, never once landing on her King.

As she stepped within arm's reach, Arius seized her wrist and drew her sharply towards him. He turned her hand, examined the cut with a stale expression, then retrieved a pocket cloth from his peach-hued jacket and pressed it firmly to her palm. The shivering girl winced as the pressure awakened the raw nerves beneath her open skin.

'Hold that there for a while,' Arius said, replacing his hand with hers. 'If the bleeding continues, take yourself to the physician. Send one of the others to clean this up.'

'Yes, My King,' she said, her voice vibrating through trembling lips.

The young maid scurried across the wide courtyard, head bowed in shame, seeing nothing of the approaching Commander until she collided with him full force.

'Watch where you're going, dumb cunt!' the Commander raged.

The girl instantly burst into tears. Saying nothing, she ran off towards the servant quarters, her sobs fading as she crossed into the towering hold.

The heavy-footed man brushed down his military coat, then resumed his steady stride toward the seated figure.

'I swear these servants are growing more incompetent by the day,' he snarled, arriving before his King.

'And what would you have me do about that?' Arius asked, raising an eyebrow and cocking his head to one side. 'You are my High Commander, Temmor, enlighten me.'

'Forgive me, Your Grace,' Temmor said, bowing. 'I've overstepped.'

Arius motioned to the chair across the table. 'Sit,' he instructed.

The lumbering man sat and straightened his posture.

'So,' Arius spoke, 'what delightful news do you have for me today?'

'Well, Your Grace, all the troops that had been stationed under false colours in Qymathor have been recalled,' Temmor announced. 'As per your command, the Qymathorian ship we seized is returning to our fort in Brag. Reports say it sustained heavy damage during their attempted retaking—but it remains salvageable, and our troops intact.'

The High Commander sifted through the catalogue of reports cluttering his thoughts, choosing to prioritise what he believed were priorities.

'With trade suspended between our nation and theirs,' he continued, 'our wheat supplies are diminishing. I have ordered crops to be planted in the western plains to account for the deficit.'

The King's eyes glazed over as if bored by the reports. He leaned forward and placed his elbows on the warm stone table, resting his head atop his interlaced fingers.

'And what of Britt Pensyr?' Arius asked, the matter of her whereabouts pressing at the forefront of his concerns.

A grin twisted the Commander's mouth. 'Her extraction from their custody was a success—silently executed before any alarms were raised,' he said proudly. 'She will be here in a few days.'

Arius let out a short sigh of relief and leaned back in his chair. His eyes dropped to his ring, and a smirk curled his lips. 'Excellent. She will prove most valuable in the war to come.'

He turned his smile upon the High Commander. 'Shall we begin?'

www.ingramcontent.com/pod-product-compliance
Lightning Source LLC
Chambersburg PA
CBHW050957210726
48287CB00004B/1271